Those Fantastic Heroes

by

Stephen M. T. Greene

The Saga of the Enforcers

Those Fantastic Heroes

Cover Art by *The Wild Rose Press, Inc.*

The Wild Rose Press, Inc.
PO Box 708
Adams Basin, NY 14410-0708
Visit us at www.thewildrosepress.com

Publishing History
First Edition, 2023
Trade Paperback ISBN 978-1-5092-4814-8
Digital ISBN 978-1-5092-4815-5

Published in the United States of America

Delveran saw what the rookie was doing. "Stop! Do not remove them!"

Accidentally freed of the nondynamis binders, Old Man Winter had his special powers of winter back. The Archvillain blew all the prison guards surrounding him from him with icy blasts from his aged hands, which had long fingers a bit crooked. All the men and women flew through the air in different directions. They landed on the floor hard, some of them crashing against force bars of holding cells first.

Stepping toward the automatic doors of the holding area, the Incarnation of Winter exploded a blizzard from his lean, ice-cold body. Icy winds and gusting snow roared through the area. Prison guards tried to draw their blasters from their holsters and fire at the foul being trying to destroy them, but the winter storm violently radiating from Wodinnol's form caused them great difficulty in aiming and shooting their weapons. Vast numbers of snowflakes blanketed the holding area in white stuff; it was getting colder and colder in the holding area. Inches of snow accumulated rapidly as Wodinnol began burying them all in it.

"If we don't stop him," Delveran said, "Old Man Winter will turn Tellus into an ice planet!"

Dedication

This is for my fellow writers of Pennwriters Area One.

Chapter 1

High Enforcer Delveran stood in the middle of the holding area of the detention facility of the Universal Prisonplex, his arms folded across his chest. Prison guards threw a bunch of new prisoners into individual holding cells. A prison guard sitting next to him touched buttons on a control console to activate force bars to hold the new prisoners in the single rooms. The force bars glowed white and hummed of high and pure energy, products of advanced science and technology, better than metal ones. The new prisoners had just been duly processed for incarceration to finally serve their long sentences in the Federation penitentiary. Each prisoner waited to be taken to their prison cells in different cell blocks and on various levels in the automated structure of the cosmic jail proper and without parole or probation.

A prison guard, a male human, came up to the High Enforcer. "All accounted for, sir."

"All right," Delveran responded. He uncrossed his arms.

Human, Delveran stood six feet even with a lean frame. His green eyes glittered coolly, reflecting the confident air about him, and his curly black hair and trim black mustache enhanced his handsome, slender face. He donned black attire—a suit, a shirt, shoes, a belt, and a cape. The Zordrak Pentacle, a very powerful amulet made of iron and attached to a silver chain, hung around his neck. On it, eight white swords touched tips in a circle, ringed by twelve mystic signs in white, all surrounded in black.

None of the new prisoners spoke. Delveran saw that all of them, except one, wore orange jumpsuits and black shoes, and were chained. Prison guards were dressed in one-piece suits—blue tops and black bottoms—with boots, belts, and helmets, all black. Simple blasters in black holsters and stun batons rested on opposite sides of their belts. Like the new prisoners, prison guards were a mixture of humans, humanoids, aliens, faerie, and miscellaneous beings, the general kinds of sentient lifeforms in the universe designated by the Federation.

Delveran pondered his present life. *I was much freer before I became the High Enforcer.* He wished to return to the days when he traveled to other worlds in the galaxy, before he joined the Enforcers and when he worked alone instead of also as the High Enforcer. *Why not leave the Enforcers and let another take my place? I have served long enough as their leader.* He felt torn between his deep desire to travel again and the great satisfaction of holding his current office.

Warden Thurjen Addarak entered the holding area and stopped beside him. The detention facility was an annexed structure to the Universal Prisonplex on its east end. Individual cells lined around the walls of the holding area to its automatic doors, not all filled. Glowpanels in the high ceiling, their contained photons activated to full intensity, brightly lit the holding area in white illumination, without giving off any heat. The silver floor shined spotless as if recently polished.

"Ten Criminals, three Villains," Thurjen remarked, a short, thin man with brown hair cropped and a brown mustache bushy like his brown eyebrows. His brown eyes smoldered, as if from the pipe smoking he puffed over the years, and he looked comfortable in a brown wardensuit with matching belt and boots. "And an Archvillain as well. It's been a while since one of their ilk graced the Universal Prisonplex."

Over a thousand years ago, the Enforcers had categorized foul beings into three distinct evil classes. Criminals were the low evil class; compared to Villains and Archvillains, they were wicked people of an ordinary nature, common scum. Villains were the middle evil class because they were greater than Criminals and less powerful than Archvillains, relying heavily on natural abilities, mastered skills, superior knowledge, science, the occult, celestory, or other resources, singly or in combination, to achieve their dark objectives. Archvillains were the last, highest, and most dangerous evil class, foul beings with special powers and unmatched malevolence, the greatest joy for the Enforcers to confront, catch, and lock away.

"Well, Sorcerer-Enforcer, did you use your special powers and magic to capture the Archvillain?" Thurjen asked half-seriously, half-facetiously.

"No," Delveran replied. "And I prefer the title of High Enforcer over Sorcerer-Enforcer."

"But you're both."

"Of course. But I am a practitioner of all the white arts, not just the occult one of good sorcery."

The Warden looked at him quizzically. "You could pass as an Archvillain."

Delveran smiled. "I believe I appear too much the gentleman to be mistaken for an Archvillain."

"Who was the last Archvillain your Universal

Marshals brought in before this?" Thurjen asked.

Delveran easily recalled. "Smoggle, the Refuse Thing."

"Didn't Mananos bring him in?"

"Yes."

"That Archvillain gave off such a stench in the Universal Prisonplex," Thurjen said, wrinkling his nose. "We had to fumigate the place just so we could all breathe again."

Delveran remembered the arrest offhandedly. "I don't care for the odorless and tasteless air in here."

"Why?" Thurjen asked. "It's very clean, completely filtered, and continuously circulated through all the Universal Prisonplex and every other automated structure on the planet."

"It's artificial," Delveran responded. "I prefer the smells and tastes of nature. The loamy fragrance of earth. The sweet smell and taste of honey by bees. The woody scent and crunchiness of a pinecone. The air in hi-tech places is lifeless and without odors in such diversity." He remembered that bees had been introduced to Tellus by Kapreece, the Incarnation of Beekeeping.

"At least the air in such places is filtered and sterilized to be pure."

"Yes," Delveran agreed. "The inmates of the Universal Prisonplex can at least breathe clean, if not necessarily fresh, air and not complain about any nasty odors and bad air quality."

The Universal Prisonplex existed on the planet Tellus—Delveran's home world and birth planet—and it was a gigantic oblong structure, surrounded by a force wall with six guard towers, a forbidding place imprisoning foul beings, doomed souls suffering eternal damnation in Hell. It stood on the southern edge of Acropollon, the largest city and capital of Tellus sprawled before the Angranadan Ocean on the west coast of Survarille, the Technoland, the civilized continent of Tellus in the planet's western hemisphere. Tellus, a melting pot world, circled the golden star Kambec as its third planet, in the Sagittarian Sector of the Milky Way Galaxy.

"Which of your Universal Marshals arrested the Archvillain here?" Thurjen asked.

"Enforcer Slennass," Delveran answered.

Thurjen grinned. "The Huntress. Who's the Archvillain?"

Delveran caught the Warden's expression and grinned himself. "Sharrack, the Black Slayer. Slennass arrested him on the planet Verkemia. It's a feudal world in the Thorrean Sector of the Milky Way Galaxy."

"Never heard of it."

Delveran sighed. "I have never visited Verkemia. The Federation does not consider it for membership."

"The Black Slayer has an army of well-armed bloodthirsty warriors," Thurjen said. "What happened to them?"

"Space troopers under the command of Colonel Zacklas Ramdar annihilated Sharrack's great host in battle," Delveran answered. "Unfortunately, it was necessary in order for Slennass to reach and apprehend the Black Slayer. Our side suffered light casualties."

Delveran and Thurjen strode over to the holding cell where Sharrack paced. It resembled the others, solely furnished with a silver bunk. The sound of the force bars reminded the High Enforcer of a fixed tone of a tuning fork vibrating perpetually; it gave off no smell to him, just a pleasant sound.

Sharrack stopped pacing and faced them. Delveran sensed the hate emanating from the Black Slayer as Sharrack looked down at them with piercing dark eyes and an aquiline nose flaring for the smell of their blood. The Black Slayer featured a black goatee and long raven hair.

Delveran studied Sharrack's black steel breastplate with a blood-red wolf loping across the middle of it. *A fitting symbol for the Black Slayer*, the High Enforcer thought. It complemented the rest of Sharrack's black garb of tunic, pants, cape, belt, and boots. Altogether, the foul being looked like a powerful warlord wanting to do battle anytime, anywhere in the universe. Sharrack was humanoid.

Before the Black Slayer, around his wrists, shined a pair of antipower handcuffs. Made of silver omnimetal, like the Universal Prisonplex, they contained the three basic energy powers—scientific, occultic, and celestic, or in simpler terms, physical, psychic, and primal—bound together. Both Delveran and Sharrack possessed special powers on the occultic level, but the Black Slayer's were neutralized by the nondynamis binders.

"One day, I shall be free of this place and build a new army to command again," Sharrack swore in a gruff voice. His tanned face flamed in rage, and his bloodshot eyes burned with fury. "Then I shall have the pleasure of smiting both of you and the others responsible for taking away my freedom. Especially that wench who put these cruel fetters on me."

"Slennass is not a wench," Delveran responded. "She is her own person."

Sharrack narrowed his eyes at the High Enforcer.

"You must be the Grand Universal Marshal. The bastard who orders the wench around."

Delveran folded his arms again and stood straight up to the Black Slayer. "I am her leader. Not her keeper."

Sharrack snorted. "When I am free again, she shall be my love slave till I take her life."

Disgusted by the Archvillain, Thurjen clenched his teeth as if crunching his pipe's stem between them. "No inmate has ever escaped from the Universal Prisonplex," the Warden stated emphatically, and the Black Slayer scowled at him. "You brought this on yourself for breaking the law." He pointed a finger at the floor. "Here you will stay for the rest of your life."

Delveran turned to a prison guard, a female human, standing near Sharrack's holding cell. "When will the Black Slayer be moved into his antipower cell?"

"In about an hour, sir," she replied. "Chief Engineer Siranan and his crew are in the subterranean section preparing it for the Archvillain."

"What sublevel?"

"Eleven, sir."

"What cell block?"

"K, sir."

Thurjen said to the High Enforcer, "Arrests of Archvillains by your Universal Marshals have drastically dwindled in the past three years."

"This is just another lull in Archvillain activity, an ebb of their evil in the universe," Delveran responded defensively. "And if not, it may be new Archvillains are rising in far fewer numbers now."

Thurjen frowned. "Wonderful. But I doubt this calm will last much longer. Archvillain activity should increase in the universe to a high level again in the future."

Delveran smiled. "A prediction?"

"An inevitability," Thurjen replied.

A terrible thought occurred to Delveran. "It has been over a thousand years since the Enforcers destroyed the supreme evil that led to our formation and that of the Federation. The next war against supreme evil is due."

Thurjen's eyes widened. "A prediction?"

"An inevitability," Delveran replied, smiling.

Thurjen snorted. "I don't think evil of that magnitude exists any longer in the universe. There have been no signs of supreme evil of a new sort rising to try and rule the galaxy, even remotely. The Universal Federation of Planets doesn't have to worry about any ultimate threat to its very existence. Take my word for it."

Delveran chose not to comment on that. He let the matter rest, for now.

A ring of prison guards entered the holding area escorting and encircling two beings, both male. The first being wore a pair of antipower handcuffs around his wrists; the other carried some nondynamis binders peeking out from under his purple robe, his leather sandals worn a bit.

"Well," Thurjen remarked, "another Archvillain to grace the Universal Prisonplex. Your Universal Marshals are doing a better job. I said this calm wouldn't last much longer."

The male in the purple robe broke from the ring of prison guards to stand before the Grand Universal Marshal. "High Enforcer."

"Ramairgan," Delveran said.

Enforcer Ramairgan, the Incarnation of Power,

appeared as an old man over seven feet tall with long white hair and a long white beard that never grew and stayed flowing and clean. His purple eyes looked at the High Enforcer with respect. In his left hand, he held his Rod of Power, long and narrow—like its owner—and silver, with a crystal at the end of it. It was a supernatural weapon of metal not as tall as the Incarnation of Power. It had energy power on the celestic level, as did Ramairgan. He wielded it as a representative of the Federation and not just his official office as an Incarnation in the universe.

"You really should stop living in the desert, Hermit Power," Thurjen said. "You look like you fast all the time."

Ramairgan looked down at the Warden, his long, narrow face with its aged, thin features formed into an amused expression. "I like the desert. Power flows through it. Desert power and my Incarnation power are in harmony."

Thurjen glanced at the new Archvillain surrounded by prison guards. "Who's he?" the Warden asked Hermit Power.

"The Archvillain Wodinnol," Ramairgan answered. "He is the Incarnation of Winter."

"Old Man Winter," Thurjen remarked. "What a battle you two must have fought. An Incarnation against an Incarnation."

"Yes," Ramairgan said. "His winter powers against my dynamic powers almost ruined a world."

"Where did you arrest him?" Delveran asked.

"Gendor," Ramairgan replied.

"Gendor?" Thurjen repeated.

Delveran explained. "It's a wilderness planet in the

Orion Sector of the Milky Way Galaxy. The Federation rates it as a pre-technological world unfortunately under the influence of polemocratic rule."

Thurjen blinked. "Polemocratic rule?"

"War," Ramairgan told the Warden. "Warring factions fight for domination of that world. A world ripe for the Incarnation of War."

Now Delveran felt concerned. "Ramairgan, did you find any signs of him harming the planet?"

"No," Hermit Power answered. "I also tried to sense his presence. Vidarius is elsewhere fomenting war in the galaxy."

"How long have you been a Universal Marshal now?" Thurjen asked the Incarnation of Power.

"Almost thirty years now," Ramairgan replied.

Thurjen looked at the Incarnation of Winter. "Didn't you arrest the opposite of Old Man Winter, Hermit Power?"

"Yes," Ramairgan answered. "Herabast, Priestess Summer, the Incarnation of Summer. I captured her on Nikrell."

"A world inhabited by an alien race of peaceful beings," Delveran explained to the Warden. "Ramairgan saved the planet before the Archvillain could cook it to death in a heat wave of such intensity, as if to destroy it in a sun."

Thurjen shivered at that. "Your arrests of Old Man Winter and Priestess Summer would have to be your biggest busts to date, Hermit Power."

Ramairgan agreed. "My service record as an Enforcer is very good."

The prison guards around Old Man Winter took him to a holding cell without force bars activated. Wodinnol stood as tall as Ramairgan and looked like an old man as well, but his eyes were white, his nose more prominent, and his white hair and white beard were longer than the Universal Marshal's. The Incarnation of Winter wore a white robe and white boots, but his icicle staff of power—on the celestic level of energy power like him— had been destroyed by the Incarnation of Power when they had battled on Gendor. A prison guard, young and an alien, new to the job, grabbed a key from a key chain on his belt and started to unlock the antipower handcuffs of the foul being.

Delveran saw what the rookie was doing. "Stop! Do not remove them!"

Accidentally set free of the nondynamis binders, Old Man Winter had his special powers of winter back. The Archvillain blew away all the prison guards surrounding him with icy blasts shooting from the long, crooked fingers of his aged hands. All ten men and women flew through the air in different directions. They landed on the floor hard, some of them crashing against the force bars of holding cells first.

Stepping toward the automatic doors of the holding area, the Incarnation of Winter exploded a blizzard from his lean, ice-cold body. Icy winds and gusting snow roared through the area. Prison guards tried to draw their blasters from their holsters and fire at the foul being trying to destroy them, but the winter storm violently radiating from Wodinnol's immortal form caused them great difficulty in aiming and shooting their weapons. Vast numbers of snowflakes blanketed the holding area in white stuff; it was getting colder and colder in the holding area.

Inches of snow accumulated rapidly as Wodinnol

began burying them all in it.

"If we don't stop him," Delveran said, "Old Man Winter will turn Tellus into an ice planet!"

Thurjen fell under the arctic onslaught of the Incarnation of Winter. The High Enforcer, his hands glowing green, raised an occult shield of green fire against the wintry attack of the Archvillain to protect himself and the Warden.

Trapped in holding cells with force bars glowing, unaffected in the blizzard, the ten Criminals and three Villains cowered under their silver bunks of their single rooms for protection against the arctic onslaught, which grew beyond the holding area outward in all directions of the planet. Even the Archvillain Sharrack went down, unable to withstand the snowy assault because the Black Slayer's own special powers were still neutralized by the antipower handcuffs around his wrists. Sharrack cursed his fellow Archvillain.

Ramairgan sneaked in and slammed a pair of nondynamis binders around Wodinnol's wrists again. Abruptly, the winter storm blasting from the Archvillain stopped as the antipower handcuffs neutralized his special powers of winter.

"No!" Wodinnol cried. "Squalls on all!"

Ramairgan shoved his Rod of Power in the face of the Incarnation of Winter. "This is not the season of winter here, foul being."

The accumulated snow melted away. The ten Criminals and three Villains crawled out from under the bunks and stood. Sharrack got to his feet as well.

Prison guards surrounded the Incarnation of Winter again. Old Man Winter pierced icicles in his eyes at everyone, especially the Incarnation of Power. Two prison guards put Wodinnol in the holding cell awaiting him. Then the prison guard at the control console touched buttons and activated force bars in place, glowing and humming.

Delveran grimaced. *Wodinnol's escape attempt is an unpleasant portent. Some great evil is about to happen. I must divine it.*

A prison guard, male and of the race of faerie, a little taller than the Warden, entered the holding area and went over to the High Enforcer. "Sir."

"Yes?" Delveran said.

"I have an urgent message for you."

"Go ahead."

"You're wanted back at the Justiceplex immediately."

Delveran addressed Thurjen after the Warden spoke briefly with a prison guard, a female humanoid. "You will have to excuse me. I have to attend to some important business. We will speak again later."

"Fine," Thurjen responded. The Warden went with two prison guards over to the holding cells of the three Villains.

Delveran left the holding area and walked down the middle corridor on the ground floor of the detention facility, pairs of automatic doors and side passages on either side of him. His dress shoes clicked on the floor and left no scuff marks. He heard no other sounds in the passageway. He passed nobody in the hallway on his way to the teleporter room in the detention facility. Glowpanels in the ceiling lighted his way.

More than halfway down the corridor, he turned left into the teleporter room. A large, square telegrid dominated the middle section of the floor. The filtered air in the chamber made the High Enforcer want to go through a forest so his nose could enjoy whiffs of natural smells. He thought the artificial ventilation in the teleporter room failed to adequately exercise his olfactory sense, like in the rest of the penal institution. The chamber looked spotless as if it could not get dirty and autocleaned itself.

Teleportist Trevv Morran, a young male human in a blue telesuit with black boots and a black belt around his waist, sat alone at the teleport console behind the telegrid on the opposite side from the automatic doors to the chamber.

"Where to, sir?" Trevv asked.

"Back to the Justiceplex," Delveran replied.

"Yes, sir. I will be with you in a moment." Trevv resumed checking his teleport log and teleport schedule for the day.

Delveran reminisced about being a Universal Marshal for over fourteen years. Seven years just as an Enforcer and seven years as the High Enforcer.

Delveran snapped out of his reverie. It had been over four years since the High Enforcer had arrested a foul being on or off Tellus. Being the Grand Universal Marshal did not afford him many opportunities to apprehend foul beings. He missed doing field work as a Universal Marshal occasionally. His time as the High Enforcer was spent as an administrator of justice. He gave the other Enforcers their assignments and did paperwork. He held and attended meetings with officials from Tellus and of the Federation, and other duties as a high-ranking official in the government system of the planet and cosmic union of worlds.

"Ready, sir," Trevv said.

Delveran nodded and stepped onto the telegrid. Instantly Trevv teleported him to the Justiceplex, the headquarters of the Enforcers.

Chapter 2

Delveran materialized in the teleporter room of the Justiceplex. The Justiceplex, an immense, T-shaped structure of golden omnimetal, pointed east from the edge of the Angranadan Ocean on the west side of Acropollon. It glittered in the harsh sunlight and was warm. Behind the Justiceplex, the vast sea stretched for miles north, south, and west with no ocean activity in view at the moment, on the surface or in the air.

Delveran stepped off the large, square, black telegrid in the chamber and found Enforcer Zorrokin, the Thunderer, waiting by its teleport console, a control podium. Glowpanels in the ceiling brightly lit the teleporter room, as throughout the Justiceplex. A large telescreen, black and off, sat in the wall across the chamber from the telegrid and behind the teleport console. Automatic doors appeared right of the High Enforcer as he stood in another spotless enclosure and breathed more filtered air.

Delveran walked over to his fellow Enforcer. He looked up at the bare face of Zorrokin, whose gray eyes regarded him solemnly. Immortal, the Thunderer had long black hair and a muscular physique in a six-foot-six frame, his chiseled features like the strong countenance of an awesome god. The gray vest, gray trousers, black belt, and black boots Zorrokin wore looked a bit dirty. Dust partly covered the steel helmet on his head, with a thunderbolt protruding from each side. In front of Zorrokin's belt rested Bronthorjal, a metal hammer—mighty tool and powerful weapon—with energy power on the celestic level—like he possessed. It featured a rectangular head and a round handle wrapped in a leather thong with a loop at the bottom. A pair of antipower handcuffs hung from the back of the Thunderer's belt.

"Where are Chryssina and Rorbash?" Delveran asked. "I sent the three of you on a joint assignment."

"They dwell on the world of Drath," Zorrokin said. "We decided that I should fly back to you quickly."

"Why?"

"I have a grave tale to tell."

"To my office."

They left the teleporter room and crossed the main corridor of the Justiceplex to Delveran's office, the High Enforcer's dress shoes clicking on the shiny floor of golden omnimetal. Pairs of automatic doors stood up and down the length of the long and wide hallway, with no side passages. Glowpanels lit the ceiling and the empty spotless passageway. Filtered air circulated throughout the place by automation.

As Delveran entered his office, glowpanels in the ceiling autoactivated to light it. Zorrokin followed behind him. The High Enforcer seated himself in his office chair behind his desk, directly facing the automatic doors of the office, as the Thunderer sat in the middle armchair before the desk. Atop his desk lay a bunch of square discs. A large black telescreen covered the wall to the right of Delveran. A storage cabinet, a computer, and a visual recorder for logs lined the wall across from the blank telescreen. The office looked clean and spotless as if dust, dirt, and germ proof, its metal surfaces shiny and smooth.

Delveran sat back in his armchair. He had sent Zorrokin, Enforcer Chryssina, the Light Being, and Enforcer Rorbash, the Dragonling, with three Federation battlecruisers following a hot trail of conquered planets. Their elusive and dangerous quarry, the Archvillain Garrax, the Beast, with his many minions, kept adding new worlds to his multiplanet empire, traveling far through the galaxy in the *Vulgarath*, his fortress ship. Delveran had firm orders from the Federation Department of Justice to stop Garrax and his minions before the Beast could claim Federation worlds for his multiplanet empire.

Zorrokin heaved his chest and rested a hand on Bronthorjal. With a gesture from the Grand Universal Marshal, he began telling his tale. "We chased the enemy through the heavens to Drath."

Delveran recalled what he knew about Drath. A world smaller than Tellus, inhabited by a primitive race of humanoids, orbiting the white star Azbruk as its fifth planet, in the Rigellian Sector of the Milky Way Galaxy. Drath was ruled by many clans and had a warrior code. The Federation had no diplomatic ties with Drath, although Drath was not on the Federation's blacklist of planets. Members were permitted to visit.

Zorrokin continued. "The Beast and his legions were in the midst of conquering Drath. This united the Drathian clans to war against the invaders. The invaders had superior weapons, but the Drathians fought like berserkers against the Beast and his legions and were not going to be easily conquered. War raged worldwide like hellfire."

Delveran thought that was natural, given the brutal

behavior of the invaders and the warrior nature of the Drathians. The High Enforcer had seen it before in the universe.

"Chryssina, Rorbash, and I helped the Drathians and battled against the enemy, aided by Federation forces," Zorrokin stated. "In time, we three fought our way into the *Vulgarath*, reinforced by an armed force of space troopers. While the space troopers swept through the fortress ship, we battled our way to the Throne Hall. After we dispatched two minions guarding its doors, we forced an entry inside. We found and fought Garrax there. But he was not alone."

Delveran leaned forward in his office chair. The last words by the Thunderer sounded rather ominous to the High Enforcer. A feeling of dread ran through the Grand Universal Marshal. "Who was with him?"

"There were three other Archvillains with the Beast," Zorrokin answered. "Unmistakable."

"Did you recognize them?" Delveran asked, sensing a possible connection with what happened earlier in the Universal Prisonplex with Old Man Winter.

"Yes," Zorrokin replied. "The other three Archvillains with him were two males and a female. Asearse, the Charybdian, was the female. Moroloch, the Monitor, and Jawsar, the Predator, were the two males. They wielded blast rifles, and she handled a blaster."

Delveran imagined the three Archvillains had not been on Drath for a social call with Garrax or to aid the Beast in conquering Drath. "Go on."

Zorrokin resumed where he left off. "We engaged the four Archvillains in battle. When we tried to arrest them, the Charybdian, the Monitor, and the Predator fled. The Beast stayed to defend his fortress ship. Chryssina and Rorbash chased the other three fleeing Archvillains while I fought Garrax in single combat. Asearse, Moroloch, and Jawsar escaped from the Light Being and the Dragonling in another ship docked behind the *Vulgarath*. The trio of foul beings flew to another part of the heavens."

"Did Chryssina and Rorbash recognize the other ship?" Delveran asked, finding the tale more and more disturbing.

"No. It was unmarked."

"What happened next?"

"I defeated the Beast in our clash and cuffed him. Then the Federation forces and the Drathians defeated his legions. Those of his minions left were taken prisoner. Chryssina, Rorbash, and I tried to get Garrax to talk, but the Archvillain refused to speak. So we looked over the prisoners, which were many, and found Wormtague, the Mouth of the Beast—a pitiful creature."

Delveran did not know about Wormtague. "I take it the Mouth was privy to everything of the Beast."

Zorrokin nodded. "Chryssina questioned Wormtague about why the other three Archvillains had wanted Garrax. But the Mouth of the Beast just sneered and refused to answer her. Then Rorbash stepped in and threatened to roast the pitiful creature with dragon fire and eat him for supper unless he started talking. That loosened the tongue of Wormtague, and he told us all."

Delveran thought the Mouth of the Beast would have made a lousy meal for the Dragonling. The High Enforcer knew that Rorbash was not like other dragons, which were huge creatures of the wild and dangerous carnivores—ferocious monsters not to cross paths with. But the Dragonling did eat meat because he was still a dragon, though he was also a civilized and intelligent being. "What did Wormtague tell you?"

"Garrax was asked by the other three Archvillains to join a great guild they belonged to," Zorrokin said. "They called it the Fellowship of Darkness."

Delveran thought the name quite appropriate for the Archvillain organization. "Did Wormtague tell you how many Archvillains comprise this evil fellowship?"

"Yes," Zorrokin answered. "They number twenty-four at present. But they seek to recruit more Archvillains and rapidly increase their numbers."

Delveran noted the figure in his mind. "What else did the Mouth of the Beast reveal about the Archvillain organization?"

"The foul beings have a stronghold," Zorrokin said. "They call it the Complex. And it is on the world of Earth."

"Earth," Delveran repeated. The High Enforcer recalled what he knew about the planet. He had never visited the Terran world, though he knew a few of the other Enforcers had, but not the Thunderer. *Earth is a planet about the size of Tellus orbiting a yellow dwarf star and inhabited by a race of humans. Not much else. I need to learn everything I can about this world.* "Any further details?"

"There is more." Zorrokin gripped his hammer. "The Fellowship of Darkness has a leader. The Archvillain Professor Magnemus."

The name invoked a dim memory in Delveran. A name he had not heard in over ten years. "What else?"

"Magnemus has an evil plan for the Fellowship of Darkness. The body of Archvillains is going to attempt to free all the Archvillains imprisoned in the Universal

Prisonplex, soon."

"How do they plan to do this?" Delveran asked.

Zorrokin straightened his helmet on his head. "By invading Tellus with a fleet of ships carrying countless legions of minions. They will be under the command of other Archvillains. Unknown how many members of the Fellowship of Darkness will lead the invasion."

"Where is the fleet of ships?" Delveran asked. The High Enforcer felt more and more uneasy the more he learned.

"Wormtague said the invasion force is gathered in the Glammarian Sector of the Milky Way Galaxy," Zorrokin replied. "It waits for word to launch the attack against Tellus."

Delveran digested all he heard from the Thunderer and began in his mind to chart a course of action to deal with the impending invasion. "Finish your story."

Zorrokin complied. "After questioning Wormtague for a while, Chryssina, Rorbash, and I held council. We agreed one of us should fly back to you quickly and tell you all that has happened. I was chosen. Thus I am here. Chryssina and Rorbash await my return with new orders from you. The Beast is ready for transport to the Universal Prisonplex."

Delveran deliberated on what the Thunderer had just told him. The High Enforcer reached his initial decisions on the important matters. "These are my instructions. Go to the teleporter room, locate and teleport Rathol, Eneysa, Procules, Lorliane, and Jagathan here. Have them meet me in the briefing room."

"As you command," Zorrokin responded.

Delveran continued. "Then you fly back to Drath immediately afterward. You, Chryssina, and Rorbash are to remove anything of value from the *Vulgarath* and load it on the Federation battlecruisers. Get some of the space troopers to help you. After that, take the fortress ship into space away from Drath and destroy it."

Zorrokin nodded. "It will be done."

"When you are finished," Delveran said, "return to Tellus with Garrax in transport and deliver the Beast to the Universal Prisonplex for due process of incarceration. Let the space troopers handle the minions. Then you, Chryssina, and Rorbash relax until I contact you."

"Yes, High Enforcer," Zorrokin responded. The Thunderer brought up another matter that needed attention. "The Drathians know of the Federation now. They are curious about it. What should I tell them if they want to join?"

Delveran already gave that some thought. "Explain to them the basic requirements for membership in the Federation. If they agree to meet these conditions, tell them they can make an official request for membership. It will be delivered to the proper party in the appropriate department for official process and serious consideration. If their request is granted, formal contact will be made in due time to officially initiate Drath into the Federation."

"As you command," Zorrokin said.

Delveran dismissed Zorrokin. The Thunderer rose to his feet and left the office of the High Enforcer.

Exercising his divination abilities, Delveran saw that the matters dealing with the Beast and Old Man Winter had appeared as signs of the upcoming invasion of Tellus by the Fellowship of Darkness. He speculated on the Archvillain organization on Earth, unknown to the

Enforcers and the Federation, until now. That bothered him. He wondered why the Universal Marshals and the Federation failed to discover its secret existence. Before he could think further on the problem, the telescreen in his office beeped. "Telescreen on."

The high-definition, three-dimensional image of a lovely young woman appeared on the telescreen. Her hazel eyes sparkled to reveal her inner beauty, and her slender and pretty face had a touch of makeup. Her long chestnut hair and curvaceous body magnified her outer beauty which easily attracted males of her species, human. She wore a blue pantsuit, the one-piece garment nicely fitting and accentuating her figure, with blue slippers. Her name etched itself deeply in his mind: Evarinia. Her high-ranking position as head of the Federation Department of Foreign Affairs matched his as the High Enforcer.

"You were supposed to meet me last night for the Federation banquet," Evarinia said.

Delveran had forgotten about it and felt a bit irritated for missing it. "The council meeting at the Occultplex extended past the time of the banquet. I apologize for not contacting you afterward. My mind was preoccupied."

Evarinia fumed. "You do this on and off. I'm tired of it. You keep putting your job as the High Enforcer and your membership in the Occultplex before our relationship. I don't do that with my appointed post."

"I don't intentionally mean to lessen our relationship and hurt you." Delveran felt trapped. His emotions became mixed.

"Then prove to me that our love for each other is real and not just another association you can do with as you like. Now."

Delveran exhaled deeply. "I cannot. I am in the middle of a crisis. A priority-one emergency."

"Cannot? Will not!"

"I'm sorry," Delveran said. Her rage at him upset him, but he did not show it.

Evarinia glared at him as if she wanted to wreak revenge on him like a Fury does to foul beings to avenge wrongs they have done in the universe. "You'd better meditate on whether or not you want this relationship. We've been together for over two years now. That is something special."

"It is," Delveran agreed.

"Because if you won't do anything to save it," Evarinia said in a bitter tone, "then it's time for me to find another man. Call me when you've reached your decision."

Delveran frowned. "All right."

"But don't take too long," Evarinia warned. "Or else you'll find that I've disappeared from your life. My life doesn't revolve around you. Good-bye." She terminated their communication.

Delveran stared at the telescreen, blank again. The High Enforcer shook his head. He sighed. Another item weighing on his mind. Her big speech made him feel conflicted.

With regret, he shoved her ultimatum from his mind and concentrated on the problem of the Archvillain organization and the threat to Tellus. He readied himself, got to his feet, and exited his office for the briefing room. The glowpanels in the ceiling faded out behind him.

Chapter 3

Enforcer Rathol, the Shepherd, stood on a hill in the great grasslands in the northwest region of gigantic Mellenroel, the Wilderland, the primitive continent of Tellus in the planet's eastern hemisphere. Below him, sheep grazed. Ahead of the sheep, a nomadic village of men, women, and children went about their daily routines. A concentric ring of various-sized tents stood halfway between him and the Glangie River, which meandered southward. On the other side of the river, more plains stretched to the horizon. He gazed up toward Kambec, the Tellusian sun, in a clear sky so blue and so fair that it caused the Shepherd to smile. The warm weather felt comfortable to him and not too humid, his face and hands tanning. He wished, though, for a nice, cool breeze on his old, weathered countenance.

Rathol wondered how much longer his aged body would last on the physical plane, his long white hair and short white beard poignantly reinforcing the hard fact of his aging. His brown-striped red robe and leather sandals made him feel humble and ordinary. He leaned on the Staff of Godpower, a divine tool he confidently and loyally wielded in the services of the Almighty and the Enforcers. A great longing for his previous life as a simple shepherd mirrored itself in his deep brown eyes. His responsibilities to both God and the Universal Marshals felt like such a heavy burden to him. He contemplated on his long life—in human terms, since he was human—reliving certain moments in his mind again.

Shebeth, his wife of many years, strode toward him in a red-striped, white robe and joined him on the hill. Her long white hair fell farther than his, her soft brown eyes filled with an unwavering love for him. Together they looked like a happy couple nearing the end of a shared journey in life. The earthy smells of green grass and rich soil made them feel at peace.

From the east, the wind picked up and blew at their backs with gentle force. No birds flew in the sky. The only animals in sight, beside the thousands of sheep grazing contentedly on the grasslands, were the sheepdogs watching the collective flocks and the mounts and packhorses tethered safely between the two farthest tents from the hill. Behind them, east, in the far distance, rose a mountain range. To the south, forestland. West of them flowed the Glangie River as its water sparkled in the bright sunlight. To the north stretched open wilderness.

"The others are concerned about you," Shebeth said.

Rathol straightened his bent posture. "I was restless." He knew she understood his mood.

Shebeth stepped around to face him. "The pilgrimage to Paradar will lift your spirits. It shall renew you." She read his uneasy expression. "What troubles you?"

"It won't be long before the Lord commands me to leave the Enforcers," Rathol replied. "Then I must hand His Almighty Staff to another to wield for Him and the Universal Marshals in service through the universe." He wished he was already retired from the Enforcers. The sheer weight of his years affected him deeply. The Shepherd felt so weary of the endless war the Universal Marshals waged relentlessly against evil.

"You have served the Lord and the Enforcers faithfully," Shebeth said. "None could have done better for God and the Universal Marshals."

Rathol appreciated her fierce loyalty to him. "After I have left the Enforcers and turned His Almighty Staff over to His new Chosen, we shall pack our belongings and return to our home world of Samaros. There we shall live the rest of our days on our former lands."

Shebeth smiled. "I shall be very happy when that happens. The good Lord has blessed us with a wonderful life together all these years, four children, all grown up and to be proud of, and plenty of grandchildren."

Rathol felt exactly the same way his wife did. "I do not wish to die for nothing. I have thought about becoming a full shepherd again after we are back on Samaros."

"I know," Shebeth said, touching his arm. "I would like that as well. At least it would pass the time until the Lord calls up to His glorious kingdom and we know the beautiful paradise of Heaven with Him."

"I pray it will be so."

"I pray it will be so, too."

The wind sighed through the grasslands, and healthy blades of green grass wavered. Strong odors of sheep drifted upward to them, the smells of the ruminant mammals normal yet a delight to them, a reminder of home. But not for the flocks to be detected by natural predators, carnivores to attack and kill sheep and force the travelers and the sheepdogs to drive hungry hunters away or kill feral stalkers. However, they stood together there in peace in the tranquility of the colorful scenery of their present surroundings, with breathtaking views to enjoy and relax in.

Below them, children played. Alert sheepdogs guarded well the collective flocks fattening themselves on the wild, abundant pasturage. The dependable canines kept the sheep from ever wandering off, always on the watch for danger to the sheep.

"Which direction are the sheep being herded next?" Rathol asked his wife, since he tended them little.

"Still west after we cross the river," Shebeth replied. "The elders have decided we should break camp tomorrow."

"That is well." Rathol leaned on the Staff of Godpower more, as if he needed it to hold himself up and prevent him from falling to the ground on weakened knees. "I would like to visit the great marketplace at Paradar. They have much in goods to offer. It shall be nice to see the sights of the city."

"I hear Paradar has plenty of entertainment for visitors seeking it," Shebeth remarked. "Places of sin abound around every street corner."

Rathol put his hand on her shoulder. "We shall avoid its dens of iniquity. How long will the journey take to visit the holy shrine at Paradar?"

"Two days journey from here." Shebeth took his hand from her shoulder and kissed it. "I must prepare the evening meal now."

Rathol nodded, and Shebeth climbed down the hill to the camp for their tent. The Shepherd swept his gaze around the area, then looked at the azure firmament. He thought of God in Heaven watching over him, his wife, and their people in the camp, trusting the Creator in everything.

"Almighty Lord," Rathol prayed, "give me strength to continue a little longer to do Thy Will. Thou art with me. Your infinite love comforts me. I am your loyal and humble servant, O God, always faithful to Your word."

Rathol sighed and climbed down the hill. He joined his wife in their tent and set the Staff of Godpower against the back wall. Then he grabbed his knife from underneath his robe and the piece of wood he had been working on near him and started whittling, sitting comfortably on plain, plush pillows. The Shepherd would fashion simple yet beautiful art out of the wood, letting it come naturally as it took shape in his hands to eventually become a small figure—being, animal, or whatever it turned out to be. Wood shavings fell onto the plain brown rug of the tent floor and made a pile before him. Few other furnishings were in the tent: a large bedroll for him, one for his wife, and extra pillows for guests to seat themselves on. Little more possessions did he and his wife have in the tent, only a small chest full of personal mementos.

****

That night Rathol and Shebeth entertained guests for supper, two middle-aged couples, Hezekiah and his wife Matila, Jacobus and his wife Nelspeth.

"How long will you be with the caravan this time?" Hezekiah asked the Shepherd.

"Until the High Enforcer summons me to service," Rathol replied. "I have been on sabbatical for a month now."

Jacobus broke a piece of bread off a loaf. "Who did you capture last time for the Enforcers?"

Rathol recalled. "Three months before my leave, I

stopped Mahussein, the Suicide Bomber, from carrying out his mission. Before that, Ililith, the Black Widow, when she tried to kill an innocent man." Both Archvillains named now served life sentences in the Universal Prisonplex.

"I hear the black wolves in these lands are extremely dangerous," Matila said, changing the subject.

"They are like the yellow wolves of Samaros," Shebeth interjected. "But they can be kept at bay."

Hezekiah ate a slice of cured meat. "Why do you and Shebeth not live in one of the great cities of Survarille, like Acropollon, Rathol? Because, after all, you are a Universal Marshal."

"Machines are part of the life of the peoples of the Technoland," the Shepherd explained. "This is not true of the peoples of the Wilderland. That is why we make a home here on Mellenroel."

Nelspeth turned to their hosts. "When shall you and Rathol celebrate the four decades anniversary of your joining?"

"After our pilgrimage to Paradar is over," Shebeth answered.

The night passed without incident. In the morning, the travelers broke camp. Rathol helped his wife take the tent down and packed their belongings on waiting horses for the next leg of their continuing journey to Paradar. Already the caravan had crossed a large part of Mellenroel.

Fluffy clouds floated and hung in the sky. The elders gave the word, and the caravan began to move out.

The travelers—proud people—and their sheepdogs herded the sheep in an orderly manner in the direction of the Glangie River, watching for strays not to leave the flocks and slow down their progress. Rathol walked beside his wife in the middle of the caravan. The sound of bleating sheep filled the air, sweet music to the Shepherd as he gladly and thankfully smelled the free and fresh air, unpolluted by vehicles, craft, and industry.

Rathol tasted no bitterness in his mouth and stayed sharp. In his hand, the Staff of Godpower looked like the ordinary crook of a simple shepherd, not the divine tool of the Chosen of God and an awesome weapon in the hands of an Enforcer.

The large caravan moved at a slow pace west across grasslands to the Glangie River. It traveled in an organized procession with the head elder and his big family leading the way. People, dogs, horses, and sheep trampled the verdant plains, but the many feet, paws, and hooves that crushed supple blades underneath caused no damage to the grasslands because of the natural thickness of the vast leas. No living beings inhabited the pasturage, which saw only regular traffic of travelers across it. Occasionally herds of wild animals, like deer and wilderox, traversed the enormous expanse.

Behind the caravan in the east, a thunderous noise rose from beyond the hill at their backs, getting louder and louder. Soon many riders topped the hill, their horses snorting in the warm air under Kambec as it shined bright yellow in a partly-cloudy sky. Their weapons drawn, swords, battle-axes, and spears with shields, the riders advanced on the travelers.

A member of the caravan, a young man, glanced back at the wild-looking bunch of horsemen eagerly eyeing the travelers as easy prey. "Marauders!"

The marauders whooped and charged down the hill after the caravan as it plodded along. A warning horn blared very loudly among the travelers. The terrified people speeded up the caravan, but not fast enough to outrun the oncoming and bloodthirsty raiders. Members of the caravan fell to the ground in the stampede to rush to the Glangie River, and fellow travelers helped them get to their feet. Sheepdogs barked at the pursuing riders as the pounding hooves of galloping steeds sounded like the footfalls of doom.

Rathol saw they were not going to make it to the river unless he stopped the marauders. Shebeth witnessed her husband change from a regular herdsman to a Universal Marshal in an instant as the Shepherd summoned the Staff of Godpower to life to do battle with the frenzied killers bearing down on them. Rathol used the Almighty power of the Staff to erect a wall of fire to block the passage of the marauders. Horses wheeled as the raiders could not chase the travelers.

The caravan approached the Glangie River. Determined and all by himself, Rathol protected the hurrying travelers from the rear now.

Tired, the caravan got to the east bank of the muttering and meandering water. The people and their animals waded quickly across the flowing course for the other side. Rathol was the last to reach the opposite bank.

Just then, the wall of fire extinguished. The marauders, mad, resumed galloping their mounts after the caravan. The travelers watched the riders closing the distance between them.

"We must flee!" a young woman screamed in the caravan.

"No!" a young man shouted. "We must fight!"

"Hold fast!" Rathol commanded in a roaring tone of voice that defied his old age. "The Almighty Hand of the

Lord shall smite them for us so they will no longer be a blight on humanity!"

"Have faith!" Shebeth yelled.

Rathol used the Staff of Godpower and made the river rise against the marauders as they crossed it. A tidal wave rushed from the north toward the marauders and drowned them and their horses. It carried the corpses and carcasses downstream, out of sight.

Afterward, the Shepherd silenced the Staff of Godpower. Members of the caravan, which was safe now, cheered at the deaths of the unlucky brigands and their hero, famous as a Universal Marshal. The aged Enforcer felt exhausted and leaned heavily on the quiet Staff.

"Rest, my husband," Shebeth said, standing right beside him, so very proud of him. "You have saved us from a terrible fate."

Rathol nodded. The Shepherd had no energy to speak at the moment. Slowly his strength returned.

The elders decided the caravan should make camp for the night by the river. Rathol lay on the ground with the Staff of Godpower beside him. Shebeth sat beside him and comforted him. The other travelers prepared an evening meal in celebration for being delivered from the marauders.

Awake, Rathol thought about Samaros, an agricultural world in the Polluxian Sector of the Milky Way Galaxy. His birth planet was a biosphere of country life, a pastoral existence on a global scale unspoiled by advanced science and technology and urban encroachment. Farmers and herdspeople lived in harmony with nature and their rural environment. The Shepherd considered Tellus his second home, but his heart belonged to Samaros, and he hoped his native world never changed its rustic ways.

Later that night, after a nice supper and a bit of revelry drinking wine, singing and dancing, and storytelling, Rathol walked a ways up the river with his wife, accompanied by their youngest sheepdog, Toggie. The Shepherd glanced up at the cloudless heavens and spotted Nembat, the only moon of Tellus, glowing white in an evening sky crowded with stars. Around them, the warm night of summer passed comfortably and peacefully, the wind still as if it needed a break to blow fresh tomorrow. The quiet around them cast a soothing effect, the earth beneath their feet not too firm, the air not too thick or thin to make their lungs work hard.

"I do not wish to meet the idolaters in Paradar," Rathol said. "Nor do I wish to meet any pagans who proclaim their gods are the only true ones and influence mortal affairs."

Shebeth smiled and touched his arm that did not hold the Staff of Godpower. "There are God-fearing people in Paradar. Those who love the Lord as much as we do."

"I have faith in that."

"We especially have to beware greedy vendors who will try and sell us worthless trinkets and useless goods. The elders have decided to market a small number of sheep in Paradar and maybe trade and bargain for things for the caravan."

Rathol understood. "That is good. Get a fair price for the sheep and add supplies for the journey after Paradar."

They walked together in silence, their young sheepdog running ahead of them and checking out everything interesting. No wild animals roamed the vicinity that night, and no fish swam in the river near them. No unusual scents in the night air, for the sheepdog would have alerted them to such smells. The loyal canine would also have indicated to them if it heard any strange sounds in the distance, like noisy people and treads of wagons approaching.

After a while, they started back to camp. When they drew near it, the Staff of Godpower broke their serenity by tingling in the Shepherd's hand. A calm resignation fell over him.

"What is it?" Shebeth asked.

"My rest period is over," Rathol replied, readying himself for service. "The High Enforcer wants me. I'm about to be taken to the great hall of the Universal Marshals once again."

"I wish the Grand Universal Marshal could have waited until after the pilgrimage to Paradar to call you to Enforcer work."

Rathol agreed with her. "Forgive me for not being able to complete the journey with you."

"I forgive you," Shebeth said, straightening out his robe unconsciously. "I will tell the others what has happened."

His eyes watered in emotion for her. Rathol did not want to part with her. "Take care, my wife. I shall return when I can."

Shebeth hugged and kissed him. Many times they had been through this. She never complained about it.

Rathol beamed with such pride and love for his faithful mate and lifelong partner, having been married to her since they were of age. Sighing, the Shepherd stepped back from his wife and waited. He vanished before her adoring eyes, teleported to the Justiceplex on the other side of Tellus.

Chapter 4

The royal entourage crossed the open plains toward an ancient forest. A herd of woolly bison migrated north of them in the huge territory, where a few villages dotted the beautiful and untamed landscape. Miles away south stood the major city of Amaron. Overhead a flock of wilderness geese flew west, and a couple of blue-tailed hawks glided in the same direction the royal entourage headed. A red-necked gopher popped up from a hole in the ground and watched in a leisurely manner as the modest procession passed. Kambec set in the west, the evening sky streaked with a few clouds. A southerly breeze blew around them like the touch of good spirits.

"I implore you, Your Highness, to wait until the light of morning to attempt the forest," Captain Fallahan said, a tall veteran of war campaigns with the battle scars on his muscular frame to prove it. His uniform looked spotless for the occasion. In the distance appeared the tree line, dark and dense. "Evil lurks in Ebongrove and haunts the forest. Creatures that devour the flesh, rend the mind, and steal the soul."

Princess Selainee laughed gaily. The young woman brushed a long lock of her blonde hair from her pretty face. The fiery daughter of King Sagememnon and Queen Decleopatra of Valdania looked prim in her white finery. "Those are foolish old tales told by feeble crones. My father grows impatient for us to arrive at Cammalain, so I can meet my future husband and king." The arranged marriage pleased her.

"Prince Xandermas will still be at Cammalain no matter when we arrive there, Your Highness," Fallahan responded as politely as he could. "Your wedding to His Highness will take place whenever it takes place."

"This marriage is very important," Selainee said. "It will ally two kingdoms in the face of an imminent attack by the Tauthans. The marriage cannot wait. The Tauths are a threat to all the lands of the Byzanmark. We need a strong alliance against those barbarians before they invade."

Fallahan understood the dire situation but shook his head in disappointment. Exasperated, he turned to the petite and pretty woman in a violet blouse, a violet skirt, and violet slippers on a bay horse to his left. "Maybe you can convince Her Highness of the folly of attempting Ebongrove after dusk, milady."

Eneysa, the Metamorph-Enforcer, unbound her long puce hair and looked at the beautiful princess with sympathy in her puce eyes. But she felt Her Highness, though well versed in the politics of kingdoms, lacked some sense beyond that, whereas the experienced captain had plenty of it. "He's right, Your Highness. We should wait until after dawn to pass through the forest, a very old place filled with unpleasant memories and much anger. There's much truth to those foolish old tales. Ebongrove is a land of shadow and dark things—eagerly desiring and waiting to prey on the unwary."

Selainee smiled disarmingly. "My dear captain. Where is your courage?"

Fallahan stiffened on his gray steed, rather offended. "My courage is fine, Your Highness. But I know better than to risk Ebongrove at night when the evil within it is most alive and most hungry."

"Posh," Selainee chided him gently.

"And as I advised you back on the lowlands, Your Highness," Fallahan said, ignoring her slight, "it would be better if we just go around the forest."

Eneysa knew the other riders behind the three of them sat tensely on their mounts, waiting for the outcome of the discussion but wanting to avoid traveling through Ebongrove. As they came in view of the forest, the Metamorph-Enforcer peered with her keenness of vision at its western edge. From Ebongrove, she read an invitation for the royal entourage to enter it in order to be consumed by the gloomy growth. She glanced up at full Nembat rising and took the natural sight of it as an ill omen tonight. Also, she thought the Tellusian moon, in its present cycle, invisibly but powerfully exuded a supernatural influence of negativity on the forest and mocked the bright lights of celestial bodies that would join it. A silvery tyrant about to dominate the darkening heavens thinning of clouds.

"I am the leader here," Selainee said haughtily. "To go around the forest would add days to our journey. We need to get to Cammalain faster. We will ride through the forest when we reach it."

Fallahan closed his eyes for a moment, as if to pray to some god to protect them, then fingered the hilt of his sheathed sword briefly for reassurance. "As you wish, Your Highness."

"It's settled then," Selainee responded, triumphant in tone. She beamed and patted the neck of her white mare. "We chance the ancient woods. With luck, we should be through it in a short enough time."

Eneysa smelled the growing fear running through the royal entourage. The Metamorph-Enforcer hoped the princess's bad decision did not become a grave mistake and cost them their lives.

By habit, she prepared for danger by considering which natural and supernatural creatures to change into if the evil in Ebongrove assailed them. Her people, the Metamorphs, dwelled on the planet Urfantasia, an imperial world in the Babarian Sector of the Milky Way Galaxy. On Urfantasia, Metamorphs were an aborigine race, subject to the planetary laws of other races—a mixture of alien races and humanoid races—now inhabiting the biosphere as one nation united around the globe. The Metamorph tribes kept to themselves, preferring not to have outsiders meddle in the affairs of their race and staying out of matters not involving other governing bodies. They were intelligent and primitive beings on Urfantasia that considered Metamorphs a far superior race, even gods. Occasionally a Metamorph served with others onworld as well as offworld.

Selainee addressed the Metamorph-Enforcer. "Do you have a king and queen to rule your people?"

"We're freely governed by a small council," Eneysa answered. "Fifteen members make it up, each from a tribe, all chosen by rite of passage. We have a chief to head the council. My great uncle Madidas."

With sharp ears, Eneysa heard whispers of discontent among riders in the royal entourage and knew they wished their whole party rode in another part of Mellenroel, out of the middle of the west coast of the Wilderland and where Ebongrove lay. The Metamorph-Enforcer stayed alert, her keen senses attuned to the natural environment around them.

The royal entourage entered the forest just after dusk, following a short stop. For the moment, the nightlife in Ebongrove remained quiet. The thick crowns of the tall trees screened out the night sky as if the forest had transported them to a kingdom of shadow. A cooler wind sighed through the trees and wafted earthen smells of the forest into their noses—raw odors strong enough to keep them awake. The night air felt warm and comfortable in sharp contrast to the chill in their bones and uncomfortable mood instilled in them by Ebongrove. Because of the conditions being practically pitch black, they were forced to let the horses pick their way through the forest. Scattered sticks snapped under the dirt-encrusted hooves of their uneasy steeds.

Bird cries echoed around them in haunting songs and made the riders in the royal entourage jumpy in their saddles. Weary but hardened soldiers guarding the princess reached for their weapons. Eneysa tensed a little, ready to shapeshift.

"We should have camped for the night back on the plains," Fallahan muttered. "This is wrong."

Eneysa agreed with the captain but said nothing, intent on sensing danger. But so far, no danger manifested, almost causing her to breathe a sigh of relief. The Metamorph-Enforcer considered whether she should shapeshift into a much bigger and more powerful form to protect and defend the royal entourage against surprise attacks from the evil lurking in Ebongrove. She finally decided it would be best to wait and react to sudden ambushes in the forest when they happened and counter them with appropriate metamorphoses.

Selainee had heard the captain as well. "We are making up for lost time in those lowlands because of the mists, dear captain. My father and mother expected us to be at Cammalain in six days, and I intend to reach it as they wish."

"They will still be glad to see us even if we're late, Your Highness," Fallahan responded, itching to draw his long sword and slay any evil in Ebongrove. "It's far better to travel slow and careful than fast and reckless."

Selainee huffed at his mild criticism. "The quicker we arrive at Cammalain, the sooner the journey is over. I do not want to prolong it unnecessarily."

"Aye," Fallahan said in general accord with the princess. "If our arrival to Cammalain is overly delayed, the king and queen will send search parties after us."

"I do not wish my father and mother to be forced to do that," Selainee stated flatly. "They should not be so burdened with worry because we simply failed to make it to Cammalain at the appointed time."

Fallahan nodded at that, while Eneysa did not respond. Later, the royal entourage heard more bird cries somewhere from the trees as the modest procession penetrated deeper and deeper into the forest. Nocturnal activity increased in Ebongrove as more sounds filled the night air from unseen sources. Bloodcurdling screams from hidden creatures spooked their mounts, and the rustlings of unseen brush made members of the royal entourage very nervous, especially those not soldiers. Fallahan silently criticized their ill-advised passage through the forest at night, foolishly awakening evil in Ebongrove to prey on them at its leisure.

The royal entourage heard a tree fall in the forest, and they stopped. All looked around toward the direction of the sound to see what had made it crash to the ground, though it was very dim around them, virtually cloaked in total darkness. But nothing appeared to take credit for the fallen timber as they waited to see if something evil would suddenly spring out to attack them. Selainee ordered them forward again, and the soldiers with her began drawing their weapons in anticipation of a bloody fight, the captain the first to wield in hand.

"Come, taste death from my naked blade, evil of Ebongrove," Fallahan growled. "I prefer a straight fight to all your scare tactics against us."

"Please, captain," Eneysa said. "Don't directly challenge the forest to send us its champions to engage us in a skirmish."

Selainee tried to maintain a dignified air as she rode, but the unfriendly atmosphere of Ebongrove weakened her aristocratic mien more and more the deeper they got into the forest. "These woods need beautiful flowers to grow in it to make it shine. It is too dreary a place."

Strangely, that made Fallahan laugh. "I suppose next you will propose that a vegetable garden should be planted in Ebongrove, Your Highness."

"My royal self is not to be made fun of, captain," Selainee retorted. She gave the military commander a scornful look.

Fallahan submitted to her royal authority. "Forgive me, Your Highness, for offending you."

Selainee blustered in the saddle. "Apology accepted. Next time remember your place, captain."

Fallahan showed no reaction to the stinging reprimand from the princess because of his military discipline, though deep down, he was a bit resentful of her reminding him that she was in a higher class of society than he was. "Yes, Your Highness."

Their passage through the forest continued with evil

lurking everywhere in Ebongrove, staying in the shadows, seemingly biding its time to strike the royal entourage. Eneysa wondered if her being a Metamorph was detected by the malevolent presence hiding in the forest and might discourage the evil lurking there from actually attacking the modest procession. They crossed the width of the forest without making camp for the night, only stopping for brief rests before moving on each time. If they had journeyed through the length of Ebongrove, it would take longer. Since they were traveling through the width of it, they could pass through the forest in less than a day, little comfort to the riders. Some animals appeared before them, small creatures like moles, muskchucks, and woodcats. A few snakes slithered into their poor view but not across their rough and winding path. Rarely did they see a bird, and when they did, it was always a black and gold crested macaw.

It looked as if they would make their way through the forest without incident. As their passage through Ebongrove neared its end, spirits in the royal entourage raised.

"Well," Selainee said, smiling. "The old tales have proven to be nothing more than false stories to frighten children to their beds at night."

At the rear of the royal entourage, a rider screamed, knocked off his horse by a dark creature. A second rider suffered the same fate right after the first one.

"Firebrands!" Fallahan yelled, grabbing his from his worn saddlebag. He pulled out a two-foot-long wooden rod with a red lighting stone and ignited the former with the latter, producing a burning torch. All the other soldiers did the same thing as Eneysa waited for the right moment to transform herself into another life form.

From all sides, large black, hairless creatures on two legs shambled toward them, revealed by the flaming firebrands. The round eyes of the dark creatures glowed white, without irises or pupils. Their jagged teeth gnashed for the warm taste of fresh meat, heightened by the awful clicking of claws on large hands. Small ears pointing out from their grotesque heads listened in delight to the frightened sounds of their victims; slit noses sniffed the pleasant scents of live prey. An unpleasant odor radiated from their broad frames, and they snarled in anticipation of slaughter for a filling meal.

Selainee utterly panicked. "Father, I need you."

Fallahan cursed. "We're trapped!" He unsheathed and swung his long sword overhead. "If I'm going to die, then let it be in battle, slaying as many of them as I can."

Quickly, Eneysa dismounted. The Metamorph-Enforcer stepped away from her horse and shapeshifted into a giant sphinx, an ancient monster with a woman's head and breast, a lion's body, and the wings of an eagle possessing energy power on the occultic level. She towered above all creatures in the forest but below the treetops.

The dark creatures attacked them with ferocity. Eneysa, in her new life form, killed the charging creatures or batted them away from her and the royal entourage with huge paws. The armed escort fought the beasts with swords, daggers, bows and arrows, and firebrands defending themselves and those of the modest procession, their mounts tight reined and battle trained.

Dark creatures shot white beams from their eyes into the faces of the riders and hypnotized their victims. They used the magical forms of the Evil Eye on the weakened minds of their frozen and helpless victims, then prepared to devour them. But before the beastly beings consumed the soft flesh of the vulnerable humans, the Metamorph-Enforcer leaped in and bowled the evil things over. Soldiers aided Eneysa and set the creatures ablaze with firebrands.

In savage fury, the dark creatures shot green beams from their eyes into the bodies of the riders, pulling souls from members of the royal entourage in order to kill them and feed on their lifeless corpses. The horses they could slaughter later if they wished. Eneysa saw what was happening and crashed on top of the beastly beings and shredded them with the lion claws of her sphinx form. Souls taken from the riders in the modest procession were restored to bodies with the deaths of the evil things. The royal entourage repeatedly repulsed the dark creatures.

Finally, unable to overpower the modest procession, mainly because of Eneysa, the evil things retreated and regrouped. A number of beastly beings lay dead on the ground, some of them hacked by sword or charred by firebrands, but most of them felled by the sphinx form of the Metamorph-Enforcer. The black blood of the dark creatures wetted the scuffed earth. Miraculously, not many of the riders were killed, and other members of the modest procession suffered just minor wounds from the terrible assault, thanks primarily to Eneysa and secondarily to the bravery of the veterans among the riders fighting beside her.

Selainee fell apart. The young woman visibly shook with fear and shed tears, speechless in the face of such horror. All Her Highness could do was sit on her horse and do nothing.

"We can't keep them off forever," Fallahan said. The captain turned his head to the Metamorph-Enforcer. "If I were them, milady, I would converge the bulk of their remaining forces on you in order to overwhelm us."

"No doubt," Eneysa agreed, still in her sphinx form.

Enraged, the dark creatures readied their next attack and started at the royal entourage again, this time cautiously, wary of the Metamorph-Enforcer, snarling at the riders. Eneysa saw their situation deteriorating fast as wave upon wave of the beastly beings advanced, hemming in the remaining riders. The Universal Marshal decided she needed to metamorphose quickly into something else different and better. Considering the endless variety of life forms she could transform into, Eneysa chose to shapeshift from a sphinx into a giantess, her head high above the treetops now and able to see in all directions.

Swiftly yet carefully, Eneysa scooped up the royal entourage in her colossal arms, horses and all, just as the evil things launched themselves at the ready party. The Metamorph-Enforcer strode through the forest, taking giant steps, carrying riders and mounts firmly in her immense limbs but not too tightly against her enormous chest, leaving the beastly beings behind them shrieking in fury and defeat.

They traveled through Ebongrove fast, Eneysa sweeping her gaze in all directions over the forest quickly, not looking down once. Instead of taking hours to finish passing through, with the tremendous help of the Metamorph-Enforcer, they rapidly cleared the forest in a matter of minutes. Once out of Ebongrove, Eneysa stopped and carefully put the royal entourage on the ground. Then she shapeshifted back into her natural state, that of a humanoid female.

North, south, and east of them stretched free territory, a vast vista of open ground. Behind them, Ebongrove quieted with their exit from the forest. They beheld no other creatures roaming the dark, yawning flatlands or flying through the night air.

"You saved us," Selainee said in astonishment.

Eneysa remounted her horse and smiled at the stunned princess. "I simply did what was called for, Your Highness."

Fallahan thanked gods for delivering them safely from the clutches of evil in the forest out loud, and Selainee did the same silently. All the other surviving riders in the royal entourage were breathless and stared in awe at the Universal Marshal.

"You're a blessed sending from the gods," Fallahan said to the Metamorph-Enforcer. "You did a deed worthy of a song."

Selainee appeared to have a new respect for the Universal Marshal. "My father will reward you for this."

Soldiers in the large procession gave a rousing cheer for Eneysa, who felt a little embarrassed by their appreciation of her saving the royal entourage from certain death at the hands of the dark creatures in Ebongrove. To her, a simple thanks was enough, for the Metamorph-Enforcer did not care for medals of valor or accolades.

"My father will bestow upon you an honorary place in the court of Valdania as well," Selainee added. "You have earned the special privilege."

"With you beside us, we are guaranteed to reach Cammalain safely, milady," Fallahan remarked.

Before Eneysa could respond to their kind words,

she found herself unexpectedly and instantly teleported to the Justiceplex on the other side of Tellus.

Chapter 5

Two robots entered the underground arena at opposite ends. Around them, spectators—human, humanoid, alien, faerie, and other beings—filled the tiered seats of the subterranean amphitheater beyond seating capacity, most having betted on the illegal robot fight.

Large glowpanels in the ceiling lit the immense place. Above it, a domed warehouse sat over the hidden stadium, located in the warehouse district of Urdanth, a major city in the northeast region of Survarille and its fourth largest. The filtered air underground was cool. No one smoked in the underground amphitheater, but some drank beverages, either alcoholic, like Nighehennan ale, or nonalcoholic, like Baltaic water. Rich people sat among the spectators, big gamblers making outlandish wagers for money, power, property, and other things. Fans cheered and booed at the two robots, and more bets were placed at the excitement in the coliseum. The arena floor had no blood spots because the combatants did not spill blood since they were not organic in nature. Instead, they lost electronic and mechanical parts and occasionally liquids like oils, chemicals, and hydraulic fluids. There were burnt marks on the arena floor from previous matches.

Rayzilla, an eight-foot, red robot with a donut-shaped head and a glassy band around it as his eyes, strode toward his opponent from the east entrance of the underground arena. Rapidly, he spun finger blades on hands attached to massive arms of heavy metal, his bulky body built like a laser tank and shaped like a refrigerator of automated design. The odd makers favored him to win the match and remain champion. They and most of the fans there expected the hulking droid to pummel the smaller one he faced into a compact heap in the deadly contest, forbidden by Tellusian law.

Procules, the Robot-Enforcer, wheeled toward Rayzilla from the west entrance of the underground arena. The Universal Marshal was working undercover on his current assignment and was at the end of it, having successfully gotten inside the illegal robot fights in and around the metropolitan area, setting up the subterranean amphitheater for a big bust. Procules stood over six and a half feet tall, about a foot and a half shorter than his opponent, a blue and silver robot with a large cylindrical head positioned horizontally and attached to a tubular neck. His neck connected to a barrel-shaped body; his body was fused to a square wheel base containing six grooved wheels. He saw through inverted triangular, crystal eyes, and his robotic hands went without finger blades. He used the identity, for the undercover operation, the name of the robot fighter Jettizinga.

"Little machine, I will shred your internal circuits with my whirling blades," Rayzilla said, spinning them faster and faster.

Procules was not impressed by the deadly display. "Fellow robot, your threatening words do not compute."

Rayzilla laughed. "My weapons systems will pound you into metallic mulch. Your only use after I destroy you is spare parts for damaged machines needing repair."

"Programmed speech from an oversized garbage disposal unit," Procules responded in the trash talk of robot fighters.

"You heap of automaton refuse," Rayzilla said. "I am the current champion. Undefeated in over two hundred matches. My maker will be proud of my mangling your electronic components and sending you home as mechanical junk."

The spectators cheered wildly as Rayzilla charged at Procules, aiming to quickly demolish the Robot-Enforcer with the finger blades of his rotating hands. Procules easily evaded the bigger robot by rolling sideways to the right, then immediately spinning around. Rayzilla shot past him, stopped abruptly, swiftly and smoothly reversed direction, and charged again at him without breaking running motion. Procules repeated the defensive tactics but to his left this time, with the same result as before as Rayzilla flew by him. Most in the crowd booed in disgust, a sign they wanted the two robots to collide into each other and whale away. Procules could tell the spectators wished either or both robots pulverized into scrap metal.

"Hold still so I can decimate your internal circuits and trash your mechanical body," Rayzilla said. The bigger robot beeped in rage at the Robot-Enforcer.

Procules beeped in return. "You're an automaton relic. I will retire you faster than permanent deactivation and see you displayed as an obsolete technology item in an antique shop."

The Robot-Enforcer wondered what held up the police raid on the subterranean amphitheater. Months ago, the sting operation had been set up and put in place. Procules had to be entered in the illegal robot fights by an owner—played by the undercover cop Serpicon, a humanoid—who had to sign an agreement to allow it with those in charge of the matches. The Universal Marshal had to prove himself in a preliminary bout to show he could hold his own against a robot opponent. Procules had defeated the robot fighter Elektranus by crippling him to be put on the fight cards. For the next couple of months, the Robot-Enforcer fought a number of robot fighters and beat them all. Some of them the Universal Marshal had deactivated in fights, some he had seriously damaged to prevent them from continuing matches, and some he had destroyed to win bouts. Eventually, he had earned a shot at the title, going undefeated himself, after beating the number one contender, the robot fighter Robotin, in a classic that spectators and fight promoters still talked about.

Rayzilla began stalking him, but Procules negated the strategic maneuver by circling the arena, staying well out of reach of the finger blades of his opponent, whirling for the destruction of the Robot-Enforcer. Those weapons of the bigger robot were very sharp and shiny, as if brand new from an automated factory and special for this match. The spectators jeered louder and louder their displeasure of the bout, the noise reverberating through the stadium in increasing volume, reaching a deafening tone. Fans shouted unkind remarks at the two robots, particularly at Procules.

"Blast that chicken machine to pieces!"

"Compact that droid into a ship hatch!"

"Disintegrate that unit into factory fodder!"

If he was an organic person, Procules would have been disgusted by their terrible manners.

The fans started acting like a lynch mob, demanding

for the destruction of the two robots for failing to entertain them, for not fighting. Some of the spectators began demanding for the next match—a better bout—to begin. They wanted to see a different pair of robots clash after the fight between the Robot-Enforcer and his opponent was terminated. The Universal Marshal was becoming more concerned about why the police raid on the subterranean amphitheater still had not happened yet. He could not understand the delay. Certainly, he could not keep prolonging this match. Eventually, those in charge would be forced to stop it.

Suddenly Rayzilla opened the left and right doors of his big chest and bombarded Procules with rapidly spinning spike balls sparking electrically. The deadly projectiles caused the Robot-Enforcer to raise his arms to protect his crystal eyes and forced him to wheel backward; a few of the spike balls hit his body and arms and stuck. He dislodged them quickly. Fans roared their approval of the attack by the bigger robot and urged the current champion to strike with more weapons against the Universal Marshal and smash him into debris. Smiles creased the faces of the fight promoters watching the match.

"Come on, champ, use your entire arsenal against him!"

"Crush him with everything you got!"

"Short circuit him and finish him off!"

Procules thought the spectators were getting bloodthirsty. To them, the Robot-Enforcer was nothing more than an expendable machine, easily replaced. They acted uncivilized, without conscience. In his view, they needed counseling.

Rayzilla pressed his advantage as the fans urged him

on. The red robot moved in and bore down on the Robot-Enforcer with finger blades in a position to drill holes into the Universal Marshal. Procules caught Rayzilla's wrists in his hands and kept the lethal weapons at bay, both locked together near the east end of the arena. The red robot closed his chest compartment and pushed closer and closer to the Robot-Enforcer with his finger blades spinning fast.

"You cannot restrain me from slicing you to pieces, puny droid," Rayzilla said. "My long cutters will chop you into metal bits for recycling material."

Procules saw himself being forced back slowly against the east wall of the arena by the red robot. "You're a defective model and need reprogramming, brother automaton."

Rayzilla beeped. "I will hack you into a mechanical mess so much even your maker will not recognize your robotic remains."

"You're a manufactured machine of low and inferior technology, factory subnormal," Procules responded, struggling against his opponent. "A mechanical being of limited capacity. As a created creature with artificial intelligence, your IQ ranks below the mind of a Tapiralean water snake."

"You will know death by deactivation," Rayzilla promised.

"Not in this existence," Procules countered.

The spectators hollered for Rayzilla to deliver the killing blow and finish Procules off fast, without mercy. Their yelling for the final destruction of the Robot-Enforcer was like Banshees wailing for the deaths of their victims.

In the stands, more beverages were served. The

sporting event was like a wild drunken party where there seemed to be no rules to obey other than having a good time. There were guards among the fans, but they did not stop the rowdiness of the spectators and only would if it got out of control too much, under orders from those in charge of the illegal robot fights. However, there were automated security devices in the coliseum, programmed to activate if emergencies arose, like the fans rioting.

Rayzilla, detecting victory within his reach, reopened his chest compartment and extended two circular saws, attached to thin shafts, toward Procules to cut into the Robot-Enforcer.

Procules reacted by firing laser beams from his crystal eyes and destroyed the two circular saws of the red robot, who beeped in surprise. Then the Universal Marshal smashed together Rayzilla's hands and caused his finger blades, still spinning, to wreck each other and the red robot's wrists. Rayzilla stepped backward, shaking in major damage.

Spectators roared their approval for Procules, but fans of the red robot booed vehemently for their robot fighter scored against in a destructive manner. Many in the crowd shouted at the Robot-Enforcer to finish off the red robot and become the new champion. The Universal Marshal refused to completely demolish Rayzilla for the victory as the mad red robot experienced a major malfunction and tried to quickly correct it.

At that moment, a joint force of local police and regional troopers in blue raided the subterranean amphitheater, armed with blasters, blast rifles, photon shotguns, and photon batons. Security personnel in the stadium drew their own blasters and started shooting at the law enforcement team. All hell broke loose as laser weapon fire flew in all directions, the place thrown into chaos.

Local police and regional troopers freed robot fighters held in single cells below the arena. The liberated droids charged into the fray on the side of the law enforcement team and paid back the foul beings who had enslaved them for gladiatorial games. Robot guards, well-armed, belonging to the sponsors of the illegal, and now busted, robot fights, entered the clash and started taking on the law enforcement team. The police robots responded to the dangerous situation and aided the pinned down police and troopers, turning the tide of battle in favor of the law enforcement team. Bodies fell everywhere dead or injured as the local police and regional troopers began rounding up those employed in the illegal robot fights for transport to a police station, there to be duly processed for arraignment. Procules saw Rayzilla ignoring the police raid and quietly assessing the actual damage the Robot-Enforcer had inflicted on him. The red robot finished determining the extent of the damage.

"You wrecked all of my finger blades and destroyed my circular saws!" Rayzilla bellowed. "You made some of my systems overheat, overload, and short circuit!"

The red robot opened his stomach compartment and produced a large pair of sharp teeth rollers, connected to two long shiny chrome handles. Beeping furiously, Rayzilla went berserk and charged the Robot-Enforcer, intent on mowing down the Universal Marshal. Having no choice, Procules opened his chest compartment and fired a spread of photon projectiles at the red robot and blew him up. The separated head of the red robot beeped once among his scattered remains, sparked, and exploded apart. Rayzilla was no more.

The police raid ended as the law enforcement team arrested all those employed in the illegal robot fights who survived the firefight in the subterranean amphitheater. Police robots shut down the robot guards remaining and lined them up against a wall. Local police and regional troopers took the arrested felons to the police hoverwagons above ground outside the warehouse. The robot guards would be separated from the other foul beings working for the illegal robot fights and taken to a police compound where other seized automatons were deactivated, tagged, stored, and waited to be reprogrammed.

Lieutenant Yar Gorodon, a tall and thin alien being, and a regional trooper, the one who led the police raid, met the Robot-Enforcer in the center of the arena, now quiet below empty seats. The Universal Marshal watched freed robots, now former fighters of the arena, leave the subterranean amphitheater as the law enforcement team closed it down. New lives awaited the freed robots as they could go wherever they wanted, beeping in joy at being liberated.

"Sorry we took so long getting down here," Yar said. "We had a little trouble neutralizing the security robots in the warehouse." In pity, the lieutenant looked at all that remained of Rayzilla, a destroyed machine turned into a pile of junk, but recyclable material. "I see you had a little trouble, too."

Procules just finished checking what had been done to him by the red robot, externally and internally. The damage was minor. "Regrettably, I was forced to terminate his robolife. His programming was flawed and solely geared for destruction in the fighting arena."

Yar holstered his blaster. "There will be no more illegal robot fights in and around Urdanth. We have seen to that. As for this sports facility, it will be dismantled. It could be remade into a storage facility for trade goods."

"Do you have in custody the mysterious figure of the crime boss who ran this entire racket?" Procules asked. The Robot-Enforcer wanted full closure to the case.

Yar nodded. "The crime boss behind these illegal robot fights was the alien Nasta Lux. He is a Thron. Small alien with big plans. We caught him trying to flee the warehouse using a teleport pod behind a clothing closet in his office here above ground. We also caught his alien mistress Shia Nim."

"My assignment is complete." Procules assessed information in his memory cells of the admissible evidence he needed to present to the Urdanth courts for trial concerning the case. All the foul beings arrested in the police raid had to be prosecuted for their parts in the illegal robot fights to the fullest extent of the law. The Robot-Enforcer found the information and internally catalogued it.

"Will you be going on another assignment for the Universal Marshals?" Yar asked. "Or will you be staying in Urdanth longer?"

"I will remain in the city until the High Enforcer contacts me for another assignment," Procules replied. "I need to give exhibits and testimony to the Urdanth courts to help convict all the foul beings apprehended in the case."

Yar ordered an Urdanth officer and a regional trooper to pack up the remains of Rayzilla for transport as evidence in the legal matter. "What will you do before the trial?"

Just then, Procules recorded himself being teleported to the Justiceplex, from the east coast of Survarille to the west coast of Survarille on Tellus.

Chapter 6

Enforcer Lorliane, the Ice Being, pursued three human thieves, two males and a female, through the major city of Darfleet, in the midwest region of Survarille. The Universal Marshal categorized them as Criminals. She did not believe any Villain masterminded the daring heist of the Crystal Sphere and thought the thieves pulled the robbery only to get a bundle of money for the stolen prize.

Lorliane, a tall woman, possessed a shapely figure. Her blue eyes sparkled like sapphires, her blonde hair long and shiny. The Ice Being wore a midnight blue unisuit with matching belt and boots. She could encase herself in ice anytime she wished.

The three humans fled in a hovercraft. A half an hour ago, the thieves stole the ancient and mysterious Crystal Sphere from the Darfleet Museum before it opened its doors to the public.

Lorliane knew the Crystal Sphere was a historical artifact of legend and mystery. It was reputed to have supernatural power of tremendous magnitude, enough to destroy planes of existence. Other tales said it radiated bioenergy—vital force of a superior nature—and could magnify the bioenergy of any living thing and make it very powerful. They were stories of it being able to heal the sick, especially the terminally ill.

The Enforcer shot a continuous beam of ice from her

left hand. It pulled her along and made a long trail of ice before and behind in the warm air, an extended track of frozen water that would eventually melt.

Lorliane chased the fleeing thieves through downtown Darfleet, all of its buildings constructed of silver omnimetal, rising all around her and them. They tried to shake her off but to no avail. People watched the pursuit in varying degrees of interest, the Ice Being ignoring the citizens for the moment, seeing no danger yet to the people of the city from the armed and dangerous felons. The thieves kept their hovercraft, a sleek and topless saucer, a safe distance above the congestion below of speeders, speeder vans, speeder buses, and speeder trucks, free to fly unhindered in the air.

The Universal Marshal dared not try to fire ice beams from her hand at the zooming hovercraft for fear of crippling it and crashing it into a building or traffic below. She might cause destruction of or damage to private or public property or bring injury or death to innocent beings. The Ice Being waited patiently for an opportunity to catch the thieves in their getaway transport, so she could encase them in ice without doing any real harm.

The chase wove around office buildings and large and small stores, plus a few apartment buildings and other structures. All the factories of Darfleet stood outside the downtown area of the city. The metropolitan area featured no stadiums for professional or amateur sports. It recently held an election and had voted for a new mayor, the alien Mimethos Huth, a Vervon.

The new mayor had requested from the High Enforcer to send a Universal Marshal to fill in temporarily as City Marshal until the current one, Jobokin, member of the faerie race called Dhanans, had returned from his leave of absence. Jobokin was expected to resume his official duties in less than a week.

Lorliane chased the thieves through Darfleet Park, the largest one in the city, the ornamented and recreation ground centrally located in the metropolitan area. Many people crowded Darfleet Park—families, friends, visitors, and others—to enjoy it. It featured a number of pathways around tall trees and big lawns to use and go through. Some sat on many of its benches of silver omnimetal or picnicked on its grass. A few pets, small and large creatures, played or walked in it with their owners.

The thieves became desperate. They started firing blasters at the Ice Being. Lorliane easily dodged their laser shots but was immediately concerned they might inadvertently or deliberately shoot innocent beings and force her to save people. The Criminals, however, did not try to harm any citizens or visitors, at least not intentionally, and they were not killers. They just hurried to get out of the city with their stolen prize.

The three humans turned south. Their hovercraft dove into the traffic below. Lorliane stayed on their tail. The chase wove through fast-moving traffic. The hovercraft bumped into a speeder, which careened out of control and threatened to cause a pile-up. The Ice Being fired a beam of ice from her free hand and formed an ice ramp before the speeder, which safely jumped it over other vehicles and managed to stop in an alley. All the occupants of the speeder were unharmed.

Lorliane tried to slow down the hovercraft by firing a beam of ice and forming a wall of ice ahead of it. The hovercraft smashed through the wall of ice, and the thieves zoomed their transport higher into the air. The Ice Being kept pace with them as their hovercraft zigzagged.

Abruptly, the thieves descended in their hovercraft for the teleporter station on Wave Avenue, a busy street east of Darfleet Park. Lorliane followed them down, staying right with them. They braked their transport in front of the teleporter station and jumped out of it, running into the immense structure, with weapons in hand and the female human carrying the Crystal Sphere in a synthon bag.

Lorliane entered the teleporter station behind them in a swooping manner as the thieves knocked people down to reach one of the teleport rooms in the public building. A station announcer informed citizens and visitors of teleporting schedules for the afternoon onworld and offworld. The station restaurant saw regular business as customers sat in it for a nice meal or a fast bite to eat or a quick drink. Other people perused the station shop for souvenirs, gifts, or trinkets.

The Ice Being gained on the thieves rapidly. They saw her closing in on them and raced as fast as they could to an available teleporter room. People made way for the Universal Marshal gliding along the promenade on a trail of ice shooting from her hand, moving in on the thieves for the arrest, her other hand ready to ice them on the spot.

Lorliane thought the thieves would figure they would not get to a teleporter room and teleport out of Darfleet unless they took care of her first. But she hoped they would surrender peacefully and not bring any additional charges against them. However, her assumption proved correct. The thieves turned around and aimed their weapons, causing innocent beings in the promenade to dive for cover in a mad scramble. They fired their blasters at the Enforcer and shot up as laser beams shattered her ice trail. Photon rays scorched the promenade, leaving black marks. The Ice Being fell toward the floor but quickly recovered by creating a new trail of ice to glide along. The thieves reoriented their weapons on her to fire again.

Before the thieves targeted her for blasting, the Universal Marshal struck first, firing a beam of ice from her hand. Instantly, the Ice Being froze them together in a big block of ice, leaving only their heads sticking out, which allowed them to breathe. Unfortunately, the Crystal Sphere got iced as well, but Lorliane knew it could not have been avoided. She thought the ancient artifact would not be damaged if it did not stay frozen in ice for too long, unless it really and truly did have supernatural power attributed to it that would protect it against such exposure.

"You'll pay for this!" the thieves sang in unison.

Lorliane dismissed their empty threat. "The city police will come and thaw you out."

Station security appeared on the scene as the Ice Being read the captured humans their rights under Tellusian law. The immobile and dejected Criminals said nothing more as a crowd of people gathered around the arrest area. Station security recognized Lorliane, who explained the situation. In time, the city police arrived to haul away the frozen felons after speaking with the Universal Marshal. The local law enforcement would see to it that the Crystal Sphere was properly returned to the Darfleet Museum. Lorliane would file a report on the robbery later.

A human male of station security shook his head in amazement and bewilderment at the sight of iced Criminals being taken out of the teleporter station. "Will they suffer any real harm in that condition?"

"Maybe frostbite to a degree," Lorliane said. "I could have very easily subjected them to cryogenic freeze. They'll just be numb for a while until warmed up."

"Have you ever frozen anyone to death?" a female human of station security asked the Ice Being.

Lorliane sighed. "Only a few times by accident in self-defense. I try not to keep living things frozen too long after I am forced to ice them. On my home world of Inglacia, I've had to kill snow beasts with my special powers. My frigid planet is home to many hostile creatures who kill for food or sport."

Station security went back to their posts, except for a humanoid male. "The Darfleet Museum might offer you a reward for recovering the Crystal Sphere."

Lorliane smiled at that. "I couldn't accept it. If the Darfleet Museum feels it has to give one, then let it be for repairing the damage caused by the Criminals during their apprehension. I'll be on my way back to my temporary office here."

As the Ice Being left the teleporter station, she suddenly found herself teleported to the Justiceplex.

Chapter 7

A bunch of commandos readied themselves to enter
Red Mountain, heavily armed with automatic weapons,
grenades, bazookas, garrotes, and knives. All around
them, the desert stretched for miles in all directions,
dotted with hardy scrub and bare mountains. High above
their heads, in a clear blue, cloudless sky, glaring
Kambec sent searing rays down to broil the arid land in
the southwest region of Survarille, making them sweat.
The only animals visibly moving on the baked earth and
its sandy and rocky sections were a few venomous
snakes, a couple of deadly spiders, and a pair of
poisonous lizards. The bleached bones of gone creatures
lay scattered in different spots on the vast wastes,
including the dry skeletons of intelligent beings, mortals
who had been foolish enough to chance crossing the hot
barrens ill-prepared for it. No wind blew, and the
humidity was low.

The well-trained soldiers stood in attack formation
behind the giant figure towering above them and before
the closed and camouflaged entrance to the Red
Mountain, leading this military operation by authority of
the regional command in Venipoor, a major city miles
north of their present location. They had followed him
for weeks on this mission, never questioning his orders,
though he was technically a civilian. But they knew him
as a Universal Marshal, and that commanded instant

respect.

Jagathan, the Titan Enforcer, stood over twelve feet tall, twice the size of the commandos, who were human and humanoid males. He was a giant figure rippling with extremely powerful, bulging muscles in a massive frame. Physically, he was the strongest of the Universal Marshals, his enormous strength derived from his immortal nature, a supernatural being possessing energy power on the celestic level. His aquamarine skin matched the color of his deep-set eyes; his thick black hair, cut short, hung bangs above a bony brow like buttressed rock. He had a dense molecular structure. Unlike the soldiers dressed in green commando garb, he wore a black jerkin, black shorts, and black shoes.

The commandos with Jagathan had been on many routine missions and covert operations. They had served as military police occasionally and assisted law enforcement to apprehend foul beings. Typically they were a special combat unit, called to act as a strike force in secret raids requiring military action of an elite status. Jagathan worked with the military before on various levels and had also fought in a few military conflicts. Once in a while, soldiers had helped him arrest foul beings when he had faced major opposition from vile minions of the latter to apprehend them.

The commandos waited for the Titan-Enforcer to bust open the big doors of the Red Mountain in order to gain entry to the hidden base inside it. Jagathan raised and smashed a huge fist through the unseen crack where the doors intersected. Then the Universal Marshal forced his giant fingers into the hole and, with prodigious effort, tore the big doors asunder as if ripping a thick book in half.

Colonel Reffic Gaskin, the ranking officer of the commandos, signaled for the military unit to penetrate the hidden base of the Red Mountain, the secret sanctum of the Villain Moshey Ravenbarr, following Jagathan inside. Somewhere within the Red Mountain lay a stolen hydrogen missile, capable of mass destruction.

Jagathan led them down a wide tunnel into a cavern, immense, and hid them behind a row of army trucks. The cavern overflowed with combat vehicles, busy personnel, military equipment, and designated buildings. Its enormous natural floor of hard earth and solid rock was uneven in spots. Its high ceiling was an artificial roof of thin steel, opened part way to let in hot and glaring sunlight. Tall lamps were spread around the cavern for artificial lighting, but none were on at the moment as solar rays provided enough illumination to see by. There was also a searchlight in the cavern, which smelled a bit like diesel fuel and kerosene.

"The buggers run an organized outfit," Reffic whispered. "And they're armed to the teeth. They appear to be a thorough bunch. But they could use tighter security."

Jagathan swept his gaze around the cavern. "A lot of military hardware. On the world I'm from, my kind doesn't use such weapons."

Reffic looked wide-eyed at the Universal Marshal as he removed the safety from his automatic weapon. The colonel checked for extra clips in his pockets. "Then how does your planet defend itself against enemy forces on your world and invading forces offworld?"

"Titans are powerful weapons themselves," Jagathan answered. "Our physical abilities of enormousness can stop and deter any enemy aggression sent against us. That is why Titans remain, to this day, unconquered."

Reffic was impressed. "How many times have they tried to invade your planet?"

"Not many," Jagathan replied. "Those who come to Titanus and try to dominate us always fail. Some come out of fear because of mistaken myths and false legends about us. Others just to invade and simply conquer."

"When was the last time your world fought a war?" Reffic asked. Unconsciously the colonel checked his other weapons—throwing knives, pistols, grenades, and garrotes.

Jagathan recalled the bloody battle his home planet last engaged in. "A hundred years ago, the Titans clashed mightily with invading monsters sent against us by evil aliens, the Harkans, to test us."

"Test you?" Reffic said.

"To see if an invasion of our world was feasible by them," Jagathan explained. "We slew most of the invading monsters. The rest fled Titanus back to their masters. That ended it."

Human personnel unloaded army trucks hauling crates of small weapons. A helicopter in the center of the cavern whirled to life and readied for takeoff. The roof opened all the way and more sunlight naturally beamed into the cavern to heat it further, and the greater illumination considerably lessened the shadows.

Instinctively, Jagathan flexed his bulging muscles in rippling waves. The Titan-Enforcer told the colonel to get his men into position to officially begin the raid. The colonel obeyed and spread out the commandos.

"Where's the missile?" Reffic asked the Universal Marshal.

Jagathan scanned the cavern by looking over an empty truck, searching in a methodical manner. "Ravenbarr must have stored it in a different place, in another cave of the mountain. I can see a row of tunnels at the other end of the cavern."

"What do you want to do about it?" Reffic asked.

Jagathan grimaced. "You and your men handle what is here. I'll take those tunnels."

In position, the commandos received the hand signal from the colonel to begin the assault. They barraged the enemy with bullets from automatic weapons, blasts from firing shotguns, and explosions from thrown grenades, only to be counterattacked in a similar manner. Buildings blew apart, vehicles shredded, equipment shattered, and men died or received wounds. Battle raged through the cavern, the noise deafening. Uncontrolled fires and choking smoke surged through the chaotic scene. Some of the enemy tried to douse the flames with fire extinguishers or foam from large canisters.

Jagathan flipped the empty truck before him onto armed men firing automatic weapons at him and crushed them underneath its weight. The Titan-Enforcer worked his way to the other side of the cavern, knocking foes out of his path. He leaped at the helicopter and grabbed hold of it as it tried to fly out of the cavern. The Universal Marshal pulled it from the air, smashed it to the ground, and completely disabled it.

Bullets bounced off Jagathan's extremely thick hide. Three men dragged out flamethrowers and expelled burning streams of liquid or semiliquid fuel under pressure in an attempt to thoroughly roast the Titan-Enforcer. But the shooting flames did not harm one inch of his supernatural skin—they just tickled a little. Calmly but quickly, the Universal Marshal lifted an army jeep and hurled the empty vehicle into the three men and flattened them to the ground. Then he tossed large crates stacked on the floor at other foes discharging weapons and felled them like mowing down stationary targets at a shooting gallery.

An army truck gunned its motor and rolled straight at him. Jagathan evaded it, kicked it on its side, jumped into the air, and stomped it. Afterward, he wove his way to the row of tunnels again, leaving the armored combat vehicle crushed like a metal drum in a useless heap as its engine died.

Jagathan reached the row of tunnels, three of them. The Titan-Enforcer studied each passageway, carefully but quickly, to decide which one to take. Finally, he decided to go through the middle one, hoping it would lead him to the prize.

The rocky ceiling of the tunnel accommodated his height. He plodded through it and emerged into another cavern, smaller than the first. The Universal Marshal saw that the natural chamber of rock served as a control center for the illegal operation. Computer and control consoles lined against its rocky walls. In the center of the cavern, Jagathan spied the object of his long search—the hydrogen missile. The armed warhead was silver and sleek and over three times his size in length. It set squarely and dangerously on a launching pad, its original carrier, for firing immediately. It was aimed in the direction of another pair of big doors thrown wide open.

The air in the cavern smelled fresher than in the other one. Before the hydrogen missile stood Ravenbarr with five other men armed with automatic weapons, grenades, and a loaded bazooka. Brimming with confidence, Jagathan strode toward the big bomb. They spotted him. The Villain ordered his men to kill the Titan-Enforcer, and they opened fire on him, but the barrage of bullets just bounced off him. A few of them threw grenades at the Universal Marshal. The grenades exploded around him but did not harm him, only raised dust. Then the man with the bazooka set and aimed it at the Titan-Enforcer and fired it at the Universal Marshal. The armor-piercing missile exploded against Jagathan's chest and slowed him down.

The man with the bazooka reloaded. His comrades fired their automatic weapons at the Titan-Enforcer, and a couple of them threw more grenades. The Universal Marshal charged at them and shrugged off bullets and blasts.

Ravenbarr turned to the hydrogen missile and set its coordinates for a specific target as Jagathan went to his knees, lifted huge fists, and hammered the floor with a mighty blow. The ground shook, and the men shooting at him tumbled to the floor, but the Villain stayed on his feet by grabbing onto the missile carrier. Ravenbarr hurried to finish his nefarious task, cursing, as the Titan-Enforcer climbed to his feet and advanced on them again. The Universal Marshal belted the armed men into the cavern walls and knocked them unconscious, then scooped up their automatic weapons, bent them, and dropped them to the floor. Next, he picked up the grenades and crushed them, causing explosions in his hands that did not harm him. Then he grabbed the bazooka, broke it in two, and threw the pieces aside. He turned his attention to the Villain, who had his back toward him.

Ravenbarr spun around and addressed the Titan-

Enforcer. "You've wrecked my plans!"

"Yes," Jagathan responded.

"Others will pay the price for your interference!"

Ravenbarr armed the hydrogen missile. The Universal Marshal stepped closer to the Villain.

"Stop!" Jagathan warned the foul being. "Don't add to your crimes."

Ravenbarr grinned at the Titan-Enforcer, then laughed. The Villain punched the launch sequence into the control pad of the hydrogen missile for firing. "Too late! This great destroyer will level the city of Monteplok. All its hopeless citizens will go to early graves. There will be nothing left of it but a gigantic hole in the earth."

"Why are you doing this?" Jagathan asked.

"To teach Monteplok a lesson," Ravenbarr replied. "They refused to meet my demands. Now they will suffer the consequences with their destruction."

Jagathan circled in front of the hydrogen missile as more of the Villain's men entered the control center, automatic weapons ready to fire. But one look at their five comrades on the floor unconscious and the towering figure of the Titan-Enforcer standing before the big bomb made them change their minds. They fled back down the way they came.

Ravenbarr ignored the cowards, giving his undivided attention to the Universal Marshal.

Then the hydrogen missile ignited in a noisy blast and flew right at the Titan-Enforcer like a rocketing juggernaut. Its firing exhaust was deafening.

"Farewell," Ravenbarr said, gleefully.

Jagathan braced himself, and the hydrogen missile rammed hard into his chest with great force, pushing him backward. Ravenbarr gasped in total disbelief and utter awe at the incredible sight of the Titan-Enforcer wrestling with many tons of blasting rocket, fighting it like a rampaging monster roaring to get through the Universal Marshal. Jagathan stopped skidding backward and blocked the hydrogen missile from ascending into the open atmosphere outside toward its intended target.

"Impossible," Ravenbarr uttered. His eyes gleamed with hatred and bewilderment. Angrily, the Villain grabbed an automatic weapon from underneath the missile carrier and fired it at the Titan-Enforcer, but it jammed. He threw it down in disgust. "You will not defeat me!"

Jagathan knew he could not crush the hydrogen missile in his grasp because that would unfortunately cause it to explode instantly and destroy everything in its destructive range, including maybe himself. The Titan-Enforcer could not afford to let go of it either, for it would automatically seek out its intended target and produce the same result. So the Universal Marshal tore the warhead off the hydrogen missile, set the warhead gently down on the ground, and drove the disarmed weapon of mass destruction into the earth to let it burn itself out, its blasting tail pointing up and firing away for nothing.

Ravenbarr ran from Jagathan only to be caught by Colonel Gaskin. The Titan-Enforcer joined them.

"You're not going anywhere, Villain," Reffic said. The foul being scowled at him. "Your operation is smashed."

"Balderdash," Ravenbarr uttered defiantly, refusing to accept defeat.

Jagathan stared down at the dejected Villain, feeling

no pity for the man. "The raid, colonel?"

"A success," Reffic reported proudly. "The men are mopping up. Red Mountain will soon be secured. Everything in it has been confiscated."

"Good work," Jagathan responded.

Reffic looked at the firing rocket, without its warhead now. "I see you have deactivated the hydrogen missile." It would burn itself out.

"It took time and effort to render it no longer such a deadly threat," Jagathan admitted. "And I saved the city of Monteplok from becoming a crater of ruins." The Titan-Enforcer stared down at the Villain again. "You will have many years to think about the error of your ways in the Universal Prisonplex."

Ravenbarr grabbed his head in his hands and closed his eyes, finally realizing it was really over, miserable about the prospect of being locked away from society. The Villain grumbled about the disastrous end to his plans. Neither Jagathan or Reffic showed any sympathy.

"Filthy giant," Ravenbarr muttered. The Villain spat on the ground.

Jagathan ignored the insult. Instead, the Titan-Enforcer glared at the foul being. Ravenbarr cowered.

Three commandos entered the cavern and reported to Colonel Gaskin and the Universal Marshal.

"The area is secured," the tallest of the commandos stated. "Prisoners have been quartered."

"Well done," Reffic said. The colonel motioned at the Villain. "Take this prisoner away."

The shortest of the commandos beamed in triumph. "With pleasure, sir." He and the other two soldiers escorted the foul being out of the cavern.

"New orders?" Reffic asked the Titan-Enforcer.

"Call for transport to haul away the prisoners to jail in Venipoor," Jagathan said. "Pack the goods we seized as evidence. Have it also hauled away but to the regional command in Venipoor. The military and civilian authorities in Venipoor can decide how the prisoners will be tried."

"And when," Reffic added.

Jagathan nodded. "Seal the Red Mountain after the transports are done."

"I will see to it," Reffic acknowledged. The colonel locked the safety on his automatic weapon. "What will you do now?"

Before Jagathan could reply, the Titan-Enforcer was teleported to the Justiceplex, miles north of his previous location.

Chapter 8

Delveran entered the briefing room with a serious expression on his face. Rathol, Eneysa, Procules, Lorliane, and Jagathan were waiting for him. The briefing room, a rectangular chamber, was on the same side of the corridor as the teleporter room, near the front of the Justiceplex. A large, crescent-shaped table of golden omnimetal stretched in the middle of the briefing room, with twenty armchairs around it. On the far side of the briefing room lay a control console before the command chair where the Grand Universal Marshal seated himself, directly facing the automatic doors. All the glowpanels in the briefing room were on, and the blank walls of the rectangular chamber hid hi-tech devices behind them. Filtered air circulated through the briefing room, as the Justiceplex was a nonsmoking facility, though a few Universal Marshals smoked a cigar or pipe. Of the group there, only Jagathan did on occasion.

Rathol, Eneysa, and Lorliane sat in three of the armchairs. Procules stationed himself in place of an armchair, not designed to sit. Jagathan towered behind two armchairs, for he was too big to sit in any of them, and the high ceiling accommodated his height. Delveran relaxed in the command chair before the control console.

The High Enforcer looked at each of them. "I have summoned you here because an unprecedented event has occurred."

The other five Enforcers focused their attention on him. All of them detected an urgency in his words. The High Enforcer told them the tale Zorrokin had related to the Grand Universal Marshal, comfortable in his seat.

"Incredible," Lorliane remarked after the High Enforcer finished telling the story. "Archvillains joined in a united body."

"We know, as a general rule, that Archvillains don't usually band together to do evil," Jagathan stated. "Unless they're of the same kind, like Spriggan Archvillains do."

"True," Delveran agreed. "It seems these Archvillains have put aside their solitary natures and enormous egos for a common purpose of malevolence."

Procules chimed in. "The possibility for an organization of Archvillains to exist was always there, though the possibility of it appeared remote."

"What was the probability for it to happen?" Delveran asked the Robot-Enforcer.

"Accessing," Procules said as he checked his memory cells. "I had calculated the possibility of such an event to be one point seven."

Jagathan laughed at that. "I would have put the odds of it happening a little higher."

"All things are possible," Delveran said. "Seemingly, it was an inevitability."

"It only needed a catalyst for it to have occurred," Eneysa added.

Rathol entered the discussion. "Evil always seeks to find ways to destroy good. I believe these Archvillains have found a way to greatly test us."

"Aye," Jagathan agreed.

"Certainly their special powers combined make them a far greater threat to deal with than as foul beings working solo," Lorliane pointed out.

"And deal with them we will," Delveran promised. The High Enforcer turned to the Robot-Enforcer. "What information do you have on the leader of the Fellowship of Darkness, Magnemus?"

"Accessing," Procules responded. In his memory cells, he found a file on the person named. "Magnemus: a humanoid born and raised in the city of Dratonia, the fifth largest on the planet of Aruvenor. He is the only child of Gerishem, his father, a chemist, and Kirilena, his mother, a psychotechnologist. Both his parents are deceased, and he has no other known family."

Delveran recalled what he knew about the planet Aruvenor. Aruvenor, a technocratic world inhabited by an advanced race of humanoids, orbited the creamy star Dirgel as its fourth planet, in the Galbraithean Sector of the Milky Way Galaxy. The High Enforcer stopped thinking about it and concentrated on what the Robot-Enforcer told him about the leader of the Archvillain organization.

"By vocation, Magnemus is a scientist. He is a graduate of Trantorus Techniversity, in Trantorus, the capital and largest city of Aruvenor. From the techniversity, he received his doctorate in biocreation, the science that deals with the making of natural and artificial life. He graduated first in his class, with honors. He was the recipient of the Drassic Award for the Most Outstanding Science Student, the Herminus Award for Best Student Science Project, and the Tyliff Award for the Top Student in Biocreation at an Aruvenor techniversity."

"A very decorated and educated person," Eneysa remarked.

Procules continued. "On leaving Trantorus Techniversity, he immediately accepted two positions to begin his career in the field of science. First, he took a job as an assistant professor of biocreation at Meccadar Techniversity in the mountain city of Meccadar, the second largest on Aruvenor, in the Silikron Province. Second, he became a biocreation assistant at the Barokeen Institute of Biotechnology on the outskirts of Meccadar."

"An impressive record already," Lorliane commented.

"There are scientists in the Federation who can easily match that," Jagathan said.

Procules resumed. "For ten years, Magnemus buried himself in biocreation work at the two positions. He made great, and sometimes radical, strides in his field of science. The trade journals of Aruvenor in science published all his articles on discs."

Delveran folded his arms. "A rather prolific writer."

Procules went on. "He became a full professor at Meccadar Techniversity a few years later. Then a sequence of events accelerated his rise to the pinnacle of success. He received a promotion and headed the biocreation department of the Barokeen Institute. Next Meccadar Techniversity named him dean of the life sciences and technologies. Later he won the Prothalamus Award—the highest award in science on Aruvenor for his contributions to the science of biocreation. To climax his rise, the following year, the Aruvenor government rewarded him by appointing him, without any political opposition, Secretary of Bioscience and Biotechnology.

This forced him to quit his two positions at Meccadar Techniversity and the Barokeen Institute. His new post made him the highest ranking official in bioscience and biotechnology on the planet."

Lorliane tapped her fingers on the table. "A scientist who became a celebrity." The Ice Being made an ice ball in her hand and played with it.

"A lord in his field," Eneysa remarked.

"Essentially correct," Procules said. "Magnemus did much for Aruvenor as Secretary of Bioscience and Biotechnology. He brought in from other planets new and radical bioscientific ideas and new and radical biotechnologies to accelerate the progress being made in those areas on Aruvenor. He eliminated outdated rules and regulations interfering in this progress. He established more conferences on Aruvenor, for bioscientists and biotechnologists to confer with colleagues in the field from other planets involving matters of bioscience and biotechnology."

"Did these invitations extend to doctors and others in the Federation?" Delveran asked.

"Yes, High Enforcer," Procules responded. "There are public and private records of this."

Rathol was not amused by all the information. "Trying to play God. The Creator is the supreme maker of all life in the universe. Above, the Lord holds dominion over all creation."

Nobody commented on the views of the Shepherd.

Procules spoke further. "Already famous and certainly a public figure, Magnemus politically aspired to be newly elected as Techarch of Aruvenor, the highest executive officer of the planet. But in his fifth year as Secretary of Bioscience and Biotechnology, less than a year before the election would take place, a scandal surfaced involving him."

"A scandal?" Eneysa repeated. "So he was dirty?"

"Corrupted," Jagathan interjected.

Rathol smiled. "A mighty fall from grace."

Procules beeped so he could finish. "This scandal caused him to vacate his government position, give up his campaign of becoming Techarch of Aruvenor, and leave the planet, banned from ever returning to his native world. The Federation has very few details of this sordid affair because the Aruvenor government covered it up. It happened over ten years ago."

Delveran thought no wonder the name of Professor Magnemus had not been heard in a decade. The High Enforcer wanted to know what the Archvillain did in all those years before he became the leader of the Fellowship of Darkness. "Magnemus must have founded the Archvillain organization for a very specific purpose in mind."

"Logical," Procules agreed.

"But how long has it existed?" Lorliane voiced the obvious question for them. None of them knew.

Eneysa raised the next one for the Robot-Enforcer. "How long has Aruvenor been in the Federation?"

"Accessing," Procules responded. It took him mere seconds. "The planet has been a member for three years now."

"Interesting," Jagathan said.

Procules beeped as more information surfaced from his memory cells about the leader of the Archvillain organization. "Magnemus is called the Scientific Being. That is because he has special powers—his ability to manipulate scientific, or physical, laws, controlling them in their original states or modifying, deleting, enhancing, changing, or adding to them to suit his purposes. On record, he owns a spaceship, the *Technokado*, the vessel he used to depart from Aruvenor. It is specially equipped with a teleport drive and is about the size of a Federation battlecruiser."

Lorliane looked at the Robot-Enforcer as she tossed her ice ball to the Titan-Enforcer, who crushed it in his hand. "Who did Magnemus associate with?"

Procules accessed memory cells to answer her question. "He had many connections in the scientific community of Aruvenor and offworld, but few friends, spending most of his time working. Seldom did he socialize, and only with other scientists and other technologists to discuss topics of vital importance to bioscience and biotechnology."

"It doesn't sound like we'll learn much about him from a personal perspective," Lorliane remarked. "The information on him seems incomplete."

"The mystery of a dark lord," Eneysa said.

Rathol rubbed his hands together and glanced at the Staff of Godpower against the wall behind him. "We must seek more knowledge about him to find the answers."

"Aye," Jagathan agreed. "All that we can."

Eneysa cut in. "We need an oracle or seer to help us."

"More like an archivist or a notary," Lorliane chimed in.

"However," Procules interrupted their talk, "among the few friends Professor Magnemus did have is a being on Tellus."

Rathol straightened up in his armchair. "Where can

this friend be found?"

"Among us," Procules replied.

"Us?" Eneysa repeated.

Procules elaborated. "The friend of the Scientific Being I am referring to is a current member of the Universal Marshals."

Delveran unfolded his arms and leaned forward in his seat, intently curious as the rest. "Who?"

"Minanket," Procules said.

Jagathan was stunned. "How does Minanket know Magnemus? He isn't from Aruvenor."

"Correct," Procules confirmed. "However, though it is true that Minanket was not born or raised on Aruvenor, his family origins can be traced back to the planet. As to how he knows the Archvillain, they attended the same techniversity, but they majored in different sciences."

"I will have to have a serious talk with Minanket on the matter," Delveran said. "Is there anything else you have on Magnemus?"

Procules checked his memory cells. "No."

Delveran changed the subject. "How does the Federation rate Earth?"

"Accessing," Procules responded. The Robot-Enforcer retrieved the specific information on the planet in his memory cells. "At this time, the Federation does not consider Earth a suitable candidate for membership and is subject to the noninterference ordinance."

Delveran sat back in his chair, relaxing, one hand on the control console before him. "In your records on file, has any Enforcer ever visited Earth in order to arrest any Criminals, Villains, or Archvillains?"

"None," Procules answered.

Delveran was not surprised. "Do you know how

often Earth has been visited by offworlders? And what kind?"

"Accessing," Procules responded. The Robot-Enforcer found the information in his memory cells easily. "Earth has been visited regularly by alien beings. None have ever invaded the planet and tried to conquer it in order to rule it. Neither have any tried to destroy it."

"Praise the Almighty Lord," Rathol said. "God must have found favor with the helpless world."

Lorliane crossed her legs. "More likely they've been incredibly lucky. Who knows what alien activity has been revolving around on Earth. It all must be happening in secret there."

"The Federation has been monitoring Earth periodically," Procules stated from his detailed files on the planet. "So far, Federation officials have reported no imminent danger to it in the foreseeable future from alien beings. In fact, visitations by alien beings to Earth have dropped dramatically to virtually zero in the past two years, according to Federation officials. No explanation for this is given on record except to say it is no concern to the Federation."

"It's obvious the Fellowship of Darkness has driven alien beings from Earth to secure the secrecy of their hidden base from everybody else," Jagathan said. "This order of foul beings wants no other outworlders to share room on Earth. They want Earth for themselves."

"Alien beings are no match for Archvillains," Lorliane agreed. "They naturally cannot defeat the special powers of the foul beings."

"A few aliens are Archvillains themselves," Delveran pointed out. "Some are locked away in the Universal Prisonplex."

"That is good," Eneysa remarked on the last statement of the High Enforcer.

Rathol appeared angry. "The evil ones on Earth must be smitten."

"Apprehended," Delveran expressed for the Shepherd to be technically correct.

Procules beeped to bring them back on track. "Besides alien beings, Earth has been visited by a number of Incarnations in its planetary history. Both good and evil."

"Like who?" Eneysa asked. The Metamorph-Enforcer had no knowledge of any of her race ever visiting Earth before, unlike Jagathan, whose people, the Titans, once had.

"The Grim Reaper, Maid Spring, and War," Procules specified. "The list is long on all kinds of different beings who have visited Earth."

"Any current Enforcer that has ever been on Earth?" Delveran asked.

"Definitely," Procules responded. "Eight of the Universal Marshals serving at present have visited the planet, before they became Universal Marshals. Also, former Enforcers."

"Very good," Delveran said. "What else?"

Procules uncovered more information on the Terran world in his memory cells, everything in his detailed files on the planet. "On the scientific level, Earth is progressive. On the occultic level, Earth is average. On the celestic level, Earth is low."

After the Robot-Enforcer gave a complete rundown on Earth, Delveran addressed them. "These are my instructions. You will take a ship and go to Earth and search for the Archvillain organization and their hidden base. Enforcer reinforcements will be sent to Earth, at different intervals, to join you in scouting for the exact location of the Complex. After you have found it, contact me, but do not enter it. I will assemble a strike force to Earth for the assault on it and backed by Federation troops."

"As you command, High Enforcer," Rathol acknowledged for them.

Delveran looked at each one of them. "Do not reveal yourselves to the people of Earth. Disguise or cloak yourselves. If you are discovered by the Earthlings, for whatever reason, contact me immediately for instructions to deal with the situation. Any questions?"

"Who will lead the Enforcer Squad?" Lorliane asked.

Delveran turned to the Shepherd. "Rathol."

Rathol nodded. "It be by God's will."

"Any further questions?" Delveran asked. No one spoke up. "You will prepare for the trip to Earth after the briefing. When you are ready, leave for Earth, but no later than tomorrow afternoon. That is all." The High Enforcer dismissed them.

They filed out of the briefing room, and Delveran watched them go, Rathol walking with the Staff of Godpower in his hand again. Soon the Grand Universal Marshal found himself alone, contemplating what could happen if the oncoming invaders—legions of biocreated creatures led by Archvillains of the Fellowship of Darkness—succeeded in conquering Tellus.

Suddenly an unhappy thought entered the mind of the High Enforcer. If the plan of the Archvillain organization succeeded in accomplishing a jailbreak of the Universal Prisonplex, the ravenous evil of thousands of Archvillains, locked away over the centuries in its subterranean section, would be free once again to ravage the galaxy. If the Archvillain organization got them and other Archvillains still at large in the galaxy to join the Fellowship of Darkness, altogether they would inevitably become the next supreme evil, threatening the very existence of the Universal Federation of Planets. United, they could rule the galaxy forever, virtually unstoppable.

Delveran realized something else about the terrifying idea. It would spell doom for the Enforcers as well. The Universal Marshals, both past and present, shared the responsibility for having put away all the Archvillains in the Universal Prisonplex. And all those Archvillains, if freed, would seek revenge against the Enforcers for their imprisonment.

Delveran left the briefing room, its glowpanels fading out behind him automatically. Very concerned now and starting to feel a little tense and a bit stressed, he headed directly for the computer room of the Justiceplex to see Nanomach, the Computer-Enforcer. The High Enforcer needed to get a complete list of names about which known Archvillains remained at large. And he also had to worry about what unknown Archvillains roamed the galaxy, doing evil as well.

Chapter 9

Delveran entered the computer room, a square chamber on the same side of the corridor as his office, near the back section of the Justiceplex. Glowpanels in the high ceiling auto-activated as soon as he stepped into the room, casting bright light. Virtual silence permeated the square chamber as no one else used it at the moment. Filtered air circulated through the computer room, clean and fresh.

Breaking the noiseless atmosphere with the clicking of his dress shoes, Delveran went over to the lone computer standing in the middle of the room. Four large, black telescreens, off, hung above it. Control consoles ringed the lone computer with swivel armchairs before them, their seats padded with black synthon, their shiny frames of golden omnimetal. Delveran stood before the computer with an agenda in mind. The High Enforcer bent down to the control console directly before him and depressed a few buttons. Then he addressed the computer. "Nanomach, I need your assistance."

"What do you require, High Enforcer?" the Computer-Enforcer asked in a male voice that sounded human.

"I need three things. First, locate in your memory banks Archvillains still at large in the galaxy and wanted by us and the Federation Department of Justice."

"Working." Nanomach found it. "I have it ready for

you."

Delveran took a deep breath. "How many Archvillains are still at large?"

"Currently on file," Nanomach responded, "eighteen."

Delveran remembered that the members of the Archvillain organization currently numbered twenty-four. He wondered how many were currently on file in the memory banks of the Computer-Enforcer. "Confirm or not the following Archvillains are on file with you: Moroloch, the Monitor; Jawsar, the Predator; and Asearse, the Charybdian."

Nanomach whirred and checked the file. "All three are listed in my memory banks."

Delveran believed they would be. "Read me the names of the remaining Archvillains in your memory banks."

Nanomach complied. "Orlin, the Grim Reaper. Yarg, the Alien Thing. Gordred, Master Horror. Usaddith, a Banshee. Brutalos, the Kraken. Hellob, a Gorgon. Ynemain, the Iron Maiden. Sorrent, a Gwillion. Quasicoatl, the Cloning Creature. Vilegast, a Gremlin. Lethesis, the Wildcat. Turiyak, the Changeling. Iosheen, the Chimeran. Cenjuno, a Keve. And Vidarius, the Incarnation of War."

Delveran thought the list of Archvillain names sounded impressive. The High Enforcer figured that if all the Archvillains in the memory banks of the Computer-Enforcer belonged to the Archvillain organization, plus Professor Magnemus, then that left at least five Archvillains unknown and unaccounted for who would complete the full membership of the Fellowship of Darkness. He knew he had better learn the identities of any and all Archvillains unfamiliar to the Enforcers and the Federation. "Add Professor Magnemus, the Scientific Being, to your memory banks of Archvillains for update."

"Affirmative," Nanomach responded.

Delveran nodded. "Later, you need to update it with more Archvillains. A new search will be conducted to find foul beings to be added to the evil class in your files. There are still unfamiliar and unknown members of the Fellowship of Darkness."

"Do you wish me to contact Federation authorities onworld and offworld of Tellus to immediately instigate such a search?" Nanomach asked.

"After I am finished with you," Delveran replied.

"Affirmative," Nanomach responded.

Delveran knew as the High Enforcer he possessed enormous power as an official of the Federation. As the Grand Universal Marshal, he gave the other Universal Marshals their assignments. They did the field work and made the arrests of foul beings of the three evil classes as he acted as their chief and only administrator. Though a duly licensed Enforcer, he still had the legal authority to apprehend such people, but rarely did. Since he had become the High Enforcer, he had actually made only two busts, one a Criminal, the other a Villain. He wished he had captured an Archvillain as well as the Grand Universal Marshal, which would have made it a complete set of the three types of foul beings.

Nanomach interrupted his train of thought. "Are you ready to state the next item, High Enforcer?"

"Yes," Delveran replied. "Next item: search through your memory banks of files of all Archvillains again for all available information on them."

"Working." Nanomach went through detailed files on the foul beings. "I have them ready for viewing or reading out."

Delveran considered carefully what information he wanted to know about them. "Besides Professor Magnemus, how many of them have minions to command?"

"Accessing." Nanomach sifted through the detailed files for the information. "In all, three Archvillains command them, but the third only technically."

"Which three?"

"Gordred, Master Horror. Cenjuno, a Keve. And technically, Quasicoatl, the Cloning Creature, because of his replications of other creatures that are him actually disguised in cloned forms."

Mentally Delveran added that there may be Archvillains of the Fellowship of Darkness, unknown, who commanded minions. "How many own spaceships?"

"Accessing." Nanomach retrieved the information from detailed files in his memory banks. "On record, four of the Archvillains listed own spaceships."

"Who?"

Nanomach whirred briefly. "Yarg, the Alien Thing, owns the spaceship, the *Xendramas*. Lethesis, the Wildcat, owns the spaceship, the *Kreshbet*. Turiyak, the Changeling, owns the spaceship, the *Dagdamorphus*. And Quasicoatl, the Cloning Creature, owns the spaceship, the *Glastronomo*."

In his mind, Delveran listed Professor Magnemus as a fifth Archvillain owning a spaceship. "How many of them are scientists?"

"Accessing." Nanomach retrieved the information

from detailed files in his memory banks. "On record, other than Professor Magnemus, only one of the Archvillains is listed as a scientist."

"Which one?"

"Turiyak, the Changeling."

"What is his field of science?"

"Topology, the science that deals with the study of places, locations, and environments."

Delveran made a mental note of both Archvillains, Professor Magnemus and Doctor Turiyak, being scientists. The High Enforcer believed there might be scientists, unknown, among the Archvillains in the Fellowship of Darkness. "How many are occultists?"

"Accessing." Nanomach retrieved the information from detailed files in his memory banks. "On record, one Archvillain is listed. Iosheen, the Chimeran. She has been an occultist since she became an adult."

"Any occult art in particular she specializes in or excels at?"

"According to the detailed file on the Archvillain, Iosheen is especially adept at certain types of black sorcery. Mental magic. Glamoury, or the magic of illusion. And projective magic."

Delveran remembered the information. The High Enforcer suspected her talent and abilities as an occultist were inherent in her, as part of her special powers overall as an Archvillain. Now he wondered how many Archvillains, unknown, in the Fellowship of Darkness were occultists. "How many are celestists?"

"Accessing." Nanomach retrieved the information from detailed files in his memory banks.

"On record, one of the Archvillains is listed. Ynemain, the Iron Maiden. As an adapt in celestory, she specializes in its negative side, particularly in inflicting harm to her chosen victims."

Delveran knew there might be Archvillains, unknown, in the Fellowship of Darkness who might be celestists. Those worked on a higher level than occultists, while occultists worked on a higher level than scientists. The High Enforcer had never been interested in becoming a scientist or celestist. "Exit memory banks on Archvillains."

Nanomach complied. "Await next item."

Bothered, Delveran recalled that imprisoned in the Universal Prisonplex there were a fair number of Archvillains who were also known as scientists, occultists, or celestists. But most of the foul beings in it were not. Villains were more likely to be one of the three learned types than Archvillains, and for that matter, Criminals, who were generally not sophisticated people. Typically, Archvillains cared simply about their special powers, not professional titles, with certain exceptions, like Professor Magnemus, Doctor Turiyak, Iosheen, and Ynemain.

Among the Enforcers, there were scientists, occultists, and celestists. Of course, Delveran was an occultist by virtue of his being a master and practitioner of the white arts. But only a minority of Universal Marshals were actually scientists, occultists, or celestists. And only a small number of Enforcers owned, in fact, spaceships. The High Enforcer did not.

Delveran broke out of his reverie. "Next item: excluding Rathol, Eneysa, Procules, Lorliane, Jagathan, and us, how many Enforcers are on Tellus at present?"

"Working." Nanomach zipped through his log of Universal Marshals signed in onworld at present.

"Eight."

Delveran wished there were more of their fellow Enforcers on the planet. "Execute two orders after I leave. First, track down the eight and have them return to the Justiceplex immediately."

"Affirmative."

"Second, search for all Universal Marshals offworld of Tellus and telebeam a priority one message for all of them to return here as soon as possible."

"Affirmative."

Delveran sighed. "All right."

"Ready for next item," Nanomach said.

Delveran thought. "Compute possible invasion strategies by the Fellowship of Darkness."

"Working." Nanomach whirred as the Computer-Enforcer computed them. "Ready with scenarios."

"What is the most likely one?"

"Accessing." Nanomach compared them simultaneously and instantly. "The Fellowship of Darkness would target major cities, military installations, the Federationplex, the Justiceplex, the Scienceplex, the Occultplex, and the Celestoryplex first. Especially neutralize the Universal Marshals because we represent their greatest foes in an invasion. The Archvillain organization would have to try to stop all of Tellus uniting against them, to prevent the various forces of our planet countering their global assault."

Delveran figured that made sense. "Another one?"

Nanomach did not need to access this time. "The most direct way is for the invasion to attack in full force where the Universal Prisonplex is. Attempt a jailbreak swiftly and decisively."

"That way, they would not have to waste time trying

to conquer all of Tellus just to free all the Archvillains in the Universal Prisonplex."

"Affirmative."

"But it would leave the legions of the Fellowship of Darkness vulnerable to the various forces of Tellus to surround them and counterattack them."

"Affirmative," Nanomach responded. "They cannot allow for such mistakes in calculating the best chance of success against Tellus. They would use the most direct way only if they were forced to. Time would be of the essence to them."

Delveran agreed with the assessment of the Computer-Enforcer. "We do not know what surprises they spring on us or all their weapons, military and otherwise, they may use against Tellus. Most important, we do not know which Archvillains will lead the invasion and whose special powers Tellus will have to contend with. We have to make certain special powers of Enforcers can stop whatever ones they use against Tellus."

"Affirmative," Nanomach said. "There is also another problem, High Enforcer."

"What?" Delveran asked, feeling that it was huge.

Nanomach paused. "If any of the Archvillains in the Universal Prisonplex are freed by the invasion, their special powers could be used against Tellus. The more of them that are freed, the greater the problem becomes. This could lead to the destruction of Tellus."

Delveran feared that. The High Enforcer remembered all too well the incident with the Archvillain Wodinnol in the Universal Prisonplex. One Archvillain alone, if powerful enough, could destroy Tellus. A bunch of them combining their special powers could do the same.

"Store all the scenarios in your memory banks for later retrieval. Add more details to them when you can. In the meantime, execute the two orders I already gave you."

"Affirmative." Nanomach went to work fast on the two orders the High Enforcer wanted him to execute.

The Computer-Enforcer scanned for the eight Enforcers on Tellus. Once he found them, he would have them teleported to the Justiceplex. Next, he would track down the Universal Marshals offworld of Tellus and would start checking for messages sent to the Justiceplex since he'd checked previously. Then he would check logs of their last known whereabouts. After that, he would check memory banks for their assignments to see where they were and what jobs they were currently working on. Those Enforcers who were not on duty he would check memory banks to see where they were if listed. Finally, after all other means had been exhausted to find them, have them telescanned in the galaxy.

Delveran left the computer room to let Nanomach complete his tasks. The High Enforcer decided to go to his quarters, near the back section of the Justiceplex, to meditate on matters, including his relationship with Evarinia, whom he had hurt terribly and felt miserable about.

Fondly, Delveran remembered how he and Evarinia had met. It had happened two years ago during a large gathering of Federation department heads on Tellus in Acropollon. They had been introduced to each other by a mutual friend, Alalime, of the faerie race of Crommons, who was the director of the Federation Department of Commerce and Trade.

During the official function, they had danced together and had eaten at the same table, right across from each other. On first meeting, they were immediately attracted to each other and began to date soon afterward. Their love affair started out as a whirlwind romance but had cooled down in the past several months, mainly because he had not shown much passion for her, and she now resented his losing interest in her. In truth, he had not lost interest in her. The official and dangerous business of dealing with the Archvillain organization was in the way now of him getting Evarinia back. As the High Enforcer, Delveran had to stop the Fellowship of Darkness—top priority for the Universal Marshals.

Delveran sighed. He needed solitude for a while.

Chapter 10

The next day the Enforcer Squad went to the teleporter room of the Justiceplex. Rathol, Eneysa, Lorliane, and Jagathan stepped onto the large square telegrid. Procules wheeled himself over to the teleport console and set specific coordinates on the control podium for the Acropollon Spaceport and immediately activated the feature of the automatic system of the teleporter to transport them to their destination. After the Robot-Enforcer joined the other Universal Marshals on the telegrid, the system engaged and sent them to their stop.

After they instantly materialized at the Acropollon Spaceport, they got their bearings quickly. They found themselves at the northwest edge of the city.

The Enforcer Squad walked through the place, very busy, late morning. Docking bays surrounded the launch field, open space, of the Acropollon Spaceport on its north, south, and west sides, while the terminal extended along its east side, marking its official boundaries. Its control tower rose in the center of its terminal, overlooking a number of stationary spacecraft of designs in individual spots on the landing field, a big rectangle. All the structures of the place were made of white omnimetal, gleaming from the golden sunbeams of Kambec, the Tellusian sun, blazing hot and brightly in blue skies on what looked like a glorious day.

Maintenance crews worked on ships on the landing field; cargo workers loaded or unloaded freighters. Other beings stood around and conversed. None of the people and activity in the area concerned the Enforcer Squad.

The air smelled unpolluted at the Acropollon Spaceport. Loud and muffled sounds of craft coming in or going from it and power tools and equipment being used made the atmosphere reverberate with noise, but decibels under shattering range. Beings ate inside the terminal restaurant and visited other parts of the facilities, such as shops, arcades, and offices. Dignitaries from other planets arrived or left the Acropollon Spaceport occasionally.

Solar rays of Kambec gleamed off metal surfaces of the Robot-Enforcer in flashes. Heated by the Tellusian sun, Procules' self-cooling system, built within his armored frame, kicked in to bring his body temperature down to normal for an automaton.

It was the season of early summer on Tellus. The Enforcer Squad, as a whole, thought nothing of it.

A parked ship began to rumble after someone ignited its big engines, across the landing field from them toward its south end. Soon a large, blue, pentagonal-shaped vessel zoomed upward, heading for space, only to have its docking spot filled by a smaller ship, shaped like a red flashlight with wings running on silent propulsion, drive unknown. Both spacecraft looked unfamiliar to the Enforcer Squad.

They stood before Docking Bay Twenty. Eneysa stepped forward and placed a hand on its touch panel for bioscanning, right of the hangar doors. The automated structure, immense and white, reacted quickly by reading her life form in complete detail for identification of her true identity, via computerized systems to accurately determine whether or not to let her enter it. It correctly confirmed her true identity as a Universal Marshal. The hangar doors slowly slid open in sound, permitting the Enforcer Squad entry.

Inside Docking Bay Twenty, the *Centaurus*, a Federation battlecruiser, was parked. The Enforcer Squad beheld it under glowpanels in the high, wide ceiling of the structure, the large vessel specially equipped with teleport drive, assigned to them by the Computer-Enforcer at the orders of the High Enforcer. A control panel was by the hangar doors, just inside the docking bay, and in the back of the covered and enclosed area were automatic doors to a storage chamber filled with maintenance equipment and other items. The ventilation system of the hi-tech hangar was on automatic control as filtered air circulated; automatic control had the normal temperature set at seventy-two degrees in the hi-tech hangar. The white omnimetal floor of the docking bay looked spotless, kept that way by a cleaning droid.

The *Centaurus* looked undamaged and needed no repairs, major or minor. It faced the hangar doors. The battlecruiser of the Zenvista Warship Class was separated, from front to back, into three sections: a disk-shaped head attached to a short and thick cylindrical neck connected to a long, triangular-shaped, arched body. Three massive legs on three gigantic feet shaped like broad, flattened blades, under her head and body sections, supported its heavy tonnage. It was a fine vessel, silver and sleek, one of a number of ships available to the Universal Marshals for official use.

The Enforcer Squad went around to the back of the

Centaurus and walked up its lowered ramp, underneath its rear part, in single file, Rathol in the lead. Once inside the ship, Procules rolled to the control touchpad for the ramp and pressed the red square on it, raising the ramp closed. The Robot-Enforcer followed the other Universal Marshals up a long passageway, glowpanels in the long ceiling auto-activated to light the way. Pairs of automatic doors lined up on both sides of the central corridor that opened to different bays, rooms, and quarters for their uses. Automatic control maintained life support systems throughout the battlecruiser. All the ship's systems were auto-activated the moment the vessel detected their presence aboard it. Its ceiling accommodated Jagathan's height, in some areas of the ship barely. No smells drifted in the filtered air circulating in the battlecruiser, and no sounds reverberated around them except their noisy footsteps, except Procules, who wheeled with a hum up the lit passageway. Glowpanels in the ceiling were auto-set at full intensity.

Eneysa frowned. "These walls need decorating. They look so drab. A few tapestries would brighten them up."

"That's what you get when you fly a Federation battlecruiser on loan to us," Jagathan remarked. The Titan-Enforcer could smash holes in the walls with his huge fists if he wanted to.

"Simple pleasures are good enough for this ship," Rathol said. The Staff of Godpower was just a walking stick in his hand at the moment.

Lorliane laughed. "Vessels like these aren't noted for their elegance and lush comfort. You would have to use an onboard replicator to produce decorations to make ships like this look and feel homey."

"Is she a fast ship?" Jagathan asked the Robot-Enforcer.

"The fastest one available," Procules responded.

"Ever see any action?" Lorliane asked the Robot-Enforcer. "She looks almost brand new."

"Not much," Procules responded. "Several escort assignments and delegate transports. Only one actual battle against an alien ship, a Vorvon vessel of the Taiprey Warship Class. It happened in an unnamed quadrant of the galaxy."

"Tested very little then," Jagathan remarked. "She could have been in more clashes to really test her mettle."

"But she has logged enough travel time," Procules told them.

They left the back of it, traversed the neck part, and went through automatic doors into the head section. Soon they found themselves on the bridge, already lit by glowpanels in the ceiling, the ship on automatic control until they engaged manual control to fly it.

"Give me a ship with sails and an open sea," Jagathan said.

Lorliane patted the Titan-Enforcer on the back. "A vessel with thrusters and the vastness of outer space will have to do, jolly giant."

Rathol, as the appointed leader of the Enforcer Squad, took his place in the captain's chair in the center of the circular bridge, laying the Staff of Godpower across its control armrests. Lorliane sat in the navigator's spot in front left of the Shepherd; Eneysa, the helmsman's seat, in front to the right of him. Procules stationed himself at the science console toward the back of the bridge while Jagathan stood at the weapons and tactical console left of the droid Universal Marshal. Neither the Robot-Enforcer nor the Titan-Enforcer could sit in station seats, the former not designed to sit, the latter too big to sit in such chairs. A view screen, large and rectangular, off at the moment, faced them in the front wall of the bridge. A railing arced behind the Shepherd, and another in front of the Ice Being and the Metamorph-Enforcer. Automatic doors stood directly behind the Shepherd.

"The infinite love of the Lord shall sustain us in the task we face," Rathol said. The Shepherd bowed his head to say a silent prayer. "Make this ship fly true to the stars!"

"As you command, squad leader," Eneysa responded crisply. The Metamorph-Enforcer manipulated the touchpad before her and ignited the big engines of the *Centaurus*. They roared to life as the ship itself remained still.

"Automatic control off," Procules reported, working the science console deftly. "Manual control on, and the vessel is under our direction now. All systems at full operation and maximum function."

Docking Bay Twenty parted its curved roof for them after receiving a computer command from the science console by the Robot-Enforcer. Eneysa activated vertical thrusters of the *Centaurus,* and they blasted and roared to life. Then the ship lifted off straight into the air and out of the opened hangar, the curved roof closing beneath them. As soon as the battlecruiser reached sufficient altitude, the Metamorph-Enforcer switched to horizontal thrusters, and they blasted and roared in activation. The *Centaurus* shot upward through the air, higher into the sunny sky, and finally into outer space.

"We enter the domain of the gods of the stars," Jagathan quipped.

Rathol uttered another command. "Let us see with the front viewer the heavens around us."

Lorliane turned on the view screen before them, and the perfect image of the dark vastness of space came into sight, permeated with white dots glowing like brilliant specks of divine sparks. It appeared like a celestial map of the heavens for them to navigate by. Rapidly the *Centaurus* put distance between it and Tellus, in the general direction of Kambec, the Tellusian sun, the largest celestial body on the view screen, a golden ball of thermonuclear energy so luminous, about the size of a discus and getting larger as they sped toward it.

"No other ships detected in the scanning field," Procules reported. The Robot-Enforcer performed a series of routine procedures for the ship as the science officer of the vessel, himself designated as such, the most qualified among them. He checked for other things in sensor range. "No other disturbances in the space-time continuum within our quadrant."

Rathol straightened up in the captain's chair. "Prepare for the quick passage to Earth."

Lorliane quickly initiated the short process to make their ship teleport to Earth. The Ice Being got the coordinates for teleportation to Earth from the main computer and fed them into the navigation system of the *Centaurus*. They would telejump in a split second and be teleported near the planet but out of reach by the Earthlings and their tracking devices, which inferior by Federation standards.

The *Centaurus* teleported to the Sol star system in an instant. One second they were in the Kambec star system, and the next, they arrived at their destination. There were a few Enforcers who possessed the ability of teleportation. None of the Universal Marshals aboard the ship did.

All stations operated normally after the telejump. On the view screen, they could see the glowing spots of countless stars in the heavens. The vessel flew past the planet Mars at sublight speed.

"Being transported like that is like riding a magic carpet commanded by the orbing power of gods," Jagathan said.

"Nothing but the application of superior technology to get you where you want to go," Lorliane remarked.

"I prefer the wings of a flying creature," Eneysa piped in.

Rathol spoke. "With God, all things are possible."

Procules added nothing to the conversation and just worked at his station. The Robot-Enforcer checked sensors and found nothing unusual in the area of space they flew in. Then he went through the memory banks of the ship's computers for all of the information on Earth he lacked, to update his detailed files on the planet. He copied the material directly into his memory cells after plugging into the ship's computers. The Robot-Enforcer processed it fast.

Rathol addressed the Metamorph-Enforcer after standing the Staff of Godpower on the floor beside him. "Make us invisible and noiseless."

"As you command, squad leader," Eneysa responded.

The Metamorph-Enforcer engaged the cloaking mechanism and silent propulsion system of the battlecruiser on the helmsman's console. The vessel veiled itself from view, and the engines and thrusters muffled in sound. Neither naked eye could see, nor naked ear could hear them, nor could tracking devices of a visual nature and a listening nature detect their presence. In complete stealth, the *Centaurus* began approaching Earth.

Soon the blue-and-white planet came into sight on the view screen as the Enforcer Squad beheld the Terran world with mild interest but strong feelings about the Archvillain organization on it. Earth was still a fair distance away but getting closer.

"Slow our approach first to Earth before we are in landing mode," Rathol commanded.

"As you command, squad leader," Eneysa responded.

Rathol turned to the Robot-Enforcer. "Tell us more about this world."

Procules accessed information in his memory cells about it. "Earth is dominated by an intelligent race of the human species. About seventy percent of its surface is covered by water. Earth has seven continents. It is the third planet from its sun, Sol, the only one inhabited in its solar system."

"What about means of far transport from its world to other parts of the galaxy?" Eneysa asked the Robot-Enforcer.

"Earth has yet to develop any modes of deep space travel," Procules answered. "Earthlings have personally ventured outer space only within their immediate vicinity. However, they have sent unmanned probes into space. They have artificial satellites orbiting their planet. Earth has one natural satellite they simply refer to as the Moon."

"Do the Earthlings have any technology where they can teleport between planets without the use of ships?" Lorliane asked.

"Negative," Procules responded. "They have no such devices or machines that can send their physical bodies to other places in the galaxy. Their technology lags behind Tellus and the Federation in general. It may take many years for them to catch up to where Tellus and the Federation are now."

Suddenly the *Centaurus* bucked. Then the ship rocked back and forth, forcing them to hang on against the swaying until an abrupt stop. The Robot-Enforcer quickly checked his science console and scanned their area of space to find out what had given the battlecruiser a bumpy ride.

"Sensors have located life forms in the infrared spectrum," Procules said as the vessel got tossed about again. In the next lull, the Robot-Enforcer tried to identify the invisible party responsible for bouncing them around at intervals. "They indicate the ship is being attacked by the Baltora!"

The Baltora inhabited the endless sea of outer space, its etheria substance as their home, at a vibrational frequency the physical eye could rarely see. Officially the Federation classified the Baltora as space critters of a malevolent nature. They varied in size, shape, appearance, color, and density, ranging from tiny to huge, beautiful to the grotesque. The Baltora propelled themselves in and out of dimensions regularly, visible and invisible, as pulsating life—foreign objects—made of etheria substance. The cosmic creatures, quite mischievous and a bit mysterious, could easily be photographed by infrared camera exposures. Federation research had indicated the plasmatic fauna had a special function to the etheria of outer space, though it was somewhat unclear as to what that was, despite numerous theories that had been offered to explain it. The natural opposites to this animal family of outer space were the Juntora, who were benevolent and rarely seen or encountered.

The Baltora resumed the repetitive shaking of the ship. Procules observed the sensors attempting to correct the problem. The space critters messed up the sensors each time the Robot-Enforcer got the science console to function properly.

Rathol clutched the Staff of Godpower tightly in one hand and grabbed an armrest with the other. "Demons of Satan, begone!"

"A banishing spell won't work here," Lorliane said.

Rathol yelled to the Metamorph-Enforcer, "Take us away from here!"

Frantically, Eneysa worked the helmsman's console. "I can't fly us out of here!"

"Teleport drive malfunctioning!" Lorliane informed the Shepherd after she tried to engage it to transport them elsewhere instantly. Instinctively, the Ice Being wanted to freeze the plasmatic fauna to stop them from shaking the *Centaurus* like a vessel caught in a gravity storm.

Jagathan grabbed onto the railing behind the Shepherd to keep his balance, looking enraged. "This is a deadly trap set for us by the Fellowship of Darkness!"

"And a warning system to detect outworlders and alert the Archvillain organization of impending visits to Earth!" Procules added. The Robot-Enforcer wheeled back and forth on the bridge with the rocking of the battlecruiser, unable to maintain a still position at his station. Finally, he was able to employ the magnetic traction in his wheel base and rooted himself to the spot at the science console. It took him much power to maintain an energized lock to the floor of the bridge.

The view screen on the bridge turned off and on, its picture going in and out. Glowpanels in the ceiling flickered wildly between high intensity and low intensity, but not out. Suddenly, the thrusters stopped firing, and the engine shut down, causing the *Centaurus* to decloak and drift into space in the direction of the Terran sun.

Procules worked his internal scanners in a wide and deep sweep pattern. His infrared sensors detected the invisible and unwelcome presence of the Baltora on the bridge. Space critters, becoming visible now, flitted through the bridge like alien spores flying through the air.

The *Centaurus* became dead in space—ship-wide systems failures. The Baltora were slowly turning the vessel into an inoperative hulk. A bunch of Baltora ganged up on Jagathan, pounding him with throbbing strikes of plasmatic energy. But the dense molecular structure—very thick hide—of the Titan-Enforcer withstood their hammering blows. They pinned him where he stood, up against the weapons and tactical console, trying to overpower him and rip him apart. However, his supernatural nature prevented them from simply tearing him to pieces, but he felt the force of their attack on his body. Coursing with energy power on the celestic level, he lashed out with huge fists and bashed them off him, left and right in fury, solid enough to effectively hit them with such unearthly force.

Procules erected a force field around himself and

blocked the Baltora, who were also raining throbbing strikes all over him. They slowly started penetrating his body shield and forced him to search for other defenses within himself.

The Robot-Enforcer shot laser beams from his eyes at them, but to no avail. He switched to electron beams, but that only stunned them temporarily. Computing fast, he next struck with plasma rays and knocked them away from him until they started absorbing the plasma rays. The Robot-Enforcer, inspired by information accessed from his memory cells on antimatter, changed his plasma rays to antiplasma rays. He increased the intensity of his shots.

Lorliane and Eneysa leaped to their feet as the Baltora lunged for them. The Ice Being dodged them, then encased herself in a thick block of ice, forcing the space critters to chip away with their throbbing stikes at her frozen shield layer by layer. This gave her time to think of some other way to stop them. She guessed she might not be able to freeze them so easily with ice blasts, though she seemed to remember a scientific fact that there was one absolute in the universe—everything freezes.

Across from the Ice Being, the Metamorph-Enforcer fought another bunch of Baltora. Eneysa shapeshifted into a giant marmog, a swamp monster with wet, shaggy, furlike moss that hid its features, a vicious creature. The space critters halted their ferocious assault on her, completely startled by her sudden metamorphosis. It seemed they recognized her similarity to themselves as they also possessed the ability to alter their shapes, though not nearly to the degree as Eneysa, who could easily shapeshift into various forms far greater in range than they could.

Rathol, hauled to his feet by the Baltora, fought them over the possession of the Staff of Godpower. The space critters bent the Shepherd to his knees with brute strength. In furious desperation, he called on the Staff of Godpower to awaken, surprising the cosmic creatures as the long stick flared white. He seized the Baltora with the mighty power of the Staff and utterly crushed them into uncreation, nonexistence for eternity. For the moment, free of their terrible onslaught, Rathol commanded the mighty power of the Staff again and blasted all the remaining Baltora from the bridge in a single strike. Then he cleared the rest of the space critters from the ship with the Staff. The ship's systems returned to normal operation.

"Will they be back?" Eneysa voiced for them.

Procules pressed touch pads on the science console and scanned for the Baltora with an infrared beam. "The Baltora are within sensor range, but at a distance of less than two kilometers. They appear to be regrouping."

"Counsel?" Rathol asked the other Enforcers.

"Would torpedoes or lasers from the ship stop them?" Jagathan suggested.

Procules spun around. "Negative. Possibly slow them down, though."

"Could we use teleportation on them?" Eneysa asked the Robot-Enforcer.

"Negative," Procules responded. "Teleportation is a kind of dimension shifting. Baltora dimension shift."

"What about using an antiplasmatic field around the ship or firing antiplasma beams at them?" Lorliane asked next the Robot-Enforcer.

"Antiplasmatic defense or weaponry would hurt

them," Procules responded. "But it is not known how powerful they must be to seriously harm them or destroy them."

"There must be a way to rid ourselves of this swarm of pests," Jagathan said.

"Freezing them probably won't work," Lorliane stated, herself being the expert on such matters among the Enforcer Squad. "They may be immune to being iced, not possibly susceptible to freezing conditions. The void of space is naturally cold, and they do live in its etheria."

"All correct," Procules concurred. "Baltora also cannot be subjected to cryogenics technology." The Robot-Enforcer scanned for the space critters again with an infrared beam. "They are moving slowly toward the ship for another attack."

Rathol thumped the floor of the bridge with the Staff of Godpower. "I shall summon again the almighty hand of the Lord to smite them from creation."

Procules could tell the Shepherd was a bit weak from the previous assault by the Cosmic Creatures. Suddenly the Robot-Enforcer got an idea. "There is another way."

"Speak it," Rathol said.

Procules explained. "The Baltora exist in the etheria of space. If we expose them to the atmosphere of a planet, it might destroy them since they would not be in their normal environment."

"In other words," Lorliane chimed in, "they need the etheria of space like carbon-based units need oxygen to breathe and live."

"In essence, yes," Procules agreed. "Baltora have never been known to enter the atmosphere of planets."

"How will we get them to chase us so we can immerse them in an atmosphere of a planet?" Jagathan asked the Robot-Enforcer. "They certainly will not blindly come after us."

"And they would sense danger to themselves when they are near enough to air," Eneysa added. "They would flee from it."

Procules computed a response. "The Baltora are dimension shifting beings. We teleport from here into the atmosphere of Earth as they pursue us and emerge from the telejump at our controlled choosing. Thus giving them no chance to sense the danger to them of exposure to the planet's atmosphere."

"And giving them no chance to escape from the air," Jagathan added.

"Correct," Procules said.

Rathol had to make the final decision on the matter, since he was the leader of the Enforcer Squad. "Let it be done."

"Better cloak ourselves first before we make the telejump," Procules advised.

Rathol nodded at the recommendation of the Robot-Enforcer. Eneysa cloaked the ship again as Lorliane set the coordinates for the telejump into the atmosphere of Earth. Procules scanned for the Baltora again with an infrared beam and found their numbers had been substantially increased with reinforcements. The Robot-Enforcer related this bit of information to the other Universal Marshals.

The *Centaurus* teleported directly to Earth. The Baltora followed its trail chasing the ship through the teledimension. The cosmic creatures suspected nothing as the vessel seemed to stay in the teledimension longer than it should.

"Now!" Rathol commanded.

Lorliane dropped the *Centaurus* out of the teledimension abruptly, and the ship entered the planet's atmosphere six miles above its surface. The Baltora rapidly emerged from the teledimension and were enveloped in the atmosphere of Earth, almost ninety feet from the ship.

The space critters screamed as the atmosphere touched their bodies like fire and entered their organic systems like poison. The cosmic creatures faded from view in a burning blur as if charred to death in an incinerator.

"Infrared scanners indicate no Baltora in sensor range," Procules reported. "They appeared to have been destroyed."

"Thank the Lord," Rathol said. "Praise Almighty God for deliverance from those demons of the heavens."

"Plasmatic fauna of deep space," Lorliane remarked.

Rathol addressed the Robot-Enforcer. "How much harm did they do to the ship?"

"Checking," Procules responded. The Robot-Enforcer used the bridge computer to assess the damage to the vessel by the Baltora. "No major or minor damage to the *Centaurus*."

"And her workings?" Rathol asked the Robot-Enforcer.

Procules quickly ran a systems check. "All systems are operating normally."

Later, after the Enforcer Squad set the *Centaurus* on full autocontrol, they retired to their individual quarters to recover from their ordeal with the Baltora. None of them had been injured in the encounter with the space critters, but the Shepherd had insisted they rest until tomorrow. The ship flew around the world at the higher edge of the stratosphere undetected by Earth tracking devices.

Next day, late morning, Rathol ordered a meeting for the Enforcer Squad in the conference room. The conference room was in the middle section of the ship toward the bridge. They had all regained their strength and sat at the silver omnimetal crescent-shaped conference table. A control console sat atop the table before Procules, who stood, since he could not sit. Jagathan could sit, so he did.

Eneysa voiced the first question on their minds. "Where do we start looking for the hidden base of the Archvillain organization?"

Rathol turned to the Robot-Enforcer. "Counsel us where to begin seeking the secret fortress of the Fellowship of Darkness."

"Acknowledged," Procules responded. The Robot-Enforcer went through all the stored information about Earth in his memory cells. He computed an answer. "Based on my analysis of this planet, we should initiate our search for the Complex in the United States of America."

"Why there?" Jagathan asked.

"It is the most powerful country on Earth," Procules stated. "The one with the greatest influence on the international affairs of the world."

"Any particular spot there?" Lorliane asked.

Procules beeped. "I will endeavor to find a starting point for us." The Robot-Enforcer commenced a process of elimination internally to reduce their range of choices to the best one. "After careful and further analysis, I recommend that we initiate our search in the city of New York in the state of New York."

Eneysa directed a question at the Robot-Enforcer. "Is it a special place?"

Procules had already formulated a logical explanation for the specific location. "Because the closest body Earth has to a planetary government is there, at what is officially called the United Nations. It is an organization of sovereign countries, its permanent headquarters are there."

Lorliane asked the next question of the Robot-Enforcer. "So where do we land in the city of New York?"

"In Central Park," Procules answered.

"What season is it there?" Eneysa asked.

Procules accessed the information from his memory cells, detailed files. "At this time, the United States is experiencing the end of spring. It has time zones. New York City is in the period of the evening hours now."

The final decision on where to land belonged to the Shepherd. They all looked at him.

"So it is counseled," Rathol said, "so shall it be done."

Lorliane brought up another important item. "How should we protect ourselves against discovery by the Terrans when we walk among them?"

Procules beeped. "I recommend we disguise ourselves to appear as a traveling party of humans to blend in with them and make them unaware of our true identities."

"I agree," Eneysa said.

"I think we should make ourselves invisible to the

Earthlings," Jagathan voiced. "We would appear as nothing to them. Their senses would not detect us."

"Being invisible would be the safest tactic, but harder to maintain," Procules pointed out. "My recommendation would enable us to mingle with them and not force us to take evasive maneuvers to avoid possible physical contact with them. Whereas cloaked bodies would risk collisions with their life forms as we travel among them."

Jagathan laughed. "I see your reasoning."

Rathol thought about it. "I agree with the counsel. It shall be done. The Staff of the Lord shall make their eyes see us belonging among them. The power of God I wield shall cloud their minds to us and make them as blind as sheep to our presence."

"The Terrans will be too preoccupied with their own affairs to take serious notice of us," Lorliane added.

"Should we take any arms with us?" Eneysa asked.

"Unnecessary," Procules said. "We are weapons enough for them. The human beings on this planet possess no equal or superior firepower that can threaten us. Their most powerful weapons are nuclear in nature, not capable of penetrating the shields of the *Centaurus*."

"It's better that the Earthlings know not the danger to them from the Fellowship of Darkness," Jagathan stated. "Else the Archvillains hiding on their world would certainly have destroyed it already."

"And the Terrans as well," Lorliane added.

"We're going to have to somehow protect them against the Archvillains here while we search for the Complex," Eneysa said. "We don't want their blood on our hands."

"Aye," Jagathan agreed. "The Earthlings are too

vulnerable to Archvillain attacks by the Fellowship of Darkness. They're like children under our care."

The Enforcer Squad returned to the bridge and took their stations after the Shepherd concluded the meeting. Eneysa disengaged autocontrol and returned the ship to her control.

"Land our ship in Central Park so we may begin our search for the evil ones," Rathol commanded. "They may still desecrate this poor world."

Eneysa complied with the orders. The *Centaurus* descended swiftly through the atmosphere toward the planet surface of the Terran world, running on silent propulsion systems, cloaked from detection. Procules worked the science console, and nothing dangerous appeared on the sensors.

The view screen on the bridge showed a vivid image of the atmosphere around them, a night sky clear and vast, magnification at normal setting. Below them was the United States of America, many square miles in size. The ship flew over the Midwest of the country toward the Northeast.

"Scanning," Procules said. "No Terran aircraft in the vicinity of sensors short range."

"None of their flying machines could catch this ship," Eneysa remarked.

Procules also worked the science console to guard the battlecruiser against missiles launched from military weapons on the ground, in the air, or from the water. Also space, particularly attacks from outside Earth by alien ships or other vessels.

The *Centaurus* swooped down from the night sky of shining stars and a waning moon, the veiled vessel leaving an invisible trail as it streaked at an angle for a stealthy landing in Central Park. The streetlamps, neon signs, and building lights of New York City illuminated the metropolitan area as an inhabited locale to the cloaked ship. Below them sprawled an urban jungle, its forest of skyscrapers rising high in the air as modern towers of human architecture. The nightlife of New York City bustled with activity, most of it friendly.

Eneysa slowed the *Centaurus* as the ship approached Central Park, the ornamented and recreation grounds an immense wilderness of trees and open areas. Less people frequented Central Park at nighttime than during the daytime, making it easier for the vessel to land with fewer witnesses. The Metamorph-Enforcer found a perfect spot in an open area surrounded by trees, large enough to land on and enclosed enough to adequately hide their cloaked ship. She switched to vertical thrusters, and the *Centaurus* landed smoothly in the tree-ringed clearing. Then she killed the engines.

Slowly Rathol rose to his feet and leaned on the Staff of Godpower. "Let us go into this strange world and know Earth. May the Lord bless us and protect us and make our search a successful one."

Eneysa and Lorliane stood up and stretched their limbs, both wearing Federation unisuits, the Metamorph-Enforcer in red, the Ice Being in blue.

The Shepherd refused to wear a formal and spotless outfit and kept on his shepherd's clothes, simple and primitive garb appropriate for him, reminding him of his rural roots. It was a sharp contrast to the two female Universal Marshals.

Jagathan wore no Federation unisuit because none on the ship fit him, so he stayed dressed as he was, but he had cleaned his black jerkin and black pants earlier.

Clothing never applied to Procules, not bothered by the fact that his fellow Enforcers wore garments and he did not.

The Enforcer Squad activated all automated systems of the *Centaurus* to run the ship in their absence. Procules turned on the autocommunicator feature of the vessel to enable the *Centaurus* to instantly communicate with them through him, like if any messages came from the Justiceplex on Tellus via telecommunications. Jagathan checked the weapons and tactical console to see if the autoweapons and autodefenses of the battlecruiser were operational, and they were activated and ready, if necessary, to stop any attacks against it. Lorliane shut off the view screen on the bridge, the clear picture of trees and green earth fading from it.

Prepared, Rathol led their exit from the bridge into the neck section, down the long passageway, and into the rear section. They stopped at the closed ramp. Jagathan stepped over to the control pad and touched the red button for the ramp to lower. The ramp lowered until it reached the ground. They walked down it, only themselves and the inside of the *Centaurus* visible. After they got off the ramp, the ship automatically raised it closed, then the cloaking mechanism erased any visibility of the battlecruiser.

The Enforcer Squad stood behind tall trees that screened them from sight. No wind blew, and they heard little sound in the vicinity. The evening atmosphere felt warm and comfortable enough to them, except Procules, who was not sensitive to any climate.

Rathol called on the Staff of Godpower to disguise them as ordinary Earthlings. Cloaked holographically by the mighty power of the Staff, they appeared as a small group of three human males and two human females, white, plainly dressed as typical Americans. Their cover in place, the Shepherd led them through the encircling trees, over to a paved walkway going east and west. Before they could decide which direction to take, a woman's scream pierced the night air and startled them.

Chapter 11

Delveran emerged from his quarters in higher spirits and a better mood after a few hours of meditating on personal and professional matters, a calm expression on his face that reflected in his eyes with a gleam. His black attire still looked clean as his cape swished behind him. With a bounce in his step, the High Enforcer walked confidently down the side corridor of the Justiceplex on its north end, automatic doors on both sides of the quiet passageway as the entries to the quarters of the Universal Marshals, no Enforcers in them at the moment. Glowpanels in the ceiling of the corridor radiated soft illumination.

Ready to handle old and new business, Delveran reached the end of the side corridor across from the side corridor on the south end of the Justiceplex. Near the back was the training room—workout chamber—where the Enforcers drilled regularly and hard as Universal Marshals. Automatic doors stood on both sides of the other passageway, also the entries to the Universal Marshals' quarters. No Enforcers in them at the moment. At the back of the side corridor he'd just walked down was an automated garage where the Universal Marshals parked their vehicles for official use and mechanical work.

Delveran turned left and strode briskly up the main corridor of the Justiceplex to the teleporter room.

Automatic doors on both sides of the longer passageway were lined with entries to different chambers for official use by the Enforcers, including several workshops and laboratories. The sublevel of the Justiceplex was a recreation area for the Universal Marshals. No foul being had ever breached the security of the Justiceplex, which was tight and automatically maintained by Nanomach— except when the High Enforcer delegated it temporarily to another Enforcer at times.

Inside the teleporter room, Delveran went over to the teleport console and saw the autoteleportist already activated for the teleporter. Smiling, the High Enforcer fed new coordinates into the control podium, then stepped onto the telegrid. In a few seconds, the autoteleportist engaged and teleported him to his destination, the Scienceplex, the top place of science on Tellus. The planetary organization of scientists headquartered there with a large membership. Several of the Universal Marshals held memberships in the Scienceplex, legal under Federation rules and regulations.

Instantly Delveran materialized on a black, square telegrid in the teleporter hall of the Scienceplex. There were ten telegrids in the teleporter hall, and a few of them were in operation. The Scienceplex was an immense rectangular structure near the downtown area of a bustling Acropollon, the busy center attracting visitors to it every day. Momentarily the High Enforcer adjusted to the change in surroundings after his system immediately and naturally shook off the temporary effects of teleportation, as if suddenly manifesting in corporeal form from an invisible dimension.

Delveran acknowledged the friendly hello of the

teleportist working at the teleport console before him, an alien being, a young male, on a regular shift. The High Enforcer stepped off the telegrid and exited the teleporter hall through automatic doors. He noticed various beings occasionally went in and out of the teleporter hall. No officials had greeted him.

Glowpanels provided light throughout the Scienceplex, which had eighty floors and twenty sublevels. Filtered air circulated through the Scienceplex by automation systems. Delveran walked across a long corridor—automatic doors stood along it to different chambers—to a row of turbolifts. These could be activated by touch using control panels next to them or by voice command. Other beings walked the corridor, but none of them said anything to the High Enforcer. He overheard snatches of conversation but concentrated on the clicking of his dress shoes on the silver omnimetal floor, which was the same color and material as the rest of the building. The Grand Universal Marshal entered a turbolift and gave it a voice command. Swiftly it took him up to the fifth floor of the Scienceplex.

Once out of the turbolift, Delveran walked to the west wing of the fifth floor and stopped before automatic doors to a particular laboratory, occupied. The High Enforcer buzzed the person inside the science chamber via the control panel to his left. A male voice, husky, told him to enter. Pushing the sides of his cape behind him, the Grand Universal Marshal entered the workroom.

Delveran crossed the laboratory to a row of working computers where Enforcer Minanket, the Molecular Being, monitored them. Minanket stood eight inches over six feet tall with a husky frame, his black hair fluffed out, his black beard long and thick but neat, his brown eyes flecked with gray. Overall the Molecular Being was a mighty man with rugged features, looking like a brawny lumberjack in a white labsuit with matching boots, polished.

Minanket was a scientist, his specific field mechanology, the science that deals with the study of machines, devices, gadgets, and apparatuses. The Molecular Being held a long-term membership in the Scienceplex. He had made Tellus his home for the past ten years.

"I must speak with you," Delveran said.

Minanket nodded. The Molecular Being took a break from his work—studying a bunch of machines, devices, and apparatuses running by routine programs to observe, test, and analyze their efficiency and operation. The laboratory resembled an automated factory.

There were open spaces in the science chamber, narrow lanes to step around the machines. Glowpanels in the ceiling shined in greater illumination than normal because of the work being done under them. The working computers compiled data and recorded information in detailed files for storage in memory banks. The deafening combination of noises would ring in the ears and make it hard to hear, but sound mufflers around the laboratory kept the racket to a low volume.

The working computers carried on their tasks as the Molecular Being and the High Enforcer grabbed a couple of stools before a worktable not far from the programmed machines.

"What do you want to see me about?" Minanket asked.

"Professor Magnemus," Delveran replied. "Your friendship with him and the scandal that forced him to leave Aruvenor forever."

The High Enforcer explained to the Molecular Being the discovery of the Archvillain organization on Earth, its plan to invade Tellus and bust all the Archvillain inmates from the Universal Prisonplex, and how the Enforcer Squad was sent as a strike force to the Terran world to find the hidden base of the Fellowship of Darkness. Minanket listened intently, frozen in his seat, a blank expression on his face, absorbing the information. After the Grand Universal Marshal finished speaking, he gauged the reaction of his fellow Enforcer.

Minanket responded momentarily. "Our association seemed inevitable. Magnemus and I had certain similarities that gravitated us to form a bond of friendship. Both of us had special powers. We both had a strong interest in what turned into a deep love of science. Intellectually, we were equal and had been ranked as the best students in our respective science majors. But what drew us to each other initially was that we resembled each other in physical appearance, as if we were genetic brothers."

"So you thought you might have been related?" Delveran asked, surprised.

"Yes," Minanket answered, a bit wearily. "We were nearly identical in height, weight, build, and facial features, except for the color of our hair and eyes. Because of our uncanny resemblance to each other, we researched for a lineage connection through our family histories for a common genealogy. We discovered we might have been related as distant cousins, but the proof was inconclusive. So we acted as if we were related by blood in some way. Thus we became best friends."

Delveran tried to form a clear picture of Professor

Magnemus in his mind. "Tell me about the scandal involving the Scientific Being."

Minanket cleared his throat before he began. "Actually, it started when we were still attending Trantorus Techniversity together. We were roommates and lived off campus, in an automated apartment building near the Tarpaignian Mountains."

Delveran relaxed as he visualized the tale of the Molecular Being. The High Enforcer folded his arms.

"During our last semester at the techniversity," Minanket continued, "Magnemus had complained to me about the restrictions placed on the use of natural and artificial creatures in both bioscientific and biotechnological work. He felt those rules considerably hindered his biocreation experiments. Day after day, he kept objecting to the laws of Aruvenor that governed his field, and I listened without commenting on the matter."

"Did he see Aruvenor officials about seriously changing the policies concerning bioscience and biotechnology in regards to his biocreation experiments?" Delveran asked, not familiar with those outside Tellus and the Federation.

"No."

"Go on."

Minanket ran a hand through his beard. "Suddenly, he stopped complaining. I wondered why. I became suspicious when he started acting too placid. At times, during the early hours of morning, he would simply disappear. So I decided to find out what he had kept secret from me."

Delveran leaned forward a little on the stool.

"I followed him next time he ventured out," Minanket said. "He led me into the Tarpaignian

Mountains, and there I, rather shockingly, discovered a secret laboratory of his under Treacher's Peak. To my utter dismay, he had been conducting numerous and extravagant biocreation experiments of an illegal and immoral nature on lower life forms. I confronted him and lectured him on the ethics of the dreadful wrong he was inflicting on innocent creatures. I told him he must abandon his unsanctioned work and immediately dismantle his secret laboratory. He agreed with me and assured me he would do it the following night and every night until accomplished. I accepted his word and let the matter be forgotten."

Minanket paused to catch his breath as Delveran mulled over what the Molecular Being had told him thus far. The High Enforcer glimpsed what the scandal that had exiled the Scientific Being from Aruvenor had entailed.

Minanket resumed his story. "Years later, as you have already learned, Magnemus aspired to become the Techarch of Aruvenor while holding the cabinet office as the Secretary of Bioscience and Biotechnology. He wanted to bring new leadership to the planet. He felt the Aruvenor government needed a change to continue and expand the growth of the planet on many fronts—economic, political, and most of all, progress on the scientific and technological levels. He thought Aruvenor was acting like an independent world too much and progress backward and had become an isolated planet again. At that time, I worked for the Garotoc Corperation as the planetary manager of the Mechanology Division."

Delveran interrupted him. "Did this corporation contract or subcontract with the Aruvenor government, including under the department Professor Magnemus headed?"

"Yes," Minanket replied. "The corporation transacted a fairly regular amount of business with the government, mostly in the area of space and mining technology."

"Proceed."

Minanket wore a grim expression on his face, his tired eyes a little bloodshot, his lips a bit chapped, his posture slightly bent from sitting too much. "In the year before the election of the Techarch, the Aruvenor Department of Law Enforcement performed a sting operation that became public shortly after Magnemus announced his candidacy to the Techarchy. It exposed illegal sales and purchases of high technology to planets having nonrelations with Aruvenor. To the embarrassment of the Aruvenor government, and public outcry, officials in the administration were implicated in the scandal."

"Professor Magnemus was one of those officials," Delveran stated.

Minanket nodded. "There were many arrests of government officials and workers by planetary authorities in law enforcement and government agencies in the intelligent branches.

"When they went after Magnemus, he fled from them and vanished. They sought me out to see if I knew where he would go because they knew of my past association with him. Our friendship had never wavered, although I saw him much less since the end of our techniversity days."

Delveran thought the scandal was a complicated affair. As an official of the Federation, no scandal had ever touched him like this one had the Scientific Being.

Never had any in the Federation ever accused him of corruption.

"Initially," Minanket went on, "I couldn't help them. Then I recalled Magnemus's secret laboratory under Treacher's Peak. I thought it highly unlikely he had not destroyed it when he gave me his word years ago. So I led the authorities to the Peak, to see if it still existed or not."

Delveran remembered the old saying that philosophy dealt with truth and science with fact. The High Enforcer refocused on the story the Molecular Being was telling.

Minanket sighed. "I was wrong. Magnemus still had it there under the Peak. Only now, he had progressed to conducting illegal and immoral biocreation experiments on higher life forms, including intelligent beings. We found him in the middle of packing computer discs containing all his biocreation notes in transport receptacles. He was in the process of relocating to another area on the planet."

Delveran thought the tale the Molecular Being told him was quite a story and a long one as well. It gave him a better idea of what the Scientific Being was like since his prior knowledge of the Archvillain had been kind of sketchy, shallow on the details. The High Enforcer felt Professor Magnemus was the right leader for the Fellowship of Darkness, sort of the opposite of him.

"The authorities tried to arrest him," Minanket said. "But he fled down a tunnel, and we gave pursuit. He went through a back entrance and sealed it behind him magnetically, then used his special powers and collapsed the rocky ceiling of the tunnel down on us. However, I changed into a molecular ball and phased rapidly through the Peak to outside."

"Was the Peak volcanic?" Delveran asked.

"No," Minanket replied. "Anyway, I spotted him running toward his ship. I wanted to catch up with him and demand why he had turned to evil and why he had lied to me. But I suddenly remembered that the authorities were trapped inside the Peak. So I rescued them from the collapsed tunnel while Magnemus escaped from the planet in his ship. Thereafter the Aruvenor government, by law, banished him from ever returning to the planet again, under penalty of arrest and trial."

The High Enforcer could see why the Aruvenor government covered up the scandal to protect its political image and hide its embarrassment over the sordid affair that had damaged its sovereign structure. He figured the Aruvenor government had repaired the damage quietly before it could cause serious harm to its relations with other planetary governments. Minanket waited for him to speak again.

"I am sending you to Earth to join the Enforcer Squad," Delveran said. "Your personal knowledge of the Scientific Being may help find the unknown location of the Complex and increase the chances of a successful raid on the Archvillain stronghold."

Minanket nodded. "When do you want me to depart for Earth?"

"Immediately," Delveran responded. "Have a Federation ship at the Acropollon Spaceport on my authority take you to Earth to join the Enforcer Squad."

Minanket climbed to his feet and left the laboratory after he instructed, by voice command, that the main computer in the science chamber shut down operations until further notice. All the machines in the workroom stopped working at once. Only the glowpanels in the ceiling were left on. Delveran rose to his feet and exited the laboratory as well. Automatically, the glowpanels turned off behind him, leaving the science chamber dark. The High Enforcer decided he must see both Tellusian and Federation authorities next to tell them about the planned invasion by the Fellowship of Darkness.

Among those officials would be Evarinia, so he could give her his answer about what he wanted to do about their relationship. He wished he could speak with her under better circumstances. A foreboding of doom hung over him.

Chapter 12

The Enforcer Squad heard the woman's scream again, east of their position. Procules used his sensors to zero in on any life forms in the vicinity, in the direction of the screams. Eneysa and Lorliane, being female themselves, were more bothered by the screams than their male counterparts in the Enforcer Squad.

"My sensors indicate four human males and one human female approximately sixty yards from us," Procules reported.

Rathol turned and faced his fellow Enforcers, who naturally wanted to go to the rescue of the woman screaming in danger and crying for help. "We must not interfere."

The noninterference ordinance kept them from rushing to the aid of the woman. It stated that no being of the Federation may interfere in the world affairs or the natural events of a nonFederation planet. But it conflicted with what they were—Universal Marshals— beings trained to fight evil in all its guises, in any and every form, the elite officers of law enforcement of the Federation Department of Justice sworn not to let evil win over good. The quandary tore at the very fiber of their beings and tested their natures as Enforcers.

Another scream reached them, louder than the last two and more desperate. When they heard the woman scream again, this time it sounded like she was in pain as if one of her assailants had hurt her in some way physically. That decided the issue. Jagathan, Eneysa, and Lorliane charged ahead to the area where the crime was being committed against the woman.

"No!" Rathol said. "Come back! We must not interfere!"

Procules beeped a few times. "Our course of action has been determined for us." The Robot-Enforcer wheeled fast behind the other three Universal Marshals.

Rathol looked up at the heavens. "Lord, give me strength. Let this be not a misjudgment."

The Shepherd moved his aged body as fast as he could, trailing his fellow Enforcers, dropping the illusion disguising them as typical Americans by the Staff of Godpower.

Jagathan, Eneysa, and Lorliane ran along a paved walkway, the Titan-Enforcer in the lead, jogging more than racing, but taking longer strides than the Metamorph-Enforcer and the Ice Being. Tall trees and bushes rose along both sides of the walkway, living things silently witnessing the Enforcer Squad coming to the rescue of a female victim the five of them knew nothing about. No animals stirred around them, quieted by the warm night. The shining stars and the glowing moon in the evening sky, clear of night clouds, mutely watched the events unfolding under them, as if putting a spotlight on the Enforcer Squad.

Jagathan, Eneysa, and Lorliane turned left off the walkway, through a patch of shrubs, and emerged in open space of mowed green grass near a stone bridge with a paved walkway below it. Jagathan pounded over the bridge like a sprinting giant, blocking the view of Eneysa and Lorliane racing behind him. Arriving at the other end of the bridge, they saw four young, thin white men wearing T-shirts, blue jeans, black sneakers, and ball caps, assaulting a white woman in a yellow shirt, red shorts, and pink sneakers. The men threw her to the ground, intent on harming her further.

Jagathan collared a man. Eneysa shapeshifted into a large beast that resembled a mountain lion the size and bulk of a rhinoceros and pounced on a man standing nearby, flattening him to the ground. The other two men took one look at the Titan-Enforcer and the Metamorph-Enforcer and fled. But Lorliane shot ice beams from her hands and froze them in blocks of ice, only their heads sticking out to allow them to breathe.

Jagathan turned to the man he held in his hand to face him eye to eye, the man's feet dangling in the air six feet from the ground, the Earthling terrified at the mere sight, the sheer size of the Titan-Enforcer. The female victim beheld the giant Universal Marshal in shock, her eyes not believing what she saw. The appearance of Jagathan overwhelmed and paralyzed her.

"What are you?" the man asked the Titan-Enforcer, not struggling in the grip of the Universal Marshal.

"You enjoy disrespecting a helpless woman?" Jagathan asked in a thunderous voice. The angry expression on his face made the man quiver in helplessness and fear. "I have in mind to drive you into the earth like I did with that hydrogen missile on Tellus. Then you would know, puny mortal, what it would feel like to be a victim, helpless and powerless."

"Please don't hurt me, man," the captive whined, his eyes practically bulging from their sockets.

Lorliane joined the Titan-Enforcer. "Why should you get any mercy, lowlife? You and your friends weren't going to be merciful with your female victim here. You are Criminals, common scum, underserving of anything."

The man panicked and thrashed in Jagathan's grasp. That annoyed the Titan-Enforcer, who clubbed the man with his free fist with sufficient force to make the Earthling behave and be quiet. "That's better. Don't do that again. I'll hammer you to pieces if you do."

Procules arrived and surveyed the scene, seeing the whole situation already under control. When Rathol caught up with the rest of the Enforcer Squad, the female victim, still hurt and on the ground, fainted. The four assailants, immobilized, could only hope the Universal Marshals did not do anything else to them. Compassionately, the Shepherd went to the side of the unconscious woman, the Robot-Enforcer assisting him.

Procules scanned the female victim for injury. "There is major damage to her stomach and ribs, minor damage to her kidneys and throat."

Slowly, Rathol bent down on his left knee and touched her forehead, wet with perspiration, with the Staff of Godpower. "In the name of Almighty God, be healed!"

The woman calmly awoke, healed miraculously of her external and internal injuries, the black and blue marks all over her gone, the trauma of the vicious assault against her cleansed from her entire system. She appeared whole, as if the terrible attack against her had never happened. Even her clothes had been mended by the Staff of Godpower.

"Relax, my child," Rathol said kindly, both hands on the Staff now. "You are among friends."

The woman gave the Shepherd a look of awe. "How

did you heal me?" she asked, unafraid.

"With the almighty power of the Lord in this simple Staff," Rathol replied. The Shepherd climbed slowly to his feet as she did. "His mighty hand has purified you of the sinful touches of these evil men."

"Our holographic camouflage has disintegrated temporarily," Procules remarked. The Robot-Enforcer caught her staring at him.

The woman gasped again at Jagathan as he came over to them, the Titan-Enforcer carrying the assailant in his hand with such ease, as if the man weighed nothing. She seemed absolutely stunned at Eneysa sitting on the back of another of her attackers, purring in feline form, as the man under the Universal Marshal remained silent and still. Lorliane, not encased in ice at the moment, did not confuse the woman with her normal appearance.

"What should we do with these puny mortals?" Jagathan asked the other members of the Enforcer Squad.

Eneysa growled and snarled in her feline form, swishing her long tail. The man underneath her closed his eyes and mouth as if expecting to be killed.

"Throw them into the abyss of Tartarus," Jagathan suggested. "Let these wicked men be forever tormented for what they did and would have done worse to the mortal woman."

Rathol came up with an answer. "If you agree with me, let the mighty power of the Lord choose how they shall be damned for their transgression against the woman."

His fellow Enforcers looked at each other and agreed with him. Smiling, the Shepherd invoked the Staff of Godpower, and it flared white in his hand as he commanded it to give the four men a fitting punishment for their crimes against the woman in the name of the Supreme Being. The four men reacted as if they were being cursed.

"It is done," Rathol said. "Release them. The wrath of God shall be swift, and justice shall be served against them."

Jagathan dropped the man he held to the ground, and Eneysa sprang off the back of the one under her. Lorliane freed the other two men from the blocks of ice they were encased in. Very frightened now, the four men fled from the Enforcer Squad over the bridge behind them, leaving only the woman for the Enforcer Squad to deal with. Eneysa changed back into her natural form, a female humanoid, astonishing the woman.

"I don't know how to thank you," the woman stammered out.

Lorliane responded for them. "No thanks are necessary. We're just glad that we were able to stop them before they did far worse to you."

"Just don't tell anyone else of your world about us," Eneysa added. "We don't need the attention."

"I don't think anybody would believe me even if I did say anything," the woman responded. "Except maybe the tabloids. But they're a joke."

"Tabloids," Procules repeated. The Robot-Enforcer accessed information about them in his memory cells. "A kind of newspaper featuring stories of crime, violence, scandal, and other subjects presented in a sensational manner."

The woman smiled. "What will happen to those men now?"

"They will be punished accordingly," Eneysa

answered for them. "And suffer the consequences of their vile act against you."

In agreement, the Enforcer Squad escorted the woman out of Central Park and to her apartment building nearby. With the Staff of Godpower, Rathol reestablished the illusion disguising the Universal Marshals as typical Americans. The modern and expensive structure towered above them like so many of the buildings of New York City. A metropolis filled with skyscrapers that reduced citizens to the size of moving dots on the urban landscape.

After the woman left them for the safety of her high-rise apartment, they conferred as to which direction they should go. They decided to continue in the same direction they departed Central Park from, north. Rathol led the Enforcer Squad, and Jagathan brought up the rear.

They traveled down streets, buildings rising on both sides of them made of concrete, steel, and glass. Parked cars and moving vehicles of different makes and models were common sights. The night air smelled foul to the Enforcer Squad due to the exhaust fumes of moving vehicles.

"The air quality here is subnormal," Procules remarked. "It is polluted to a degree."

A lost dog peed by a tall tree near a street curb, a Labrador retriever, male, with a short, dense, chocolate coat. Then it bounded over and sniffed the Enforcer Squad. The strongly built, compact canine wagged its tail and barked a few times. Eneysa petted the friendly creature and scratched behind its ears. With a last yelp, the Labrador retriever ran along down the street as the Enforcer Squad continued along under the glare of streetlights that illuminated their path. Neon signs advertised and promoted businesses and products and related messages to the public, but the Enforcer Squad had no interest in what they said.

The Universal Marshals passed flights of wide stairs leading down to subway stations. They decided to remain above ground in their exploration of New York City, yet watched people entering and exiting the underground public transit system. Traffic lights blinked red, yellow, and green, green, yellow, and red as cars, a few trucks, and a bus drove by, their occupants simply ignoring the Universal Marshals. The five Enforcers heard honking horns and saw taxi cabs picking up a few fares. A police car spotted them and drove on.

"This place seems to have plenty of nightlife," Lorliane remarked. "A city that never seems to sleep."

The Enforcer Squad heard a groan from a dark alley and went to investigate. Rathol, Eneysa, Lorliane, and Jagathan wrinkled their noses at the sour odor emanating from the alley, but Procules analyzed the smell. A black-and-white cat jumped from a garbage can near the Robot-Enforcer and ran out of the dark alley.

"Very unclean and unsanitized," Procules said. "This thoroughfare needs to be cleaned and sanitized before it becomes more of a health hazard."

The Universal Marshals found a drunk Terran behind a trash bin in the dark alley, holding an empty bottle of beer. The rotten smell of spoiled food wafted in the night air from the trash bin.

Empty bottles, waste paper, and cardboard boxes littered the dark alley. The drunk looked terrible and needed a bath and a shave. The man reeked of heavy liquor, body odor, and the stink of his vomit.

"Poor soul," Rathol said. "May the Lord find pity on

you in His infinite mercy and save you."

The Enforcer Squad left the drunk where he lay and exited the dark alley the way they came, almost bumping into two kids on skateboards racing down the sidewalk.

"This is like the Tellusian city of Hellakesh," Lorliane remarked. "An urban maze unpleasant to visit."

Procules beeped. "By my data, New York City could use an Enforcer sweep to rid this metropolis of its evil element."

The Enforcer Squad found another crime in progress as a fight erupted on a basketball court between two rival street gangs. A high wired fence enclosed the basketball court, except for the open gateway on its west side. They watched gang members fighting each other with knives, chains, baseball bats, and bare hands.

"How barbaric," Eneysa remarked. "They don't know how to battle like skilled and honorable warriors."

"Wretched beings," Jagathan agreed. "A fine kill in battle takes real artistry. They fight like primitive pygmies."

In the middle of the rumble, a few teenagers spotted them and yelled to alert the other gang members to the unwanted intrusion by the Enforcer Squad. The rumble stopped, and both gangs turned on the Universal Marshals now, seeing only five adults to victimize. Evilly, gang members smiled, clearly indicating to the Enforcer Squad that those young punks were going to really enjoy hurting the Universal Marshals.

As both gangs charged at the Enforcer Squad like rabid animals let loose, Jagathan stepped forward, raised his right foot high, and stomped the basketball court with earthquake force. The basketball court shook and toppled all the gang members to the cement. When the young punks tried to get up, the Titan-Enforcer stomped the basketball court again, shaking it and knocking the juvenile delinquents to the cement again. Jagathan had to stomp the basketball court four times before both gangs got the message to stay on the ground, bewildered and scared by the awesome display of physical strength by the Titan-Enforcer.

"Cease your feud and make peace," Eneysa advised the teenagers. "Your fight will only lead to death and despair."

The Enforcer Squad left the two gangs to ponder their bad situation, the young punks too stunned to resume the rumble after what had just happened to them. Both gangs decided to call it quits for the night.

Five blocks and two streets over, the Universal Marshals encountered a third crime in progress. Two men held up a convenience store, the taller robber wielding a shotgun, the shorter a Saturday Night Special handgun. Procules wheeled into the place, the unpleasant odor of cigarette smoke lingering in the air, his fellow Enforcers waiting outside for him, and his scanners registering the layout of the licensed business. The convenience store had three aisles between stocked shelves of products and a back section of cold and frozen goods. It sold liquor and newspapers and magazines as well. Behind the cash register stood the frightened owner, a fat, balding, elderly man, arthritic hands raised at shoulder level.

"What the fuck is that?" the man with the shotgun said as Procules appeared to the two robbers in his true form, a robot.

The other man laughed. "Hey, maybe it's looking for its mama, eh?"

Procules identified their weapons and determined that their firearms could not damage him if they shot at him. Analyzing the entire matter, the Robot-Enforcer deduced logically that he should neutralize the taller robber first because he wielded the more powerful weapon. The Universal Marshal bore down on the bigger man.

"You know," the other robber said, waving his pistol, "it looks like a refugee from a sci-fi movie. Shoot it, Jose."

Jose opened fire on Procules with the shotgun and whooped. The shotgun blasts deflected harmlessly off the Robot-Enforcer and left no marks on his omnimetal frame, not even slowing him down. Jose emptied the shotgun at the Universal Marshal, who then ripped the weapon, by the hot barrel, from the man's grasp and broke it into pieces. Procules tossed aside the remains as Jose ran from him, only to be clotheslined by Jagathan just outside the establishment and knocked unconscious.

The other robber blinked in disbelief and lowered his gun. Procules wheeled over to him and he gave the Robot-Enforcer his weapon and dropped to his knees, pleading with the Universal Marshal not to hurt him. Procules beeped at him and gave the convenience store owner the gun.

Surprised, the proprietor carefully took it from the Robot-Enforcer and pointed it down at the man kneeling on the floor in fear, mumbling words in Spanish.

"Call your local police," Procules said to the owner. "Have them deliver the two Criminals to the proper facility."

"Yeah," the proprietor responded, reaching for the telephone behind him. "Thank you."

After the owner completed the call, Procules rejoined the Enforcer Squad outside. Jagathan hurled the unconscious man into the convenience store, where he landed at the side of the kneeling one. The proprietor covered both robbers with the pistol. Nobody on the street paid much attention to the Universal Marshals or what had happened in the convenience store. The illusion disguising the Enforcer Squad by the Staff of Godpower included the Robot-Enforcer again. Satisfied, the Universal Marshals left the crime scene and continued on.

The Enforcer Squad met more of the dregs of society in the metropolis. Homeless people slept in doorways and other grimy spots, and a bag lady walked by pushing a grocery cart full of junk. Two hookers stood near a street corner, both young females, a blonde and a brunette.

"Hey, baby," the blonde called to the three males of the Enforcer Squad. "Want to have a little fun?"

"A little fun?" Procules repeated. "That does not compute."

"Tainted ladies," Jagathan remarked.

Eneysa seemed irked by the pair of prostitutes and yelled to them, "Stop wasting your life, peasant women." The two hookers gave the Metamorph-Enforcer the finger.

The Universal Marshals witnessed many evil happenings taking place as they journeyed through the city. Some major crimes, some minor crimes. They had seen worse. The Enforcer Squad felt New York City needed cleaned up.

"Disgraceful," Lorliane remarked. The other Universal Marshals agreed with the Ice Being, all of them wondering why the citizens of New York City tolerated these deplorable conditions. "There should be a public outcry against this urban decay."

In some ways, New York City reminded the Enforcer Squad of Acropollon, both major cities on their respective planets. But to the Universal Marshals, the Tellusian capital looked far more clear and much less dangerous than the Earth metropolis. Also, Acropollon appeared larger in area and population than New York City, the former way more advanced than the latter, as if there were any comparison. Of the two cities, the Tellusian capital had existed longer than the Earth metropolis, less than a thousand years, but the Terran world predated the Federation planet in terms of civilization. The Federation had officially recognized Tellus as a colonized world, originally, whereas Earth was not because life evolved naturally and independently on it.

"This city seems to be an environment for foul beings of all kinds to thrive in," Eneysa remarked.

"It would be a perfect place for the Complex to be erected," Lorliane added.

Procules beeped. "There is a distinct possibility that the hidden base of the Archvillain organization could be located underground, beneath a building or buildings in the metropolis."

"It would make obvious sense for the foul beings to simply operate from a subterranean headquarters," Lorliane said. "What better way to hide from apparent sight of the unsuspecting Terrans."

"Aye," Jagathan agreed.

The Enforcer Squad came to a clothing warehouse district. It seemed quiet all around them, no Earthlings in the vicinity, buildings shut down for the night. No sooner did they turn a corner when a warehouse exploded. Fire erupted from the destroyed building, threatening to spread through the business zone and cause the potential loss of millions of dollars in property, including facilities and merchandise, to the commercial area, and maybe cost lives. Seeing the danger the conflagration represented, Rathol summoned the Staff of Godpower to extinguish the flames. Rathol shrank the blaze smaller and smaller until the remains smoldered.

Jagathan grinned. "Well done."

Procules used his sensors to check the razed structure for any bodies. "I detect no life forms in the destroyed building, either alive or dead."

Lorliane shot ice beams from her hands to instantly cool the smoldering wreckage of the leveled warehouse. "This was the work of a Criminal, no doubt. Probably hired by a Villain to do it."

"We must not expose ourselves too much to the Earthlings," Procules stated. "Otherwise we violate the noninterference ordinance to a major degree."

"I think our encounters with the Terrans so far haven't endangered the search," Lorliane said. "As long as we keep direct contact with them to a minimum, we should be able to complete our mission without any serious complications."

"The real problem is not letting the public masses of this world know of our presence," Jagathan chimed in.

"Agreed," Eneysa said. "We really don't want to endanger them because of our presence here. The Fellowship of Darkness would use that to their advantage against the Enforcers and the Federation."

"We shall bring the foul beings from the shadow of

evil into the light of good to face justice," Rathol promised them. "They will know damnation for what harm they have done to the lives of others."

"Yes," Lorliane agreed. "For all the death and destruction they have caused for so long."

The Enforcer Squad walked some more through New York City. No further incidents occurred, but their sightseeing of the Earth metropolis was not altogether pleasant. The most familiar thing to the Universal Marshals was the foul beings that had crossed their path, who were Terrans, all Criminals and no Villains. Earth was not known to have any Archvillains originally from it.

"I hope the culture of this world is better than what we have seen of it so far," Eneysa said. "It seems poor."

Procules accessed information in his memory cells about it. "Earth does have a rich and diverse culture, by normal standards, for human beings."

Just before dawn, the Enforcer Squad returned quietly to the *Centaurus*. The Universal Marshals relaxed and rested for a while. Their sojourn through New York City proved stimulating, eventful, and interesting, but also disappointing. Their search to find the Complex yielded nothing, but they were still hopeful. They each went to their private quarters to gain strength and prepare for another jaunt into the Earth metropolis. Next time they would venture out by day. And they knew that that would be a greater risk to themselves than their previous excursion around the major city.

Chapter 13

Delveran materialized on a large, black, square telegrid of the teleporter hall in the Federationplex, a skyscraper gleaming of blue omnimetal with many windows, towering over every other building in Acropollon, in the heart and center of the downtown area of the Tellusian capital. The High Enforcer stepped off the telegrid and was greeted by the teleportist on duty at the station, a female android, who sat at the teleport console. The teleporter hall had fifteen telegrids, all in use at the moment by diplomatic parties and other beings teleported to and from the Federationplex. Glowpanels in the ceiling lit the teleporter hall, a huge chamber on the ground floor of the immense building. After exchanging a few friendly words with a diplomatic party from the Federation planet Zionia—inhabited by a race of humanoids—as they prepared to teleport to the Acropollon Spaceport, the Grand Universal Marshal exited the teleporter hall through automatic doors.

Delveran walked down a long corridor, glowpanels above him at moderate intensity, and thought about his family tree. His bloodline was not that special—no one in it, except himself, famous. Federation employees worked in the Federationplex, which featured offices for every department. Automatic doors on both sides served as entries to the various chambers.

The council hall of the Federationplex was annexed

to the building where delegates from all the planets of the Federation held their meetings. Planet representatives regularly worked in the Federationplex, which was also the largest building on Tellus. Embassies of different worlds were spread across Survarille but not Mellenroel. Tellus attracted offworld visitors the most of all Federation planets because of it being the planet capital of the Federation—and the home of the Enforcers.

A number of beings passed Delveran in the long corridor, people from alien, faerie, human, humanoid, and other races of the basic types in the universe. The High Enforcer, though human, had the most associations with those of the race of faerie, mainly because of magic, since he practiced it, and the race of faerie was the one known most to practice magic. There were members of his bloodline that had and still did practice magic, notably an uncle who had first taught him the white arts before learning from other teachers in the occult field.

Delveran took a turbolift up, other passengers in it, to the forty-fourth floor of the Federationplex. Other turbolifts, in different sections of the building, conveyed passengers either up or down to other floors. Turbolifts were in constant use in the Federationplex, freight ones not as much as passenger ones. All the floors of the Federationplex hopped with the activity of Federation business.

After getting off the turbolift, Delveran walked a short distance up a long corridor with half of the glowpanels in the ceiling on above him. The High Enforcer met other beings in the extended passageway but exchanged no words with them, though they knew who he was.

Automatic doors on both sides of the Grand Universal Marshal opened and closed to certain offices of Federation departments as people walked in and out of them up and down the wide hallway at intervals. He stopped at the entry to the office of the director of the Federation Department of Foreign Affairs, where Evarinia worked. The High Enforcer felt a bit nervous, so he steadied himself for the coming scene with her, figuring groveling would certainly be involved on his part. In his mind, he rehearsed what he wanted to say. After taking a few deep breaths—not of the mystical kind, just simply heaving his chest—he boldly entered her office as if possessed.

In the outer office, Delveran stopped before the desk of Evarinia's personal secretary, Drusilla, an elderly humanoid woman. Office machines occupied all the spaces of the outer office. Drusilla worked on her computer, busy transcribing documents of the Federation addressed to and for the lady director. She looked up from her routine task when she noticed him standing before her desk. The only sounds in the room were from another, larger computer autorecording news of Federation happenings in the galaxy via subchannels from other planets, humming, and a televised broadcast on a telescreen showing the council hall of the Federationplex where representatives met in session, not open to the public, as a debate raged about peacekeeper missions involving Federation forces. Diplomats were taking turns speaking, among them, Chukkikat Espock, the Tellusian ambassador, a male humanoid of middle age, who had served the government post for the past ten years. Delveran glanced at the view screen with little interest, for politics did not interest him, unless it concerned matters involving the Universal Marshals.

"I'll let her know you're here," Drusilla said.

Delveran held up a hand. "Don't tell I'm here. Let me surprise her. It's very important." He lowered his hand.

"Okay, sir," Drusilla responded. She resumed her work, not showing curiosity as to why the High Enforcer did not want to be announced to the lady director.

Quietly Delveran walked into the inner office, looking calm on the outside, but fear gnawing on the inside. Evarinia sat at her desk with her back to him, facing the automatic door. She read to herself a long memo on a computer notepad, her office computer off at the moment.

There were fewer office machines in the inner office than in the outer one. To the right of her desk hung a telescreen. Before her office desk sat two armchairs and a window appeared behind her desk. Evarinia did not look out of the window, which showed a view of downtown Acropollon.

Delveran crossed the inner office to her desk as she spun around in her office chair and faced forward. Evarinia looked up from her computer notepad as he remained standing instead of taking a seat.

"Evarinia," Delveran said. The High Enforcer tried to smile, but the effort was half-hearted, and he gazed at her with sudden longing.

"Have you come to a decision about us?" Evarinia asked. She gave him the look of a woman still scorned.

"Yes," Delveran replied, sensing the fury emanating from her. "First, I wish to say that I admire and respect you. I always have. But I know I have been taking you for granted, and my actions of the last few months have been unconscionable. Forgive me for my unacceptable handling of our relationship."

Evarinia relaxed a bit after being so tense at his entrance. "I accept your apology. Now, what is your decision?" She put her computer notepad on her office desk.

Her directness was like an arrow piercing his heart, but Delveran liked her fine qualities of openness and honesty. He swallowed his pride and almost hesitated in answering her. "I do not wish to part with you. You are the right lady for me. I cannot live without you, and it makes me miserable not to have you by my side. I want you with me always."

Catching him by surprise, Evarinia flew into his arms and wrapped her legs around him, hugged him fiercely, and kissed him passionately. Delveran embraced her tightly and kissed her deeply in return. She unwrapped her legs from around him. They undressed while kissing. Then they lay on the floor and made love. Her beautiful body excited him, and his sophisticated manliness turned her on. They caressed each other from head to toe with loving touches. He inhaled the fruity fragrance of her long hair and body perfume; she loved the smell of his clean frame and herbal cologne. Their lovemaking session lasted an hour.

Evarinia smiled at him. "You have made me the happiest woman in the whole galaxy."

Delveran grinned. "That pleases me beyond words."

"You are such an animal in bed." She stroked his chest, then straddled him. "My lover for life."

Delveran knew they would work to maintain harmony in their relationship. They had intimacy again and did not want to lose it. He played with her firm breasts, then they made love one more time. Spent, they lay side by side facing each other.

"You know, darling, we have been together over a year," Delveran began. "We have the eternal fire between us. Our official positions are well-matched."

Evarinia gazed into his eyes and pressed up against him, ran a hand through his hair. "What are you saying, my sweet man?"

Delveran sweated a little. "I guess what I am asking you is will you be my mate."

Evarinia was speechless. Moments later, she was atop him and kissing him madly, crying in joy. She stopped smooching him to respond to his last words. "Yes, I will marry you, Delveran. I thought you would never ask me to be your wife!"

Eventually, they got off the floor and put their clothes back on. She straightened his collar. They held each other close for a time.

"We will have to make an official announcement about our formal engagement," Delveran remarked. He could not take his eyes off her and temporarily forgot everything else.

Evarinia beamed. "We will have to set our wedding date."

Delveran nodded. "We will."

"We must have a big wedding." Evarinia positively glowed like a million stars. "Send out wedding invitations. Decide where to have the wedding. A thousand and one details."

"Yes." Delveran laughed, happily. Then he remembered his official duties as the High Enforcer. "My darling, there is also another reason why I came to see you."

"What is it?" Evarinia asked.

Delveran looked grim as he told her about the Archvillain organization and its planned invasion of Tellus. "Federation and Tellusian officials must be informed about the matter."

Evarinia was alarmed. "Do you know when the invasion will happen, sweetheart?"

"No."

"Did you look into the future about it?"

"Yes. But my mantic work unfortunately has yielded me insufficient information regarding the matter."

"How come?"

Delveran sighed. "Because some of the members of the Fellowship of Darkness have and are combining their special powers to thwart my attempts at receiving visions."

"Oh, sweetheart," Evarinia said, rubbing his back. "I'm sorry."

Delveran cupped her cheek in his hand. "I will find a way to see the oncoming invasion with my mantic and magic efforts. It may be necessary to combine my special powers with other Enforcers to break through the veil."

Just then, the telescreen in her office beeped. Evarinia verbally commanded it on. Nanomach appeared on it in perfect three-dimensional color.

"Your pardon, director," the Computer-Enforcer said. "I must communicate with the High Enforcer."

Delveran stepped over to the telescreen. "Proceed."

"Eleven of the other Enforcers have returned to the Justiceplex, eight onworld and three offworld," Nanomach told him. "I have related to them what has transpired. They await your orders."

"Who are now available?" Delveran asked.

"From onworld: Molton, Vartagal, Slennass, Mananos, Neisie, Arboron, Wardelorean, and Isisis," Nanomach replied. "From offworld: Kennedrill, Brinivere, and Ulleric."

Delveran considered what instructions to give Nanomach. "Have Vartagal taken on a Federation ship to Earth to join the Enforcer Squad. Tell Kennedrill to prepare his ship for a mission."

"What is the mission?" Nanomach asked.

"To search for the Archvillain space fleet," Delveran replied. "Kennedrill will lead a team of Universal Marshals to find it. And on my authority, assign Zorrokin to form a fleet of Federation ships ready to strike after the enemy one is found."

"Affirmative," Nanomach responded.

Evarinia watched the High Enforcer in action, a little amazed by his official performance because she had never really beheld him being the Grand Universal Marshal before. Such pride showed on her face for him, though he forgot about her for the moment. Delveran relayed further orders to Nanomach. "I need some assistance here. Teleport Molton and Brinivere to this office after I have finished giving my instructions."

"Affirmative," Nanomach responded.

"Since it is assumed that the Archvillain space fleet must conquer all the areas on Tellus," Delveran said, "an Enforcer will each oversee the defense of the land, sea, air, and space. I will coordinate it all. Those of the Universal Marshals remaining are to help find the other Enforcers offworld. That ends my commands for now."

"I will implement them immediately." Nanomach signed off.

Evarinia went to him. "I never before really appreciated the great responsibility you carry as the High Enforcer. Or the heavy burden on all the Universal Marshals."

Delveran smiled. "Such power I have as the High Enforcer demands my utmost respect for the important position. The heavy burden we carry as Universal Marshals is forever because of the eternal war between good and evil, always coexisting in conflict, in relation to each other as opposites. There can never be one without the other, fortunately and unfortunately."

Evarinia moved in close to him and brushed his hair back gently with her hand. "You speak almost in riddles, sweetheart."

Softly, Delveran caressed her face. "I am speaking of truth in a philosophical way, my darling."

At that moment, two Universal Marshals materialized in the inner office and interrupted them, but Delveran greeted the pair. The first was Brinivere, the Cellular Being. She stood half a foot shorter than the High Enforcer, a slender young woman with short, dark brown hair and deep brown eyes. She wore a white labsuit and white labshoes, befitting her other occupation, a scientist, her field biology, in line with her special powers.

The other Universal Marshal was Enforcer Molton, the Lava Being, a male eight feet tall. He dressed in nothing, not required to wear clothes since molten lava composed his entire massive body. His reddish-brown eyes glowed, and he controlled the great heat his unusual form radiated at will, his huge frame cool to the touch at present. He made his home in volcanoes, his natural environment, though he had his own room in the

Justiceplex.

"What do you wish of us?" Molton asked.

Delveran addressed the Cellular Being first. "I want you to inform the proper Federation officials of the invasion. Help them with measures needed to deal with it."

"Will I get any help from the others?" Brinivere asked.

"I will send you assistance when there are more of us on Tellus," Delveran responded. He turned to the Lava Being. "You are to inform the proper Tellusian officials about the invasion. Help them initiate defense and emergency procedures for our planet. The same with assistance for you."

"Understood," Molton acknowledged. "I am ready for the eruption of evil we will face."

Delveran addressed both his fellow Enforcers. "Coordinate everything with Nanomach. If you need to communicate with me, do it through him." Both of them nodded in obedience to his authority as the High Enforcer.

"Will you invoke the Pamarantha ordinance?" Brinivere asked.

Delveran had not thought about using the ordinance at all but considered the option now. Named after the first Grand Universal Marshal, it stated that a High Enforcer may take command of the Federation and Tellusian forces on Tellus to defend the planet against offworld aggression, such as an invasion if the threat was great enough and fell under the jurisdiction of the Universal Marshals. It also applied to the Federation itself if it had to fight evil of extreme magnitude powerful enough to threaten its existence. He weighed the facts of the dangerous situation involving the Archvillain organization to determine, under Federation and Tellusian regulations, if he could invoke the ordinance. After he briefly deliberated with himself, he decided it would be necessary because the coming invaders, minions of an Archvillain under the command of other Archvillains, definitely fell within the obvious jurisdiction of the Universal Marshals.

"I must invoke it," Delveran finally replied. "This grave matter demands it. Therefore the Federation and Tellusian heads should grant me the power of authority to take complete charge of this impending situation."

Brinivere and Molton left the office to execute his official orders. Delveran returned his attention to Evarinia. He sensed a disquieting feeling of isolation from her, that she could not be a part of his world now.

"Do not fear," Delveran said to reassure her. "I will not cast you out of my life. The words I spoke privately to you regarding our relationship are irreversible."

She embraced him again, tightly, his words comforting her and laying her fears to rest. He held her as before, tenderly, drawing strength from the love she felt for him. When they separated, he saw tears of joy in her eyes and her face beaming because of his love for her. He smiled, then kissed her passionately; she responded with intense desire for him.

"When will I see you next?" Evarinia asked.

"When the evening begins," Delveran replied. "I will work until then. If I do not contact you first, contact me wherever I am. I will come to you."

Evarinia smiled. "I'll make certain you do."

Delveran grinned. He knew she surely would see to that. The High Enforcer departed from her company after they kissed and hugged some more and said their last words of love to each other until evening.

Delveran strode down a long corridor to a turbolift. He found one open and zoomed in it down to the ground floor, where he returned to the teleporter hall he arrived in at the Federationplex.

"Where to, sir?" a female humanoid teleportist asked him, sitting at her teleport console.

"Send me back to the Justiceplex," Delveran answered.

He stepped onto the telegrid. She teleported the High Enforcer to his chosen destination.

Delveran went to his office. He sat in his office chair and contacted Nanomach through the telescreen in his office. "I have another task for you. It must be initiated immediately."

"Yes, High Enforcer?" Nanomach responded.

"Push through a request both to the Governarch and the Federation President that I wish to invoke the Pamarantha ordinance. Include all the information relating to the Archvillain organization and the invaders coming to Tellus."

The Governarch was the highest executive officer of Tellus, the current holder of the office Mhiri Salis, a female human. The Federation President was Sethremus, a male alien from the planet Duskelion.

"Affirmative," Nanomach acknowledged.

Delveran turned to the next thing on his mind. "Have any more of the other Enforcers reported in?"

"Negative," Nanomach replied.

Delveran wondered, if the invasion occurred now, would there be enough Universal Marshals to deal with it? The High Enforcer thought not. He felt at least a third of the Enforcers should be on Tellus when the enemy space fleet arrived, preferably all of them. Of course, he knew the invaders would first have to get past the warding device of Tellus, a machine that erected a protective shield around the planet, comprised of the three basic energy powers—scientific, occultic, and celestic. However, Delveran planned to find the enemy space fleet before it reached Tellus and annihilate it. Otherwise, Tellus better have its planet defenses established by the time the invaders arrived.

The High Enforcer meditated further on the whole matter, considering what all must be done about it. But his uneasiness increased as he waited for more Universal Marshals to return to Tellus. He knew it was a race of time now.

Chapter 14

In Biolaboratory Two of the Complex, exotic plant life, such as tall ferns in emerald colors and banyan trees, and exotic animals, like different families of parrots and monkeys, teemed in a natural laboratory of biocreation, a carefully constructed biome of a tropical rain forest, the most prolific and richest ecosystem in nature. The biome packed the place under created sunlight controlled by automation. Illumination was provided by a ceiling machine generating solar energy and alternating with a ceiling machine generating lunar energy and other ones providing starlight. Computer control extended to the constant recycling of clean air in the untainted environment and the regulation of steady temperatures, the cycling of day and night, and changing weather conditions normal for a tropical rain forest. At the moment, the biome experienced daylight, midmorning, weather sunny and the temperature hot at eighty-five degrees Fahrenheit.

Loamy and earthy smells wafted through the biome in powerful waves of natural odors. Many sounds of animals reverberated in the air, bird cries and the chattering of monkeys the loudest. The creatures of the biome did not know they were not in their natural habitat when it looked like they were. Safeguards prevented any of the animals from leaving the biolaboratory as computers monitored their activity and activated force fields to block any creature from accidentally wandering out of it and into other sections of the Complex.

The Archvillain Professor Magnemus, the Scientific Being, began working in the biolaboratory, a biocreation study of how well the biome was evolving. He grew the biome from root, and it was fruitful and multiplied under his careful supervision. His husky frame, eight inches over six feet, tromped through the lush greenery around him, carrying a pocket recorder to gather new notes and log progress on the biome. Occasionally he fingered his long beard, thick and red as his fluffed-out hair, his violet eyes scanning the dense vegetation of the biome for abnormalities in the heavy growth. His rugged features were well-suited to the jungle scenery, but the white labsuit, black labbelt, and black labshoes he wore belied that.

Broad-leaved trees with high green canopies rose around him like a sylvan tribe he interacted with. Green ferns and bushes crowded underneath the treetops, vying for space to get needed sustenance of sunlight, soil nutrients, and rainwater, which was provided by automated systems to pour at least a hundred inches worth per year on the biome to match the minimum dumped on rain forests on Earth naturally, constantly irrigating them. Black and brown soil formed the huge, undulating floor of the biome, rich and smelling strongly earthy. A small, clean, and sparkling river meandered through the biome, supporting over twenty species of fish and other aquatic fauna. Passing near the river he spotted a small school of bony puffers— blowfish— swimming along in the river. He did not populate the natural stream of considerable volume with piranha, for any animal in the biome, including fish, could fall victim to the little balls of fury. But he himself could not be harmed by piranha because his special powers as an Archvillain protected him against their frenzied attacks.

The balmy odor of the loose soil under his feet assailed Professor Magnemus' wide nostrils. A warm wind, blowing mildly by holographically-covered wind machines hidden in the walls of the biolaboratory brought a honey-sweet fragrance to him, pleasing to his large nose, and tangy-tasting. He listened to the natural sounds of the biome and heard the loud squawking, screeching, and wailing of exotic birds, mixed with the loud croaking of tropical frogs, the buzzing and droning of different insects, the chattering of monkeys, the infrequent roars of big cats prowling through the contained area, and other animal noises. Together they combined into an unrehearsed symphony of nature, playing music to the sole audience of the Scientific Being.

Magnemus stood near a clear pool near the center of the biolaboratory and started speaking into his pocket recorder, a silver rectangular device activated, controlled, worked, and deactivated by voice commands. "The natural genetic mutation of the rain forest in Biolaboratory Two proceeds at an accelerated rate." He nodded to himself. "Its gene pool continues to receive new biomaterials for new biocreations, aided by new bioprocesses to produce new bioforms for further and extensive experimentation of natural evolution. The by-products of this intricate ecosystem include foods, medicines, fuels, and timber. The production rate of this biome steadily increases at a natural pace, and its diversity widens in quality and quantity. So far, I have catalogued, by my estimations, about thirty percent of the many botanical and zoological species and subspecies within this biolaboratory."

The professor reached down and grabbed a handful of dark, rich soil. The soil felt cool to him, sitting loose in his big hand with a granular texture. He smelled it; it exuded an earthy odor strong enough to awaken a sleeping being to do handsprings. Satisfied with the excellent condition of the soil, he dropped the handful and stepped over to a palm tree to his left. He ran a hand up and down its rough, dark brown, long unbranched trunk, then looked up and studied the large, dark green, pinnate leaves, noting no defects in its growth.

The Scientific Being continued through the biome to find animal life. Soon he spotted a black and yellow bowerbird on the high branch of a banyan tree just ahead of him, the brown branches of the hulking tree sending down roots into the soil, growing new trunks. He crossed the path of a jaguar, the large feline instinctively knowing not to attack him because it could not harm him, its orange-yellow, black-spotted hide weaving through the abundant flora in search of prey. He could easily kill it with his special powers.

Magnemus stopped at the small river of the biome. He studied schools of yellow, pancake-shaped sunfish swimming with the slow current. A group of freshwater turtles caught his attention, paddling underwater near him with their flippers, occasionally surfacing for air. A silver and red-scaled water snake glided through the clear water against the lazy flow of the winding river in a side-to-side motion. He spoke into his pocket recorder again, voice-activated as before.

"By my observations, the creatures of the rain forest appear healthy, prolific, and well-adapted to their loosely controlled and untainted environment. Note: specimens are to be taken from Biolaboratory Two for bioengineering experiments and internal scanning for health checks."

Magnemus turned back. He exited the biome through automatic doors hidden in the wall by a holographic projection. The Scientific Being walked down a long corridor with automatic doors on both sides and glowpanels in the ceiling. He was alone in the high and wide passageway, and it was very quiet. The professor turned left and entered a different laboratory, not a biological one.

Inside the laboratory, a desk with a swivel chair sat in the middle of the room. To his left, a large telescreen and a computer each covered half a wall, both off at the moment. On his right, a worktable was against the opposite wall. A storage closet dominated the back wall, filled with building materials to biocreate androids. Right of the automatic doors stood a tool cabinet full of biocreation instruments used to help construct androids. To the left of the automatic doors stood four androids, incomplete and nonfunctioning, two males and two females. Glowpanels in the ceiling brightly lit the chamber, automatically activated by his entrance to it.

"Need to work on more androids," Magnemus said to himself.

Magnemus lifted and carried a male android over to the worktable, where he carefully laid it on its back. He opened the chest cavity, removing a square panel and setting the panel by its feet, then turned its head sideways, facing away from him, and flipped its head panel open and up to expose its positronic brain. The android before him neared completion, only its brain and chest sections remaining to be finished.

The Scientific Being went to the tool cabinet, touched an entry code on its keypad to open it, retrieved a black case of small instruments—biocreation tools—for intricate work, and resealed the cabinet. He returned to the worktable and laid the case on the android's legs.

Shortly Magnemus opened the magnetic lock on the case, whereby he took several instruments from it, laying them on the android around its chest cavity. He first examined the chest microcircuits of the android to determine those that needed adjustments.

"Microprocessors in chest cavity should work much faster," Magnemus muttered to himself. "Alternate source of power in chest cavity has to be much faster when power is rerouted after main source of power is lost or damaged."

Someone buzzed him outside the laboratory.

"Enter," Magnemus said.

Automatic doors opened, and the Archvillain Asearse, the Charybdian, stepped into the laboratory. Webbed hands and feet, pointed ears, smooth and flawless skin the color of the deep blue sea, and thin and slanted eyebrows particularly marked her physical features. Her black hair fell past her shoulders, shiny and thick; her eyes sparkled, the same color as her skin. The black gown and black slippers she wore heightened her evil beauty, and around her slim wrist ticked a silver wristwatch from Earth.

"What is it?" Magnemus asked.

"I have important news," Asearse replied. She once had remarked to the Scientific Being that he looked like an Earth Viking in a labcoat and he had oddly laughed at that image of himself.

Magnemus stopped in the middle of his biocreation work and gave her his full attention. "What do you have to report?"

"An Enforcer Squad has landed on Earth, in New York City." Asearse was not interested in the android on the worktable, for the Charybdian did not care about science and technology.

"Inevitable," Magnemus responded. He heaved his big chest. "How many Universal Marshals?"

"Five." Asearse waited for him to speak again.

Magnemus considered how to deal with the Enforcer Squad. He knew it would have to be very carefully. "The High Enforcer, no doubt, will send additional Universal Marshals to strengthen the Enforcer Squad."

"A standard procedure," Asearse agreed.

Magnemus picked up a circuiting fork and tinkered inside the android's chest cavity. It was a two-pronged tool for making circuits in machines of a biocreation nature to modify activity in them. In this instance, he used the precision instrument to increase the speed of circuit operation in the android. It partly activated the android, but not enough for the android to move. "We must intercept them and stop them."

"How?" Asearse asked.

Magnemus turned his attention to the positronic brain and activated it with the circuiting fork. The Scientific Being weighed his options to deal with the Enforcer Squad. "Send a squad of our own."

Asearse smiled at that. "How many should be on our squad, and who do you want on it?"

Magnemus laid the circuiting fork back on the android's chest and checked microchips in its positronic brain. "Have any of our fellowship members tried to prognosticate the near future concerning the Enforcer Squad?"

"Yes," Acirce replied, unconsciously a bit distressed that her beauty did not affect him. Her body language indicated she desired him through her firm posture, the dilation of her pupils, her hands resting gently against her flat stomach, and her slender legs spread apart. Consciously, she remained unaware of her personal interest in the Archvillain leader. She acted as his second-in-command. "Usaddith has foreseen three more Universal Marshals arriving tomorrow to join the other Enforcers here."

"Then we will match their number of the next day and face them that same day," Magnemus said, removing a few microchips from the positronic brain of the android with a special pair of tweezers. "Eight of them against eight of us. Who are their eight?"

"The five here now are the Titan-Enforcer, the Ice Being, the Robot-Enforcer, the Shepherd, and the Metamorph-Enforcer," Asearse answered, straightening her gown at the shoulder. "The three Usaddith foresees joining them will be the Great Archer, the Occultic Being, and the Molecular Being."

Abruptly, Magnemus stopped in the middle of his delicate work on the android and turned to face her. "So the Enforcers know of my past association with Minanket. Logical for the High Enforcer to send him."

Asearse seemed shocked and confused. "Minanket? You were friends with a Universal Marshal?"

"That was before the Molecular Being became an Enforcer and I an Archvillain," Magnemus responded. Fingering his red beard, the Scientific Being reminisced about his past association with Minanket.

Asearse cleared her throat to cut short his pleasant recollection.

"Minanket knows me very well. The Enforcers will use that to their advantage."

"Undoubtedly," Asearse agreed, uncomfortably.

"But it has been over ten years since the Molecular Being and I spoke." Magnemus closed the chest cavity on the android. "Who is available?"

Asearse smiled. "Quasicoatl, Eveinnen, Usaddith, Moroloch, Sorrent, Namprey, Ynemain, Gordred, Jawsar, and us."

From those she named, Magnemus decided the composition of the Archvillain Squad. "You lead our squad. Collect Quasicoatl, Jawsar, Namprey, Sorrent, Moroloch, Ynemain, and Eveinnen and intercept them."

"What about the armada?" Asearse asked as he resumed working on the android.

Magnemus paused, disliking changing their plans for their space fleet. "The timetable for the invasion of Tellus is forced to commence sooner. I will send a message to the space fleet and inform them of the new developments and alterations in our plans."

"All right," Asearse said.

"Unquestionably, Tellus will be readying itself against the invasion," Magnemus remarked. "They will be erecting defenses against it. We will have to neutralize their defenses so the invasion can succeed. The Archvillain commanders of the space fleet will handle it."

Asearse left to carry out her mission. Magnemus returned to the android to work more on its positronic brain and attached new microchips to it. Suddenly he stopped and went over to the intercom. "Attention. All combat units be on alert status. Marshal all forces for possible deployment around Earth. Battle may be imminent with Federation forces coming to the planet." He signed off and finished working on the android.

The professor was not pleased losing the advantage of secrecy and surprise to the Universal Marshals. Nor was he happy about having to deal with an Enforcer Squad. But the Archvillain, though ruffled a bit by the Enforcers, felt confident of achieving victory over their triple adversaries in the invasion—the Tellusians, the Federation, and most of all, the Enforcers.

Chapter 15

The Complex, an immense L-shaped structure of white omnimetal, existed in a demesne outside the physical plane and was created by a realming device inside the Archvillain stronghold.

Asearse walked up the corridor in the longer stem of the Complex, glowpanels in the ceiling illuminating the passageway as she passed automatic doors to various rooms on either side of the hallway, a control panel on the left side of each entry. The Charybdian breathed in the clean air recirculating throughout the Archvillain stronghold, her slippers clicking quietly on the floor. She turned right, passed through automatic doors, and stood in the armory of the Complex, where she found the second member of the Archvillain Squad she would lead against the Enforcer Squad. Glowpanels in the ceiling lighted the chamber. The burnt smell of melted metal caused by a fired laser weapon lingered in the room.

Many weapons, of different types, from the primitive to the hi-tech, filled the arms racks and the weapons cabinet of the armory. Bunches of weapons lay on two tables of the armory in the middle of the room. All the walls featured weapons on display.

At one of the tables, inspecting a pack of photon grenades and a pair of modified blasters, was the Archvillain Jawsar, the Predator. Jawsar stood over seven feet tall, muscular, with mottled skin. Prey looking into his oval lavender eyes saw intensity for the kill, his sharp claws ready to tear. His long nose and large ears contributed to his keen senses, like his sight, and his big bare feet featured wicked talons. Featherlike hair, braided, reached down his broad shoulders. He had long, powerful limbs with visible veins, sinewy. The Predator wore a black meshsuit with long sleeves, which resembled chain mail, and on his thick wrists were black rectangular devices, each with five buttons on them. His special powers resided on the scientific level.

Asearse drew his attention away from his inspecting weapons. "We have a mission." The Charybdian told the Predator about the Enforcer Squad.

"Conflict to experience," Jawsar responded after she finished giving him the details. "A special weapon I need for this combat."

"There is plenty in the armory to choose from," Asearse remarked, noticing the chamber had so many. She did not use weapons that much herself. Her special powers resided on the occultic level.

Jawsar went through the weapons in the armory. In particular, he looked over blasters, blast rifles, photon bazookas, and other kinds of laser weapons. "Weapons galore to choose from."

"How was your last hunting trip?" Asearse asked.

"Successful," Jawsar answered. "A few humans I bagged on it."

Asearse smiled. "How would you rate Earth on a hunting scale?"

Jawsar thought about that as he reached out and grabbed a blast rifle off a wall. "Rather good."

"How does it compare to your home world of Praetoria?" Asearse asked, checking the time on her wristwatch.

"Not as good." Jawsar examined the blast rifle. "Praetoria has more and larger game than does Earth. My planet has more jungle than the Terran one." After a moment, he shook his head. "This won't do." The Predator put the blast rifle back on the wall and grabbed a pair of blasters next to it. He aimed the twin weapons at another wall.

Asearse had never visited his home world. "The planet I am from, Tharacia, is a water world."

"Are there hunters on it?" Jawsar asked, curious. He examined the two blasters carefully.

"The sport of hunting is a luxury on my home world," Asearse replied, remembering her place of origin fondly. "It is dominated by races that are aquatic."

"Praetoria has none like that," Jawsar said, eyeing another pair of blasters. "These are too common for such a clash." The Predator wanted a weapon worthy of fighting the Enforcer Squad with.

"Tharacia is ruled by courts of king and queens," Asearse stated. "Underwater kingdoms prevail on it. Those intelligent creatures on dry land are primitive."

Jawsar went to a different wall displaying weapons of low technology in the forms of swords, spears, and other arms of a primitive nature. "My planet is ruled by hunters. It has no governing bodies of courts or other kinds of rulers. There are only predators and prey. Only the strongest survive on Praetoria."

"Your home world sounds barbaric," Asearse remarked.

Jawsar laughed. "Maybe. But it is simple. Politics does not play a part, make everything complicated. Simple is best for Praetoria."

Asearse could not argue that. "Tharacia would be in chaos if not for lord and ladies to rule it. It could not survive if it was like your home world."

Jawsar took a sword from the wall and swung it. Then he returned it to its place and grabbed and hefted a spear. The Predator liked the spear better than the sword, but neither seemed right for the job, though the spear was a good weapon for hunting. He put the spear back. On another wall, he spotted automatic weapons, including a few of Earth design, plasma rifles, neutron shooters; any and all forms of arms. He strode to the wall and grabbed an automatic weapon, a Terran one, and examined it.

"Trouble deciding which weapon to use against the Enforcer Squad?" Asearse remarked. The Charybdian would use her special powers in the upcoming fight against the Universal Marshals.

Jawsar sighed. "This weapon was made for slaughtering. Not honorable combat." But his hunting instincts told him to take weapons that could fell prey instantly. He liked quick kills the best, so he could continue his carnage of creatures on Earth. The Predator knew, however, the upcoming fight against the Enforcer Squad would not see any quick kills, for it would be an even match with the Universal Marshals.

Asearse hoped he would not take too long to decide the right weapon to take into combat against the Enforcer Squad. Patiently, she waited for him to arm himself. "Is it so hard a decision what to carry in combat against the enemy?"

Jawsar grunted. "Great adversaries are the Enforcer Squad. Against them will special weapons be needed to fight." The Predator dismissed the arms he beheld as not good enough to engage the Enforcer Squad in battle. To him all the weapons he looked at seemed conventional and not worthy to kill Universal Marshals with.

"I wish you would just pick some so we can get on with the mission," Asearse said. "We still have to find the others for our squad. Only Quasicoatl is here."

"The rest?" Jawsar asked.

"In different spots on Earth." Asearse gazed at a few of the weapons and appeared to consider whether or not to take arms herself for the showdown with the Enforcer Squad. "We may have to make an extra stop or two on the way before we get them."

Jawsar brightened. "To combat, I will take my *krillja*. Long while it has been since I carried it. My quarters I get it from. Outside meet you at the ship. Which vessel?"

"The *Glasnostromo*," Asearse replied. "Quasicoatl already has his ship ready for flight. He was planning on taking a solo trip later today into Earth for his special needs."

"Special needs I have, too," Jawsar said.

Asearse smiled. "Did you not work out in the holochamber?"

Jawsar grinned. "Good exercise is simulated combat. Best exercise is live combat. Also best for hunting."

Asearse cared not for hunting, but destroyed her victims in other ways than the Predator. "Maybe you will get a chance to hunt live prey before our squad meets the Enforcer Squad."

"That, good," Jawsar said and laughed.

A female Archvillain entered the armory. She was Wuminga, a Fox Maiden, who looked like a tall oriental woman with black and white streaked red hair. Her nails were long and her eyes red. Wuminga wore a long black dress with a red shawl and white slippers. The Fox Maiden, an evil beauty, was armed with a dagger. Her special powers resided on the occultic level.

"You returned sooner than expected," Asearse remarked.

Wuminga frowned. "Recruiting others of our kind for our fellowship is proving difficult."

Jawsar sighed. "Like us, know few."

"Maybe I should have used my wiles on the Incarnation of War to have gotten him to join us," Wuminga said. "But the professor has Orlin speaking with him now."

"That makes sense since the Grim Reaper and War were members of the Four Horsemen of the Apocalypse," Asearse stated. "Any luck with anyone else?"

Wuminga nodded. "Lethesis is speaking with the Hellcat."

"Understandable that," Jawsar said.

Wuminga seemed dejected, but got over it quickly. "There is a member of an Archvillain race I may be able to get for our fellowship."

"Who?" Asearse asked. The Charybdian was also trying to think of other Archvillains they could get for the Fellowship of Darkness.

"One of the Tengus," Wuminga answered.

"Winged warriors Tengus are?" Jawsar asked.

"Yes," Wuminga replied. "Tengus are supernatural master swordsmen. Honor and duty are part of their traditional code. If we can get a Tengu to join us, he would be very loyal to our cause."

"Where do you find them?" Asearse asked.

"They live within the mountains and forests of a few worlds," Wuminga said. "Tengus are well disciplined and have a set of moral principles they follow."

"Moral principles?" Asearse repeated. "They don't sound like Archvillains."

"Moral principles of their own making," Wuminga explained. "Handed down to them by their ancestors."

"That of the hunt only code I have," Jawsar said. "Predator and prey."

"You have a simple code," Wuminga remarked.

"Simple code only need," Jawsar responded. "My weapons live and die by."

"Both natural and manufactured," Asearse finished for him. Unconsciously the Charybdian straightened out her gown.

Jawsar beamed. "Yes. Kills I live for. The hunt is all."

"If we need to stalk game, you can handle it," Asearse said, half jokingly, half seriously.

"A quick workout in the holochamber maybe before we leave?" Jawsar asked the Charybdian.

"You can do your exercise program in the new holochamber on the *Glasnostromo*," Asearse replied. "Quasicoatl had it installed with a little help from the professor."

"Good," Jawsar responded. "Practice, intense. Enforcers fight warm up for."

"I have seen you practice," Asearse said. "Brutal."

Jawsar laughed. "The better, more violent."

"You lack sophistication," Wuminga remarked, teasing the Predator in part. The Fox Maiden smiled like a lady.

"Brute am I," Jawsar admitted. "My technology

except for."

"Obviously," Asearse agreed. "A hunter like you doesn't need to be a lordly being. You're just a killer without much of a conscience."

"In hunting conscience no help," Jawsar stated. "Ferocity and tenacity best."

"I prefer the company of male beings who are gentlemen," Wuminga said. "Being a lady, they would appreciate my fine qualities.."

"Until they see your Archvillain nature," Asearse remarked.

"True," Wuminga agreed.

"Like me you be then," Jawsar said.

Wuminga laughed. "Only not as savage and as gory as you are when taking a life."

"Archvillains not many like me in that," Jawsar boasted.

Asearse chimed in. "Basically I just drown my prey."

"Be more like me you two," Jawsar kidded. "Bloody get in body count of victims. Keep trophies of victims."

"You are so sadistic," Wuminga remarked. "No wonder you and the Incarnation of Horror get along so well. Both of you are quite grisly when it comes to delivering death to creatures you slaughter."

"Good comrades me and Gordred," Jawsar said. "But he more bloody than me in prey killed."

"Gordred is," Asearse agreed. "By his nature, the Incarnation of Horror is king in the galaxy at making victims suffer ghastly deaths. Especially when he does it on a broad or grand scale."

"Master Horror tends to be fanatical in his work," Wuminga added. "Overzealous at times."

"Crazy he is," Jawsar interjected.

"Anyway," Wuminga said. "We need to find other Archvillains to persuade to join us. The main computer of the Complex could help locate them."

Asearse sighed. "I already checked its memory banks for a list. It had a short one of those known and not imprisoned in the Universal Prisonplex."

"Then it will have to conduct an extensive search to help find those unknown and new to us," Wuminga said.

Jawsar cut in. "Planet I recall where could be some."

"Where?" Wuminga asked.

"Pintar," Jawsar answered. "Secret sanctuary for scum said it is."

"Archvillains are not scum," Wuminga huffed.

"To good citizens in the galaxy, all foul beings are scum, including Archvillains," Asearse stated. "They consider our kind the greatest of the type."

"I will ask the professor if I should go to Pintar and try to find Archvillains there," Wuminga said. The Fox Maiden left them to find the Scientific Being.

"Hunt scum below us," Jawsar muttered.

Asearse heard him. "Plenty of scum to hunt among the people of Earth. Lots of Terrans who are Criminals and a few Villains."

That pleased Jawsar immensely. "Kills galore."

They exited the armory. Jawsar jogged down the corridor to the short stem of the Complex to his private quarters to fetch his *krillja* as Asearse went in the opposite direction to the menagerie bay, toward the front of the entrance of the L-shaped structure.

Inside the menagerie bay, Asearse located the third member of the Archvillain Squad. Omnimetal cages, each exhibiting a single or several specimens from different planets in the galaxy, crowded along the walls. The zoo chamber housed both natural and supernatural creatures. She spotted some she knew; others were unfamiliar to her. Glowpanels in the ceiling shined on the room, built by the Fellowship of Darkness, based on co-designs by the Scientific Being, the Changeling, and the one she sought in there for the Archvillain Squad. She ignored the roars, growls, howls, and shrieks of the caged creatures; animal odors from the enclosures made her nose twitch.

Asearse went to the back of the menagerie bay where the Archvillain Quasicoatl, the Cloning Creature, observed the wild specimen before him, a huge saber-toothed cat with black fur and a single horn protruding from the center of its forehead. He favored the zoo chamber in the Complex, just as Jawsar favored the armory and Wuminga the entertainment room. Asearse loved the swimming chamber best.

Quasicoatl, whose special powers resided on the scientific level, possessed the ability to mold his massive body into geometrical shapes when he exercised his cloning faculty. Currently, he retained his natural form, a four-legged alien with a huge head crested. His physical features included ear holes, a round, slitted nose, and a huge, protruding circular mouth. His blue-white skin felt rubbery, and his blue-white eyes utilized inner and outer eyelids. He stood nine feet high.

The Charybdian told the Cloning Creature what she related before to the Predator. He listened to her with puckered lips as if to spew cloned creatures from his orifice.

"I need new creatures to ingest for cloning," Quasicoatl said. "All those here I have cloneable cells for, inside me."

"We'll stop at an Earth zoo before we face the Enforcer Squad," Asearse promised. "You may select the animals for your replicating needs."

"That will do," Quasicoatl acknowledged, turning away from the caged creature before him.

"You seem a little dejected," Asearse remarked.

Quasicoatl cocked his head back. "I was thinking of my home world."

"I never knew you had one," Asearse said. "You seemed to be from whatever place you clone creatures from."

"The planet I originally came from orbits a blue-white star in the Orion Sector of the Milky Way Galaxy," Quasicoatl stated. "It has a harsh climate. Life forms of a normal state cannot survive long on it. A creature needs a biology suited to such conditions. One with a mutable anatomy."

"I come from a water world," Asearse said. "A place with a better climate than yours."

Quasicoatl believed her. "I can adapt to any climate. Neither heat nor cold bothers my metabolism, even in extreme temperatures."

They left the menagerie bay and exited the Complex through its front entrance—a big automatic door that raised like a garage door on Earth. Asearse walked beside the larger Quasicoatl as biocreated minions of Professor Magnemus organized a heavily-armed defense force on the roof of the Complex to stand watch. Outside the Archvillain stronghold, within the domain maintained by the realming device, no natural sky or any geological or topographical feature existed, as if the place resided in a void. But artificial sunlight and moonlight appeared alternatively by a huge glowglobe suspended in the sustained atmosphere high above the Complex, utilizing an antigravity system. Its cycle of day and night matched Earth where the gateway from the created world opened onto Earth. At present, the demesne experienced the phase of day, just after dawn.

Behind the Archvillain stronghold towered an atmosphere processor supplying a breathable atmosphere in the created world, a pyramid constructed of silver omnimetal. Biocreated minions on the roof of the Complex made the only noise in the domain outside; no particular smells permeated the exterior atmosphere. The place created by the realming device appeared to be vast and without boundaries, like a holochamber on the deck of a ship creating the reality of a programmed world for beings to move around in and interact with. A gravity machine in the Complex supplied gravity to the demesne for all to walk in.

Asearse and Quasicoatl approached the transportation field spread toward the inner side of the Archvillain stronghold and in sight of the atmosphere processor. The transportation field, immense, rectangular-shaped, and constructed of silver omnimetal, held at the moment a shuttlecraft, two speeders, a hovercraft, and two ships, the *Glasnostromo* and the *Technokado*, ready for use. They entered the *Glasnostromo* through its wide circular aperture expanding open to admit them. The flying saucer, blue-white and large, docked on the ground without supporting legs. The aperture contracted to close behind them.

"Your ship is conventional in design from the outside," Asearse said. She had not flown in his ship before.

Quasicoatl did not take offense or respond to her remark. His ship had four corridors in concentric rings, surrounding the circular bridge in the center of it. Assorted bays, chambers, and other facilities spiraled inward toward the bridge. They went through four portals, high and wide, like the aperture they entered the vessel through, to pass the concentric passageways to get to the bridge. Light plates in the ceiling and walls illuminated all the areas of the ship.

Around the bridge functioned different consoles, control boards, and other devices without seating before them. But in the middle of the bridge operated the command center of the ship, around a blue-white alloyed, cup-shaped seat, the captain's chair. Before the captain's chair rose a view screen, big and square.

Quasicoatl lowered himself slowly into the captain's chair, naturally shaped to fit his life form, an alien being. Asearse stood behind him. The Cloning Creature activated his ship for travel on the control console before him, ignoring the system panel for superluminal drive, since they would not be needing it, because they were not going on space flights of long distances. He readied his vessel for inertialess drive for normal speed, but fast enough to get to the first of their destinations.

Jawsar joined them on the bridge, carrying his *krillja*. The hi-tech weapon, resembling a multipurpose lance of photon power, measured six feet at regular length, eight feet if stretched to its full length, a two-foot section hidden in the larger, grooved part. Five buttons adorned it on its shaft near the middle of the weapon. Along with his *krillja*, the Predator brought a few small devices attached to the black meshbelt—a kind of utility belt—he now wore. "Combat I am ready for."

"Where first?" Quasicoatl asked the Charybdian.

"To an Earth zoo to get animals for you to clone," Asearse replied. "A big one so you can get all the animal cells you need for your replicating system."

"Then we need to stop at a major city of Earth," Quasicoatl said. "It would have a large zoo keeping plenty of animals. Enough to satisfy me."

"Then we will go to the closest one on the way," Asearse responded.

Jawsar twirled his *krillja* a few times. "After zoo?" he asked the Charybdian.

"To Komodo Island to get Moroloch first," Assearse answered. "Then Egypt for Namprey. Followed by Germany for Ynemain. After that Wales for Sorrent. Finally Baltimore, Maryland in America for Eveinnen."

Quasicoatl contacted the control room of the Complex on his control console. "*Glasnostromo* ready to enter Terran reality."

"Understood," the voice of Usaddith, an Archvillain who was a Banshee, responded through his communications channel. "Opening gateway to realm of Earth."

"Acknowledge," Quasicoatl said.

Jawsar itched to go to the new holochamber aboard ship and get a quick workout. He might create a new program for it to test his fighting and hunting skills. The Predator did get a ship of his own recently—the *Parahunter*—but had not time to build a holochamber on it. His vessel was not ready for regular flights in space.

Jawsar stood his *krillja* on the floor of the bridge. His blood boiled for battle, his eyes lighting up in anticipation of killing prey in the form of higher beings who were formidable opponents. "Enforcers or Archvillains—now we see who stronger!"

Chapter 16

On the island of Komodo, in Indonesia, lived the largest of all modern-day lizards on Earth, Komodo dragons, massively built creatures up to twelve feet long with forked tongues and powerful jaws. The natives feared them, though none attacked man unless provoked, and their diet included goats, deer, and wild pigs.

Now, a new monitor terrified the natives even more than the Komodo dragons. The natives called it a lizard god. The natives believed the monitor a brother to the Komodo dragons, seeing it in the company of the large lizards. They worshipped the new monitor, referring to it as the "King of the Lizards" in their own language. But the greatest act that subjugated the natives to the new monitor occurred over two weeks ago when it talked to them as if it belonged to the human race, confounding their minds.

Moroloch, the Monitor, felt amused by their deification of him. As an Archvillain, he thought they should worship him because he was a superior being. Regarding the Komodo dragons, he visited the island to associate with the closest living creatures akin to him on Earth, those lizards. The natives knew not to anger him, and especially not to harm his monitor cousins on the island or any other lizard subspecies, or else they would suffer punishment.

Moroloch rose to over seven feet tall, a lizard being

massively built. Spiny combs stretched along the backs of his long arms and from the top of his reptilian head down to his long tail. His long tail and long legs counterbalanced his dense, elongated frame. A subtle intelligence glimmered in his emerald eyes, their pupils rounded like a lizard. His special powers resided on the scientific level. Among his special powers was the ability to change colors. At the moment, his scaly skin was gray, his natural color. His reptilian snout displayed rows of sharp teeth. The Monitor wore no clothing, though he normally donned a sleeveless and legless green worksuit—with a hole in the back to let his tail out—when laboring for the Fellowship of Darkness.

The scenery of Komodo Island delighted Moroloch. Tall trees with thick crowns, brown to black barks, and thick trunks formed a canopy over the brown and green matting of the island floor. Underneath the timber, green ferns and shrubs flourished. In the open spaces of the island, smaller sun-baked vegetation dominated, except where villages stood on bare ground. Loamy smells of earth and vegetation pervaded the heated air, affecting the Monitor like a natural drug and making him feel in harmony with nature. The varied cries of exotic birds and the chattering of skinny monkeys sounded heartening to him. But what he enjoyed most about the island centered on devouring prey. Like his fellow lizards, the Komodo dragons, he behaved as a ferocious carnivore, save he acted bloodthirsty when hunting. His monitor cousins lacked the intelligence to be murderous predators, going only on their natural instincts as meat-eaters. For him, nothing compared to the succulent taste of a fresh kill.

At that moment, Moroloch stalked prey with two male Komodo dragons, a twelve-footer and a nine-footer, but not as a team, among the trees. They targeted wild pigs. Both the four-footed lizards charged at the pigs, and each managed to sink their teeth and claws into one. The two monitors pulled their squealing prey to the ground, finally killing the pigs, seizing their necks in crunching jaws, their teeth puncturing the throats.

Moroloch prepared to jump a pig. But he caught sight of an island deer out of the corner of his eye, a brown and white doe ahead. In stealth, he closed in on the doe, camouflaged his scaly skin to match the dark brown color of the trees, and maneuvered patiently to strike. The doe chewed on an edible green bush before a clearing, not yet realizing or sensing danger from the Archvillain. No wind blew at the moment to carry his scent to the deer, an advantage to the Monitor.

Moroloch crashed on top of the doe as it sensed the danger too late. The Monitor bore the thrashing deer to the earth hard and fast, into the clearing, quickly locking an arm around its slender neck. He raked it with curved claws of his big hands. Then he ripped the back of its neck with his sharp teeth, his large mass effectively pinning it on the ground, toying with it, slashing it with his claws, and spilling rivulets of its warm blood on the earth. When he'd teased the doe long enough, he grabbed it in his hands and crushed its neck, snuffing out its life. He proceeded to feed on the fresh carcass, tasting the juicy warmth of raw flesh as he shredded with his teeth and claws, swallowing strips of it. Blood dribbled down his chin.

"Deliciouss," Moroloch said. The Monitor ate all the meat off the doe, relishing every bite.

The two monitors he had been with dined contentedly on their wild pigs. They moved on after they were finished.

Moroloch heard human voices far off. The Monitor went to investigate. He blended in with the brush using his special powers—his chameleonic ability—to help disguise his approach to the party heading his way. The Archvillain stopped when he caught sight of them. He bent down and hid farther in the brush.

The party consisted of five white males, two white females, and a bunch of natives. The Caucasians dressed like they were on safari. One of the white men carried a movie camera. Two of the white men held rifles. All the natives wielded spears.

"It will be splendid to capture this creature," Boris Rinne said, the white male in the lead. "It must be a freak of nature. A mutation of lizard evolution."

"Could be a missing link," Richard Spasky suggested, a white male younger than Boris. "Or it might be a small dinosaur."

"A prehistoric park here," Melody Stein remarked, younger of the two women, blonde. She filed her nails as she walked.

The other woman, Janet Neilson, a brunette, laughed. "It could be a kind of Creature from the Black Lagoon."

"Whatever it is," Will Sutcliffe, one of the two men holding a rifle, said, "it has to be dangerous. Anything that large usually is."

The other man carrying a rifle, Josh Remington, frowned. "It would be better just to kill it than to capture it. Easier to handle a lifeless carcass than a living beast."

"Nonsense," Boris responded. "If we capture it, we can put it on display and make money off it. Give audiences a chill and a thrill at beholding a refugee from the prehistoric age."

Josh snorted. "If it were caged, it could escape. It could go on a rampage if it got loose in a city."

Boris grinned. "Then we tie it in chains so it cannot attack anyone during a show."

Moroloch hissed. They talked about him. The Monitor wanted to kill them all for planning to capture and exhibit him to other Terrans so they could gawk and marvel at him as a feature attraction of a show. "SStupid humans. You will wishsh you had never ssearched for me."

"This creature will provide quality entertainment," Boris said. "We can bill it as a rare find, one of a kind."

The elder of the white males, Miles Thorton, spoke. "The natives say it is a god. They worship it with an occasional sacrifice." A native talked in his tongue to Miles, who asked a few questions of the native in a dialect of the Indonesian language. "He says we should not disturb the god or we will make him very angry. His people don't want to placate the god for an intrusion."

Melody giggled. "Superstitious baloney. It probably is the world's largest living lizard. We could have it put in the *Guinness Book of World Records* as such."

Richard checked the movie camera he hauled. "Filming its capture will be headline news."

"We will get all the credit for it," Boris remarked.

"Provided it doesn't kill us first," Josh said.

Boris smiled. "You worry too much."

"How do you plan to capture it?" Miles asked.

"We will use nets and tranquilizers," Will explained. "A trap will be set."

Moroloch flicked his tongue out in rage. In his mind, the Monitor planned his own trap for them before they sprang theirs against him. He would teach them not to mess with an Archvillain.

"When do you think it will come so we can capture it?" Richard asked Will.

"Night," Will answered. "Best time."

Boris agreed. "We need to set up camp ahead. I believe there is a gully not far from here that would make a good spot."

Moroloch followed. The Monitor stalked them from the brush, careful to be quiet so as not to alert them to his hidden presence. He knew he must not let them use their weapons against him because tranquilizers could put him to sleep, if they gave him enough of a heavy dose, and the spears could penetrate his scaly hide if thrust into him hard enough. It would take them much to capture him, more if they tried to kill him. The Archvillain was more than a match for the whole lot since they were inferior beings.

Normally Moroloch did not feast on humans or other kinds of beings. The Monitor ate wild animals according to the diet of his lizard nature, though he was intelligent. Very rarely did he consume the flesh of beings, but when he did, it was not because of his lizard nature. It was because of his Archvillain side.

"This thing could have come from somewhere else," Melody remarked.

Josh chuckled. "Like outer space?"

Moroloch did come from outer space. The Monitor was from the planet Gaiagos, a pre-industrial world in the Avanautu Sector of the Milky Way Galaxy. Gaiagos was primitive compared to Earth, not united, yet civilized to a degree. A race of lizard beings existed on it, but only Moroloch was an Archvillain with special powers. He could have ruled his home world easily, since none on Gaiagos could have challenged him. Instead, the Monitor had left his native planet to travel among the stars for adventure, to be a terror in the galaxy as an Archvillain.

Before night fell, Moroloch watched them make camp. The Monitor watched them set the trap. He watched them settle in. The Archvillain would make his move against them when he felt ready.

Deep into the night, Moroloch leaped into action. The Monitor hurled a rock into their trap to spring it. A big net rose in the air without him in it. The men from the party rushed in to secure what they thought they bagged but were disappointed when they found the net empty.

"We have to set the trap again," Boris said.

"I'll do it," Will offered. Josh helped him.

Moroloch crept up behind a native holding a spear and killed him quickly by breaking his neck. Then Moroloch slew another native by snapping his spine. One by one, the Archvillain took out the natives.

A native raised the cry of the party being attacked by the lizard being. Two natives threw spears at Moroloch, who blocked the weapons. The Monitor charged them and raked their throats with his claws, killing them instantly. A native got behind him and tried to ram a spear into him.

The Archvillain whipped his tail and sent the native flying into a tree, knocking the native out. Both white males aimed their rifles at the Monitor. The women cringed behind the remaining men. Moroloch slowly came toward them, towering over them.

"What a monster," Boris remarked. "Shoot it."

"SStupid humanss," Moroloch said. In shock, the men with the rifles froze. "SStinking beingss no match for me."

"Oh, my God!" Janet exclaimed. "It talks!"

Moroloch advanced on them closer. "I talkss. You lisstenss."

"What is it you want?" Boris asked, fear on his face like the other humans there.

"Me no prizze for you," Moroloch said. "You die."

Will and Josh fired tranquilizers at the Monitor. The darts had trouble penetrating the scaly hide of Moroloch, but they did barely. Enraged, the Archvillain used his special powers and neutralized the drug in his system.

"You should have given the thing a stronger dose," Miles remarked.

"We gave it enough to put an elephant to sleep," Will said. He pulled out his pistol at the same time Josh did.

Moroloch grabbed the rifles from the males and broke them apart. The Monitor tossed the pieces aside as the humans before him backed away. Surviving natives drop their spears on the ground and ran away.

The two women fled with Miles. Will and Josh fired at Moroloch, but the Monitor whipped his tail and made them miss. Boris ran as the Archvillain grabbed the two remaining men by their throats and lifted them in the air.

"Messs with me and ssuffer," Moroloch spat.

The Monitor crushed Josh's throat, killing the human. He discarded the body. Will struggled in his grasp, trying to kick him. The Archvillain bit the human in the arm, then threw Will to the ground and stomped his head.

"Tassty human fleshsh," Moroloch said. The

Monitor retrieved all the human corpses and piled them up. In the morning, he began eating them.

Moroloch paused in the midst of feasting when he heard what sounded like the eerie beacon of a commercial airliner flying toward the island. He checked the partly cloudy sky above and saw nothing, only the atmosphere, but the noise persisted. The Monitor dismissed it and returned to dining on human flesh.

Suddenly there appeared before him Asearse, teleported down to Komodo Island from the cloaked *Glasnostromo* in the midmorning sky overhead.

Asearse explained the situation. It churned his stomach.

"Cursse the Enforcerss!" Moroloch said, snapping his tail. He debated whether or not to take his food with him. He decided to let the Komodo dragons on the island have it. "They have sstolen my appetite."

Jawsar teleported Asearse and Moroloch up to the ship. The Monitor would avenge himself on the Enforcer Squad for abruptly ending his island vacation and robbing him of a filling meal when the two squads clashed in New York City.

Chapter 17

In the Serbonian, a large marshy tract in northern Egypt, a legend stated that in ancient times it swallowed up entire armies. In present-day Egypt, two squads of Egyptian soldiers disappeared after venturing into the low-lying wetland. Now a platoon of Egyptian soldiers searched through the Serbonian to find their missing comrades.

High green reeds overflowed the Serbonian. Palm trees, surmounted by crowns of fan-shaped leaves, populated the marshy tract. Waterways veined through the wetland and connected to the Nile River via a tributary. The glaring sun in the cloudless sky overhead contributed to the rapid plant growth of the Serbonian, which favored long reeds.

Wildlife thrived in the marshy tract. Nile crocodiles lay on shore or glided through the waterways of the wetland, waiting to snare unwary prey. Flamingoes, aquatic birds with very long necks and legs, webbed feet, bills bent downward, and pinkish to scarlet plumage, whooped their majestic cries in the Serbonian, an exotic sight. Emerald-green tree frogs croaked. Mosquitoes buzzed, and marsh flies droned in the marshy tract, instinctively ready to bother any humans brave enough to traipse through the wetland. Silver-scaled and golden-scaled fish swam in the waterways, alone or in schools, occasionally splashing to the surface. An asp, a small venomous snake, slithered through the reeds.

The platoon did not fear any of the natural creatures of the marshy tract, except for the crocodiles. Armed with M16s, grenades, pistols, and Swiss army knives, courtesy of the United States government, they tested the legend of the Serbonian. The men sweated in the still, hot, dry air. They acted as if murderous humans were responsible for the disappearances of their comrades, moving in stealth through the reedy oasis. The soldiers would rather be elsewhere than in this spooky water-saturated area, as they remembered the old horror stories of their youth.

The platoon deduced the wrong truth about the missing men; humans were not the culprit. Namprey, the Nodrone, watched them combing the wetland for their missing comrades, hidden in the tall reeds near the south edge of the largest waterway in the Serbonian, his lower half submerged in the water. His existence unknown to the platoon, the Archvillain knew the answer they sought pointed to him. Knowing about the Serbonian legend, he deliberately brought it back to life by killing the two military units a day apart.

Namprey attained a height over eight feet, an insect being with a long body. Four arms extended from his chitinous frame. The holes at the fingertips of his long hands and at the ends of his antennas shot silken thread when he exercised that particular ability. His special powers resided on the scientific level. Poisonous fangs protruded from his large mouth below a small nose; black eyes bugged out of his large head forward instead of sideways; two long legs attached to two large feet carried his ponderous weight. A long stinger aimed at a downward angle from his tailbone, and he was the color of a praying mantis, pale green. When the Nodrone wanted to, he flew in the air on large diaphanous wings, folded against his towering figure for the moment.

Silently, Namprey moved through the water and reeds. The Nodrone selected a soldier as the platoon fanned out farther to cover more ground. Slowly the Archvillain came up behind his intended target, stopping to glance up at the palm tree near the bank. He seized the young man with all four arms and snapped his spine, instant death; the Egyptian had no chance. He then cocooned the corpse and hid it in the reeds.

One by one, Namprey took out the platoon until the surviving soldiers decided to flee the Serbonian. The Nodrone decimated their number, reducing them to six. The Archvillain killed and cocooned fifteen members of the platoon. As the remaining men desperately ran across the sea of trampled reeds, Namprey shot silken threads from all his fingers and both antennas and roped them from behind, causing them to drop their automatic weapons. The Nodrone cocooned them simultaneously as he closed in on them, and then used his stinger and stung five of them to death before they could grab their Swiss army knives and slice their way out of his cocoons. He lifted the last wrapped soldier, the platoon commander, searched for his throat under the silken casing, and sank his poisonous fangs through the fibrous material into the neck of the human. Instead of poisoning to death the last victim, he drank the life juices from the helpless Egyptian until drained and dead.

Namprey took the discarded body of the Terran and other human corpses to a secret hiding place in the marshy tract, a deep pool screened by palm trees and rocks. He dragged each lifeless body into the water and swam down to an underwater cave. After removing the huge boulder blocking its entrance on his first dive, he stored the corpses, piling them on top of the dead bodies of the two missing squads, amused by the number of killed soldiers stacking up higher in the lair. Then he resealed the cave with the boulder and returned to the surface in triumph.

On land again, Namprey fetched the cocooned corpse of the first member of the platoon he killed. The Nodrone unwrapped it and carried it in search of Nile crocodiles. He found a bunch of them swimming in the waterway north of him. In a single heave, he tossed the dead body to them to consume. They responded in a feeding frenzy, tearing the corpse apart to swallow chunks of it. Later he disposed of another one in the same manner, almost as if the crocodiles were pets to feed. He continued this procedure and stopped when all the remaining bodies disappeared into the stomachs of the large reptiles.

Six days later, Namprey spotted a battalion of Egyptian soldiers approaching the Serbonian from the east in jeeps and tanks, heavily armed. The Nodrone considered whether or not he could handle the larger force. As the Archvillain mulled it over from reeds, Asearse materialized before him. She related the latest news concerning the Enforcer Squad.

"So," Namprey said. "The Universal Marshals have buzzed to Earth. Do we swarm them?"

"It will be an even match when we face them," Asearse replied as she ignored the oncoming battalion. "Archvillains versus Enforcers on this inferior world."

Namprey preferred to swarm the enemy. But pitted against Enforcers at the same strength appealed to him because the Universal Marshals were unique beings like the Archvillains. The Nodrone believed it would be a contest of who possessed the greater wills—the Fellowship of Darkness or the elite law officers of the Federation. He began to relish the feeling of doing battle with the Enforcer Squad.

The Egyptian battalion closed the distance between it and the Serbonian. The soldiers failed to spot Asearse and Namprey, angling toward the wetland away from them, south. The Nodrone wanted to see if he could wipe out an entire ground-force unit of Earthlings, but he sensed maybe he was overmatched this time. He knew the Charybdian would probably agree with his assessment.

Moroloch teleported Namprey and Asearse up to the cloaked ship. The invisible *Glasnostromo* flew away after the Nodrone and the Charybdian were on board. One consolation to Namprey was that the Egyptian battalion would never find him, the sole party responsible for their missing and dead troops. But the Nodrone would never get a chance to test himself against the military unit. However, the Archvillain hungered to suck the organic fluids from an Enforcer in agonizing death. Namprey buzzed at that. The Nodrone would get a golden opportunity soon.

Chapter 18

In the city of Quedlinburg, as in other parts of Germany, unrest flourished because of the sagging economy and influx of immigrants. The leaden sky reflected the frustration and anger of the German citizens in Quedlinburg, typified wrongly by the rebellious and racist skinheads—who rioted and protested in the city and throughout the country.

A mob of eighty skinheads marched down a main street that stretched from one end of the city to the other, heading for the apartment complex housing foreigners new to the country. Armed with rocks, clubs, and Molotov cocktails, the Neo-Nazis, ranging in age between eighteen and twenty-five, demonstrated what they clearly wanted to do. People moved or stayed out of their way, watching them zeroing on their chosen target, some folks cheering them on in silence, others sick of their disgusting behavior. Tension filled the air on a warm day, a mild wind blowing from the west behind them as if egging the skinheads on.

Ahead of the Neo-Nazis, the Quedlinburg police stood ready to meet the skinheads to prevent them from rampaging through the city. The law officers wore full body armor and helmet with plastic visors, armed with riot shields, police batons, tear gas guns, and service revolvers. Trained men held ground ready to combat the immature punks when they finally arrive at the apartment complex. Quedlinburg police form a barricade of living bodies in order to stop the skinheads from attacking the building.

Ynemain, the Iron Maiden, followed behind the tromping Neo-Nazis. The Archvillain gloated over her accomplishment at instigating, with her special powers, which resided on the celestic level, the inevitable confrontation between the two sides. Even now, she deviously affected the skinheads with torturous thoughts, emotions, words, and actions planted within and without them. She planned to do the same with the Quedlinburg police to turn the coming clash into a terrible fight and disaster for Germany.

Ynemain stood just under six feet tall with a gorgeous body, fit and supple. Her long arms and shapely legs accentuated her height, and her long, dark fingernails growing from her long, slender fingers enhanced her dark beauty. Her chocolate eyes lit up when she witnessed or felt torturous things happening in the galaxy; her sensuous ruby lips stiffened, and her small, slender nose flared when the reverse occurred. Long chocolate hair hung past her shoulders. Her ruby cheeks and long eyelashes highlighted a narrow, classically chiseled face as a famous actress out of the golden age of Hollywood. At the moment, she wore a long red dress with black shoes, a black coat, and a black fedora.

Ynemain listened in rapture as the Neo-Nazis repeatedly shouted two slogans, "Foreigners Out!" and "Germany for the Germans!" The Iron Maiden wished she could do physical torture to the skinheads. She excelled and specialized in physically torturing victims.

As the Neo-Nazis approached the apartment

complex housing new immigrants, Ynemain intensified her mental torture, exciting them to violence. The angry skinheads stopped at the front yard on the west side of the building. Between them, most of the Quedlinburg police stood in a phalanx with riot shields, and the rest readied to fire tear gas at the young men. All together, the Neo-Nazis hurled rocks at the uniformed officers and struck their unbreakable plastic shields. Then the skinheads ignited their Molotov cocktails with lighters, charged, and cocked their arms to throw them at the apartment complex. Quedlinburg police fired tear gas at them to disperse them. The young men did not disperse. Uniformed officers moved forward and swung their police batons at the Neo-Nazis.

Ynemain affected both sides with the full extent of her special powers and caused a full melee to ensue. The Iron Maiden loved the brawl between the punks and the officers, a wild affair getting more out of control. Molotov cocktails smashed against the apartment complex and fire licked the front of the building. Quedlinburg police clubbed skinheads before and after they threw the Molotov cocktails, whacking them into submission or causing them to flee in pain with possible injury. Other Neo-Nazis fought the Quedlinburg police, kicking and punching the officers or hitting them with sticks. Both sides battered each other as they felled bodies bloodied, bruised, and broken, weapons dropping to the ground. Bystanders watched it all happen, shock and dismay on their faces. The Archvillain enjoyed the entire episode.

More police arrived, supported by water cannons on armored vans. Skinheads scattered in all directions on seeing the arrival of reinforcements. Water cannons fired streams of water at the escaping Neo-Nazis, knocking some of them down.

Quedlinburg police pursued those fleeing the area, tackling any they could and placing them under arrest. A water cannon doused the flames scorching the apartment complex.

Screams of horror arose from bystanders. Their cries were sweet music to Ynemain.

Finally, the Iron Maiden ceased radiating torturous forces over the skinheads and the police. Pleased with herself, the Archvillain walked away from the ending clash, a fiendish smile on her face.

Ynemain went to and got into a silver sedan parked before the Black Forest Tavern, five blocks down from the riot scene. The Iron Maiden got her key out of her coat pocket, jammed it into the ignition, and started the car. She drove away laughing. A good day.

Humming to herself, Ynemain stopped at an intersection. Suddenly Asearse materialized on the passenger side of the car. The teleportation startled the Iron Maiden only for a second.

She continued to drive as the Charybdian informed her of the new development involving the Enforcer Squad.

"How quaint of them to visit this little corner of the galaxy," Ynemain said. "Positively delightful. We must give them a smashing welcome to this small world of Earth befitting their high place in universal society."

"We will," Asearse vowed.

Ynemain chortled. "It is rather dreadful of the Universal Marshals crashing our party. Simply rude of Enforcers trying to wreck the big bash we have planned for Tellus. Really, they have spoiled the surprise."

Asearse generally agreed with the Iron Maiden on that. Soon Ynemain spied an alley in the next block and turned the vehicle into it. It appeared deserted. The Iron Maiden parked the car under a fire escape. Both Archvillains climbed out of and stood away from the sedan.

With no one watching, Moroloch teleported Asearse and Ynemain up to the cloaked ship high over Quedlinburg. Thereafter the *Glasnostromo* flew away to pick up the next Archvillain on the way.

The Iron Maiden looked forward to greeting the Enforcer Squad in New York City. She hoped the Archvillain Squad would give the Universal Marshals an unforgettable welcome to Earth.

Chapter 19

On the night before the Archvillain Squad formed, a pair of human travelers, two young men from America, dared to hike the mountain roads of Wales. They dismissed the beliefs held by Welsh elders that evil faeries inhabited the jagged mountains overlooking the Gwynedd River to the south, in northern Wales. From the mountains, they saw lush green land rolling east and west of their present position and forestland stretching beyond the river for miles. A full moon glowed in the cloudless and starry night sky above. Westerly winds whistled through the mountains.

The mountain roads, well-worn by centuries of human trekking and winding above, below, and through familiar passes of the weathered range, remained unpaved despite progress. Stands of oaks pocketed the mountains, tall trees with spreading branches, rounded crowns, stout barks, and bearing large acorns. Tarns glimmered in the moonlight, scattered in the mountains. Animal life prevailed in the forestland—red deer, rabbits, and many species of birds. Nature ruled in this area devoid of human habitation.

The two Americans wore backpacks strapped across their backs. They dressed in short-sleeved shirts, pants, and hiking boots. They talked of trivial things, unconcerned about any threats to their lives because they figured there was nothing dangerous around. The mountain road they traveled spiraled downward, wide, dusty, and uneven, past the durable, hardwood oaks silently watching them enjoying their long journey. Raw smells dulled their senses, particularly of dirt. The only sounds they heard echoed from their thumping footwear on the mountain road and occasional squawks and hoots respectively from hawks and owls hidden in the forestland. There was not much nocturnal activity.

The Archvillain Sorrent stayed with the two Americans, unseen by them among the trees shrouding her in darkness. She cackled to herself, thinking how foolish they disbelieved in the stories of faeries dwelling on the mountains. Sorrent herself belonged to faerie, a magical race called Gwillions. Ironically, the word Gwillion appeared in the Welsh language, but Sorrent knew it actually derived from a tongue of her native planet, her home world, Phantasma, a magicratic world in the Keltian Sector of the Milky Way Galaxy. Some of her people visited Earth in the distant past, Wales in particular, leading the Welsh to use her race name in their lexicon.

Sorrent looked hideous. She stood five inches over five feet tall, her ugly body scarred and lumped, unattractively clothed in a blood-red robe, with blood-red slippers on her deformed feet. Her crooked nose flared above a twisted mouth filled with yellow and black teeth, below sooty narrow eyes. Dirty black hair falling to the base of her bent spine framed a wrinkled and withered face and covered her pointy ears. Her thin, aged, black-splotched hands featured long, curving fingernails with jagged tips. She walked a bit bowlegged.

Sorrent saw the two Americans stop at a crossroads. Before the young men stretched two roads, the first angling up, the second arcing down. They discussed which road should they take. Seeing her chance to waylay and mislead them, she emerged from the trees and came up behind them.

"Good evening, my dear friends," Sorrent said, startling them. She read revulsion on their faces to her appearance. Then their expressions changed to bewilderment.

"Hi," both of them replied.

Sorrent grinned wickedly. "What brings two nice boys like you to travel these mountains at night?"

The taller American answered her. "We're hiking across the United Kingdom on our summer vacation from college."

"Very interesting," Sorrent remarked. "What lore are you mastering?" Both of them looked quizzically at her.

"Oh," the shorter American said. "What are we studying. Well, I'm a history major. He's an English major."

The Archvillain found their choices of majors funny in light of the true history and native language of Wales. She recognized them as two bright men, young and virile, who remained ignorant of many things in the universe. "Are you in need of help?"

"Kind of," the taller American replied for them. "Do you know which of these roads leads in the direction of Dyfed?"

Sorrent knew about the place named. "The path on the left points you toward Myrrddinfed. The path on the right takes you toward Dyfed."

"Thank you," the shorter American said. "Are you heading toward Dyfed by any chance?"

"Indeed I am, dearie," Sorrent responded.

"Would you care to travel with us, since you're going that way anyway?" the taller American asked.

Sorrent anticipated the question. "Company would be nice. It's so lonely traveling by yourself."

The Archvillain misled them as they took the road on the right. She walked between them as they spoke with her, the night around them still and eerie. The wind died, and the night air felt less warm and smelled and tasted bitter.

Sorrent brought them to a tarn in a rocky bowl. They stood at its eastern edge, the spot too quiet around them.

The shorter American turned to the Gwillion. "You brought us to a dead end."

Sorrent cackled. "Yes indeed."

The Archvillain pushed them both into the small lake. Using her special powers, which resided on the occultic level, the Gwillion put a glamour over them. Their eyes beheld the illusion of a hundred Gwillions on the shore where she stood, all cackling at them.

Both men screamed in disbelief as they drowned in the water, struggling to save themselves and weighed down by their heavy backpacks. Their disregard for the stories, old tales, about evil faeries in the mountains cost them their lives. After Sorrent completed her foul deed, the glamour ceased, and the Gwillion stood alone before the tarn.

"Pathetic humans," Sorrent remarked as she walked away from the mountain lake, back the way she came. She enjoyed killing those two mortal fools. In her twisted mind, she'd won a victory for the faerie realm over humankind again. The pleased Archvillain went back to the mountain oaks she lodged in and rested till late morning when Asearse materialized before her and called her name.

"Why do you disturb me?" Sorrent asked. The Charybdian told her about the Enforcer Squad. The Gwillion suddenly perked up and spat on the ground. "Universal Marshals. Always waylaying us. Bah!"

The sun shone down on the rich land below in a partly cloudy sky. A cool wind gusted from the north, rustling the dark green leaves on the trees. The mountains, majestic and ancient, rose over the soft earth like stone giants guarding the undulating countryside. Unhurried, time passed the fertile region by as if it had existed forever.

Huffing, Sorrent rose to her feet and nodded to Asearse that she was ready to go. Jawsar teleported the Gwillion and the Charybdian up to the cloaked ship high above the blessed land. The mountains no longer contained any evil faeries now.

Sorrent wanted to waylay the Enforcers for a change. She looked forward to trying soon enough.

Chapter 20

Inside a crack warehouse in Baltimore, Maryland, in America, Gris-Gris Eyes, leader of the Jamaican posse, held a special meeting to discuss business. His men, twenty in number, sat in wooden chairs before a small table in the center of the meeting room with a deck of playing cards on it. Sliding doors stood closed behind Gris-Gris Eyes. Painted on the walls, in white, the posse displayed symbols of their group and voodoo. The air in the crack warehouse smelled of tobacco smoke as a few of his men puffed cigarettes.

Gris-Gris Eyes grasped a long wooden tube in his right hand, sheathing a special sword, its plastic hilt carved with voodoo and personal signs. He looked at each of his men, attempting to read their souls from their eyes as they focused on him, none of them uttering a word, transfixed by his charismatic presence. The posse leader began to speak.

"Let no man here stray from the path I have prepared. The way is true and clear before us. No man here need question the path, nor fear it."

His words held them spellbound. Not a man stirred, as if hypnotized. Gris-Gris Eyes stood close to the table, the secret of his magic like an impenetrable shield around him. They waited for him to ensorcell them further with his speech. He glanced at the deck of playing cards, then resumed talking.

"If a man hurts you, he must be paid back in pain and agony a thousand times! His wife, his children, his entire family must be killed. They must be marked for death and sacrificed to the spirits. The spirits are on our side and against our enemies."

His men agreed with him fervently. Their devotion to him bordered on blind faith, fanatics to his cause. They willingly accepted anything he stated as correct, no matter how far it stretched away from reality. He fired them up with his words and controlled them as if they served him like zombies. His eyes sparkled with confidence and the makings of destiny.

"I have the power!" Gris-Gris Eyes shouted, raising his ritual sword in the air briefly. "Let no man doubt me. Follow the—"

At that moment, a white man entered the meeting room and interrupted the posse leader's speech. He stood as tall as Gris-Gris Eyes, with a slim build, his black hair cut short and combed back. The stranger appeared handsome, his gray eyes bright, but regarding the posse leader with an icy stare. His clean-shaven face gave him a youthful look, his small nose and thin lips reinforcing that impression of him. His small ears flattened against his boxlike head, featuring a tight chin. No blemish or other mark tainted his smooth, untanned skin. He wore an electric blue outfit with black shoes.

The posse pegged the stranger as either a cop or a crook. They fingered pistols in their belts, the only weapons at their immediate disposal. But the stranger appeared unarmed.

"You are a foolish man or a brave one," Gris-Gris Eyes said to the stranger. His men rose from their seats and stood beside and behind him. "No man enters here without my permission, unless he wants to go to Heaven or Hell. Do you want to be dead?"

The stranger stepped toward them. He smiled and kept silent. Some of the posse positioned themselves on either side and behind him. The stranger seemed not bothered by their obvious tactic of encircling him.

Gris-Gris Eyes fingered the hilt of his ritual sword. "The spirits sent you to us as an empty shell. I want your soul, man. Speak, for the goddess of death will claim you soon."

"I'm not worried about your goddess of death," the stranger responded. He looked at the ritual sword of the posse leader. "Say, that's a fine weapon you have there. Really fancy."

The posse burst out laughing. Gris-Gris Eyes quieted them down by raising his ritual sword in the air, then pointed it at the stranger. The stranger raised an eyebrow at the gesture as if the posse leader cursed him with it.

"Prepare to meet the spirits, hollow one," Gris-Gris Eyes said. He unsheathed his sword.

The stranger frowned. "You talk too much."

The posse burst out laughing again.

The stranger raised his arms. Suddenly his limbs changed into gleaming sword blades and froze the posse in disbelief by what their eyes beheld. His action revealed him not as an Earthling but as an Archvillain. Before them stood Eveinnen, the Liquid Metal Being.

In a swift stroke, Eveinnen lashed out with both arms and slit the throats of the Jamaicans within reach on either side of him, killing two of their number. Gris-Gris Eyes let his men deal with the Archvillain as he fled from the meeting room upstairs to another floor. The Liquid

Metal Being befuddled the Jamaicans, who could not figure out what he represented. Eveinnen thrust his sword arms through the stomachs of two more of the posse, sending another pair to the world of spirits. The men who were still alive pulled out their guns from their belts and pumped the Liquid Metal Being full of lead. Metallic holes opened in the Archvillain's body.

He absorbed the bullets, the holes vanishing after. Quickly he reacted by chopping off fingers, hands, arms, and heads. In glee, he hacked the Jamaicans to death, littering the cement floor with sliced corpses, staining it red with human blood.

Three members of the posse survived Eveinnen's onslaught and ran out of the meeting room. The Liquid Metal Being pursued them upstairs to the next floor, a storage level. Rows of stacked metal shelves seven feet high clogged the area, crowded with cardboard boxes marked with black stenciling. Black marks scuffed the cement floor, and there was dust everywhere. Near the stairway, a large window filtered sunlight, and coupled with the overhead lights, lit the floor.

Confident and fearless, Eveinnen searched for the remaining Jamaicans. The Liquid Metal Being halted at a wooden table piled with documents, order pads, service manuals, and memos. He dismissed it all as a waste of paper. A Jamaican jumped out at him with a shotgun and blasted his midsection. A gaping hole appeared in his stomach. Before the man could get off another shot, Eveinnen hacked off his hands, and then beheaded him. The Archvillain willed his damaged midsection to shrink the hole to nothing.

Another Jamaican leaped at him with a crowbar and bashed his head. The Liquid Metal Being recoiled against the table. With his sword arms sparking, he blocked the succession of blows the Jamaican rained on him with the crowbar. Eveinnen retaliated by slashing the man's gut. The posse member retreated as Eveinnen transformed his sword arms into long hooks causing the man to blink in bewilderment.

"The spirits have sent you against us," the Jamaican said.

"Wrong," Eveinnen responded. The Liquid Metal Being ripped the crowbar from the man with a hook limb. He buried the other in the man's skull, slaying the Jamaican.

The Archvillain climbed the wooden stairs to the third floor of the warehouse, a recreational level. It split into four different compartments: the barroom, the kitchen and dining area, the billiard room, and the television room.

Eveinnen found himself in the barroom. Five wooden tables, each surrounded by four black-cushioned wooden armchairs and a metal ashtray on top of each, all sat toward the staircase. The wooden bar stretched between two doorways, metal ashtrays spaced apart on it.

Behind the bar, bottles of liquor packed the wooden shelves. Underneath the bar, glasses of different sizes and shapes crowded several shelves, all empty and clean and a few with beer logos on them.

The last of Gris-Gris Eyes' men stormed into the barroom from the doorway nearest him, armed with a submachine gun. The scared Jamaican riddled the Archvillain's body with bullets and emptied the weapon. His perforated form looked like metallic Swiss cheese. The man reached for another cartridge in his jacket pocket after ejecting the empty one, hurrying before the Archvillain could kill him. But the Liquid Metal Being remolded his hook limbs into spear arms and charged at the Jamaican, ramming the left and right appendages respectively through the man's heart and throat to terminate his life. He yanked his spear arms from the corpse and let it fall to the floor of the barroom, and then cleaned his bloodied limbs on the clothing of the dead Jamaican. Finished, he exited the barroom and entered the dining area.

Three long wooden tables connected together and extended down the length of the dining area. Padded wooden chairs sat at the ends of the joined tables and ran along both sides. At the far end of the dining area stood a wooden door leading to the kitchen. The overhead lights of the dining area flickered occasionally.

As Eveinnen moved toward the kitchen, left of the tables, Gris-Gris Eyes emerged from the kitchen carrying his ritual sword. The posse leader threw aside the sheath and mumbled a quick prayer to the spirits. The Liquid Metal Being stopped and faced the Jamaican boss.

"I island awaits me," Gris-Gris Eyes said, twirling the sword. "You an evil spirit, a man of no flesh. You have no teeth. You have no soul. I spirits send you back to the hell you came from. You a creature of the darkness."

Eveinnen cocked an eyebrow, amused by his lingo. The Liquid Metal Being changed his spear arms back into sword arms as the posse leader gripped the hilt of his own sword with both hands. The foul being raised his weapon appendages in an on-guard position after saluting the scared man.

Gris-Gris Eyes struck first, slashing at him.

Eveinnen easily blocked the blows, retaliated by hewing at the posse leader with both sword arms. The Jamaican boss deflected all his strikes.

They exchanged blows, neither able to penetrate the defense of the other. The combat moved into the barroom.

"You fight like a man," Gris-Gris Eyes remarked during a lull in their duel. "You a demon sent to take my soul."

"I am no demon," Eveinnen responded. His special powers resided on the scientific level.

Gris-Gris Eyes twirled his sword once. "You no demon sent to take my soul. You no zombie commanded to kill me. What are you, man?"

"Unique," Eveinnen answered, simply.

The posse leader stepped from behind the bar. Eveinnen thought the man still talked too much. Their clash resumed as sparks continued to fly and metal sliced against metal.

Gris-Gris Eyes kicked a chair at the Liquid Metal Being, who evaded it. The posse leader picked up a table and smashed it into the Archvillain, knocking him tumbling down the stairs to the ground floor.

Eveinnen sprawled on the cement floor as Gris-Gris Eyes ran down the stairs. As the man tore by him, the Liquid Metal Being lashed out and cut the posse leader on the back of his right thigh. Gris-Gris Eyes yelled in pain, crashing into a wall and bouncing off it to the dirty floor with his sword. Eveinnen leaped to his feet as the injured man rose to his in time to meet the Archvillain's renewed attack.

In fury, the Liquid Metal Being hammered blows against Gris-Gris Eyes, who barely kept up blocking the combination of thrusts and slashes launched against him by the Archvillain.

Eveinnen moved faster than before, his lightning assault forcing the posse leader to backpedal rapidly toward the elevator doors, which stood open, exposing the lift positioned above on the second floor. The elevator shaft loomed closer as a death trap for the Earthling as the Archvillain attacked with tireless ease.

The posse leader cried out as the Liquid Metal Being opened several cuts on his body. Eveinnen pressed him to within a few feet of the elevator shaft. The Jamaican boss could see his doom approaching as the Archvillain became the goddess of death in his eyes.

"Spirits, do not desert me, I servant," Gris-Gris pleaded as he looked like he was going to collapse. The posse leader tried to catch his breath.

Eveinnen grinned. "No spirits to help you."

"I curse you, soulless creature," Gris-Gris Eyes spat at the Liquid Metal Being. "I join the spirits and see you in Hell."

"Brave talk," Eveinnen responded. "Death becomes you."

Gris-Gris Eyes, desperate to save his life, bleeding too much, took the offensive. Eveinnen intercepted the posse leader's initial blow by parrying the man's overhead slash downward, and then hacking off both the Jamaican boss' hands. With a clang, the severed hands fell to the floor, still clinging to the ritual sword. Such agony overtook Gris-Gris Eyes.

Eveinnen thrust a sword arm through the Earthling's chest, lifted him high in the air, and carried him over to the edge of the elevator shaft. The posse leader screamed and did not call on the spirits for any more help.

Merciless, the Liquid Metal Being disengaged his blade appendage from Gris-Gris Eyes' body and dropped the Jamaican boss down the elevator shaft. Eveinnen watched, without emotion, as the fall impaled the posse leader on a metal rod at the bottom of the shaft, instantly and violently killing the man.

"I have sent you to your spirits," Eveinnen said to the corpse of the Earthling.

The Archvillain changed his sword arms back into human-looking ones. Then he grabbed the ritual sword on the floor and snapped it into two pieces. Lastly, he tossed the broken weapon and severed hands down the elevator shaft to join the dead body of the Jamaican boss.

As Eveinnen turned his back on the elevator shaft, hands still bloody, Asearse materialized before him. The Liquid Metal Being listened as the Charybdian talked to him about the Enforcer Squad. Eveinnen nodded in understanding. Then Moroloch teleported them up to the cloaked ship, the Archvillain Squad complete. After that, the *Glasnostromo* flew away in the direction of New York City.

The Liquid Metal Being was ready to battle the Enforcer Squad. He ached to chop a Universal Marshal to pieces, never successful in the past in clashes with Enforcers. Now he looked forward to redeeming himself against them.

Chapter 21

Procules entered the teleporter room of the *Centaurus* and wheeled over to the teleport console, a control podium, in the center of the chamber. Behind the Robot-Enforcer a telescreen was off on a wall. Before him and the teleport console, a black square telegrid raised off the floor two steps. Glowpanels illuminated the room from the ceiling.

A short time ago, Procules worked alone on the bridge and received a telebeamed message. That brought the Robot-Enforcer to the teleporter room, where he activated the telecom on the teleport console to communicate with the teleporter room on a cloaked ship in space near Earth, the *Starfarer*.

"Ready," Procules said into the telecom.

"I'm sending them to you now," a male voice responded from the other end.

Three Universal Marshals materialized on the telegrid before Procules. The tallest of the three, Minanket, seemed a little disturbed. The Robot-Enforcer understood his reaction because of Professor Magnemus. Procules had expected the High Enforcer to send the Molecular Being to Earth for that very reason.

Left of Minanket stood Enforcer Isisis, the Occultic Being. What special powers Magnemus possessed on the scientific level, Isisis had the equivalent on the occultic level. Five inches under six feet tall, the Occultic Being looked, in Earth terms, thirty-five years old. Her dark brown hair she kept cut short, like her polished fingernails. Her deep brown eyes held a hypnotic stare to those gazing into them. Her round face featured wide lips, a short, round nose, and a flat chin. A white robe clothed her modest-shaped figure, and white slippers hugged her feet.

The remaining Universal Marshal leaned on the half natural, half supernatural golden longbow that the Federation identified as his trademark. Federation citizens called him the greatest archer that ever lived, a legend even before he became an Enforcer. That title fitted him truly and accurately. He knew it, too, a bowman of supreme skill. Other beings recognized him as Vartagal, the Great Archer.

Vartagal rose to his full height of two inches over six feet. A golden tri-peaked cap rested on his narrow head with a golden feather sticking out of the back of it. His blond beard and mustache were kept trimmed and matched the color of his keen eyes. His nose and chin looked like chiseled arrows in flesh, and between them, his thin mouth neither smiled nor frowned. His physically fit body, he dressed in a golden tunic and golden breeches with golden moccasins on his feet. Strapped around his back, his golden quiver held thirty arrows. He wore a golden belt around his slim waist. Five pouches hung from it, filled with various items.

The three new members of the Enforcer Squad stepped down from the telegrid, greeted by Procules. The Robot-Enforcer led them out of the teleporter room and assigned them individual quarters on the ship. After that, Procules went to his quarters as each member of the Enforcer Squad relaxed for a couple of hours before resuming duty.

The Enforcer Squad gathered in the rear section of the ship by the closed ramp. Rathol commanded the Staff of Godpower to life, flaring white. The Shepherd disguised them all as ordinary Americans—now five white males and three white females, the former dressed in casual suits, the latter in similar wear. Procules worked the control pad to lower the ramp. After it stopped, touching the ground, Rathol led them down it, Jagathan bringing up the rear. Once outside, the *Centaurus* automatically closed the ramp after them and engaged its autodefense system, still cloaked. They emerged from the trees surrounding the vessel and headed east across mowed grass.

Daytime activity in New York City differed considerably from the night kind. Children ran playing, some tossing balls, some flying kites, others enjoying games. Adults sat on wooden benches, reading books or newspapers, in conversation, eating and drinking, lovers holding hands and kissing, or just sitting and relaxing. Mothers watched their kids having fun. A young black man passed the Enforcer Squad, carrying a box blaring loud music.

Eneysa shook her head. "What kind of music is that?" she asked the Robot-Enforcer.

Procules searched through his memory cells and found the answer. "The Earthlings call it reggae."

"It sounds like tribal music," Vartagal remarked.

"The Terrans may have a few strange customs," Lorliane said.

Above them, the Earth sun, Sol, shone in a nearly-cloudless blue sky. A cool breeze from the west blew around behind them. The temperature registered seventy-five degrees.

Minanket addressed the Titan-Enforcer. "What all transpired before we came?"

"Evil activity," Jagathan responded. "Last night we clashed with Earth scum. Criminals."

"It was a learning experience," Lorliane said. "Earth is a very interesting planet."

Rathol joined the conversation. "Earth is a world greatly touched by the Lord. A wilderness of sin has taken root in her."

Isisis spoke. "I sense the evil hand of an Archvillain in her. She has been infected with the foulness of the Incarnation of Horror. His evil has been planted here. I do not know how long his seeds of horror have been sown on Earth."

"Or what shall be reaped from them," Eneysa added. "Those seeds have had plenty of time to take shape and grow."

"Another's wicked hand has touched it as well," Rathol said. "Asathain."

His companions understood. Asathain was the Samarosian name for Satan. They all knew that he warred with God over the planet because the Supreme Being considered it as one of his favorite worlds in the universe.

Lorliane looked at the Molecular Being. "You know the leader of the Fellowship of Darkness. If he had made the final decision in choosing where their hidden fortress would be, where would he have had it built?"

Minanket pondered the question. "New York City is a place Magnemus would have considered because he would want it near the seat of power on the planet, the political base of the Earth government."

"The United Nations," Procules said.

Minanket nodded. "He would not want the Complex to be in proximity to a primitive place on the planet. He would prefer to be near an area of high technology and advanced science on Earth. Especially if it involves bioscience and biotechnology."

"Because of his biocreation work," Procules said.

"Yes," Minanket responded.

"Could the Complex be an underground stronghold?" Eneysa asked.

"Possibly," Minanket replied. "In the past, Magnemus has worked in subterranean facilities."

Internally Procules analyzed detailed files he had on all the nations of Earth. "If we do not discover the location of the Complex in the United States, then the country of Japan is the second prime candidate for its location."

"That deduction is logical," Minanket agreed. "I reviewed information discs on Earth before coming here. If I were Magnemus, I would have had the Complex built somewhere in the United States, either on its east or west coast. New York City or a major city in the state of California."

The Enforcer Squad exited Central Park. They crossed a busy street congested with traffic when the stoplight their way turned red. People flowed around them in both directions. They felt the crush of bodies, which reminded them of Acropollon in some ways, though only humans existed as the intelligent beings and dominant species on Earth. In the Tellusian capital, all kinds of beings used its various walkways, including walk belts moving them along through it.

Wisely the Enforcer Squad went with the flow of

traffic of the walking masses and tried to avoid physical contact with the Earthlings, especially Jagathan and Procules. The Titan-Enforcer could see over everyone's head and reported what he saw ahead to his fellow Universal Marshals. They passed different businesses, open with people walking in and out of them, some carrying purchases in paper or plastic bags. At the sight of a restaurant, Jagathan had a desire to try its cuisine, and then decided to try the food replicator later on the *Centaurus* to see if it could produce Earth food to satisfy his huge palate. Parked cars lined both sides of the street.

Noise rose all around them. Honking horns, the rumbling engines of vehicles, jackhammers, a police whistle, and snatches of conversation between people or on cell phones jumbled in their ears. Exhaust fumes from small and large vehicles, cigarette smoke, the aroma of food, body odors, perfume and cologne assaulted their noses. The air tasted on the foul side, as if the Incarnation of Horror claimed sole responsibility for its uncleanliness due to air pollution. It made the Enforcer Squad almost gag for oxygen. They wondered how any beings on Earth could breathe in the unhealthy content of the air and live. The sights of New York City in the daytime overwhelmed them. Signs drew their attention everywhere. To them, the American metropolis appeared crammed, as if to leave no space unfilled with someone or something.

The Enforcer Squad stopped at a street corner and waited for the light to change green. Isisis suddenly stiffened as if she got a premonition. Her fellow Enforcers noticed her strange reaction and turned to her, recognizing the warning sign.

"What is it?" Eneysa asked the Occultic Being.

Isisis held up a hand. "I sense Archvillains in the area."

"Where?" Vartagal asked, ready to use his longbow.

Isisis tried to sense the location of the foul beings and met resistance. "Close by."

Jagathan swept his gaze around their vicinity. "I see only Earth mortals around us."

"They must be in disguise like us," Lorliane remarked.

"An illusion or holographic projection," Procules added.

The low drawling voice of Ynemain reached them, where only they could hear. "You're so right, darling."

"Who is it?" Vartagal asked, not recognizing the voice.

Procules identified her to the other Universal Marshals. "The Iron Maiden."

The Enforcer Squad heard Ynemain giggle. "Greetings and felicitations, Enforcers. I and my dear companions here give you a warm welcome to dreary Earth."

"Our meeting is not a friendly one," Jagarthan responded for the Enforcer Squad.

"Pardon us if the reception we give you is not to your liking," Ynemain said. "We did not expect your company, although it is not surprising."

Isisis responded next for the Enforcer Squad, focusing her voice so only the Archvillains could hear her. "What is it you want?"

"Why, a smashing party with you," Ynemain replied, the other Archvillains with her letting her do all the talking for them.

"Party?" Isisis repeated.

They did not see Ynemain smile. "A match between your universal class and ours. A fair one. Your eight against our eight in a high stakes game."

The Enforcer Squad then knew that they faced an Archvillain Squad, but not which Archvillains comprised it other than the Iron Maiden. On a microcosmic scale, the two sides represented good and evil, clashing again for supremacy of the galaxy.

"And if we refuse?" Isisis asked.

"Then, my dear companions and I will just have to rid this world of an inferior universal class and claim its property for ourselves."

Their foes put the Enforcer Squad in a delicate situation, a real predicament. On one hand, their true identities must not be revealed to the entire planet—it would complicate their mission. But on the other hand, they could not let the Archvillains obliterate Earth and its inhabitants, who were helpless against the foul beings. They conferred. The Enforcer Squad faced a tough decision.

"Very well," Isisis said after the Enforcer Squad all agreed reluctantly. "You win. We will fight."

"Splendid!" Ynemain responded. The Iron Maiden gloated, along with the rest of the Archvillain Squad. "Show yourselves. We will do the same."

Rathol stopped the illusion disguising the Enforcer Squad as Sorrent did with the glamour covering the Archvillain Squad. The two squads spotted each other on opposite corners across the street. With no false images hiding either squad, the startled Earthlings suddenly beheld sixteen beings who were not Terrans, each unique and different from all the others.

Both squads approached each other toward the

intersection of four lanes of traffic. Above the intersection blinked a traffic light. The Earthlings froze, fascinated yet concerned by the sight of the two squads, standing or sitting in vehicles, unable to react or think clearly, caught up in a major event on their planet. The noise level fell a little, the air tense as the two squads halted and stared at each other less than fifteen feet from each other.

Without warning, the Enforcer and Archvillain Squads paired off and clashed. Jagathan tangled with Quasicoatl, Minanket battled Namprey, Isisis fought Sorrent, Lorliane engaged Asearse, Vartagal contested with Eveinnen, Eneysa scuffled with Ynemain, Procules combated Jawsar, and Rathol opposed Moroloch.

The Cloning Creature grabbed the Titan-Enforcer and dragged him toward his opening mouth. Quasicoatl intended to consume Jagathan so the Archvillain could collect cells of the Enforcer to clone him. The Titan-Enforcer broke the grasp of the Cloning Creature, who only grabbed him again. Quasicoatl pulled Jagathan within inches of his waiting mouth and teeth in multiple rows, ready to shred his flesh into bits for clone processing. The Archvillain bent the head of the Universal Marshal to crunch it.

In a rage, Jagathan smashed both his fists against the cheeks of Quasicoatl, jarring the Titan-Enforcer free of the grasp of the Cloning Creature again and loosening a few teeth of the Archvillain as well. Quasicoatl shook his head, feeling pain in his jaw from the blow of the Universal Marshal. Before the Cloning Creature could seize him again, the Titan-Enforcer picked up the foul being and hurled him over and down stairs into a subway station.

Isisis dueled Sorrent with special powers. The Gwillion lay a glamour of mist around the Occultic Being, who countered by shredding it to nothing with the fabric of reality magically.

Then the Archvillain surrounded the Universal Marshal with twenty images of herself and her real self before the Occultic Being could find her. Twenty Gwillions converged on Isisis rapidly, jagged fingernails ready to tear into the Enforcer. The Occultic Being could not tell who the real Gwillion was from the false ones. All the Sorrents cackled like evil hags. Instinctively, Isisis reacted by snuffing out the glamour replicants of the Gwillion one by one with the occult law of magic reversal. Before the Universal Marshal could reduce the Archvillain down to the live one, the real Sorrent slipped around and raked the back of the Occultic Being, ripping through the robe of the Enforcer and leaving claw marks and blood flowing from the wounds. The Gwillion clung to Isisis' back and reached around to tear out her eyes.

In quick defense, the Occultic Being grabbed Sorrent's thin wrists, then flopped backward on top of the Archvillain, knocking the wind out of the Gwillion, forcing the dark faerie to relinquish the gouging attack on her eyes. Isisis let go of Sorrent's wrists and rolled away from the foul being. She rose to her feet to face the Archvillain. Sorrent climbed to her feet in fury. Shrieking, the Gwillion launched herself at the Occultic Being. The Universal Marshal met the charge and locked bodies with the Archvillain, each trying to get the upper hand.

Namprey shot silk lines from his holed fingertips and two antennas, cocooning the Molecular Being. Minanket changed into a molecular ball of white particles, escaped the white cocoon, and in blazing speed, rammed into the Nodrone. The Archvillain flew backward ten feet and crashed to the street on his back. The Universal Marshal reverted to humanoid form and moved in quickly to finish off the foul being.

Namprey rose and instantly caught the Molecular Being in a death lock, pinning the Enforcer's arms behind his back with three of his arms. The Nodrone used his fourth arm to twist Minanket's head around to expose his neck. Instantly, the Archvillain opened his mouth and sank his fangs into the Universal Marshal's jugular vein, attempting to inject poison so he could proceed to drink the organic fluids, live and warm, from the mortal body of the Molecular Being.

Minanket anticipated the deadly move. Namprey bit into white particles of molecular energy as if eating air. The Nodrone could not find another spot to try and suck the life juices from the life form of the Enforcer. Minanket next changed into a white chain of molecular energy and chained the Archvillain to the pavement of the intersection. Namprey shrieked and yanked on the powerful fetter with all his strength to break it. The Molecular Being stretched back and forth, but would not break his hold on the foul being. For the moment, the Enforcer had neutralized the Nodrone.

Vartagal faced Eveinnen. The Liquid Metal Being transformed his arms into sword blades as the Great Archer nocked a special arrow from his quiver to his longbow in one fast motion. At lightning speed, Eveinnen charged Vartagal. The Enforcer loosed the arrow, and it exploded in the Archvillain's chest, which sent the foul being reeling. Eveinnen discovered a hole in his chest and willed it gone, whole again. The Liquid

Metal Being attacked again, and the Great Archer shot a magic arrow this time, designed to paralyze the Archvillain. But Eveinnen reacted by vertically splitting his body down the middle to his crotch, and the arrow missed its mark. Before the Enforcer could notch a third arrow to his bowstring, the Liquid Metal Being unsplit himself and slashed both arms of the Universal Marshal. The Great Archer backpedaled in pain, blood welling from the cuts.

Eveinnen came at the Enforcer to fell him swiftly. Immediately, Vartagal willed the supernatural power of his longbow to life as the Archvillain bombarded him with stabs and slashes, all blocked by the Great Archer with his magical weapon. Eveinnen seemed confident of slaying the Enforcer simply because Vartagal was mortal and the Liquid Metal Being was not.

The Universal Marshal whacked the foul being across the face with his longbow when he found an opening to counterattack. Its supernatural power flipped the Archvillain to the ground. Eveinnen jumped to his feet, shaken but unhurt. The two extraordinary beings exchanged roles as attacker and defender repeatedly, stalemated.

Lorliane grappled with Asearse. The Charybdian backhanded the face of the Ice Being, who retaliated likewise. Asearse kicked Lorliane in the stomach and aimed a second for the exposed chin of the Universal Marshal. The Ice being caught her foot, lifted her leg up, and threw her backward to the ground. Then Lorliane stepped back five feet as the Charybdian rolled to her feet to face the Enforcer again. The Ice Being shot ice beams from her hands at the Archvillain and encased her in a block of ice.

Asearse melted the ice with her special powers, then turned the water into a whirlpool around her. The Charybdian hurled the whirlpool at Lorliane and trapped the Ice Being inside it, but the Universal Marshal froze the whirlpool and shattered it into ice shards. They circled each other, wary of each other's special powers. Suddenly, they locked arms, trying to get the better position. Their fight stalled, each attempting to finish the other off.

Jawsar jabbed his *krillja* at Procules. The Robot-Enforcer wheeled away and aside from the lancelike hardware and blocked it with his arms. In surprise, the Predator vaulted into the Universal Marshal with his weapon and knocked the Enforcer back ten feet. Jawsar immediately followed up by swinging the *krillja* at Procules to knock his head off. Procules intercepted the blow and locked his hands on the shaft of the weapon. Then the Universal Marshal shot bolts of electricity along the *krillja* and shocked the Predator, who writhed in the volts dancing up and down his body. Finally, the Archvillain let go of it before the electricity felled him. Procules bent the *krillja* into a U shape and tossed it aside, enraging Jawsar.

The Predator pressed a button on each black rectangular device around his wrist and camouflaged his entire body in a shimmering cloak of opaque, silver light. Jawsar pressed another button on both devices and out popped a pair of serrated, deadly two-pronged forks.

The Robot-Enforcer could not register the blurred appearance of the Archvillain on his normal sensors, nor could he tell what the foul being was up to. Procules switched through light sensors to find the frequency of light to match that of the devices of the Predator which bent light rays to service the Archvillain's purpose.

Jawsar did not wait for the Universal Marshal to find the right frequency. The Predator ran at the Robot-Enforcer in a flash and punctured four holes in Procules' body with the two forks.

Rattled, Procules instantly activated a force field around himself, still working on the light frequency of the Predator's devices but with much difficulty. The Archvillain darted around the Universal Marshal so fast, striking the force field with the two forks, testing it, searching for weak spots to exploit and finish the Robot-Enforcer with other hidden weapons in his devices. Procules maintained his defenses.

Eneysa squared off with Ynemain. The Iron Maiden sent thought waves of torture to the Metamorph-Enforcer to disrupt her mind, to cause confused and conflicting thoughts. Utter torment racked Eneysa's mind and an awful headache throbbed in her head. The Metamorph-Enforcer knew her brain might hemorrhage if she failed to stop the mental assault. In desperation, the Universal Marshal shapeshifted into the first life form she could think of, a roc, a gigantic brown and white bird with huge wings. The thought waves of torture struck her long legs now instead, each of her huge feet featuring wicked talons.

Ynemain shifted the thought waves of torture upward toward Eneysa's head. The Metamorph-Enforcer flapped her wings furiously and propelled the Iron Maiden through the air like a rocket, to crash into a section of wall above the big window of a restaurant. Surprised, the Archvillain crumpled to the ground but recovered shortly. In fury, Ynemain rose to her feet, stamped back to the Universal Marshal, and with her special powers, materialized a torture device of immense size. Energy power on the celestic level ran through the shape of an iron maiden. In an instant, the foul being began enclosing it around Eneysa.

The Metamorph-Enforcer felt the Iron Maiden trying to impale her with the deadly spikes of the torture device. Instinctively, the Universal Marshal changed from a roc into harmful bacteria and zoomed through the air at light speed to enter the body of the Archvillain. It forced Ynemain to make the torture device vanish and radiate torture rays inside herself against Eneysa, who tried to make the Iron Maiden sick with a disease. A standoff resulted, each trying to destroy the other.

Rathol locked eyes with Moroloch. The Monitor lumbered over to the Shepherd, who raised the Staff of Godpower before him in defense against the Archvillain. Moroloch stopped two feet from Rathol, then spun around and whipped his tail at the Universal Marshal, lashing the right side of the Enforcer's head. The Shepherd rocked to his left, wobbling on his feet. The Monitor advanced, hands before him to claw the old body of the leader of the Enforcer Squad.

The Archvillain underestimated the Universal Marshal. Rathol struck upward into the unprotected throat of Moroloch, causing the foul being to gag. The Shepherd cracked the snout of the Monitor with the Staff, then in rapid succession, whacked the arms and legs of the Archvillain, driving Moroloch back.

Abruptly the Monitor retreated from the onslaught, then lashed his tail at the Universal Marshal, who blocked the blow. The Archvillain timed his move, stepped inside of Rathol's next strike, and grabbed the Staff outside the hands of the Shepherd. The Monitor forced the Enforcer to his knees, much stronger physically than the elderly mortal.

In defense, Rathol verbally commanded the Staff to life. The Staff flared white along its length as the foul being began twisting it from the Shepherd. The Universal Marshal engulfed the Archvillain in the white fire of the Almighty Lord, roasting the Monitor alive while he hissed in pain and frustration. Moroloch released his grip on the Staff before it could cook him completely. Recovering, the Archvillain stalked Rathol, wary of the Staff and staying out of its range, the foul being looking for a way to defeat the Enforcer.

The street suddenly exploded underneath in the intersection, hurling cars aside. Chunks of pavement flew in all directions and scattered around a large hole in the street. Quasicoatl altered his natural form into the geometric shape of a giant cylinder and thrust upward through the hole. His body, now huge, cracked in four places. Cloned creatures poured forth from the Archvillain.

The living replicas resembled what they naturally appeared to be on the outside, but on the inside all being the Cloning Creature in disguise. His fellow Archvillains retreated behind him, including Namprey, when Minanket unchained the Nodrone from the fetter. The Molecular Being transformed himself back into his humanoid form to face the new threat as Eneysa did as well. Quasicoatl would deal with the Enforcer Squad his way.

"This is not good," Lorliane remarked.

"Now they fight in a cowardly way," Jagathan said.

First a wave of lions, tigers, jaguars, leopards, and pumas rushed at the Universal Marshals as the Cloning

Creature produced a horde of natural predators. Jagathan met the cloned beasts head on, belting them in every direction as they pounced on him. Vartagal nocked an exploding arrow on his longbow and blew up a line of big cats converging on him. Rathol blasted large felines with the Staff of Godpower as Lorliane froze them in blocks of ice. Minanket changed into a molecular wheel of white particles and wreaked havoc among the unnatural carnivores. Eneysa shapeshifted into a griffin, a large lionlike monster with white and brown eagle wings, and batted aside the big cats attacking her.

Quasicoatl stopped replicating large felines when the Enforcer Squad neutralized them all. The Cloning Creature next produced grizzly, Kodiak, brown, black, and polar bears, only to be annihilated by the Universal Marshals. He cloned a third batch of Earth animals, white, black, and Indian rhinos, and they all suffered the same fate as the previous two series of natural creatures.

Quasicoatl realized he needed to clone extraterrestrial beasts to crush the Enforcer Squad. As he began to replicate copies of animals alien to Earth, Jagathan closed in on him and tore the Cloning Creature bodily from the hole and body slammed the Archvillain on the street over and over. Jawsar intervened, drop-kicking the Titan-Enforcer in the back, jarring Quasicoatl loose from the Universal Marshal's grasp. The Cloning Creature and the Predator joined their fellow Archvillains at a corner of the intersection as Jagathan did with his fellow Enforcers on the opposite corner.

"This is getting us nowhere," Sorrent said.

Lorliane spoke for her side. "It is becoming a draw."

Ynemain acted. The Iron Maiden bathed all the

Earthlings in the vicinity with feelings and thoughts of being tortured, and they reacted in agony. Isisis held the Enforcer Squad back as she sensed those malevolent influences radiating around them. All the Terrans within the area of the intersection swarmed toward the Enforcer Squad to attack the Universal Marshals, barehanded or wielding some kind of makeshift weapon, purses, pieces of broken pavement from the damaged street, pocketknives, and anything else they could get their hands on.

The Archvillain Squad escaped from the city as the Enforcer Squad contended with Earthlings attacking them by forming a defensive ring. The Universal Marshals did not want to hurt the Terrans but needed to protect themselves. Humans blindly struck at them, under the tormenting control of Ynemain. A rock thrown gashed the forehead of Vartagal. Rathol commanded the Staff of Godpower to life to destroy the evil hold the Iron Maiden over the Terran mob. The Almighty power of the Staff swept away the malevolent influences of the Archvillain.

The Earthlings awoke from the mind control of Ynemain bewildered. New York City police arrived at the strange scene and surrounded the Enforcer Squad before the Terrans could surge forward to greet the Universal Marshals in a more friendly manner, finally realizing the members of the Enforcer Squad were the good guys. The police led the eight of them away through the multitude of people, slow because of the size of the crowd, to escort them somewhere.

The Universal Marshals did not rejoice in their victory over the Archvillain Squad. They had won the battle of the squads but lost their advantage of secrecy, the foul beings having forced the Enforcer Squad to reveal themselves to the planet. All the Universal Marshals could really think of was how badly they had compromised or complicated their mission after their exposure to the people of Earth.

"We will clash again," Jagathan remarked in reference to the Fellowship of Darkness.

The Archvillain Squad fled in the *Glasnostromo* back to the Complex to regroup.

Chapter 22

In Docking Bay Seventeen, its entrance facing south, Enforcer Kennedrill, the Interstellar Pilgrim, made a final check of his ship for space flight, the *Aurora Moth*, raised up on three landing legs. She appeared a sleek vessel, smaller than a Federation battlecruiser, being readied to see action again.

Kennedrill stood six feet, four inches tall, his muscular body bulging in the jet black flexsuit he wore with matching boots and attached cape. His black beard was trimmed and his gray eyes steely. His rugged features conveyed the impression that he traveled through space as a way of life, thus his special title. But his trademark he wore around his forearms, a pair of black powerbands, each with four silver buttons on them. When pressed singly or in combination, the buttons activated a variety of offensive and defensive rays he used to fight evil, ranging from a freeze ray to a plasma one. To go along with his two powerbands, he wore a powerbelt around his waist. When he pressed any of the buttons on his powerbelt, they activated other powers, from a body shield to invisibility. His special powers resided on the scientific level, such as his ability to fly.

Kennedrill completed the maintenance routine of the outside of his ship. The *Aurora Moth* featured a long cylindrical body, silver and black, with a conical nose. Unbreakable glass formed the roof over the bridge of the vessel. Silver and black wings tapered from the middle of the ship to the rear thrusters. A silver and black fin rose atop its exhaust pipe. The Universal Marshal built the ship himself with help from factory robots when he was younger and had flown in it ever since. Already he'd logged many flights in space, having traveled millions of light years in the galaxy.

"Give me a solar sail, and I will fly to the stars forever," Kennedrill quoted the famous space explorer, Dak Tarnis, a human from the planet Vitune. The Interstellar Pilgrim himself was humanoid and originally from the planet Hestril, an industrial world in the Wutheron Sector of the Milky Way Galaxy.

The Acropollon Spaceport, where Docking Bay Seventeen stood, saw increased activity. More visitors from outworld came to Tellus, and vessels took off at regular intervals.

Kennedrill took equipment from a storage room in the docking bay to help prepare his ship for a mission with a team of Universal Marshals. The side door of the docking bay opened, and two beings entered the hangar structure, one male, the other female. They met Kennedrill and exchanged greetings with him.

The female was Enforcer Barbrielle, Lady Luck, the beautiful Incarnation of Luck, an immortal who possessed special powers on the celestic level. Five feet six, she had curves in all the right places, her blonde hair long and thick, so soft and lustrous as if she shampooed and conditioned it daily. Her blue eyes sparkled like gemstones; her cute nose twitched in a tantalizing manner. She clad her exquisite figure in a golden robe with matching slippers.

The male who had come with Lady Luck was

Wankatanuka, the Manitou-Enforcer, an immortal being with special powers on the celestic level like her. Wankatanuka resembled an Indian chief, tall and lean. His aquiline nose was like the snout of a bloodhound, his brown eyes like the sight of an eagle, his large ears like the hearing of a bat.

"Is she ready for the journey?" Wankatanuka asked.

Kennedrill flew down from the top of his ship. "The *Moth* is set for take-off. All systems check out fine."

"Have the others gone already?" Barbrielle asked.

"Soon," Kennedrill replied.

The Interstellar Pilgrim had spoken with the Universal Marshals who each commanded another ship with a team of Enforcers. The joint mission of the three teams: locate the space fleet of the Fellowship of Darkness that would invade Tellus.

Kennedrill led Barbrielle and Wankatanuka underneath the *Aurora Moth* to a big hatch in the middle. The Interstellar Pilgrim pressed a button on his powerbelt and the hatch opened. A lift beam—a white shaft of transporting light—carried them up through the hatch into the ship. The hatch closed under them before the lift beam vanished.

They stood in the main corridor of the ship. Behind them stood automatic doors to the rear section of the vessel that led to other compartments. Glowpanels in the ceiling lit the passageway and various panels appeared on the walls. Before them stood the automatic doors to the bridge.

"Have you outfitted your ship with additional upgrades?" Barbrielle asked the Interstellar Pilgrim.

"She has more features," Kennedrill replied. "Periodically, I improve her. The *Aurora Moth* now has increased power to the thrusters, a tractor beam, and expanded weapons systems. Plus better facilities for lab work."

Wankatanuka smiled. "A faster ship is good. Did you give her changes besides technical ones?"

"No," Kennedrill replied. "The *Aurora Moth* is a simple vessel for space travel. She does not need features extravagant for space flight. Or to be burdened with too much technology."

Kennedrill led them onto the bridge, which was nothing more than a large cockpit that seated six people. The Interstellar Pilgrim sat in the helm chair, also the captain's seat, in the very front of the bridge. Lady Luck and the Manitou-Enforcer took a seat on either side behind him as they all strapped in. Kennedrill touched a button on his control console before him and ignited the upgraded engines of the *Aurora Moth*. The engines sounded quieter.

"Where are we off to?" Barbrielle asked. She monitored sensor readings from a control console.

"The Glammarian Sector of the Milky Way Galaxy," Kennedrill replied. "That is where the space fleet of the Fellowship of Darkness is hiding. We have to find it before they start the invasion of Tellus."

"A force of ships from the Federation may have to engage theirs to stop them," Wankatanuka added.

Kennedrill used his control console and opened the roof of the docking bay. Activating her thrusters, the Interstellar Pilgrim piloted their ship out of the hangar structure. Thereafter the *Aurora Moth* soared into outer space. He set coordinates in the helm computer to his right for the Glammarian Sector, and in a moment, engaged the superluminal drive of his vessel to jump to faster-than-light speed. The ship disappeared from normal space in a blur.

****

In Docking Bay Thirty-Eight, its entrance facing east, Enforcer Galamagne, the Space Chevalier, finished readying his ship, the *Nebula Stallion*, for the joint mission. Galamagne stood three inches over six feet and wore a special suit of armor, hi-tech and lightweight, shiny silver.

Under his helmet, his blond hair was combed back; the sights of his visor showed blue eyes. His handsome face sported a blond beard trim only around his chin and above his upper lip.

The *Nebula Stallion* was the same size as the *Aurora Moth* and as well armed as the latter. His ship resembled a battering ram with wings—Galamagne designed her that way. The vessel did not stand on legs, but she was open on her left side to permit entry. She had the same color as his suit of armor, as if they were made from the same alloy, which they were not. The *Nebula Stallion* was more like a warship than the *Aurora Moth* though because Galamagne was more of a warrior than the owner of the latter.

A pair of Universal Marshals arrived at the docking bay to join the Space Chevalier for the mission. The first, female, was Enforcer Neisie, the Unicornling. She looked like a unicorn who walked upright like a woman, an intelligent being as tall as a big horse with special powers on the occultic level. Being of the unicorn species, she was a magical creature. She wore nothing.

With Neisie was Enforcer Lucane, the Peryton, human, a middle-aged man with long gray hair streaked with white, thin, brown eyes mirroring a mystical soul.

He wore a deerskin robe over a tunic and breeches with deerskin boots. On his head he wore a deer head with its neck flaps open for him to see.

"Is your ship ready to gallop to the stars?" Neisie asked the Space Chevalier, who took his gauntlets off for a moment.

"Yes," Galamagne replied. "She is outfitted extra in case we encounter battle with the ships of our foes."

Lucane understood that need. "The light and dark shall meet again in decisive conflict. We must gain victory for the light against the dark."

Galamagne put his gauntlets back on after checking the hi-tech metal gloves for the improvements he made to them. "And vanquish this evil we fight before it vanquishes us."

The three Enforcers boarded the ship after the Space Chevalier was satisfied with the inspection of the vessel. Galamagne led the other two Universal Marshals onto the bridge and sat in the command chair as Neisie and Lucane took the two seats in front of him. The *Nebula Stallion* ran on automated systems, and the Space Chevalier pressed buttons on the armrests of the captain's seat. Engines ignited, and thrusters blasted. The roof of the docking bay opened, and the ship lifted off and out of the hangar structure.

"All systems running normal," Galamagne reported. "We are ready to speed to our destination."

"Which is?" Neisie asked.

"The Glammarian Sector of the Milky Way Galaxy," Galamagne replied. "We will be searching through it for the space fleet of the Fellowship of Darkness. It must be found before it can invade and destroy Tellus."

Lucane tried to sense where in the Glammarian Sector it was hiding. "My mystical sense cannot get an exact reading on them. I may need the balanced powers of light and dark to help us find them."

When the *Nebula Stallion* was far enough from Tellus, the Space Chevalier engaged teleport drive. The ship telejumped to the Glammarian Sector.

****

In Docking Bay Thirty-Two, Enforcer Darthan, the Marveltrooper, readied his ship, the *Quasar Storm*, for take-off to join the other two vessels carrying Universal Marshals on the mission to locate the space fleet of the Archvillain organization. Both the *Aurora Moth* and the *Nebula Stallion* had a head start.

Darthan stood six feet one. He wore a unisuit like a space trooper, except his was blue. The helmet over his head hid his sandy hair, brown eyes, and a clean-shaven face. In fact, his unisuit covered his entire body and hid his human appearance. Around his waist hung a utility belt with equipment on it. He carried a blast rifle.

The *Quasar Storm* was a vessel the size of a battlecruiser. His ship was a warship that could also be used as a military transport. She was shaped like a bullet flattened on top and bottom, winged, standing on four short legs with a ramp that lowered in the front. It was lowered at the moment. Darthan waited at the bottom of the ramp after he finished his maintenance check of the vessel, his blast rifle fully charged, but the safety on.

A pair of Universal Marshals walked into the docking bay and met Darthan. The first was Sharminival, the Energy Being, who appeared in the life form of a female humanoid. She was made of pure energy and looked thirty years old in Earth terms. Her auburn hair was long and never bound, her auburn eyes bright and clear. She wore a pantsuit, casual wear off-white, like her comfortable shoes and the thin belt around her slender waist. Unlike the Marveltrooper, she went unarmed. Her special powers, which resided on the scientific level, were the only weapons she needed.

With Sharminival was Enforcer Ramairgan. The Incarnation of Power carried his Rod of Power with him. Hermit Power had been assigned to the mission by the High Enforcer after he returned to the Justiceplex from the Universal Prisonplex.

"Where do we begin our search in the galaxy for it?" Sharminival asked the Marveltrooper.

Darthan hefted his blast rifle over his shoulder. "The space fleet of the Fellowship of Darkness is based somewhere in the Glammarian Sector of the Milky Way Galaxy. We need to locate it for a space fleet of the Federation to intercept it and stop the invasion of Tellus from happening."

Ramairgan frowned. "Take your best guess where you think in the Glammarian Sector it could be stationed."

"All right," Darthan responded. "My guess is it is near an inhabited planet there. A world with a primitive culture where it can visit without suspicion."

"Any other possibilities?" Sharminival asked.

"Certainly," Darthan replied. "It could be hiding in an asteroid belt. Or it could be hiding inside a nebula. Another possibility is it could be hiding in a dimension outside the normal space of the Glammarian Sector. There are a number of possibilities."

Sharminival agreed. "One of those possibilities has to be it. All we have to do is find the one that is right."

"It is a riddle to solve," Remairgan remarked.

"We can find it by process of elimination," Darthan said. "When we come to the correct one, we stop looking."

Sharminival seconded that. "Then the Federation sends its own ships and clashes with the space fleet of the Fellowship of Darkness to destroy the enemy vessels."

"That is the plan," Darthan said.

"Sounds simple," Sharminival remarked.

Ramairgan nodded. "But accomplishing it is not."

"All right," Darthan said. "Come aboard, and we can travel."

The three of them walked up the ramp of the *Quasar Storm*. They went to the bridge of the ship. Darthan sat in the captain's chair as Sharminival took a seat at the communications console while Ramairgan stationed himself before the navigation console. The vessel ran on automated systems for the mission, and the main computer on the bridge operated both helm and navigation and the science console. The Marveltrooper had manual control over the weapons and tactical console from his seat, but in an instant could switch it to automatic control and let the bridge computer handle it, if the ship were under attack by enemy vessels.

"Computer, close ramp," Darthan ordered. It complied with his verbal command, and the ramp raised closed. "Ignite engines. Thrusters on."

"Affirmative," the bridge computer acknowledged in a female voice.

"Open roof, computer," Darthan ordered.

"Opening roof of docking bay. Ship ready to enter the atmosphere for space."

"All right," Darthan said. "Take us out of the hangar structure at impulse power. Increase to regular speed once we are high enough in the atmosphere."

"Affirmative," the bridge computer acknowledged.

Darthan set his blast rifle on the floor behind his chair. "Set telejump coordinates on the navigation system for the Glammarian Sector of the Milky Way Galaxy. Engage the teleport drive when the *Quasar Storm* is out of the orbiting range of Tellus."

"Telejump coordinates set. Teleport drive will engage in three minutes."

The ship left the docking bay, and the roof closed behind the lifting vessel. Next, she zoomed through the atmosphere and into space. When the *Quasar Storm* went beyond orbiting range of Tellus, the bridge computer engaged the teleport drive, and the ship vanished from normal space into the teledimension. The vessel reappeared instantaneously in the Glammarian Sector of the Milky Way Galaxy.

****

The *Aurora Moth* entered and began searching through the Glammarian Sector of the Milky Way Galaxy.

"What is known about this part of the galaxy?" Barbrielle asked the Interstellar Pilgrim.

"There are a small number of inhabited planets in this sector," Kennedrill replied. "None that are members of the Federation."

Wankatanuka closed his eyes and concentrated with his special powers. "I do not feel them yet. By the power of the Great Spirit, their ships will become known to me. I will know where they harbor in this area of the heavens."

"Are there any outposts?" Barbrielle asked the Interstellar Pilgrim.

Kennedrill checked with the ship's computer about all the information he had on the Glammarian Sector. "One Federation outpost. Several nonFederation outposts. Visits by Federation ships in this sector are infrequent. Few contacts made by the Federation with sapient species of inhabited planets."

"What about Archvillain activity?" Barbrielle asked.

Kennedrill looked at the information on the ship's computer. "Hardly any Archvillain activity in this sector has been recorded by the Federation. Most of the activity in this sector has been by alien races."

"I sense a force in this part of the heavens," Wankatanuka remarked.

"The data banks here list a wormhole in the center of this sector," Kennedrill told them. "Unexplored by the Federation."

"Any other ships in this part of the galaxy in sight?" Barbrielle asked the Interstellar Pilgrim.

"Scanning," Kennedrill replied. "No vessels in sensor range at this time."

The Interstellar Pilgrim continued a sensor sweep of the sector. His ship flew at a regular—sublight—speed as they searched far and wide for the space fleet of the Fellowship of Darkness. He checked on his ship's computer for any other astronomical phenomena in the sector. Besides the wormhole, nothing else was listed in the data banks.

"What about reports of space pirates?" Barbrielle asked the Interstellar Pilgrim.

Kennedrill checked with the ship's computer. "Very

little activity. This sector has a low rate of evil existing in it."

Barbrielle seemed pleased by that. "What about waves of invasions by alien races?"

"This sector has had its share of them," Kennedrill replied after a glance through the data banks. "None of them had spread beyond the boundaries of this sector. All minor in degree."

Wankatanuka sensed the supernatural in the Glammarian Sector. "I sense no presence of magic or higher forces in this part of the heavens either. It is relatively peaceful here. No scent of coming evil here and no past danger here in the last ten seasons to attract attention."

They traveled a distance across the Glammarian Sector of the Milky Way Galaxy. Their sensors detected nothing unusual in range in that part of the galaxy, only natural occurrences in the extensive area of space, like a passing comet and solar flares from a sun. The sensors did pick up a gravitational distortion in space, a very large star in the process of going supernova in the future, but that was not a concern to them. It would only be a concern to them if an Archvillain had triggered the upcoming explosion of the celestial body of enormous mass. Wankatanuka sensed that the supernova was a natural occurrence in the galaxy and not the handiwork of a foul being. The Manitou-Enforcer mentioned it to Lady Luck and the Interstellar Pilgrim.

Their search through the Glammarian Sector started to look like a waste of time. The only ship they had encountered so far was an alien freighter traveling between two sister planets in a solar system of no real consequence to the Federation. The only other thing they ran into, briefly, was a mining operation by a humanoid race in an asteroid belt near a quasar.

"This is fruitless," Barbrielle said.

Kennedrill piloted his ship in a new direction. "The information we received about the location of the space fleet could have been in error."

"The ships of the Fellowship of Darkness have to be harbored somewhere in the heavens," Wakatanuka stated. "They have to begin their attack from some point of origin."

Kennedrill agreed. "It would seem logical if their armada of vessels were based in space near their Archvillain stronghold on Earth."

"But that would seem too obvious," Barbrielle pointed out. "The Fellowship of Darkness would not want their fleet of ships easily found."

"True," Kennedrill acknowledged. "We need to pick up their trail. Either as a group or an individual vessel returning to the group."

"I still sense nothing of them in the heavens," Wankatanuka said, a bit frustrated.

"Patience, you supernatural force," Barbrielle responded. "With a little luck, we will find the enemy fleet before it leaves their spaceport to invade Tellus."

"They are on the warpath already," Wankatanuka remarked.

Barbrielle could not disagree with that. Lady Luck used more of her special powers to help them in their search. She asked the Manitou-Enforcer, "As a highly evolved soul-mind, how often have you had to communicate through shamans in the galaxy to bring healing methods, continual knowledge, and true prophecy to their tribes?"

"I was called upon many times by them to help their tribes before I walked the path of a Universal Marshal," Wankatanuka answered. "When I am no longer an Enforcer, they will be able to call upon me again to help their tribes."

Kennedrill jumped in his chair when he scanned long range in the solar system nearest them. "Sensors indicate a large vessel is leaving a planet identified as Exxonor for its smaller moon."

"What is so unusual about that?" Barbrielle asked.

"Exxonor is a small planet inhabited by a primitive people," Kennedrill explained. "According to my computer, it is a forest world with a simple culture and no technology."

"Then let's go check it out," Barbrielle said.

Kennedrill changed course and piloted the *Aurora Moth* for Exxonor. As the ship approached the solar system where the planet orbited, the Interstellar Pilgrim ran a spectral analysis on residual traces of particle trails left by ships in the solar system with the ship's computer. "This area of space has seen heavy traffic of vessels flying through it."

"Still tracking that ship?" Barbrielle asked.

"Yes," Kennedrill replied. He scanned and picked up a new reading. "Sensors indicate a rift has appeared near the smaller moon of Exxonor."

"Is it a wormhole?" Barbrielle asked.

Kennedrill checked it with the ship's computer. "No. It registers as a gateway to space."

Wankatanuka sensed it. "I feel the presence of another world beyond that gateway. Not normal."

Kennedrill swore. "The vessel has disappeared into the rift, and the rift has vanished. Sensors detect nothing now."

"We should investigate this," Barbrielle said.

The Interstellar Pilgrim and the Manitou-Enforcer agreed. Kennedrill piloted the *Aurora Moth* to the spot where the rift had opened and closed. The view from the bridge window showed them only normal space where the rift had been.

"I don't think we should get too close to the spot," Barbrielle suggested.

Kennedrill maneuvered the *Aurora Moth* to be between the spot where the rift had been and the smaller moon of Exxonor. "If necessary, we can hide behind the natural satellite in case the rift opens again and something comes through it that we best hide from. Especially avoid being forced to go to battle station."

The rift suddenly reappeared as they neared it. From the bridge window, they saw space beyond the rift. From the rift, issued five ships in a tight formation.

"Space destroyers!" Kennedrill remarked. "The space fleet of the Fellowship of Darkness is using a spacing device!" A spacing device was a machine that created an area of space beyond the fabric of reality, normal space.

"Quick!" Barbrielle said. "Cloak us!"

Wankatanuka frowned. "Too late. They know of our presence. Attack is eminent."

The space destroyers detected them and converged on the *Aurora Moth*. No communication from the attacking vessels for them to surrender. Instead, the enemy ships fired lasers at the *Aurora Moth*.

Kennedrill piloted his ship in evasive maneuvers.

"Shields up," Wankatanuka said. "Weapons ready."

Laser fire struck the *Aurora Moth* from behind. The

space destroyers spread out to try and encircle the vessel. Kennedrill prepared to engage the superluminal drive of the ship, but before it could jump to faster-than-light travel, laser fire pounded the *Aurora Moth*. Sparks flew on the bridge of the fleeing vessel.

"Any damage?" Barbrielle asked the Interstellar Pilgrim.

Kennedrill grimaced. "The superluminal drive has been hit. It needs to be repaired fast."

"We're easy prey now," Wankatanuka remarked.

Kennedrill shot to his feet. "Lady Luck, take the helm. I'm going to engineering to repair the superluminal drive."

Barbrielle piloted the ship as the Interstellar Pilgrim ran off the bridge toward the back of the vessel to engineering. The Manitou-Enforcer operated the weapons console and fired lasers from the *Aurora Moth* at the enemy ships. He scored a hit on one of the space destroyers, striking its bridge section.

"We need reinforcements," Barbrielle remarked. She piloted the ship with one hand and, with the other, sent communications to the other two ships of Enforcers in the Glammarian Sector of the Milky Way Galaxy via telespace channel.

The space destroyers chased them through the solar system. Lasers from the five ships could not destroy the *Aurora Moth* with a single shot, but they could pound it to death, which was what the enemy ships were trying to do. The rift stayed open though nothing else issued from it.

"How are the shields holding up?" Barbrielle asked the Manitou-Enforcer.

"Shields down to ninety-six percent," Wankatanuka

replied.

The Manitou-Enforcer fired a spread of antimatter torpedoes aft. Behind the *Aurora Moth*.

Space destroyers banked sharply to avoid the path of the torpedoes, but one vessel was too slow and got hit. Blasts rocked it and damaged it in several places, including the engineering section. It careened to a stop and listed in space.

Three space destroyers appeared ahead of the *Aurora Moth* and forced the ship to make a 180-degree turn back in the direction of the rift. The enemy ships tried to lock tractor beams on the *Aurora Moth*, but Lady Luck dodged them, and the Manitou-Enforcer fired lasers to try and knocked them out from the attacking vessels. The space destroyers retaliated with laser fire and scorched the *Aurora Moth* as the ship zigzagged in defense to minimize hits against it.

"Is it repaired yet?" Barbrielle asked the Interstellar Pilgrim over the intercom. "Things are getting desperate here."

Kennedrill replied over the intercom. "Not quite. You must give me a little more time."

"We're running out of time," Barbrielle said. Lady Luck used her special powers to help them a bit.

The remaining four space destroyers were starting to close the net against the *Aurora Moth*. They continued pounding the ship with laser fire. As it looked like the *Aurora Moth* was about to be snared, a space destroyer exploded a distance off the starboard side of the vessel.

Into sensor range flew the *Nebula Stallion* and the *Quasar Storm* to the rescue of the *Aurora Moth*. The two ships evened the odds against the enemy ones. The three vessels of Universal Marshals battled the space destroyers, which were bigger than the former.

Barbrielle received a communication from the *Nebula Storm*. "News?"

Neisie spoke on the telespace channel from the bridge of the *Nebula Stallion*. "I sent a message to Tellus before we arrived. We may have Federation ships coming to our aid."

The *Quasar Storm* linked to the telespace channel between the *Aurora Moth* and the *Nebula Stallion*. From the bridge of the *Quasar Storm* Sharminival communicated to the other two ships. "After this, we might be sent to Earth to help the Enforcer Squad."

From the rift issued more ships. Three battlecruisers and a spacecraft carrier flew to reinforce the space destroyers. From the spacecraft carrier, enemy fighters launched in numbers to help capture or destroy the three ships of the Enforcers. The battlecruisers fired lasers at the vessels of the Universal Marshals.

"We have to retreat!" Sharminival communicated to the *Aurora Moth* and the *Nebula Stallion*. "We cannot win this fight without aid."

"Agreed," Neisie responded for the *Nebula Stallion*.

"Yes," Barbrielle seconded for the *Aurora Moth*. Over the intercom, she contacted the Interstellar Pilgrim. "We need it now, or the ship faces destruction."

"Almost there," Kennedrill replied over the intercom.

Laser fire from enemy fighters and ships began overwhelming the three vessels of Universal Marshals. The *Nebula Stallion* and the *Quasar Storm* fired parting shots before they engaged their teleport drives. Both ships disappeared from normal space to fly back to Tellus.

Hostile craft closed a noose around the *Aurora Moth*. Lady Luck piloted the ship in evasive maneuvers as the vessel returned fire. Now from the rift, another space destroyer appeared. The Manitou-Enforcer shot another spread of antimatter torpedoes.

"We need to leave this instant," Barbrielle said over the intercom to the Interstellar Pilgrim. "Our luck is about to run out. They are readying to finish us off."

The *Aurora Moth* got pounded by laser fire. Enemy ships prepared to destroy it with a bombardment of antimatter torpedoes.

Kennedrill spoke over the intercom. "Drive restored. Punch it!"

Lady Luck engaged the superluminal drive of the *Aurora Moth,* and then it disappeared from normal space at faster-than-light speed. The vessel escaped the trap of the enemy ships as their torpedoes destroyed nothing but empty space. Multiple blasts shook the solar system as the *Aurora Moth* flew back to Tellus.

Chapter 23

Delveran let Nanomach keep track of the three ships of Enforcers the High Enforcer sent to search for the space fleet of the Fellowship of Darkness in the Glammarian Sector of the Milky Way Galaxy. Right now, the Grand Universal Marshal turned his attention to emergency procedures for the possible invasion of Tellus. He worked from his office in the Justiceplex.

After reviewing emergency procedures, Delveran used the telecom on his desk and contacted authorities at the Defenseplex, where it housed the warding device of Tellus in Acropollon, not far from the Militaryplex at the northeast edge of the planet's capital.

"Sergeant Teppon Damus here," a male voice answered over the telecom.

"This is the High Enforcer."

"Yes, sir. What can I do for you?"

"Have you increased security around the warding device?"

"Yes, sir. Colonel Ramdar gave the order after learning of the invasion plan by the Archvillain organization."

"Thank you, sergeant. That will be all for now. Good-bye."

The communication ended. Logically, Delveran figured the first target of the space fleet of the Fellowship of Darkness would be the warding device, a machine that erected a defense shield of the three basic energy powers around Tellus against any and all external threats to the planet. Nothing could enter or leave the world once the warding device was activated. That would force the space fleet of the Archvillain organization to lay siege to Tellus from space.

Delveran used the telecom again and immediately contacted the Teleportplex. The High Enforcer got the alien Akmosh Natiki, chief of teleportation. "Good day, chief."

"High Enforcer. How may I help you?"

"Have evacuation plans been completed for Tellus in case the invasion succeeds?"

"Yes. Per instructions of our government and the Federation Assembly on your word."

"Good. I shall contact you later. I will need the use of a telechamber."

"As you wish, High Enforcer. Until later."

Delveran ended the communication. He switched from the telecom to the intercom and called for Enforcers Chryssina and Rorbash. In five minutes, the pair of Universal Marshals entered his office to stand before him.

The smaller of the two, Enforcer Chryssina, the Light Being, looked really puny compared to her giant companion. Chryssina brushed a few strands of her long, strawberry-blonde hair from her sapphire-blue eyes, her lithe figure clad in a white jumpsuit and white shoes. Her pretty face seemed that of a child. She was the youngest of the Universal Marshals and had served as an Enforcer for the shortest time thus far, barring any new Universal Marshals. Her antipower handcuffs rested in the back pocket of her jumpsuit. Her special powers resided on the scientific level, involving light.

Enforcer Rorbash, the Dragonling, towered above both the Light Being and the High Enforcer at over eleven feet tall, the third largest of the Universal Marshals. Rorbash swished his long tail behind him, his leathery wings folded tight against his large frame at the moment. The green eyes of the High Enforcer paled in color in comparison to the emerald-green scaly body of the Dragonling, whose big black eyes rolled in deep sockets like shiny liquid. Rorbash split his reptilian snout to show sharp teeth. His antipower handcuffs were locked around the bottom of his white horns. The Dragonling wore no clothing.

"I have a task for the two of you," Delveran said. "Go to the Defenseplex and guard the warding device." His two fellow Enforcers understood the job fully. "Later, I will send two other Universal Marshals to relieve you."

They acknowledged him and left his office. Delveran watched them go as they went to the teleporter room of the Justiceplex to teleport to the Defenseplex and carry out their assignment.

The High Enforcer felt much better that Universal Marshals guarded the warding device. If the machine was made inoperative or was destroyed, Tellus would be open to invasion from the space fleet of the Fellowship of Darkness.

Delveran contacted Nanomach on the intercom. "How are all the preparations against the invasion progressing?"

"By my calculations, they will be completed before the attack of the space fleet of the Archvillain organization commences," Nanomach responded.

That bit of news lightened Delveran's mood. "Increase security measures around the Justiceplex."

"Affirmative," Nanomach acknowledged.

"How many Universal Marshals are now on Tellus?"

"Eighteen."

"Any word from our search vessels?"

"Negative. The last report from the three teams of Enforcers was thirty-six hours ago."

This worried Delveran. The High Enforcer thought they should have reported in again already. "Locate Medeordese and Thayla."

"Working." Nanomach searched Tellus for them via his own scanners. "I have located them."

"Where are they?"

"In the Universal Prisonplex."

"Relay a message to them. Tell them to relieve Chryssina and Rorbash at the Defenseplex in seven hours."

"Affirmative." Nanomach signed off and implemented his orders.

Delveran got to his feet and left his office. He headed for the teleporter room of the Justiceplex, leaving Nanomach in charge of the place. When he was away from headquarters, he usually left the Computer-Enforcer in charge. The High Enforcer punched in the teleport console coordinates for the Militaryplex and activated its autoteleportist, then stepped onto the telegrid after giving Nanomach additional instructions over the intercom. Instantly, the autoteleportist engaged itself and teleported him to the teleporter room of the Militaryplex.

"Greetings, sir," a military teleportist said, a female

humanoid, sitting behind a teleport console. "Who do you wish to see?"

Delveran smiled. "Colonel Ramdar."

"I'll let him know you're here."

"Thank you." She notified the colonel of his visit over a telecom.

Delveran left the teleporter room and walked over to a turbolift. Its doors opened for him and he entered it, taking it up to the fifth floor. He got off the turbolift and walked down a long corridor to the office of Colonel Ramdar. On both sides of him stood automatic doors to other rooms.

Delveran entered the office. Colonel Ramdar greeted him. Ramdar, a middle-aged man, human, as tall as Delveran, wore a green unisuit, green boots, a green belt, and nothing on his head at the moment. Before the colonel spread a holographic globe of Tellus over his desk in three-dimensional color. Ramdar mapped out military strategy on the globe through the control console before him—red stars, yellow lines, and green arrows marked on the globe to indicate strategic moves.

Right of the colonel a telescreen covered the wall. To his left, against the wall, operated a military computer sandwiched between a file cabinet and a storage cabinet. Behind the colonel, two monitors with large screens showing three-dimensional images, one inside the Militaryplex, the other outside the building. Across the desk stood automatic doors. Ramdar sat in a swivel chair, green padded. Glowpanels in the ceiling lighted the office.

Delveran lifted his cape out of the way and sat in one of the three armchairs before the desk. "How many combat vessels do you have on Tellus?"

Ramdar answered momentarily. "There are seven battlecruisers."

Delveran wondered how much of the Tellusian armed forces and Federation units remained on the planet. The Tellus military consisted of four main branches: land troopers, sea troopers, air troopers, and space troopers.

"Any information about the size of the space fleet of the Archvillain organization?" Ramdar asked.

"Not yet," Delveran replied. "But we figure it must be very large in order for the Fellowship of Darkness to succeed in conquering Tellus and breaking out all the Archvillains in the Universal Prisonplex."

Ramdar agreed. The colonel served as a military advisor to the High Enforcer concerning the coming invasion. In fact, a number of military advisors on both Survarille and Mellenroel served the Grand Universal Marshal.

"Have you already assigned a Universal Marshal to set the defense for each of the battle areas where we will combat the invasion?" Ramdar asked.

Delveran nodded. In his name and by his orders, Enforcer Bolan Trevarre, the Noble Soldier, oversaw the land defense. Enforcer Wardelorean, the Dreadnought, oversaw the sea defense. Yauriga, the Avatar-Enforcer known as the Charioteer, oversaw the air defense. Lastly, Ulleric, the Dynaman, oversaw the space defense.

"Are all military vehicles for land and craft for sea and air ready for combat?" Delveran asked.

"Yes," Ramdar replied. "All are set to defend Tellus."

Delveran was satisfied with the progress of the defense of Tellus. "Relay orders for all combat vessels for space to ring Tellus in defensive positions fairly distant from the planet."

"Yes, sir. Anything else?"

Delveran thought about what other moves to make. "Put a military unit around the Defenseplex outside and inside the structure, particularly the room housing the warding device. The machine needs ample protection against open assaults or sneak attacks to destroy it by the Fellowship of Darkness."

Ramdar relayed both orders on the intercom to subordinates to carry out. "They might try suicide squads to destroy the warding device."

"I would not be surprised if they did," Delveran responded. "The greatest threat to the warding device would be if the Fellowship of Darkness sent Archvillains to try and destroy it."

"That makes sense," Ramdar said. "Do you wish to assign ships for other duties in space against the oncoming invasion?"

"Yes," Delevarn replied. "For patrol and for reconnaissance of our sector. One of the battlecruisers here will have to be spared."

"Yes, sir," Ramdar said. He relayed more orders over the intercom. "Do you want any Universal Marshals on our battlecruisers in space?"

Delveran considered it. "I will assign Ulleric to be on the warship for patrol and reconnaissance of the sector."

"Where is the Dynaman?"

"Contact Nanomach for his whereabouts."

"Yes, sir," Ramdar called the Computer-Enforcer on his telecom. "This is Colonel Ramdar at the Militaryplex. The High Enforcer is with me. Where is Enforcer

Ulleric?"

The Computer-Enforcer responded in a moment. "He has just returned to the Justiceplex."

"The High Enforcer is assigning him to a battlecruiser for patrol and reconnaissance of our sector," Ramdar said.

Nanomach beeped. "I will inform the Dynaman."

The communication ended.

Ramdar turned to the High Enforcer. "What about magic for the defense of our planet?"

"I am working with the Occultplex to coordinate it," Delveran said. "There are plenty of practitioners, namely from Mellenroel."

"What about the Celestoryplex?" Ramdar asked.

Delveran smiled. "It is involved in the defense planning of our planet." He rose to his feet. "I shall leave you now."

Ramdar saluted him. "Where will you be, sir?"

"At the Justiceplex."

Delveran exited the colonel's office and took a turbolift down to the first floor of the Militaryplex. He went to the teleporter room and traveled to the Justiceplex. The High Enforcer went to his office.

Inside his office, Delevran checked messages on his telecom. There were two of them. The first came from the head of the Occultplex, the occult master Pallandon. He played the message.

"High Enforcer, the membership awaits further instructions on what defense plans for Tellus you want the Occultplex to enact on your behalf to stop the invasion. Contact me. We wait to hear from you."

Delveran sighed. The High Enforcer listened to the second message. It came from the head of the

Celestoryplex, the celestory master Vishnumars. "High Enforcer, your associates of the Celestoryplex are inquiring what additional measures for Tellus you wish for us to take to aid in the defeat of the space fleet of the Fellowship of Darkness. Get in touch with us. We are standing by, ready to serve you."

Delveran deleted both messages from the telecom. The High Enforcer already formed more defense plans for Tellus involving the parts the Occultplex and the Celestoryplex would play to help stop the oncoming invasion. He called Selmajase, the Glaistig-Enforcer, on the intercom.

She assisted him with what part the Occultplex would play in the defense plans for Tellus against the invasion. "Are you finished?"

"Yes," Selmajase answered. "All drawn up in detail to show them now."

Delveran smiled. "Teleport to the Occultplex. Explain to its membership what all their roles are in the upcoming fight against the space fleet of the Fellowship of Darkness. The defenses of Tellus must be completely set before the enemy attacks our world."

"Aye," Selmajase agreed.

"If the membership of the Occultplex makes any suggestions about the overall defense plans, inform me," Delveran said. "We will incorporate any changes to them they advise that are appropriate."

"By your command," Selmajase responded. She signed off. The Glaistig-Enforcer carried out his orders.

Delveran called Enforcer Glyndalyn, Mother Nature, on the intercom next. She assisted him with what part the Celestoryplex would play in the defense plans for Tellus against the invasion. "Are you finished?"

"Already done and ready to present," Glyndalyn replied.

"Good," Delveran said. "Teleport to the Celestoryplex. Explain to its membership what all their roles are in the upcoming fight against the space fleet of the Fellowship of Darkness. As I told Selmajase, the defenses of Tellus must be completely set before the enemy attacks our world."

"Naturally," Glyndalyn responded.

Delveran wanted to update progress regarding the matter of the Archvillain organization. "If the membership of the Celestoryplex makes any suggestions about the overall defense plans, inform me. We will incorporate any changes to them that are appropriate."

"It will be done," Glyndalyn acknowledged. She signed off. Mother Nature carried out his orders.

Delveran pondered what to do next. Just then, his telecom beeped. The High Enforcer answered it. "Yes?"

"This is Fahren Galileia." He was the chief scientist and head of the Scienceplex. "We request what you want the Scienceplex membership to do in the defense plans for Tellus against the invasion."

"Your part is already decided in them," Delveran responded. "Brinivere has been assisting me in regards to what help you will provide against the invasion." Enforcer Brinivere, the Cellular Being, besides being a Universal Marshal, was also a biologist and a member of the Scienceplex. "I shall have her teleport to you and present the overall defense plans to your membership. She will also explain all your roles in the upcoming fight against the space fleet of the Fellowship of Darkness."

"Very well. We will hold an emergency meeting and let her relate the details of them to the membership."

Fahren signed off.

Delveran called the Cellular Being over the intercom. "You are to teleport to the Scienceplex and tell its members the overall defense plans for Tellus against the invasion and what all their roles are against the space fleet of the Fellowship of Darkness."

"On my way," Brinivere acknowledged. She signed off. The Cellular Being carried out his orders.

Delveran contacted the Computer-Enforcer over the intercom. "After Brinivere, Selmajase, and Glyndalyn have finished speaking with the respective memberships, have them coordinate the parts of the defense plans for Tellus involving the Scienceplex, Occultplex, and Celestoryplex."

"Affirmative," Nanomach responded.

"Then coordinate all parts in the defense plans for Tellus. The quicker they are all set and unified, the better they will be and the stronger we can oppose the enemy space fleet."

"Affirmative." Nanomach signed off. The Computer-Enforcer carried out his orders.

Deleveran tried to relax. The High Enforcer felt much strain and a lot of stress commanding the defenses of Tellus against the impending invasion. He took ten slow, deep breaths to still his body and calm his mind. When he finished, Findall and Arboron entered his office.

The two Enforcers were an extreme contrast in size. Findall was the smallest of the Universal Marshals, while Arboron was the largest of the Universal Marshals. Delveran thought that quite odd, the pairing of a giant being with a dwarf being.

Findall belonged to the race of faerie. Known as the

Habble-Enforcer, he stood only three feet tall. His thick white hair curled around his pointy ears, and bangs draped above his silver eyes; his small nose twitched as if casting a spell. He wore a brown vest over a white tunic with brown pants and brown shoes. A tool belt around his small waist held delicate and shiny instruments, for Findall was a master craftsman who could fix or create magical objects. Inside his vest, he hid his magic slingshot, and hanging from the back of his toolbelt was a pair of antipower handcuffs.

Arboron, in comparison to his diminutive companion, wore no clothing and towered over fourteen feet. He looked as if he could step on Findall and squash him underfoot. In truth, he and Findall were best friends. Called the Treeling-Enforcer, Arboron belonged to the ancient race of tree beings, the Dendronii, or Treelings. He walked on roots like feet, his grayish-brown trunk was serrated, and long branches served as his arms with huge hands. A thick crown of leaves constituted his hair above a long face featuring big grayish-brown eyes, a bulbous nose, a large mouth, and a short beard of moss. He had thick eyebrows of moss, and his tree bark was of a dense hardwood. Like Delevarn and Findall, he possessed special powers on the occultic level. The three of them were magical creatures.

Delveran looked at them both and thought. "You can help me in the magic chamber."

"A magical creation?" Findall asked.

"Yes," Delveran replied.

Arboron shook leaves on his crown. "What creature are you going to sprout?"

Delveran rose to his feet. "A sending."

Findall fingered an instrument on his tool belt.

271

"What purpose?"

"To command it against the space fleet of the Fellowship of Darkness," Delveran explained. "It may not stop the invasion from happening, but it can slow it down a little."

"Root and twig," Arboron said. "Our acorn will be a growing thing that will instill fear in the enemy. Maybe plant a seed for their destruction."

"We shall see how much damage it can inflict against them," Delveran promised.

Findall grinned. "Enough to give them pause."

Delveran led Findall and Arboron from his office down the main corridor of the Justiceplex to the magic chamber. The magic chamber was for the use of Enforcers who could perform magic rituals on the occultic or celestic level for professional reasons— Enforcer business. Universal Marshals performed magic rituals of a private type in their own quarters.

The magic chamber was large and was automated with hologram programs of magic. Panels opened in the walls to cabinets filled with tools of the occult arts and celestic sciences. The floor was bare for the moment. Glowpanels lit the room as they entered.

"Computer, we need a circle on the floor and a pentagram in the circle," Delveran said.

The computer of the magic chamber responded in a feminine voice as it began operation. "What circumference and color for the circle and pentagram?"

"A nine-foot ring and both mystic symbols are to be white," Delveran replied. "Also, an altar for magic use with a white cloth on it."

The computer complied. A magic circle and a pentagram of white appeared in the middle of the floor.

Near the mystic symbols materialized an altar with a white cloth on it. The High Enforcer went to a wall cabinet, opened it, and took out of it occult tools for the magic ritual to create a sending. He put a gold candle in the upper left corner and a gold candle in the upper right corner of the altar. In the center of the altar, he put a briarwood incense cone in a censer. A bowl of water he put in the lower left corner of the altar, and a bowl of agomorrah oil he put in the lower right corner of the altar.

"We can begin the Sending Creation Ritual," Delveran said.

The High Enforcer stood behind the magic circle near the top of the pentagram as the Habble-Enforcer and the Treeling-Enforcer formed with him three points of a triangle around the mystic symbols. He had more experience than them in creating sendings, which in the occult were made most by sorcerers and alchemists. Faerie beings were second in creating sendings, usually by those who were masters of magic. Though Findall was of the race of faerie and versed enough in magic— but not as experienced as the Grand Universal Marshal— the Habble-Enforcer did not specialize in creating sendings, for he practiced magic of a different sort. Arboron practiced magic the least of the three— Dendronii were not occultists generally, though occasionally they did do it—the Treeling-Enforcer had practiced magic to a degree, enough to be familiar with it and skilled enough to work with serious practitioners.

Delveran had created sendings many times while Findall and Arboron had done it a few times.

"*Aglamour ock hovah enth,*" Delveran intoned. "The veil is lifted which separates the two worlds of the natural and supernatural."

The High Enforcer took the bowl of the agomorrah oil, walked around the magic circle, and anointed each point of the pentagram with the agomorrah oil. After he returned the bowl to its altar place, he took the bowl of water and sprinkled drops inside the pentagram. Then he returned what was left of the water to its altar place.

Delveran continued. "The power of spirit shall bring forth life to be created. *Cree ack espiri gno biosh.*"

The High Enforcer lighted the two candles on the altar with green fire from his glowing hands. Next, he lighted the incense the same way. Then he nodded to the Habble-Enforcer and the Treeling-Enforcer. They all closed their eyes and together concentrated on creating the sending, which in part was a magical extension of their own selves. Their combined magic gave life energy to the birth of the magical creature.

"Euboreas, Spirit of the East Wind, I call thee," Delveran intoned. "Nafujinni, Spirit of the South Wind, I call thee. Vahtar, Spirit of the West Wind, I call thee. Aeoborg, Spirit of the North Wind, I call thee. *Mahteh rawkoth tiber familia.*"

A blue mist coalesced in the center of the pentagram. It glowed and vibrated with supernatural force. The three of them concentrated harder to mold the blue mist into the magical form of a sending. They recited in unison mystic words.

"The power of we three command thee to shape and be our servant. *Rustique cabal nahiyah pyrexus.*"

The blue mist took solid form. Their combined magic molded it into the shape of a bull. The sending snorted, an advanced version of a spirit familiar.

They spoke in unison again. "We command thee to do our bidding. Go forth and wreak havoc on the space fleet of the Fellowship of Darkness. *Manji espiri grammaton felish.* So mote it be."

The sending stamped its feet and roared like a bull. It obeyed them and disappeared. The magical creation proceeded to its task. They hoped it succeeded against the enemy.

Chapter 24

The Enforcer Squad busied themselves in the *Centaurus* with officers of the NYPD surrounding it to keep other Earthlings from disturbing the Universal Marshals. The ship was decloaked, but its autodefenses were activated as a precaution. Since Earth had discovered their presence, the Enforcer Squad waited for further instructions from the High Enforcer.

Procules worked on the bridge of the vessel. He operated the communications console and established contact with the Justiceplex on Tellus. The Robot-Enforcer also monitored global communications of the Terran world, recording any useful information in the memory banks of the bridge computer and in his memory cells.

"*Centaurus*, this is the Justiceplex," Nanomach said. The Computer-Enforcer telelinked to the bridge computer.

"*Centaurus* here," Procules responded.

Nanomach continued. "The High Enforcer orders that you hold a news conference on Earth. Be very careful what you say to Earth. Do not tell Earth anything that would compromise the security of the Federation or endanger your mission."

"Understood," Procules replied. "Will we be receiving any additional members to the squad?"

"Affirmative," Nanomach said. "Severrin and

Orissa will be joining you in an hour. They will be aboard the battlecruiser *Horizon*."

"Acknowledged," Procules responded.

Their communication ended. The Robot-Enforcer used the ship intercom and informed the rest of the Enforcer Squad of their orders from the High Enforcer and the Universal Marshals that were being sent to join them. Then Procules contacted officials of New York City at City Hall through the communications console and made arrangements for a news conference to be held by the Enforcer Squad there in the near future.

An hour later, in the teleporter room of the *Centaurus,* Vartagal stood at the teleport console to greet the two new members of the Enforcer Squad. The pair of Universal Marshals materialized on the telegrid after being teleported from the *Horizon*.

Orissa, the Sylph-Enforcer, waved at the Great Archer. She was an air elemental, made of air, visible as if someone exhaled cold air and created a female form with their breath. Her figure was slim and sexy, her hair long and buoyant. Orissa wore no clothes, and she hid her antipower handcuffs inside her body. The Sylph-Enforcer was a tall lady with special powers on the occultic level.

Beside her towered Enforcer Severrin, the Colossus. He looked like an animated bronze statue. His bronze skin showed no blemish or mark, his bronze eyes were deep-set, and his bronze hair was cropped. His beardless face was chiseled with distinctive features and altogether he appeared a god among men. Severrin wore a bronze unisuit with a bronze cape and bronze boots. Besides being a Universal Marshal, the Colossus was also a renowned scientist—a metallogist. Metallogy was the science that dealt with the study of metals and alloys. He possessed special powers on the scientific level.

Vartagal led Orissa and Severrin from the teleporter room and showed them their individual quarters. The Great Archer returned to his own room.

In the evening, the Enforcer Squad gathered in the mess hall for dinner and to talk about the news conference they would be holding on Earth. The ten of them discussed how they were going to proceed and what they were going to say to the Terran world. The people of the Terran world would be asking them questions, some of which they already had answers for, others they would have to give on the spot. All agreed that Procules should be the spokesperson for the Enforcer Squad. As the leader, Rathol should be doing it, but the Shepherd knew that the Robot-Enforcer was best qualified to handle the role. They had a pleasant meal despite the situation they were in.

A few days later, the news conference was scheduled. When they were ready, the Enforcer Squad teleported from the *Centaurus* to City Hall in a corridor leading to its hall. Officials of New York City met them and led them into the chamber.

The hall had a lofty ceiling and windows. City Hall was a smoke-free environment.

Reporters sat or stood in the hall waiting for the Enforcer Squad to appear and start the news conference. A long table, with ten microphones on it but only eight chairs behind it, faced windows across the hall. Police ringed the inside of the hall providing heavy security. It was an anticipated and exciting event.

The Enforcer Squad took their places at the table and seated themselves in the chairs, except for the Robot-

Enforcer and the Titan-Enforcer, who stood at opposite ends of the table, unable to sit in chairs. Cameras flashed as photographers took pictures of the Enforcer Squad and television cameras rolled to record live the news conference. A female Earthling, middle-aged with dark hair in a blue pantsuit of formal wear, stepped up to a podium near the table where the Enforcer Squad relaxed and being eyed by a lobby full of Terrans.

"Good afternoon, ladies and gentlemen. I am Monica Franken. This is a momentous occasion for our planet. First contact has been made with other intelligent beings in the universe. We know now that we are no longer alone."

Terrans sitting and standing talked among themselves. The Enforcer Squad looked at the Earthlings without concern.

Monica held up her hands, and the audience became quiet. "So without further delay, let's begin the questioning."

Procules had been designated by the other members of the Enforcer Squad as their chief speaker. The Robot-Enforcer fielded questions from the floor. He pointed at a young white female in a black outfit, sitting in the front row of chairs, holding a tape recorder.

"I'm Carol Stevens of the *New York Times*. Who are you, and why are you here?"

"We are Universal Marshals of the Universal Federation of Planets," Procules answered. He introduced each member of the Enforcer Squad to the Terrans, including himself. "We have come here to arrest a group of foul beings known as Archvillains, who have established a hidden base on your world and threaten our home planet of Tellus."

"What are Archvillains?" Carol asked.

"The most powerful and dangerous of the three evil classes of foul beings in the universe," Procules stated. "The other two evil classes are Criminals and Villains."

Carol crossed her legs. "Just how powerful and dangerous are these Archvillains?"

"They could easily conquer your planet," Procules replied. "Or simply destroy you. You could not stand against them."

That brought shouts from the Terrans as they talked among themselves. The Enforcer Squad remained calm. The Earthlings quieted down after several minutes. Monica restored order.

The Robot-Enforcer pointed at an older white male in the fifth row from the front to address the Enforcer Squad.

"Barry Reasoner, *Times Magazine*. Why didn't you contact us sooner?"

"We were not supposed to contact you at all," Minanket said. "Our mission was a secret one here. Your biosphere was not to know of our existence. Only the battle with the Archvillain Squad—the foul beings we fought on your streets—forced us to reveal ourselves to you."

"As intelligent beings, you should have contacted us," Barry responded.

Procules beeped. "That is not logical. We did not have to contact you. It was our choice if we wished to."

"Why didn't you want us to know of your existence?" Barry asked.

Procules was not rattled by the question. "The Federation has classified you as a planet for noncontact. You are not a member of the Federation. The Federation only communicates with nonmembers that are safe to contact or can meet its basic requirements for possible admission into the Federation." The Robot-Enforcer pointed at a middle-aged black male in the last row.

"Thurgood Gibson, *WKBT news*. What are the requirements to become a member of your Federation?"

Severrin responded to the question. "First, you must have a united world under a planetary government. Second, you must be willing to practice and show, accept and adhere to the guiding principles the Federation follows."

"Does a world have to be technologically advanced to be a member of your Federation?" Thurgood asked.

"No," Severrin replied. "There are planets in the Federation not as advanced as others."

Another white male got the green light from Procules to ask questions of the Enforcer Squad next, sitting four rows from the front. "Henry Mason, *Boston Globe*. What mode of space travel did you use to get here?"

"Teleport drive," Procules answered for the Enforcer Squad. "The instantaneous travel between two points in space anywhere in the universe."

"Do all the members in the Federation use this to travel in space to other worlds?" Henry asked.

"No," Procules said. "There are a number of supernormal ways of space travel, not counting all the regular modes of interstellar flight, in use by the Federation."

That brought gasps from the gathering of Earthlings. It overwhelmed them, including a few scientists among them, especially the one who worked for NASA. The Enforcer Squad said nothing to each other as the members watched the Terrans' reactions.

Henry cleared his throat. "What are some of the other ways of space travel your Federation uses besides teleport drive?"

Procules answered the question. "A few have been written about in your books of science fiction— hyperspace, superluminal drive, and space folding. Others you have not written about in science fiction, such as space juxtaposing, space transposing, and space rifting."

"Would you care to elaborate?" Henry asked.

"That would take too long to explain," Procules said.

The Robot-Enforcer pointed to a young black woman sitting six rows from the front. She stood up.

"Teresa Johnson, *Philadelphia Enquirer*. How many planets are members of your Federation?"

Procules checked his internal files for the correct figure. "The current number of planets that are members of the Federation stands at 1,379. But eleven other planets are being considered for membership in the Federation at this time."

Procules pointed to a Japanese-American male, in the third row from the front. The Terran bowed in respect to the Robot-Enforcer before he spoke.

"Masatsu Toyama, *Los Angeles Herald*. Do you know about alien abductions of people from Earth?"

"Yes," Procules answered.

"Did any planet of your Federation abduct citizens from our world?" Masatsu asked.

"No," Procules replied. "The Federation does not abduct beings from other worlds."

"Could your Federation help get people from Earth

that have been abducted by aliens back?" Masatsu asked.

"The Federation could," Procules said. "But it will not help you."

"Why?" Masatsu asked.

Procules beeped. "Because the Federation will only rescue beings who are citizens of the Federation that have been abducted by aliens."

Masatsu thought of his next question. "How much do you know about alien abductions that have taken place on our planet?"

Procules turned to the rest of the Enforcer Squad. They conferred with the Robot-Enforcer. The Terrans started to become restless.

Vartagal spoke. "The Federation knows everything about it."

"Then why won't the Federation help us get back our citizens who were abducted by aliens?" Masatsu asked.

"Because it's not a problem of the Federation," Minanket answered for them. "It's a problem you should solve."

A young Korean-American male, nine rows from the front, stood up after the Robot-Enforcer pointed at him to talk next. "David Nuyen, *WKXZ news*. Could you help at least solve some of the problems our world faces?"

Severrin responded to the question this time. "All the problems you face on your planet have been faced at one time or another by members of the Federation. They solved all the problems in time. But the Federation will not help you."

"Why not?" David asked.

"Because you must solve your own problems,"

Severrin said. "If the Federation has to solve them for you, your planet will never learn, grow, and develop into a more civilized, more united, and more advanced world."

That stirred the Terrans into an explosion of dialogue among themselves. Some of the Earthlings yelled angry words and more questions at the Enforcer Squad, who were collected before the upset humans. The Universal Marshals could hear many issues being talked about among the Terrans, topics like terrorism, the environment, climate change, the crime rate, and other subjects of importance to the Earthlings. It took federal and city officials to get the news conference going again after they got the throng to quiet down.

A young Hispanic woman got to ask the next question of the Enforcer Squad as she stood up with tape recorder in her hand. "Elizabeth Lopez, *Dallas Gazette*. Does this mean you will just complete your mission and leave our world as if you were never here?"

A bit of rage filled her voice, representing the resentment the Terrans began to feel toward the Enforcer Squad and the Federation. The Universal Marshals were not surprised by the sudden attitude of the Earthlings toward them and the Federation. It did not bother the ten Enforcers, yet it did alert them to growing hostility by the humans.

"There is one thing the Federation might allow," Lorliane said. "The exception the Federation makes to nonFederation planets involves the Enforcers. If you needed legitimate help against evil attacking your world, and if you made proper contact with the Federation, Universal Marshals might be permitted to aid Earth to stop foul beings or whatever evil was attacking your world. Since the Universal Marshals fight evil in all its guises in the universe, your request as such to the Federation falls under the jurisdiction of the Enforcers."

"That's really nice of you," a white male of middle age with glasses on responded from the front row. "Too bad no one from here is a citizen of your Federation."

"Actually," Minanket said, "there is an Earthling who is a citizen of the Federation."

Suddenly excitement shot through the Terrans. The Molecular Being asked his fellow Enforcers if he should have mentioned that fact to the Earthlings. The other Universal Marshals were divided on it.

Elizabeth asked the next question that was on all the minds of the Terrans after they stopped talking to let the news conference continue. "Who?"

Severrin told the Earthlings. "Enforcer Bolan Trevarre, the Noble Soldier."

"How did he become a citizen of your Federation?" Elizabeth asked.

"He was abducted by alien beings visiting, in secret, the Earth," Minanket answered for them. "Universal Marshals rescued him from his captors. The Enforcers discovered he had the potential to become a Universal Marshal. Bolan was given a choice: return to Earth with his memory erased of the abduction or join the Enforcers and become a citizen of the Federation and sever his allegiance to his native planet. He chose us."

Another white woman, in her thirties, stood up to ask the next question after Procules pointed to her in the second row from the front. She wore glasses and a blue dress with black shoes. "Christy Holmes, *Chicago Daily*. How come you speak English so well?"

Orissa spoke for the first time at the news

conference. "The language is spoken on a number of worlds, notably those with races of humans. Before Bolan became a Universal Marshal, beings from the Federation studied your world and learned to speak it. There were even those in the Federation who visited your world before they became citizens of the Federation, including several Enforcers currently serving."

"Like who?" Christy asked.

"Enforcer Milantheus, Father Time, and Enforcer Glyndalyn, Mother Nature," Orissa said.

"Father Time?" Christy repeated. "Mother Nature?"

"Many of the beings and creatures in your myths and legends are real inhabitants of the universe," Eneysa stated.

"Unfortunately, that also includes Archvillains," Vartagal added.

"What Archvillains?" Christy asked.

"Faerie beings and wereanimals who are evil," Lorliane said. "There are a vast number of foul beings from your myths and legends who are Archvillains."

"And a vast number of foul beings not from your myths and legends who are Archvillains," Minanket finished for the Ice Being.

"Enough of both to give you plenty of nightmares," Eneysa added.

Christy, like the other Terrans, seemed a little nervous now. "How often have Archvillains victimized Earth?"

Procules beeped. "Occasionally. Not enough to warrant the Federation to send Universal Marshals to Earth to arrest any. Until now."

"So Universal Marshals have come to save our world from a bunch of Archvillains," Christy said.

"Yes," Severrin responded. "They might decide to move their stronghold to another planet and destroy your world if they are given a reason to do so."

Christy perspired, along with the other Terrans, at that. "Then you better save our world from them."

"Aye," Jagathan agreed for the Enforcer Squad.

"Anyway," Lorliane interjected, "Bolan becoming a Universal Marshal caused—as your world would say—a craze to speak English. All the current Enforcers can converse in it. It's now the most popular language in the Federation."

Procules pointed at a Native American male, middle-aged and tall, sitting toward the back. "John Sunbird, *Arizona Sun.* You mean you don't have a universal language spoken by all the citizens of your Federation?"

"No." Procules answered this time. "It is unnecessary. We have the means to intercommunicate the different languages in the Federation, particularly through devices. The Federation does not believe everyone has to speak only one language, and by law, beings have the right to speak any language they wish. They are not forced to speak a particular one."

John nodded. "How many do you Universal Marshals number?"

Procules checked his memory cells for the correct figure. "Currently, the Enforcers number eighty-three."

"How old is your Federation?" John asked.

Internally Procules calculated the exact figure. "By Earth measurement, the Federation has existed for 1,107 years now."

"Last question," John said. "What kind of society is your Federation? A democratic one?"

Minanket fielded it. "Basically, yes. But our rule is far more reaching."

Just then, a mass of right-wing Christian fundamentalists pushed their way into the lobby, many of them carrying signs, all of which were negative toward the Enforcer Squad. They screamed at the Universal Marshals. Police intercepted them.

"Leave our planet alone!" a protestor shouted, a young white female. "This is our planet!"

A middle-aged white male shook a fist at the Enforcer Squad. "Go back to where you came from! We don't want your kind here!"

"You have come to invade us!" a young white male spat. "Get off our world, you heathen aliens!"

A middle-aged white woman yelled out from the group. "God shall strike you down if you try and harm us! The Almighty Lord will protect us from you!"

Rathol rose to his feet and grabbed the Staff of Godpower behind his chair. "Earth sinners, how dare you speak of the Lord in vain!" The Shepherd looked at the group in fury. Angrily, he willed the Staff of Godpower to life, and it blazed white end to end. "If you do not humble yourself before the Almighty power of the Lord I wield in His great service, I will smite you in His supreme name and humble you before Him! God will be merciful if you humble yourselves."

Police tried to get control of the situation with the angry Christian fundamentalists before it got out of hand. The rest of the Enforcer Squad remained cool and did not react or respond to the venom being spewed.

Beholding Rathol with the Staff of Godpower threatening them with consequences if they did not heed him, the Christian fundamentalists were reminded of

Moses when the biblical hero wielded a similar staff. "Bow down to the Lord and ask for His forgiveness, Earth sinners. His almighty power is before you!"

The protestors kneeled to the floor, save one lone man, a young white male.

Instead, the Earthling pulled out a .32 caliber revolver and shot at the Shepherd three times before the police could restrain him. Rathol stood still as if to await the angel of death to take the Shepherd to Heaven. But Severrin snatched all three bullets in the air in front of the leader of the Enforcer Squad and saved the life of his fellow Universal Marshal.

"It is the will of the Lord that I live to do His mighty work," Rathol stated. The Shepherd walked over to the cowering group, accompanied by Severrin and Minanket. "God forgives your transgression against Him and me. I also forgive you. You were blind, and now you see." The leader of the Enforcer Squad swept the Almighty power of the Staff over the entire group. The Christian fundamentalists felt the loving touch of the Creator. They all smiled and knew God was truly represented in the person of Rathol.

"The Lord watches over your Federation," a middle-aged white female remarked, the closest Terran kneeling before the Shepherd.

Rathol beamed. "He does."

"Actually," Minanket said, "the Federation classifies God as just another being existing. Albeit a supremely powerful one."

"Yet there are those in the Federation who obey His will," Rathol interjected quickly.

Severrin chimed in. "The Federation features many different religions, belief systems, and philosophies. It believes in the freedom of religion like your nation. But it is not allowed to go beyond boundaries as outlined by Federation law. Any religion that does evil will answer for it and face Federation justice."

Abruptly the news conference ended. The Enforcer Squad teleported back to the *Centaurus* after Procules telelinked to the ship. Once on board the vessel, the Universal Marshals left the teleporter room, wondering how well the news conference had gone in their eyes and the eyes of the Terrans. None of them spoke about it, and each went to their quarters to relax a while.

Later, the Enforcer Squad would report back to the High Enforcer. But deep down, they feared for Earth. They did not want the planet doomed by the Fellowship of Darkness, especially since Bolan Trevarre, their friend and fellow Enforcer, came from the Terran world. They hoped they could foil any plan hatched by the Archvillains hidden on Earth to implement the destruction of the planet. A question loomed over the Enforcer Squad, though. When and where would their enemy strike next on the Terran world?

Chapter 25

Earth gave the Enforcer Squad a warm welcome, sending the Universal Marshals gifts and celebrating a parade in their honor. The Enforcer Squad took a little time off from their mission and explored the Terran world to experience its global culture.

The first thing the Universal Marshals experienced, a bit ironically, happened when boxes of comic books, novels, and graphic novels were delivered to the *Centaurus*. In the conference room of the ship, they met to look over the reading material piled on the conference table. They ate lunch together, except Procules, who did not need to.

"Did you notice," Lorliane remarked, "that almost all of the superheroes in this stuff are terrestrial in origin? Many Terrans in costumes?"

"While almost all of the Enforcers are extraterrestrial in comparison, by Earth definition," Severrin finished for her.

They all found that interesting. The various materials flattered the Universal Marshals. No planet in the Federation had anything like this.

"There is plenty here," Vartagal remarked, holding a graphic novel.

"There are some stories with archers in them," Severrin told the Great Archer. "But you are still the most famous in the galaxy."

"Hey," Eneysa said, holding a fantasy novel. "There are many tales here about wizards in these books."

The Enforcer Squad discovered a bunch of fictional counterparts to the Universal Marshals altogether. They learned that Archvillains had fictional counterparts in the reading material as well. All this amused the Enforcer Squad.

Their readings prompted them to search for other sources to find fictional Earth counterparts to the Enforcers and also Archvillains. Aided by the bridge computer of the *Centaurus*, they came across characters in the television and films of the Terran world. The Enforcer Squad began to wonder how much of the Universal Marshals and everything else associated with them in the universe existed in fictional form on Earth. They began to question how much was coincidental and how much was not. However, not all of the Universal Marshals—or Archvillains for that matter—had fictional counterparts on the Terran world.

Later, the Enforcer Squad received a telebeamed message from Tellus. The High Enforcer was sending two more Universal Marshals to Earth. They arrived there in the *Horizon*, ready to transport to the *Centaurus*. In the teleporter room of the ship, Procules met the two new members of the Enforcer Squad—Enforcer Averriol, the Chakra Being, and Raquella, the Gothic Being.

Raquella, a tall woman, featured long dark hair and brown eyes. She wore a black outfit with matching shoes and black lipstick. Her special powers resided on the occultic level.

Beside Raquella, Averriol stood a few inches taller than her. He wore a rainbow robe of the seven major colors of the seven major chakras, or psychic centers: red, orange, yellow, green, blue, indigo, and violet. On his feet, he wore leather sandals. His black hair was cropped short, and his thick black mustache and goatee were neat. His large and glossy purple eyes radiated mystic power, under thick black eyebrows. His small, narrow nose pointed like a dowsing rod as if he could find things hidden from normal senses. The Chakra Being wore a golden rainbow-shaped amulet around his neck as thin as his wiry body.

The Enforcer Squad now numbered twelve. They all got together in the conference room.

"We still have no idea where the Complex is hidden," Lorliane said.

Minanket spoke. "But we know it is here, on Earth. The question is where."

"Do we ask the Earthlings for their help?" Eneysa asked.

"No," Rathol said. "We must find it on our own."

Isisis voiced a question. "What if they offered to help us?"

"We will deal with it if it happens," Rathol responded.

Their meeting lasted an hour. Afterward, they went to their individual quarters.

Next, the Enforcer Squad experienced the wonders of Earth. They visited museums, libraries, movie theaters, concert halls, game shows, Broadway shows, restaurants, colleges and universities, amusement parks, and many more places on the Terran world. Procules recorded all the various sensations, so much information pouring into his data files that it seemed he might explode his circuits in super overload. They accepted graciously and met the President of the United States and the First Lady and foreign dignitaries and U.S. officials who all wanted to have conversations with them.

One night, when the entire squad sat together in the dining hall of the *Centaurus*, they talked about their experiences on Earth since they started to explore the culture of the planet. Three food replicators had been programmed by them to synthesize assorted Earth cuisine. Procules did not need to consume organic substance like his fellow Enforcers.

"The food on this planet tastes quite good," Jagathan said. He dug into a T-bone steak, hot Idaho potatoes, garden salad smothered in Italian dressing, and hard rolls with tall glasses of chocolate milk to wash it all down with. "This drink is sweet nectar from the gods."

Vartagal laughed. "Titans have enormous appetites. They don't worry too much about the food they eat or the beverages they drink. They swallow enough at a meal to feed an entire army." The Great Archer ate a bowl of New England clam chowder with pumpernickel bread and a few cans of cherry cola to drink. "On my home world we have no such fare."

Procules entered the conversation. "I have sampled their variety of edible solids and drinkable liquids. Their alcoholic beverages are crude and caused my geomatic circuits to malfunction temporarily."

"Did any other biofuel disrupt your mechanical sense of taste?" Minanket asked the Robot-Enforcer.

Procules checked his memory circuits for data on the subject. "Their chewing tobacco left an unpleasant residue in me. I had to clean my system of the undelectable organic material."

"The foods I like most are their icy products,"

Lorliane said. "Ice cream, frozen yogurt, frozen fruit bars, Italian ice, and assorted frozen desserts." The Ice Being rose from her chair and stepped back to the food replicator behind her. "Make me a hot fudge sundae." The food replicator complied and materialized on its silver shelf a hot fudge sundae. She picked up her dessert, sat back down again, and began devouring it.

Severrin watched the Ice Being eat. "That hot fudge looks like brown molten lava." The Colossus picked up a mug of decaffeinated coffee with cream and sugar in it and drank it. "A fine refreshment, this is. It has a strong aroma."

Averroil looked at his companions in wonder. "I think we're being Terranized. Maybe too much."

Later, Isisis worked the communications console. On the floor of the bridge lay a toolbox. As she listened intently to telephone chatter her console picked up around Earth, her console beeped red. The Occultic Being answered the call. "This is the *Centaurus*."

"My name is Colonel Colin Langhorn," a male voice said on the communications console. "I'm calling from the Pentagon."

"How may I help you?"

"The President of the United States has instructed me to offer the services of our country and the United Nations to help you and the rest of the Enforcer Squad to find and capture the Archvillains you've been sent here to arrest."

"Your offer is very kind."

"Thank you. What do you say?"

"I will have to confer with the others of the squad. I will contact you when we have an answer for you."

"When can we expect your reply?"

"Within two days, at the most."

"That sounds very reasonable. Call me back here. Over and out."

Isisis activated the ship-wide intercom. "Attention, everybody. We need to meet in the conference room immediately. I have just been contacted for a very serious proposal. See you there." She rose from her seat and left the bridge for the conference room.

In the conference room, all except Procules and Jagathan sat. Rathol brought the meeting to order.

Isisis explained the offer she'd received from the Pentagon to her fellow Enforcers. They listened to her without interrupting. After she finished, they all turned to the Shepherd.

"We must speak with the High Enforcer," Rathol said.

Isisis contacted the Justiceplex on Tellus by telespace channel on the control console she sat before. They established communications with the Computer-Enforcer. "We must speak with the High Enforcer."

"I will connect you to him," Nanomach responded.

Soon Delveran was on the line. "What do you have to report?"

Isisis told him about the offer from the Pentagon.

"Because of your discovered presence, I had hoped not to have to have such a possibility arise, to avoid their involvement in the matter of the Archvillains there. But it is their world. Their request is legitimate since their very lives may be endangered." The High Enforcer paused a moment. "I will have to relate the matter to the Federation. We don't want the Terrans to get hurt because of us. I will get back to you as soon as I can. Out."

Another thing disturbed the Enforcer Squad. Their fellow Universal Marshal, Bolan Trevarre, came from Earth. How would Bolan take it about his native world in possible danger of extinction by the Fellowship of Darkness? They all knew he would probably want to return to his home planet to help it and the Enforcer Squad stop the Archvillains. In the meantime, until they received word from the Grand Universal Marshal, all they could do while they waited was to continue their routines aboard the vessel and experience a little more of the Terran world.

The Enforcer Squad did not neglect its duty to the Universal Federation of Planets. They kept searching for the hidden stronghold of the Fellowship of Darkness, but without success. The High Enforcer had not gotten back to them yet. They began to worry. After a week had passed, they all agreed they would wait one more day before reestablishing contact with Tellus.

Another matter concerned them. The Archvillains on Earth had not made a move against them or Earth since the Enforcer and Archvillain Squads had clashed in New York City a while ago. They wondered why their enemies did not lash out at the Earthlings for the defeat the Enforcer Squad had inflicted on the Fellowship of Darkness. To them, it seemed uncharacteristic that their foes did not avenge themselves against the Enforcers in some way. What were the Archvillains up to?

The next morning after breakfast in the dining hall, Rathol ordered that they contact Tellus to find out what was happening. They went to the bridge to give the *Centaurus* a systems check. One by one, it was done.

Isisis completed her systems check of the communications console. The Occultic Being contacted

Tellus by telespace channel. "I'm not getting any response."

"Does the system check out?" Minanket asked.

"It works perfectly," Isisis replied. She kept trying as her fellow Enforcers surrounded her after they each finished their individual tasks, except the Sylph-Enforcer.

"Well?" Vartagal prodded the Occultic Being.

Isisis look at them, dismay on her face. "Something has blocked off all communication with Tellus. We won't be getting any reinforcements, nor will Federation forces be sent here. We're on our own."

Chapter 26

Inside an area of outer space created by the spacing device of the Fellowship of Darkness, beyond the reality and fabric of normal space, their fleet waited to invade Tellus. There were many ships in the armada, filled with biocreated minions manning the vessels. Aboard a battlecruiser the Archvillain commanders of the space fleet held a meeting in the conference room of the vessel. In the chamber, a large oval table filled the middle of the room.

Orlin, the Grim Reaper, sat in a swivel chair facing the automatic doors. The Incarnation of Death stood six feet, four inches tall, thin in build and long of limb. A black cloak wrapped his jet-black body with matching loafers on his long feet; a black cowl hid his face. The only visible part of the Archvillain were his jet-black hands with long fingers and curved nails. Behind him, his shiny scythe of power stood against the blank wall. Both it and he possessed celestic power.

"I have received a message telebeamed from the Complex on Earth," Orlin said. "There is an Enforcer Squad on Earth looking for it. The Universal Marshals know of the existence of the Fellowship." His unseen gaze fell on the other eight Archvillain commanders there, three others missing from the meeting.

Brutalos, the Kraken, hammered the table with a huge fist. "Sea rot! They're a bane to us." The

Archvillain towered twelve feet when standing, the largest member of the Fellowship of Darkness. Sea blue skin hued his massive frame, matching the color of his deep-set eyes. His gills bloated in rage at the Universal Marshals, who he wished he could crush the life from with his four huge arms. He wore no clothes over his dense hide.

"Mmm, I wish you could send a tidal wave to destroy their headquarters," Rheabenj, the Delilahan, said. Her ravishing beauty exuded sensuality bioenergetically at will, her long dark hair, soft hazel eyes, and sensuous mouth heightening the special power of her gorgeous state. She wore a pink dress with pink slippers. "Couldn't you just die to see the Enforcers retire and find another line of work?"

"I'd rather turn them to stone," Hellob, a Gorgon, stated. She wore special red glasses that hid her ruby eyes. The many snakes making up her hair hissed. She dressed in a black robe with black slippers. "They would make fine sculptures for my growing collection."

Orlin raised a hand to stop their chattering. "We will travel to Tellus as soon as Turiyak, Cenjuno, and Vilegast relay news to us. The invasion will begin after they have completed their mission." The Grim Reaper addressed the Archvillain across the table from him. "Are the photon bombs ready?"

"Yes," Yarg, the Alien Thing, replied. He stood ten feet tall, when erect, his black eyes sticking out of their wide sockets like giant black marbles. Four huge feet, each with four large toes, attached to four thick legs, supported his ponderous, jellylike mass. His eight oarlike arms quivered in agitation at the news of the Enforcers, wanting to lash out and grab a Universal

Marshal to throttle. His vertical-scooped jaws opened and closed like a bird beak; his big triangular-shaped ears projected out like the roof slabs of a building. Like Brutalos, he wore no apparel. "When do you want to use them?"

"When the time is right," Orlin responded. He looked at the Archvillain two places from his right. "Are the fighters ready?"

"They're waiting to wing," Kalliki, the Batling, answered. The Archvillain rose over seven and a half feet tall and resembled a bat with long arms and long legs. His black leathery wings folded tight against his body, his blunt snout split to reveal sharp teeth and needlelike fangs. His black eyes held the power of the night to terrify his victims. Deadly claws on his thin fingers and wicked-looking talons on his slender toes enhanced that effect. He wore no garments. "My sonar is keen, my fangs are pointed, my claws are sharp for the enemies of the night!"

Orlin faced the Archvillain two places left from him. "Are our land forces all ready?"

"All hungry for battle," Ragnar, the Berserker, replied. He stood a muscular six and a half feet tall with blue eyes filled with intensity; his long hair and beard were blond. He wore a brown tunic with matching pants and boots. Against the wall behind him leaned his battle-axe of power. "Battle vehicles have been equipped with extra firepower. Enough to raze Tellus to a wasteland."

Lethesis, the Wildcat, smiled sinisterly on the immediate right of Ragnar. "I like the sound of that." She sported an athletic build, her long hair thick and red. Her reddish-brown eyes burned in anticipation of the brutal action she expected on Tellus when the invasion commenced. She wore a red jumpsuit with black shoes. "I just want to romp all over Tellus."

Iosheen, the Chimeran, held similar feelings, sitting across from the Wildcat. "The whole planet is so vain. They fancy themselves better than us." She wore a tan unisuit, a tan belt, and tan boots. Her golden-honey hair was short, tied in a pigtail at the moment. Her yellow-brown eyes held only contempt for Tellus, especially the Enforcers. Between her eyes, her flat nose flared in disgust of the Federation, her thin mouth twisting and untwisting until she calmed herself down. "I yearn to riddle Tellus with the wrath of my special powers."

"Death shall come to claim them," Orlin vowed. "They will be cut down like crops with my scythe. They will experience my special powers of death to their dismay." The Grim Reaper itched to turn Tellus into a planet of death. He resumed where he left off. "We will simultaneously invade all parts of Tellus to conquer it." That included the area of space around Tellus as the outside part of the planet. The Incarnation of Death talked of minor details of the invasion with his fellow Archvillains.

The meeting lasted over two hours. Afterward, the Archvillains split up and headed for different vessels in the space fleet. Orlin materialized in the flagship of the armada, a space destroyer. The Grim Reaper walked up a long corridor for the bridge, carrying his scythe of power.

A female android walked up to the Incarnation of Death. She told him of the battle that had occurred in normal space outside the created area of the spacing device.

"Relay news throughout our fleet to immediately

prepare for the voyage to Tellus," Orlin commanded.

The female android ran up the corridor to the bridge to execute his orders. She went to the communications console and informed the rest of the space fleet.

The Grim Reaper continued on. Twenty steps later, a silver and blue robot came up to him.

"What now?" Orlin asked.

'We are under attack!" the droid said.

"What strikes us?"

"We don't know. We haven't been able to identify the intruder."

The Incarnation of Death hurried to the bridge. The bridge had two floors. Control consoles arrayed along the walls of it operated under the diligence of biocreated minions sitting at the stations.

Orlin strode down steps to the first floor of the bridge to the front of the ship. Out the window ahead, the Incarnation of Death witnessed the explosion of a twin engine of a battlecruiser on its starboard side, then the destruction of the other one on its port side. Slowly the damaged vessel sank into the fabric of created space like a sea ship sinking in water, then a final explosion shredded it to tons of floating scrap metal.

"How many ships have we lost?" Orlin asked the female android at the navigation console.

"Two," she replied.

At the helm console a male clone addressed the Grim Reaper. "Sir, another vessel is exploding off our starboard."

The Incarnation of Death heard the booming destruction of another battlecruiser reverberating through the created area of the spacing device and the death crises of hundreds of biocreated minions from it.

Ironically, this was something that would generally be credited to the Grim Reaper. Orlin felt as if his domain had been violated by someone or something, though he admitted to himself that he had to admire the method of death employed to claim many lives.

The female clone at the science console saw red lights flashing at her station. "Sir, we're being attacked within on Deck Four!"

Orlin went over to her. "What do your sensors show?"

"It can't identify what it is invading us."

"Then tell me what it is not."

"It's not electrical, nuclear, photonic, ionic, plasmic, or mechanical. It doesn't read in the infrared or ultraviolet spectrum. All I'm getting are emanations that may be some kind of strange energy."

The Incarnation of Death fingered the shiny blade of his scythe. "What physical readings do you get from it?"

The female clone looked up at him wide-eyed. "It doesn't appear or read as anything physical, sir."

Orlin used his special powers to sense who or what the intruder was aboard the flagship. He hit the floor of the vessel with the bottom of his scythe, and it clanged against the surface. "It's a sending."

The female clone seemed puzzled. "Sir?"

"A creature sowed of supernatural energy and power to do a specific task, created by magic," Orlin explained. "This one has been sent to reap destruction on our fleet. I must confront it and claim its supernatural life."

Orlin left the bridge quickly and used his special powers to draw himself and the sending together. He turned right into a turbolift and verbally commanded it to take him to Deck Four. It obeyed him and took him down to the requested level.

After getting off the turbolift, the Grim Reaper sensed which direction to take. He strode down a corridor aligned with pairs of sliding doors on either side of him and glowpanels above him providing sufficient light to see by, though he could have moved around easily in total darkness. When he reached the sliding doors to a storage bay, he stopped. Sensing the supernatural creature inside the chamber, he readied his scythe.

Orlin entered the storage bay. Long, high metal shelves formed six rows from the sliding doors to the back. Different colored containers filled with items from probe components to organic materials were piled atop the shelves in neat stacks.

Orlin felt the presence of the sending as it sensed his being. The Grim Reaper watched as the supernatural creature charged him from the other end of his aisle. It appeared to him as a blue bull—large and dangerous. The sending rammed him and sent him flying backward to land on his back, caught off guard.

The Incarnation of Death recovered and jumped to his feet. "I am Death, creature. I have come to claim your supernatural life."

The sending bellowed in defiance and pawed the floor of the storage bay, leaving burn marks on it. It whipped its short tail in a frenzy. Its blue eyes glowed with fury. Its breath came out in blue puffs of supernatural energy and power.

Orlin walked toward the magical creation. Suddenly stacks of containers fell on him, burying him. The sending roared in quick triumph. But the Grim Reaper emerged from the pile on top of him unharmed. The bull looked confused by this development, acting as though the Incarnation of Death should not have survived its second attack.

Orlin berated himself. He had allowed himself to be struck when he should have first made himself insubstantial. The sending had caught him by surprise twice. Now he changed his substance from solid to ethereal, so if the bull hurled any other physical objects at him, they would pass through him. The magical creation sensed his transformation and bellowed in challenge, its hooves glowing hot-white now.

The bull charged the Grim Reaper. Orlin faded from sight, and the sending skidded to a halt at the other end of the aisle. It snorted and could not see him. Pawing the floor in rage and frustration, it tried to detect where the Incarnation of Death was.

Orlin materialized in the middle of the aisle, facing the bull. The sending walked a few steps toward him, cautiously, wary of him. Blue electrical charges of supernatural energy and power radiated from its massive body, its powerful thick limbs stomping the floor with each step sounding like a hammer hitting an anvil. The magical creation stopped and eyed him, stalking him. The Grim Reaper wielded his scythe like a lance, its blade deadly and whirling in an argent blur.

"Come to your death, creature," Orlin said. "I, Death, await you."

The sending reared on its hind legs, roared, and dropped back on the floor with such force it shook the storage bay, jarring containers from shelves to hit the ground and roll to the other side of another aisle. If the bull thought the Incarnation of Death would fall to the floor, it wasted its time. Orlin remained firmly planted on the ground. The magical creation lowered its head and thundered down the aisle at him.

The Grim Reaper stopped the bull as soon as it touched his scythe. His tool and weapon of power started to absorb the magical essence of the sending, draining the life from it. The bull raged in its death throes as it began to shrink. Finally, nothing remained of the sending except a roar of agony ringing in the storage bay. Then silence fell in the chamber, the Incarnation of Death all alone.

Orlin ceased the spinning blade of the scythe, then clicked its blade back into its handle. He exited the storage bay and returned to the bridge.

On the bridge, the Grim Reaper went to the communications console, where a female cyborg operated it. She looked up as he addressed her.

"Relay a message to the Complex," Orlin ordered. "Tell them the invasion will begin soon."

"Yes, sir."

The Incarnation of Death went forward to the helm and navigation consoles. "Is the fleet ready to travel?"

"Yes, sir," the male clone manning the helm console answered him.

Orlin went back to and addressed the female cyborg at the communications console. "Tell the Ward Room to shut off the spacing device. Then inform the entire fleet to follow the flagship to Tellus."

"Yes, sir."

The Grim Reaper beheld the spacing device deactivated as the fabric of reality wavered before him and changed to normal space, a blackness dotted with glowing white spots scattered unevenly around the space destroyer. "Engage the hyperdrive."

"Hyperdrive engaged, sir," the female android at the navigation console said.

Every ship in the space fleet activated its hyperdrive, winked out of existence in normal space, and sped into hyperspace. A number of vessels flew toward Tellus, heavily armed, carrying legions of biocreated minions, battle vehicles, and other items of war. When the Federation capital and the armada of the Fellowship of Darkness collided, the reverberations of battle would ring like the explosion of the Big Bang throughout the entire galaxy.

Chapter 27

Aboard the battlecruiser, the *Ranging Falcon*, Enforcer Ulleric, the Dynaman, stood on the bridge. Beside him, Captain Loric Markan, human commander of the vessel, sat in the command chair, his arms on its control armrests, his fingers near their two sets of four buttons colored red, green, blue, and yellow.

Around the bridge, personnel worked at different consoles as the ship reconned through space, a distance from Tellus. Before the two men, a view screen displayed an image of space, a black fabric dotted with white spots representing celestial bodies, heavy concentrations of them in the middle and lower right corner of the view screen. Behind them stood sliding doors to a turbolift.

At the moment, Ulleric appeared in his natural lifeform, a human male just over six feet tall with a fair build. He kept his thick light brown hair cut short, his narrow face clean-shaven, and wore wire-rimmed glasses. His eyes, light blue, locked on the view screen before him, looking for any anomalies to indicate unnatural disturbances in the quadrant. He wore a white unisuit with matching boots.

"So far, nothing unusual out there," Loric said.

"Nevertheless we must keep searching," Ulleric responded.

A humanoid female at the science console addressed

the captain. "Sir, sensors have picked up emanations a half-parsec ahead of us."

Loric rotated in his command chair back toward her. "What kind of emanations?"

"Unusual energy patterns."

Loric swung in his command chair forward to address the helmsman. "Set a course for it, Mr. Voh. Engage the superluminal drive."

Ooloo Voh, an alien, complied. The *Ranging Falcon* jumped to ultralight speed. In a short span of time, the vessel reached the area of the disturbance and reentered normal space. The science officer manipulated her console to identity specifically what the sensors had found. Before them on the view screen glowed an immense, dense white band.

Loric addressed the science officer. "Report, Lura."

"It's an energy barrier of some kind," she responded. "My sensors show a distortion in the fabric of space-time where it is."

"Odd," Loric remarked.

Ulleric agreed with the captain. "This barrier must be the work of the Fellowship of Darkness."

"You must be right, doctor," Loric said. "Lura, how far does this barrier extend?"

"I'll check," she responded. The science officer used her console, and the sensors detected the range of the energy barrier. "Sir, it envelopes an area of space around the Kambec star system."

"What!" Loric said, disbelief in his tone.

She repeated her findings.

The captain frowned. "This telebeam's trouble." He spoke to the communications officer, a female human named Celene Quay. "Contact Tellus and inform them of the barrier. Ask for instructions on what to do about it."

"Right, sir," Celene acknowledged.

Ulleric studied the energy barrier on the view screen. His normal sight distinguished nothing unusual about it nor giving him a clue to its unique nature, given the probable fact that Archvillains had constructed it. "Captain, I would like to inspect it close-up from outside the ship."

Loric looked at the Universal Marshal. "What do you have in mind?"

"Explore the barrier as the Dynaman," Ulleric answered.

The captain considered his idea. "All right. But be careful."

"I will." Ulleric left the bridge and entered the turbolift. It took him down to Deck Seven.

After exiting the turbolift, Ulleric walked down a corridor until he reached the shuttle bay. He entered the chamber and turned into the Dynaman, a silver and blue superbeing. His transformed skin looked smooth and synthetic and formed his clothing, as if sewn into his altered flesh. His large silver eyes resembled blank coins. No hair existed on his head, just a silver and blue patch like a helmet outlined as synthetic skin. His hands appeared as a pair of blue and silver synthetic gloves sewn into his synthetic skin to match the color of his synthetic boots merged into his feet and lower legs.

The shuttle bay housed a pair of shuttles. Some ship personnel worked in the chamber. A male alien stood at the control stand that operated the space door of the shuttle bay. Ulleric walked up to the alien, a Teuthii, a squidlike being, and told him to open the space door for the Enforcer. The Universal Marshal stepped over to the entrance, and the alien opened it enough for him to pass through the field, keeping the effects of space out.

Ulleric willed his body bioshield on, a transparent field of bioenergy encasing him to protect him from the physical effects of naked exposure to outer space. He flew from the shuttle bay into space toward the energy barrier. The Teuthii monitored him on the control stand from the ship.

Totally aware and fully alert to his cold, dark surroundings, Ulleric jetted. Through his normal vision, the energy barrier increased in size as he closed the distance between him and it, making him feel like a dust mote compared to a supergiant star. His highly sophisticated dynadetectors registered nothing other than the energy barrier and the ship. It seemed like he was trapped between an immense pair of space monsters that could crush him between them into a two-dimensional being.

Ulleric stopped close to the energy barrier, about three feet from it. Still nothing else appeared on his dynadetectors. The Dynaman studied it in the mode of his normal senses, but could not fathom the intricacies of it. He switched to his microsenses to analyze it.

First, he looked at it with his supersense of microvision. He discerned its molecular structure, a dense bunch of white molecules bound together tightly. Further he observed that the energy barrier disobeyed the scientific laws of the conservation of energy—it replicated and reversed those laws. Ulleric knew it had to be the handiwork of Professor Magnemus because the feat fell within the special powers of the Scientific Being. The Archvillain created a new scientific law. That made the Dynaman wonder how many other physical laws the energy barrier broke and reversed.

Next, he listened to the energy barrier with his supersense of microhearing. His normal hearing could hear nothing from it. But his microhearing filtered any intruding noises from space and recognized a low, sharp ringing from it. Then he used his supersense of microsmell to sniff any odors. His normal sense could smell nothing, but his biomechanical sense caught the whiff of what reminded him of charred synthon—a synthetic fiber of high-quality fabric used as material for garments—that reeked sickly bitter.

He skipped his supersense of microtasting—it did not apply to the energy barrier—and floated in to touch it. First, he touched the energy barrier with a normal feel and it felt like to him smooth and impenetrable. Now he did the same with his supersense of microtouching. The energy barrier vibrated low under his special fingers and still met powerful resistance; it reminded him of the force bars at the Universal Prisonplex.

The energy barrier utilized scientific and maybe occultic and celestic levels of energy power. Ulleric confirmed this with his supersense of microvision. The Dynaman wondered if laser or other particle beams or antimatter or other kinds of missiles could destroy it, or at least puncture holes in it. And if neither tactic worked, what would happen? Nothing? Or catastrophic results?

Ulleric flew along the energy barrier for five kilometers in one direction, returned to his starting point, then jetted five kilometers in the other direction. Nothing different about it or the surrounding area. Unable to solve the problem of the energy barrier, the Dynaman returned to ship. Afterward, the Teuthii closed the space door behind him.

Returning to the bridge, he did not bother to change back into his natural state, figuring it would be better to stay as his alter ego for a while. The captain turned to him as soon as he stood beside the man.

"Discover anything about it?" Loric asked him.

Ulleric related everything he learned about the energy barrier to the captain. Loric's expression became grim after the Dynaman finished relating the details. The Enforcer showed no emotion, but remained in a thinking mode.

"Any communication from Tellus?" Ulleric asked.

Loric snorted, looking skeptical. "Nothing yet. I think they should send another vessel here to back us up. We might encounter something we might not be able to handle alone."

Ulleric said nothing. He glanced at the view screen, impressed by the great design of the energy barrier. In his mind, he analyzed all the data he had gathered about it from his close-up inspection of it. He considered fresh solutions to the problem. An idea of merging it with an opposite kind of energy barrier to neutralize it might work, he thought.

"Sir," the communications officer addressed the captain. "Message from Tellus."

"On channel," Loric responded.

Celene Quay manipulated her communications console and put the message on audio. A male voice spoke to the ship.

"*Ranging Falcon*, you are ordered to examine the barrier and try to penetrate or destroy it. The problem is being dealt with here. Keep in constant communication with us until you receive new orders. Out."

"Well," Loric said, "we'll have to try and break the barrier somehow." He whirled in his command chair to face the science officer. "Give me a complete and detailed reading on the barrier and exclude what Doctor Ulleric has already told us."

"Yes, sir," Lura responded. She used her science console to analyze and examine it. "The barrier has energy power on the scientific level in different bands: photonic, ionic, plasmic, and nuclear. I cannot get a reading on what is holding it in place. It could be ships or satellites on the other side of the barrier."

Ulleric pointed out something. "Her readings do not indicate energy power on the occultic or celestic levels."

"Marvelous," Loric said. The captain frowned. "Any life form readings on your console?"

Lura checked. "None, sir, of the barrier internally or externally."

"I find that rather unusual," Ulleric remarked.

Loric looked at the Dynaman in surprise. "Oh?"

Ulleric collected his thoughts to explain himself. "Considering the fact that Professor Magnemus is a biocreationist and that some of his fellow Archvillains in the Fellowship of Darkness command subordinates, in all probability they would set some sort of life form units to guard it. Unless they rigged the barrier with booby-traps."

Lura used her science console to sweep through the energy barrier for any indications of that possibility before the captain asked her. "I find no anomalies to that effect, sir."

Loric seemed to be weighing his options on how to deal with the barrier. "Recommendations?"

The helmsman Ooloo Voh suggested an idea. "We

could try to send a probe into it."

"I would not advise it," Ulleric said. "I doubt the probe could penetrate the barrier. The barrier acts like an enormous force bar."

"Why not fire some torpedoes at it to test it," Aworfis, the weapons and tactical officer, suggested. He was a big male Khargan, a humanoid. His control console was behind and right of the captain.

Loric addressed his science officer. "Are there any weak spots in the barrier?"

Lura used her control console to find any. "I detect none. The barrier is uniform."

Loric turned to Ulleric. "Torpedoes?"

"It is unknown what the reaction would be if any kind of torpedoes were exploded on it," Ulleric replied.

"How about cutting it with our lasers," Sulune said, the engineering officer. He sat at his station behind and left of the captain, a humanoid male. "It's a safer way than blasting it with torpedoes."

Loric smiled. "That might work."

Ulleric felt unsure about that, given the unusual nature of the barrier. But he could not offer any alternatives to the captain. Loric waited for him to state his opinion on the idea. "If we attempt lasers against it, then I would advise we move to maximum laser range. If a negative reaction occurs and threatens the ship, we might have time to stop or outrun it."

"Agreed," Loric said. He faced front. "Mr. Voh, take us to maximum laser range. Mr. Aworfis, ready lasers."

Both officers complied. The ship flew to maximum laser range, circled 180 degrees, and prepared to fire on the energy barrier. Ulleric stared at it, pondering its complex structure, dissecting it in his mind.

"Lasers ready," Aworfis said.

Loric gripped his control armrests. "Fire."

Twin continuous beams from the ship flashed through space and hit the energy barrier in a cutting motion. It seemed impervious to the attack and remained unchanged, but the lasers kept slicing at it. Ulleric watched as nothing happened, not surprised by the initial reaction, and wondered if his special powers as Dynaman could penetrate it. But in all probability he believed they could not.

Without warning, the lasers caused an explosion on the energy barrier.

"Cease firing!" Loric commanded.

From the energy barrier, huge blue-white waves radiated outward like swift ripples of a rock dropped in a pond. They headed toward the ship.

"Shields!" Loric ordered.

Aworfis used his control console and raised them around the battlecruiser. Everyone on the bridge braced for impact from the waves. The waves slammed into the ship, and it convulsed and tossed some of the crew members around. Electric sparks jumped from control consoles on the bridge and shocked members of the crew. A fire erupted on the helm console. Ulleric shot a silver ray from his right hand and snuffed it.

The waves ended, and the ship recovered. Loric touched the red button on his left armrest and called for emergency procedures for the vessel and a doctor to the bridge. The rest of the bridge crew resumed their stations, except Ulleric. No one appeared seriously hurt.

"What attacked us?" Aworfis asked to no one in particular.

"Shock waves," Ulleric told him. The Dynaman

knew he dare not change back into his normal state now. The situation made it too dangerous for that. He wished another Enforcer had been assigned aboard the ship with him.

Loric wore a grim expression. "This barrier is one huge problem."

Ulleric could not agree with the captain more.

Chapter 28

In the northeast corner of Acropollon stood the Defenseplex, an octagonal, one-floor silver omnimetal building not far from the Militaryplex. Within the structure, in its circular center room, the warding device of Tellus functioned. The diamond-shaped apparatus, made of coppery omnimetal, locked into a computer under it on automatic operation, and a long coppery omnimetal tube connected it to the ceiling. It measured four and a half feet long and two and a half feet wide in the middle. It erected a vast shield of scientific, occultic, and celestic energy powers around the planet to defend against attacks from space, natural or artificial. Right now, it operated with its force field on. But if a ship wanted to enter or exit the planet, it first received clearance from the computer, whereby openings appeared temporarily in the shield to allow vessels in or out. It was late afternoon.

Nothing else was in the chamber with the warding device or the computer. Except for the two Universal Marshals guarding it from possible sabotage from the Fellowship of Darkness.

Overhead, glowpanels in the ceiling lit the room in bright light. No sound came from the warding device or the computer.

Thayla, the Valkyrie-Enforcer, did not like the silence. To the semidivine warrior handmaiden, it seemed ominous. She tossed her long blonde hair to straighten it out as her indigo eyes blinked. She wore light armor over a golden tunic with a matching belt around her trim waist. A golden scabbard hung from the left side of her belt, sheathing a sword. A round shield strapped around her shoulders in back glittered as if newly made. Yellow boots completed her outfit.

Across the warding device from her, Enforcer Medeordese, the Speedster, guarded the contraption with her. He stood a little taller than her, slim in build. His short hair matched hers in color, but he was not a semidivine or supernatural being like her, only a natural humanoid entity. He stared at the elevating door before them, the only entrance to the room, his violet eyes locked on it as if he could see through it to the corridor outside the chamber. His clean-shaven face gave him a boyish look; his thin-lipped mouth turned up slightly in an amused smile at their situation. He placed his hands on his hips, his right foot forward a half-step, his body relaxed for explosive speed. He wore a special blue white-trimmed tracksuit with matching running shoes. As his title indicated, he was the fastest of all the Universal Marshals—speed his trademark.

"This is not exactly what I had in mind for us to be alone together," Medeordese said in a mischievous tone of voice. "It's not exactly a place for lovers."

Thayla smiled. "Still your hot blood, my swift warrior. Save it for battle. We might have to fight."

"You lower my expectations of a romantic rendezvous."

"Battle comes first. Lovemaking later."

The two Enforcers had been lovers since shortly after the Speedster had joined the Universal Marshals.

Medeordese had impressed Thayla with his special powers of speed; he had admired her fighting ability. Some thought the inherent conflict of him being mortal and her being immortal would make their affair short-lived. It did not, and they kept their personal and professional lives distinct and separate from each other.

The intercom by the door came on. A male voice spoke from it. "This is Lieutenant Greever. I need to see one of you. It's important."

Medeordese looked annoyed. "I'll go. My legs are starting to freeze on me. They need recirculation."

The Speedster exited the room and left the Valkyrie-Enforcer to guard the warding device. Medeordese turned left from the corridor to the chamber and down a longer passageway between sliding doors and under glowpanels lighting the hallway at high intensity, especially because of the threat of sabotage from the Fellowship of Darkness to the defense machine. The muffled tapping of his footsteps echoed in a corridor devoid of other sounds.

Medeordese reached the sliding doors to Lieutenant Greever's office. He entered it and looked straight at the man. "Now what is—"

A blow from an unknown and unseen assailant knocked him unconscious. The Speedster sprawled face down on the floor. Over him stood a male and a female Archvillain.

"He'll sleep for a while," the female Archvillain remarked. She was Cenjuno, a Keve, an evil-bearing goddess who inflicted all kinds of ills on mortals, from diseases to natural disasters. Her long black hair hung loose around her shoulders; twisted joy filled her glossy black eyes at the sight of her evil deed—having rendered

Medeordese unconscious. She wore a black robe with black sandals. In her hand, she held the instrument of her crime, a black box of power on the celestic level containing all ills that could be released against mortal creatures, called a Curdatch.

The male Archvillain grinned. "It's unfortunate he wasn't a gadget. I'd have some fun with him." He was Vilegast, a Gremlin. He stood five feet tall, shorter than Cenjuno. Huge ears stuck out from his head with tufts of white hair on them, his hairless, dark brown body covered by rough, serrated skin. White eyebrows bristled above his large, deep green eyes; claws protruded from his long fingers and toes. Spikelike teeth filled his wide mouth and a few hairs sprouted from his small round nose. He wore a green workshirt with four pockets and green pants. A black work belt, strapped around his waist, held tools.

Lieutenant Greever sat totally paralyzed in his swivel chair, his arms gripping its armrests tightly, unable to do anything. He looked like a living statue. To the right of him, a telescreen sat in the wall, off, and two chairs faced his desk. Vilegast had already made the telescreen and the control console on the desk inoperative.

One of the chairs before the desk melted into the lifeform of a male being, only changing in outline. "This silver coating itches." The Archvillain Turiyak, the Changeling, looked down at the unconscious Speedster. Turiyak was a contour shapeshifter, possessing the ability to transform into the outline of anything animate or inanimate. A scientist like Professor Magnemus, his field was topology, the study of places, locations, and environments. He stood under six feet tall with a thick, wide body. The silver coating covering him hid the tan color of his short, thick hair and shaggy eyebrows. His other specific features included a flat nose, a broad chin, and the part of his body not painted in silver, his wide-set tan eyes. He addressed the Keve. "That was a primitive way of putting him into an unconscious state."

"It was simple and effective," Cenjuno responded.

Vilegast looked at both with a gleeful expression on his face. "Let's get to the device. I want to play with it a little before we destroy such a beautiful machine."

Turiak gave the Gremlin an annoyed looked. "We're here to accomplish a mission. Not for your mechanical amusements."

Gremlins were a faerie race that loved to tinker with machines, devices, and other mechanical objects. No supernatural creature knew technology like they did. The worst flaw in their occultic make-up was a tendency to do twisted pranks with all kinds of gadgets, sometimes fatal. Vilegast frowned in disappointment. "Not even one?"

Turiyak turned away and led them from the office, Disgusted, he pounded steps down the corridor. "Of all the supernatural beings in the universe, why do Gremlins have to be the ones with the gift of being master technologists?"

Cenjuno followed behind the Changeling. She laughed. "Gremlins need to have pleasure in something. The only thing they like are mechanical objects." She herself did not understand Gremlins' obsessions with gadgets, and she was a supernatural creature like Vilegast. All other kinds of supernatural beings thought it incomparable that mechanical objects, products of science, should be so attached to Gremlins, creatures of magic.

Behind them, as they receded from Lieutenant Greever's office, the three Archvillains left an unconscious Medeordese to complete their assignment. Ahead, they knew only a single Enforcer stood in their way now.

****

Thayla began to worry about Medeordese. The Speedster had been gone too long. He should have called her over the intercom and told her he would be a while. She debated whether or not to contact him in Lieutenant Greever's office. Finally, she lost patience, went over to the intercom panel left of the entrance, touched a green button on it, and spoke. "Medeordese, are you there?" She got no answer from the lieutenant's office. "Where is he?"

A momentary thought of leaving the room of the warding device entered her mind, but she shoved it quickly aside. She had to stay and guard the apparatus. So she went back over and swept her gaze up and down it.

The elevating door behind her opened. She turned around and said, "Where have you—"

The words froze in her mouth. At first, she believed she imagined the three Archvillains standing before her. But a look at them told her all she needed to know about the situation. In a swift motion, she drew the sword from her scabbard in her right hand. She dared not reach for her shield. It would take too long to get from her back if the foul beings attacked her quickly.

"Well, sister goddess," Cenjuno said. "I see you are ready to be tested. Your warrior skills against my Curdatch."

The Keve opened the black box in her hand. Turiyak showed no expression, but Vilegast chortled. Thayla knew what ills that evil thing contained. The Valkyrie-Enforcer took a defensive stance to battle whatever ill Cenjuno unleashed against her.

Out of the Curdatch a gray smoke emerged. It hovered a second, then struck rapidly before Thayla could decide how to fight it. She felt strange and looked at her sword hand. Her hand aged. Then her whole body aged, at an accelerated rate. She tumbled backward against the wall right of the warding device, dropping her sword as she fell to the floor, trying to fight the ill of premature aging with her special powers on the celestic level. Thayla managed to slow the process down, but it kept eating at her.

"Felled by time," Cenjuno remarked. "Go to work, eager Gremlin."

Vilegast skipped over to the warding device and marveled at its ingenuity. The Gremlin eyed it like a lover as he programmed the computer connected to it for an overload of power to the control console. "A shame to waste such a great invention. I could work with it for days and make it do things its makers never thought of."

After Vilegast finished his task, the three Archvillains left the chamber. Thayla watched them depart, unable to stop them, fighting for her life against the ill ravaging her with rapid aging.

The Defenseplex began to shake as the warding device built up an enormous charge of power overload. On the computer, a rectangular screen measured the amount of power building up in the defense machine, now at the halfway point. Steadily the silver hand arced across the small panel, nearing the danger point.

The elevating door opened, and in rushed Medeordese. A quick look at the measuring meter told him the warding device would blow in a few minutes. The Speedster swore, knowing not how to disarm the power overload. He wished he had a good grasp of the technical knowledge of computers. Spotting Thayla, who reached for and gripped her sword and sheathed it, Medeordese dashed over to her, picked her up in his arms, and sped from the room in a blur of motion, trying to outrace the coming explosion of the apparatus.

Medeordese zoomed through corridors of the Defenseplex and reached the exit of the place. The Speedster pumped his legs at the top speed he could manage carrying Thayla, hoping he could escape in time from the building and get a safe distance away from it before the warding device blew up. He instinctively knew it would be close. When he reached the outside, not more than fifty feet from the structure, the warding device exploded and blew the Defenseplex apart, hurtling debris in every direction. Jagged metal chunks flew after Medeordese like missiles targeted to destroy him and Thayla. The Speedster proved too fleet for the pieces and left them to fall on the ground in defeat.

Medeordese ran up the avenue with military houses on either side of him, made of omnimetal and painted different colors. No vehicles parked in sight of him. But a crowd of people came running to see what happened and saw only the shredded remains of the Defenseplex.

Medeordese gently laid Thayla on the ground. The Speedster saw her rapid aging reversing, due to her special powers on the celestic level fighting off the attack and rejuvenating her. When she finished restoring herself, the Valkyrie-Enforcer opened her eyes and beheld him with a tear in each of his eyes.

He laughed. "This is not the way I wanted to sweep you off your feet and carry you. Too much strain."

Thayla smiled. "My swift warrior." She hugged him, and he did the same.

While the two Enforcers ignored their surroundings and took comfort from their embrace, the three Archvillains fled Tellus in Turiyak's cloaked ship and rendezvoused with the Archvillain space fleet. As the foul beings increased their distance between them and the planet, Vilegast grinned at the success of their mission. The Gremlin hoped he would get a chance to have fun with some of the other gadgets in the Federation capital. He believed he would. Then he would achieve thrills beyond his wildest expectations, and Tellus would suffer immeasurably.

Chapter 29

Delveran felt very upset at the destruction of the warding device and the Defenseplex. The planetary shield being gone opened Tellus for the oncoming invasion. But there was a bright spot. There were now thirty-two Enforcers on the planet.

The High Enforcer assigned Universal Marshals to different parts of the planet, namely on the continents of Survarille and Mellenroel. Land troopers, sea troopers, air troopers, and space troopers were also deployed for the defense of their world. The Tellusians were ready for the space fleet of the Archvillain organization.

****

The armada of the Fellowship of Darkness entered space around Tellus. Battlecruisers engaged ships of the enemy. Transport vessels from the space fleet landed on planet to begin the invasion properly. Robots, cyborgs, androids, mutants, clones, and other biocreated minions under Archvillain commanders poured out and marched on places on Tellus in order to conquer the planet. This would make it easier to bust the thousands of Archvillains imprisoned in the Universal Prisonplex out. The invaders met strong resistance from the inhabitants of the world.

The war for Tellus began.

****

Biocreated minions moved on the city of Paradar on

Mellenroel. Before the gates of the place forces stood in their way, led by two Universal Marshals, Enforcer Zithell, the Amazon, and Estephone, the Horae-Enforcer.

Zithell was the biggest female of the Universal Marshals. She featured long dark hair and hazel eyes, dressed in a blue unisuit and matching boots. Armed with a light sword and force shield, she uttered a battle cry in defiance to the enemy.

Estephone was smaller than her fellow Universal Marshal. She was a Horae, or Season, an attendant of gods. Blonde with blue eyes, she wore a brown robe with matching shoes. The Enforcer held a shorter blade—made of metal forged by deities—and swung it once over her head.

The biocreated minions halted a hundred yards from the defenders of the city. They seemed a bit surprised by the Tellusians making a stand against them.

"They will attack shortly," Zithell said.

Estephone agreed. "May the gods find favor with us in battle."

Warriors from around Mellenroel comprised the defenders, all armed and ready for battle. Their weapons consisted of swords, battle-axes, spears, and other arms. Some carried shields. The defenders, a mixture of humans and faerie, formed an alliance to oppose their common foes. Among the faerie, a few wielded magic for the fight. A male cyborg among the biocreated minions barked a command. The enemy charged at the defenders.

In response, the Tellusians rushed the enemy, and the two sides clashed. In the cloudless sky above the fray, Kambec shone hotly, and no wind blew. Open ground stretched for miles from the city.

Zithell sliced through foes with her light sword. The photonic blade cut down biocreated minions like a scythe mowing down crops. A male android fired at her with a blast rifle. Her force shield intercepted the shots. Then she leaped in and slashed him with her weapon in the head and disabled him.

Estephone fought a male clone. He fired at her with a blaster, but she evaded the shots. She moved in and stabbed the biocreated minion in the chest and finished him off.

The battle raged back and forth. The invaders kept pressing the advantage with their tech weapons. Defenders fell, but the Tellusians slayed their fair share of foes.

The enemy drove the defenders back toward the city. A stone wall enclosed Paradar. The biocreated minions outnumbered the Tellusians. Soon the fight reached the gates of the city.

"Do we retreat into Paradar?" Estephone asked the Amazon as they fought side by side.

Zithell felled a female mutant. "It is not a good idea to battle in its streets. We need to push them back away from it."

The defenders halted the enemy before the gates of the city. With great effort, the Tellusians shoved the biocreated minions into a retreat. The invaders went backward, but it lasted temporarily. Then the enemy moved forward again.

The battle poured into the streets of Paradar. People in the city scrambled for safety as opponents collided in deadly combat. Bodies fell in the streets. Biocreated minions also killed a few civilians as the fighting went into buildings. The fighting went on for a while.

****

On the plains near Cammalain, biocreated minions landed from transport ships. They marched on the kingdom led by the Archvillain Ragnar. The Berserker hefted his battle-axe of power, looking to spill Tellusian blood.

Overhead in a partly cloudy sky, Kambec shone hotly. Ahead of the invaders, they saw opposing forces come toward them. Yauriga, the Avatar-Enforcer, known as the Charioteer, led the defenders. The Universal Marshal rode a chariot pulled by a team of white horses, his whip of power in one hand. Yauriga stood over six feet tall, his long blond hair waving in the wind. He wore a white tunic with a black belt and leather sandals. His blue eyes locked on the foul being leading the enemy.

Both sides halted a hundred yards from each other. They sized up each other. The Tellusians rode horseback with the Enforcer. The invaders had no transport, either beasts or vehicles.

"I will take the Archvillain," Yauriga said to the Tellusian commanders beside him. "He has a magical weapon, I sense."

Captain Braddis unsheathed his sword. "They must not capture or raze Cammalain. We must stop them here."

"That is true of Tellus all over our world," Yauriga remarked. "The invaders must not accomplish the goal of their attack on us."

Lord Jaredic spoke. "Do you sense the battles going on around Mellenroel?"

"Yes," Yauriga replied. "The enemy is engaging us

on many fronts. It seems they want to conquer different areas of the planet simultaneously."

Ragnar raised his battle-axe of power, then chopped down with it. He signaled for the biocreated minions to charge the defenders. In response, the Tellusians rushed at the invaders as the distance between them shrank. Soon both sides clashed. It seemed the Berserker slayed defenders at will. Humans made up the Tellusian forces, except the Universal Marshal. The Avatar-Enforcer fought his way to reach the Archvillain, not to arrest the foul being but to fell him in combat. Biocreated minions kept crossing his path to prevent the Universal Marshal from getting to the Berserker.

Yauriga cracked his whip of power, and lightning bolts shot from it to kill foes. The invaders wielded blasters and blast rifles and managed to shoot Tellusians off their mounts. The tech weapons appeared to make the battle a mismatch against the defenders.

Yauriga saw Lord Jaredic go down after being pulled from his horse by male androids. The Avatar-Enforcer came to his aid and destroyed the automatons with his whip of power.

"Thanks," Lord Jaredic said to the Universal Marshal. He got his horse and remounted his steed, then resumed fighting the enemy.

Yauriga spotted the Archvillain not far from him. In fact, the foul being sought him out in the battle. Swinging his battle-axe of power, the Berserker charged at the Universal Marshal, uttering a battle cry. Yauriga cracked his whip and sent lightning bolts at him. Ragnar intercepted the shots, his magical weapon absorbing the energy from them. Soon they faced each other at close range after Yauriga got off the chariot.

"You are not like your allies," Ragnar stated.

Yauriga grinned. "The same can be said about you."

"It will be a great pleasure to slay you, Enforcer. Your world will fall to us."

"Not if I have anything to say about it."

Ragnar swung his battle-axe of power sideways to slice the Universal Marshal's torso. Yauriga jumped back to avoid the blow. Then the Avatar-Enforcer cracked his whip of power and lashed the right forearm of the Archvillain. The blow stung the Berserker.

Ragnar shrugged off the pain. He started swinging his battle-axe of power in a combination of strikes to land on the body of Yauriga. The Universal Marshal dodged the attacks and looked for an opening to retaliate. But the foul being struck relentlessly at the Avatar-Enforcer, giving him no chance to counterattack.

"I will spill your blood," Ragnar vowed.

A horn sounded. Another transport ship landed on the plains. Out poured more biocreated minions. This gave the advantage to the invaders, who now outnumbered the Tellusians.

"Retreat!" Captain Braddis shouted. The defenders followed his orders and began riding back in the direction of Cammalain.

Yauriga ran to his chariot and hopped on, pursued by the Archvillain. The Universal Marshal sped his horses after his comrades and left the Berserker to howl in frustration.

Yauriga caught up with Captain Braddis and Lord Jaredic. The enemy did not chase the Tellusians, but still marched for Cammalain.

"Do we make a last stand at the castle?" Captain Braddis asked the other two.

Yauriga heaved his chest. "Where else?"

****

Next the transport ships of the invaders landed near Amaron. Systematically the enemy sent biocreated minions to many parts of Mellenroel, bent on conquering the continent quickly.

But wherever the invaders appeared, they met resistance from the Tellusians. Battles raged. Nanomach kept track of the war for Tellus and informed the High Enforcer of anything related to it. Delveran knew the Archvillain organization did not want to prolong the fighting sweeping the planet. The Fellowship of Darkness preferred to conquer in one fell swoop, knowing Federation forces would attempt to destroy the energy barrier and come to the aid of the Tellusians. The sooner the invaders conquered Tellus, the better to accomplish their objective of busting out the Archvillains imprisoned in the Universal Prisonplex.

****

Time passed. Now the enemy started landing biocreated minions on different parts of Survarille. They met resistance from the Tellusians.

The invaders prepared to storm Urdanth, led by the Archvillain Kallaki. The Batling flew in the air at the head of biocreated minions. Ahead waited the defenders of the city, Tellusian land troopers led by Enforcer Rorbash. The Dragonling spotted the foul being in the air.

"The Archvillain is mine," Rorbash said to the commanders with him. The Dragonling extended his wings and took off in the sky.

Both sides fired weapons at each other in the form of blast rifles. Bodies fell in battle. The morning sky featured a few fluffy clouds as the noise of fierce fighting rang in the air. The enemy tried to push the Tellusians back into Urdanth, but the lines of the defenders held.

Rorbash flew toward the Archvillain. The Dragonling shot fire from his mouth at the foul being, hoping to burn him and knock him from the sky. But Kallaki evaded the fire and collided with the Universal Marshal in the air, locking arms in aerial combat. They spun around, each trying to gain an advantage, neither giving ground.

They began spiraling down toward the earth. The Archvillain tried to bite Rorbash in the neck, but the Dragonling stopped the foul being. Soon the ground approached, and the two let go of each other before they crashed.

Kallaki shrieked. Rorbash roared in response. The Batling flew upward, and the Dragonling pursued him. Below them, the battle continued, the invaders surging forward and making the defenders retreat a bit.

The Archvillain changed course and flew toward Urdanth. The Universal Marshal followed. Not long, they entered the city and flew between buildings. Then the foul being dove and landed on the ground amid startled onlookers. The Enforcer landed on the ground himself, not far from the Batling.

"Your world is doomed," Kallaki said.

Rorbash advanced toward him. "Not in my lifetime."

The Archvillain grabbed a parked speeder and hurled it at the Universal Marshal. The Enforcer caught the vehicle and set it down.

People scrambled to get out of the way of the fight between the two. The foul being shrieked and launched himself at the Dragonling. Rorbash caught him and hurled the Batling into a building. Unfortunately, the Universal Marshal did not have a pair of antipower handcuffs with him to put on the Archvillain.

Kallaki recovered and took off in the air again. Rorbash took flight and chased him. Outside the city the battle moved closer to it. Soon the fighting spread into Urdanth. The enemy got reinforcements as another transport ship brought more biocreated minions into the fray. But the Tellusian land troopers fought hard to prevent the enemy from taking the city.

****

Transport ships from the enemy landed near Darfleet. Biocreated minions rushed out, led by the Archvillain Lethesis. The Wildcat hungered for some action and would get it.

Tellusian land troopers, led by Enforcer Slennass, intercepted the enemy. The Huntress stood five foot six with brown hair and brown eyes, slim in build, an immortal being. She wore a white tunic with white boots, armed with a bow and a quiver of arrows.

Battle began. The invaders charged at the defenders, blast rifles firing. Tellusian land troopers responded with their own weapons. The morning sky held a few wispy clouds and a breeze blew from the west. Overhead a flock of birds flew.

The Archvillain leaped and stomped a Tellusian land trooper. She moved fast and struck down more. After she killed one by breaking his neck, she met with Slennass. The Huntress loosed an arrow at the Archvillain, who dodged it. A couple more arrows flew from the bow of the Enforcer, all missing their mark.

"Bad aim," Lethesis said.

The Wildcat leaped at the Huntress. Slennass rolled out of the way of the attack. Then the Archvillain ran into the Universal Marshal, and they fell to the ground, the bow knocked from the hands of the Enforcer.

Both got to their feet and faced each other. Lethesis attacked the Huntress and tried to claw her face. Slennass caught her arms and threw her. The Wildcat flipped in the air and landed back on her feet.

"You are good," Lethesis said. "But not good enough."

Slennass smiled. "I will not be defeated by the likes of you."

They locked arms, and each tried to get the advantage. The Archvillain attempted to trip the Universal Marshal, but the Enforcer blocked it. Slennass went to sweep the legs of the foul being, who avoided the technique. On and on they fought, neither giving ground to the other.

The Tellusian land troopers advanced against the biocreated minions. The enemy did not retreat. Another transport ship landed, and more foes poured out against the defenders. This increased the threat of Darfleet being stormed by the biocreated minions. But the Tellusian land troopers held their ground, and the enemy did not advance toward the city.

Eventually, the defenders found themselves being pushed back by a surge of their foes. The Tellusian land troopers were outnumbered by the enemy. Darfleet was in danger of being overrun by the invaders.

****

In space near Tellus, battlecruisers from Tellus engaged enemy ships. The space fleet of the Archvillain organization outnumbered the ships from the planet.

Battle favored the Fellowship of Darkness.

Laser fire shot all around in space near Tellus. Battlecruisers from the planet scored on enemy ships but took a pounding themselves. More transport ships departed from space destroyers and headed for Tellus. The battlecruisers targeted and managed to destroy a couple.

Enemy fighters from spacecraft carriers launched and joined the fray. Fighters from Tellus took off and flew toward the battle in space. Tellusian space troopers manned the fighters of the defenders and engaged the enemy.

None of the Enforcers took part in the battle in space. Instead, they fought the enemy on the planet. Some Universal Marshals owned ships that could join the fighting in space. They still might if the High Enforcer ordered them to.

****

Back on the planet, transport ships flew over the Angranadan Ocean for Survarille. Ahead of them, riding on a whale, stood Enforcer Mananos, to bar their way. He stood three inches over six feet, with a short white beard, long white hair, and sea blue eyes, wearing a white robe and matching boots. The Aquabeing raised his trident of power and summoned a tidal wave. He sent the tsunami to crash into the transport ships, and they fell into the water.

More transport ships came, this time accompanied by fighters. The small ships fired lasers at the Universal Marshal, but the Enforcer dove under the surface and avoided the shots.

Mananos rose onto the surface again and summoned a hurricane against the enemy. The cyclone struck his foes and disabled the transport ships and the fighters.

Transport ships kept coming. From one, the Archvillain Brutalos jumped into the ocean. The Kraken swam fast toward the Aquabeing to stop the Universal Marshal from mainly disabling transport ships. The immortal Enforcer fought the foul being.

****

Delveran stood before the Computer-Enforcer. "Report."

"The invaders are making headway against our forces all over the planet," Nanomach said. "They are mostly targeting major cities on Survarille and Mellenroel."

"Have they committed to attacking Acropollon yet?" Delveran asked, crossing his arms.

Nanomach checked. "So far, the invaders have not sent any of their forces against the capital itself."

Delveran found that disturbing. "Sooner or later, they must in order for them to accomplish the jailbreak of the Universal Prisonplex."

"Affirmative," Nanomach agreed.

"Have troopers been employed to guard the metropolis and the Universal Prisonplex?" Delveran asked. The High Enforcer uncrossed his arms.

"Affirmative," Nanomach responded.

Delveran nodded. "It's only matter of time before the enemy attacks us here."

Chapter 30

The Archvillains in the Complex met in the meeting room. A long table stretched from one end to another. Behind one end of the table, a telescreen hung on the wall. On the end of the table sat a control console. Professor Magnemus seated himself before the control console.

"We must do something about the Enforcer Squad," Xiaosu said. The Fox Maiden sat left of the Scientific Being.

Magnmeus addressed the Banshee. "What do you see?"

"The Enforcer Squad is getting closer to finding the Complex," Usaddith replied. Dressed in a white robe with matching shoes, she had long white hair and white eyes, long fingernails, and sharp teeth. "It may be inevitable they find the gateway of the realming device."

Eveinnen spoke. "I agreed with the Fox Maiden. The Enforcer Squad must be dealt with before they find our hidden stronghold."

"And we will," Magnemus responded. The Professor thought a moment. "We will attack Earth. The Terrans are vulnerable."

"Yess!" Moroloch agreed.

Magnemus turned to Master Horror on his right. "You will have your chance to unleash new horrors on Earth."

"Yes!" Gordred said with glee. He looked deformed with black eyes in a white cloak and matching shoes. "The Terran world will feel the full extent of my special powers of horror."

Magnemus nodded. "First, we will send biocreated minions out to attack Earth. This should keep the Enforcer Squad busy for a while."

The meeting lasted a short time. The Archvillains prepared the attacks on Earth.

****

The Enforcer Squad continued to search for the hidden stronghold of the Archvillain organization. They pursued some leads, but none panned out yet.

They ate lunch in the mess hall of the ship, except Procules. He did an internal systems check on himself.

"Their citadel is so well hidden," Isisis remarked.

Minanket agreed. "It must be somewhere we have not considered." The Molecular Being consumed a hamburger with French fries and drank iced tea.

"The real question is how are they hiding the Complex from us," Severrin said. The Colossus devoured a bacon, lettuce, and tomato sandwich with a bowl of vegetable soup.

Raquella ate a tossed salad with slices of wheat bread. "It must be cloaked from sight. That is why we have been unable to find it." She drank a tall glass of root beer.

"So how are they cloaking it from sight?" Averriol asked. The Chakra Being downed a chicken salad sandwich with a bowl of macaroni and cheese. He gulped a carton of milk with his meal.

Rathol chimed in. "We shall eventually find where they are hiding. It is only a matter of time."

The other Universal Marshals agreed with the Shepherd. Sooner or later, they would get a break to where the Complex hid. The Archvillains could not avoid them forever.

****

The Archvillains launched their first attack on Earth. Biocreated minions stormed New York City and fired blast rifles at anything that moved as well as caused destruction to property. People scurried for safety.

The Enforcer Squad responded. They came to the Terrans' rescue and took on the biocreated minions.

"This a bold move by the foul beings," Eneysa remarked. The Metamorph-Enforcer shapeshifted into various life forms to combat the enemy.

"They must not succeed in this attack," Vartagal stated. The Great Archer loosed arrows at foes. He scored every time. Then he switched to the supernatural half of his bow and shot arrows of energy at them, felling the biocreated minions left and right.

"This is a calculated strategy by the Archvillains," Minanket remarked. The Molecular Being turned into a molecular ball, white and glistening, and rammed into a bunch of male clones firing blast rifles at the Enforcer Squad.

Jagathan fought a group of androids. The Titan-Enforcer smashed his fists into them, rendering them inoperative. A male android jumped on his back. The Universal Marshal grabbed him and ripped him in half.

Lorliane froze a bunch of male mutants in ice. The Ice Being kept freezing biocreated minions as they attacked her.

Rathol used the Staff of Godpower to blast the enemy. The Shepherd wiped out a bunch of male and female cyborgs as they charged at him.

Averroil, Raquella, and Isisis fought back with blast rifles to match their foes. Orissa used wind power to combat biocreated minions. Procules took them out in different ways with his offensive capabilities.

"They are like pests," Severrin remarked. The Colossus fired bronze beams from his eyes at them to destroy them. He flew at a bunch of clones and knocked them down.

Down the street, a gigantic robot strode. It smashed cars in its way and proceeded toward the Universal Marshals.

"I got this," Severrin said. The Colossus took off and fired bronze beams from his eyes at the huge droid. The shots damaged it but did not slow it down. The Enforcer flew at great speed and went through the chest of the automaton, leaving a gaping hole in it. The robot collapsed to the ground, inoperative. "That is how you do it."

The fight with the biocreated minions lasted a while. In the end, the Enforcer Squad triumphed over the enemy. Their foes were all destroyed. New York City was safe again.

The Enforcer Squad wondered what the next attack on Earth by the Archvillains would be. It could come in any form.

****

The Archvillains gathered in the meeting room of the Complex again.

"The biocreated minions failed," Namprey said. The Nodrone wanted another crack at the Enforcer Squad.

Quasicoatl addressed the Scientific Being. "Let me send cloned creatures at them. Not of Earth."

"All right," Magnemus responded. "Launch your attack against them."

Gordred spoke. "When do I get my chance?"

"Soon, Master Horror," Magnemus replied. "If the Cloning Creature does not succeed, then you can unleash your first horror on the Terran world."

Gordred laughed. The foul being would choose what the first horror would be from a number of options at his disposal.

"I foresee the Enforcer Squad will eventually find our hidden stronghold," Usaddith said.

"What do you see in regards to our invasion of Tellus?" Ynemain asked. The Iron Maiden might want to launch an attack herself against Earth.

The Banshee concentrated to see a vision of the invasion. "Our forces are making progress against the Tellusians. But resistance from them is strong. Enforcers are leading it."

"Can you foresee the outcome of the invasion?" Xiaosu asked.

"Not yet," Usaddith replied. "In time, I will. Right now, I see battle waging across Tellus. On the planet itself and in space near it."

Quasicoatl prepared to launch his attack on Earth.

****

The Enforcer Squad rested after the battle with the biocreated minions. But they stayed vigilant.

In the meeting room of the ship, the Universal Marshals gathered. Procules updated his memory cells with information on the Terran world.

"Are we getting any closer to finding the Complex?" Raquella asked her fellow Enforcers.

"We have eliminated a number of possible locations

for their hidden stronghold," Averroil remarked. "But there are still plenty of places it could be. It is a process of elimination to find it."

Eneysa spoke. "Where haven't we looked?"

"We have concentrated our search around populated areas on Earth mainly," Minanket said. "Maybe the Complex is hidden in an unpopulated area of the Terran world."

****

The next day, Quasicoatl unleashed extraterrestrial creatures on Earth. New York City again suffered the assault. The Enforcer Squad came to the aid of the Terrans once more.

"This is the second deadly attack by the foul beings," Vartagal remarked. The Golden Archer shot arrows of energy from his bow at animals that looked like big cats with horns and spiked tails. He cut them down as fast as he could.

Jagathan wrestled with a bearlike creature with tusks. It tried to bite him, but the Universal Marshal kept it from succeeding. The Titan-Enforcer lifted it in the air and slammed it on the ground. Then he snapped its neck, killing it.

The other Enforcers contended with the extraterrestrial creatures. A variety of them fought the Universal Marshals, of different sizes, from various worlds.

Eneysa shapeshifted into a huge armor-plated animal with a club tail and took out a few of the alien animals. The Metamorph-Enforcer charged at another bunch of them and bowled them over. Then she changed into a dragon and finished them off.

Severrin shot bronze beams from his eyes at more of

them. The Colossus felled them in succession. A huge apelike creature jumped at him, but he dodged it. Then he grabbed it and flew into the air at a high altitude and dropped it from the sky. It crashed to the ground, dead.

The battle with the extraterrestrial creatures lasted several hours. Afterward, Terrans got out from under cover and thanked the Enforcer Squad for saving them.

****

The Universal Marshals returned to the *Centaurus* and gathered in the meeting room of the ship again.

"The Archvillains are sorely testing us," Averroil remarked. "That is now two times we had to fight their attacks on Earth."

Lorliane spoke. "I think we will see more of their attacks on the Terran world."

"They are trying to distract us from finding their hidden stronghold," Minanket said. "We must be getting close to finding it."

"They are attacking Earth because the Terrans are vulnerable," Severrin stated.

"Aye," Jagathan agreed.

Rathol entered the conversation. "We must protect the people of Earth from them. They must not destroy this world."

"They already victimized this planet even before we arrived here," Isisis said. "I sensed this."

"How much harm have they done then?" Raquella asked the Occultic Being.

"Enough to cause concern," Isisis replied.

Raquella smiled. "Now that we're here they won't be victimizing Earth so easily."

"Do you think they may challenge us to a fight again?" Vartagal asked his fellow Enforcers.

"I don't think they will," Minanket responded. "But I could be wrong. They might decide to confront us again to be rid of us."

"They are not cowards," Severrin said. "If they think taking us on again in a fight would suit their plans, they will."

"Once we find their hidden stronghold and penetrate it, they will be forced to battle us," Orissa stated. "It will be unavoidable."

Rathol chimed in. "Pray we find where they are hidden before they launch more attacks on this world."

****

The Enforcer Squad continued searching for the Complex. But before they could find it, the Archvillains launched another attack on Earth.

Gordred unleashed his first horror on the Terran world. Master Horror sent a swarm of African killer bees to attack people in New York City. Earthlings got stung by the four-winged, deadly insects, some fatal.

The Enforcer Squad responded again. Lorliane shot ice beams from her hands and froze bees. Severrin shot bronze beams from his eyes and killed more of the insects. Suddenly the swarm turned its attention on the Universal Marshals and buzzed toward them. Rathol used the Staff of Godpower and raised a wall of fire that consumed the remaining ones. That ended it.

"I sense this was the work of the Archvillain Gordred," Isisis said. The Occultic Being paused. "Master Horror is not finished yet."

****

"Your first horror failed," Eveinnen remarked. The Liquid Metal Being wore a grim expression.

The Archvillains stood in the main corridor of the

Complex. Biocreated minions went in and out of the place.

"I am just getting started," Gordred said. Master Horror seemed not bothered that his initial attempt did not meet with success. "My next horror will be a better one."

Xiaosu spoke. "Three times we have launched attacks against the Earthlings, and three times we have come up empty. The Universal Marshals are making us look silly."

Magnemus turned to the Banshee. "What do you see in how the invasion of Tellus is progressing?"

"Progress is slow," Usaddith replied. "We are not conquering the planet fast enough. The Federation will soon try to eliminate the energy barrier."

"Not good," Sorrent commented. The Gwillion shook her head in disgust.

"We must change our invasion plans," Magnemus said. "We must contact our forces there and have them attack Acropollon to get to the Universal Prisonplex."

****

The second horror Gordred launched against Earth took the form of monstrous plants. The walking vegetation attacked people and animals. It happened around the globe.

The Enforcer Squad acted. With the help of military forces of the Terran world, the Universal Marshals fought the botanical nightmares. Earth soldiers used flame throwers on the monstrous plants to burn them. Rathol wielded the Staff of Godpower and summoned fire to consume the walking vegetation. Other weapons employed against the botanical nightmares, like bazookas, were effective against them.

The battle against the monstrous plants lasted a while. When it was over, there were casualties to the Terrans. None of the Enforcer Squad suffered any wounds or injuries. The Universal Marshals returned to the *Centaurus*.

"Gordred is being creative in his horrors," Isisis said.

Minanket addressed the Robot-Enforcer. "What is the full extent of the abilities of Master Horror?"

"His special powers of horror are wide-ranging," Procules answered. "There is no limit on what he can unleash against Earth."

"Does he have any tendencies in his horrors?" Lorliane asked.

Procules checked his memory cells. "He enjoys scaring his victims before he kills them. His horrors take the shape of either organic or inorganic forms. He is particularly fond of monsters for his horrors."

"What horror will he send against Earth next?" Eneysa voiced.

Severrin sighed. "Whatever it is, it will be different than the last two."

****

The Archvillains gathered in the Complex. They sat in the mess hall.

"The Terrans have paid a small price so far because of our attacks against Earth," Usaddith said. "But the Enforcer Squad has prevented a larger cost to the planet."

Magnemus was not pleased with that. He addressed Master Horror. "Have you planned your next attack on Earth?"

Gordred chortled. "Yes. There are several more horrors I can bring against the Terran world. Let's see how they handle the next one."

****

The next horror Gordred sent against Earth was in the form of a pandemic. The Terran world had previously suffered a pandemic that was the coronavirus. Now Master Horror spread a new disease around the world rapidly.

The enemy the Enforcer Squad fought this time was vastly different than the last two attacks. Conventional weapons were useless.

"I sense Gordred has unleashed some kind of plague against Earth," Isisis said. "Master Horror is trying to devastate the world population as much as possible."

"How do we stop it?" Averroil asked his fellow Enforcers.

"With the healing power of the Lord," Rathol interjected. "God can vanquish this blight the foul being has sent against Earth."

The Shepherd brought the Staff of Godpower to life. He commanded it to cure the people of the planet. From the heavens, white light poured down and bathed every Earthling in healing rays. The pandemic disappeared.

"I sense great relief from the Terrans," Isisis said. "The Archvillains have been beaten again."

"They will be back with another attack on Earth," Lorliane remarked. "They will not stop until they have succeeded in ruining the Terran world somehow."

"Aye," Jagathan agreed. "Their malevolence knows no bounds."

****

In the Complex, Gordred appeared a little frustrated. Master Horror thought his third horror against Earth would succeed.

"The only reason your pandemic didn't work was because of one Enforcer," Usaddith said. "The Universal Marshal Rathol, the Shepherd, thwarted you."

"Curse him," Gordred responded. Then Master Horror brightened. "I will try another horror against Earth. Something the Terrans fear."

"What do you have in mind?" Eveinnen asked.

Gordred grinned. "The Earthlings fear a number of things. I have looked through their information bases for scenarios they are afraid of. One of them involves a nuclear winter."

"The Terrans do have nuclear weapons," Magnemus stated. "They keep many in silos."

"True," Gordred agreed. "The Earthlings fear nuclear war."

****

The Enforcer Squad waited for the next attack by the Archvillains against Earth. Their search for the hidden stronghold of the Archvillain organization narrowed. So far they eliminated a number of possible places for it.

The next attack on Earth by the Archvillains happened just after dawn Eastern Standard Time. Nuclear missiles in silos in the United States and Russia began launching without warning and not by the military personnel responsible for them.

"Alert," Procules said from the science console. "Nuclear missiles in the air and targeted for different locations."

Severrin left the *Centaurus* and flew in the air. He zoomed toward nuclear missiles in the sky. When he caught up with some over the Atlantic Ocean, the Colossus redirected them for outer space. He kept going after nuclear missiles, faster than them in flight.

Severrin could not get all the nuclear missiles in time. So the *Centaurus* took off and went after the nuclear missiles going the other direction—for the Pacific Ocean. The ship traveled very fast to catch up with them.

"Missiles in laser range," Procules said.

"Fire!" Rathol ordered.

Jagatahan shot lasers from the ship and destroyed nuclear missiles high in the sky, one by one. "Got them all."

"Praise God," Rathol said.

The battlecruiser returned to Central Park. Severrin returned to the ship. The Universal Marshals gathered in the meeting room.

"The sooner we find the Complex, the sooner we can stop these attacks on Earth," Lorliane remarked.

Averriol agreed. "Where have we not looked?"

"The Arctic and Antarctica are two places we have not searched," Minanket stated. "But I think the hidden stronghold of the Archvillains is unlikely to be at either location."

"We should check them out anyway," Raquella suggested.

Rathol nodded. "We shall."

****

In the Complex, the Archvillains sat in the meeting room. All eyes turned to the Scientific Being.

"Once again, an attack against Earth failed," Magnemus said. He addressed Master Horror. "Do you have any horrors left to try against the Terran world?"

Gordred grinned. "One more. This is something I used before on other worlds with success. It might work on Earth."

"Proceed," Magnemus ordered.

****

The Enforcer Squad searched through the Arctic and Antarctica for the Complex. It proved unsuccessful.

The next attack on Earth was a favorite horror of Gordred. Master Horror raised the dead, both ghosts and zombies, to terrorize the Terran world. People got scared and were attacked by the Walking Dead and phantoms.

The Enforcer Squad battled the new foes. So did Earthlings. The dead could not be killed so easily since they were not living beings. On they marched to wreak death and destruction.

Finally, Rathol summoned the Staff of Godpower to exorcise the spirits of the dead. White light from the heavens shot down, and all the specters disappeared in it. Now the Shepherd turned his attention to the zombies.

The Walking Dead could not be dealt with the same way as the apparitions. So the Enforcer Squad and the Terrans had to destroy the zombies instead. Fire worked well against the creatures. Eventually, all the animated corpses were annihilated.

That evening, the Enforcer Squad gathered in the mess hall for supper. They discussed many topics.

Isisis stiffened. "I sense danger to the ship."

The Universal Marshals hurried out of the vessel. They spotted a male clone planting a bomb on the *Centaurus*. The biocreated minion fled, but Severrin flew after him and caught him. Jagathan crushed the bomb in his hand without exploding it.

The Enforcer Squad interrogated the male clone on the ship.

"Where is the Complex?" Lorliane asked.

The male clone refused to answer. Rathol roasted

the male clone in white fire from the Staff of Godpower until the biocreated minion cracked.

"It is in Hawaii," the male clone said. "It is hidden by a realming device."

The Enforcer Squad locked him up in the brig. Soon the Universal Marshals would confront the Archvillains in their hidden stronghold and try to arrest the foul beings.

Chapter 31

Delveran stood before the Computer-Enforcer. "What is the latest news?"

"The invaders are withdrawing," Nanomach answered. "Federation forces are trying to break through the energy barrier."

"The enemy is changing their plans," Delveran said. The High Enforcer thought. "They will gather their forces and attack Acropollon next in order to reach the Universal Prisonplex."

"That is logical," Nanomach agreed.

Delveran let out a deep breath. "We must gather our forces to meet them in battle. All Enforcers on the planet must return here to prepare for the enemy attack."

"Acknowledged," Nanomach responded.

"How many of us are at the Justiceplex at present?" Delveran asked. The High Enforcer knew a few of the Universal Marshals were at the headquarters.

"Counting us, four," Nanomach replied. "Zorroquin and Brinivere are also here."

Delveran nodded. "Put me on the intercom to speak with the two of them."

Nanomach complied. Both the Thunderer and the Cellular Being answered on the intercom.

"I want you to go to the teleporter room and teleport the other Enforcers on Tellus to the Justiceplex," Delveran ordered. "This is a priority matter. Have them all meet me in the training room. Join us after you are done with your task."

"As you command," Zorrorquin and Brinvere responded in unison. The Thunderer and the Cellular Being went to the task.

Delveran addressed the Computer-Enforcer again. "Contact the Militaryplex, General Jaylor Manthen's office."

"Affirmative," Nanomach acknowledged. "Communication established."

"What can I do for you, High Enforcer?" Jaylor asked.

Delveran sighed. "We need to gather our forces to defend Acropollon and the Universal Prisonplex. The enemy is massing for an attack on the capital in order to accomplish the jailbreak."

"I will order all our military units to the scene," Jaylor said. "Land, sea, air, and space troopers will be deployed as quickly as possible."

"Thank you, general," Delveran responded. The High Enforcer ended the communication.

Nanomach beeped. "Is there anything else?"

"No," Delveran said. "Keep monitoring the situation, though."

"Affirmative," Nanomach acknowledged.

Delveran left the computer room and went to the training room of the Justiceplex, located at the south end of the shorter corridor. Enforcers gathered in the huge chamber. One by one Universal Marshals entered the training room and stood in lines. After all the Enforcers arrived, the Grand Universal Marshal looked them over.

"The invaders have been forced to alter their plans," Delveran began. "Federation forces are at the energy barrier and should eventually eliminate it. The enemy is gathering their forces to attack Acropollon. They are in a hurry to accomplish the jailbreak of the Universal Prisonplex."

"So we will meet them head-on," Wardelorean said. The Dreadnought stood six feet, four inches tall, with light brown hair and hazel eyes, in an armored suit of his own design.

"Yes," Delveran responded. "We must prevent them from unleashing the thousands of Archvillains imprisoned in the Universal Prisonplex. The galaxy is depending on us."

There was a murmur of agreement from the other Universal Marshals on that.

"How much time do we have before they strike?" Voltar asked. The Electrobeing stood six feet, two inches, with black hair and blue eyes, in an electric blue unisuit with matching boots.

Delveran closed his eyes. The High Enforcer looked into the future. "I foresee their attack coming in three days."

"I foresee this also," Selmajase added. The Glaistig-Enforcer, of the race of fairie, appeared as an old woman with long white hair and white eyes, in a green robe with matching slippers.

"What about our forces?" Molton asked. The Lava Being stood in line in the back.

"The Tellusian military is deploying as we speak to defend Acropollon," Delveran replied. "We will join them in two days. In the meantime, we will get some training in to ready us for the coming battle."

"Bust my bark!" Arboron exclaimed. The Treeling shook a few leaves in his crown. "These minions and their foul masters need to be split like rotted timber."

"What about Earth?" Bolan asked. Trevarre stood six feet, one inch, clean-shaven, with sandy-brown hair and brown eyes, dressed in military garb from the Terran world. The Noble Soldier looked very concerned about his native world.

"The Enforcer Squad will have to protect your home planet against the Archvillains there," Delveran replied. "We cannot help them."

For the entire day, the Enforcers worked out in the training room. Over and over again, they simulated combat—via hologram programs—in all kinds of terrain, surroundings, and battle situations, both invasion and noninvasion types. The High Enforcer pushed his fellow Universal Marshals to be up to par. He wanted the Federation and Tellus to be able to rely on them when the time came for the battle of Acropollon. Deep within himself, he sensed there should be more Enforcers for the task. Then the idea of recruiting and training new beings to become Universal Marshals sparked in his mind. Finally, he decided that there were enough Enforcers for the coming battle. He worried about how many Archvillains would lead the assault on the capital.

The Enforcers gathered in the mess hall for dinner. Only Nanomach could not attend. The Universal Marshals got food and drink from synthesizers in the walls.

"Now, this is fellowship," Findall said. The Habble-Enforcer ate a rice dish with fish and drank ale.

Ulleric sat across from the small faerie. The Dynaman munched on a salad and dark bread with ice water for a beverage. "This is pleasant to be together."

The High Enforcer excused himself and went to his

office. Meanwhile, the other Universal Marshals enjoyed the evening as a group, something they did not do often.

In his office, Delveran sat back in his chair. Then the telescreen beeped, and he answered it.

Evarinia appeared on it. "How is the defense of the planet going?" she asked.

"The enemy is changing their strategy," Delveran replied. The High Enforcer leaned forward in his chair. "I expect an all-out assault on the capital by them soon. Their energy barrier is being threatened by Federation forces as we speak. Hopefully, we will have help from the Federation before the enemy get a chance to reach the Universal Prisonplex."

Evarinia smiled. "I take it you have employed our military forces for Acropollon already."

"Yes," Delveran said. "I will have the Universal Marshals in position with the troopers by tomorrow."

Evarinia brushed back a lock of her hair. "It's a shame the warding device and the Defenseplex were destroyed."

"Yes," Delveran agreed. "A new warding device will have to be made and a new Defenseplex built. After we have dealt with the enemy."

Evarinia nodded. "I am confident you and your Universal Marshals with the troopers will stop them. They cannot win against us."

Delveran grinned. "The enemy did not succeed in overrunning our planet with the invasion. That is a good sign."

"Will I see you for dinner, sweetheart?"

"Where would you like to dine?"

"My place."

"What time?"

"Nine?"

"Nine it is."

****

Back in the mess hall, the Universal Marshals laughed and talked of many things. They thoroughly enjoyed their meal and time together.

"How is your family?" Kennedrill asked the Dreadnought. The Interstellar Pilgrim had no family of his own.

"My wife, daughter, and son are doing fine," Wardelorean replied. "Why have you never mated?"

"I was too busy exploring the galaxy," Kennedrill answered. "Never really had a chance to find a mate."

Findall chimed in. "I have been married for thirty years." The Habble-Enforcer drained more of his ale.

"Do you have any children?" Wardelorean asked.

Findall smiled. "I have seven children. Four girls and three boys."

"I am the only one of my kind," Molton interjected. "As far as I know."

Rorbash spoke. "I find it hard to mate with a female of my species." The Dragonling felt down about that.

"Why?" Wardelorean asked.

Rorbash huffed. "Because of the size difference. Among dragons, I am a pygmy."

"All of nature is my children," Glyndalyn said. Mother Nature was a tall woman with short blonde hair and green eyes. She wore a white robe with matching slippers. The Incarnation ate a bowl of mushroom soup.

Ulleric spoke. "I don't have a spouse or kids. But I do have siblings. A brother and a sister."

Zorroquin changed the subject. "I thought our workout in the training room earlier was much more intense than usual." The Thunderer dined on a steak with beer to drink.

"Yes," Voltar agreed. "Our situation with the invasion called for it. Very rigorous." The Electrobeing consumed a pork sandwich with milk as a beverage.

"The coming battle of Acropollon has us all on edge," Wakantanuka remarked. The Manitou-Enforcer devoured a bowl of venison stew with wine as refreshment.

Lucane chimed in. "We may see all the Archvillains with the enemy space fleet leading the assault on the capital." The Peryton feasted on lamb chops with cooked green beans and mead to drink.

"That seems likely," Yauriga agreed. The Avatar-Enforcer worked on a dessert of apple pie.

Ydiart entered the conversation. "Emotions are running high among us." The Empath-Enforcer specialized in them. She featured long strawberry-blonde hair and blue eyes, wearing a pink unisuit with matching boots. "The atmosphere for the coming battle here will be quite tense."

Some of the Enforcers had been in a war before they became Universal Marshals. But none ever experienced an invasion of a planet. Until now.

"We do know most of the Archvillains who will lead the attack on Acropollon," Selmajase said. The Glaistig-Enforcer ate a plate of raw vegetables with water to drink. "They had led the invasion on Tellus before the enemy withdrew."

"Can you foresee how many of them there are to lead the assault on the capital?" Darthan asked. The Marveltrooper had already finished his dinner.

"Yes," Selmajase answered. "There are a dozen of

them."

"Who is the chief commander among them?" Wardelorean asked.

Selmajase concentrated her vision. "The Grim Reaper. Formerly of the Four Horsemen of the Apocalypse."

"Aren't two of them in the Universal Prisonplex?" Neisie asked. The Unicornling munched on wheat cakes.

"Yes," Zorroquin confirmed. "Pestilence and Famine. They were arrested by the High Enforcer before he became the Grand Universal Marshal."

"What about War?" Estephone asked. The Horae-Enforcer ate a cherry ice treat.

"Still at large," Zorroquin replied. "The Four Horsemen of the Apocalypse did much harm in their day as a band."

"Then War is not with the Archvillains in the invasion," Zithell stated. The Amazon had just finished her meal.

"My vision does not show him with them," Selmajase said. "I do not sense him with the Archvillain organization at all. He may join it later if it is still around."

Kennedrill voiced a thought. "The Archvillain organization may have already tried to get the Incarnation of War to join it."

"True," Zorroquin agreed. "The Grim Reaper is the obvious one to try and recruit him for it, since they know each other very well."

"War would have been the perfect commander for the invasion," Wardelorean said. "It fits right in his specialty of war."

In the Universal Prisonplex, few of the Archvillains

imprisoned there had any associations with fellow Archvillains. One involved a group of inmates who were Spriggans, belonging to the race of faerie and known particularly as thieves. Archvillains did socialize with members of their evil class occasionally.

****

Delveran ate dinner with Evarinia in her apartment in Acropollon. Their meal consisted of pasta with meat sauce and rye bread and white wine to drink. Her place was modestly furnished, with a few holographic paintings on the walls.

Evarinia noticed his demeanor. "You seem worried."

"I am," Delveran admitted.

"You fear you will fail to stop the enemy from busting out all those Archvillains in the Universal Prisonplex." Evarinia took a bite of pasta.

Delveran sighed. "Yes. Over the centuries, Enforcers have arrested them and locked them away. The important work by the Universal Marshals could be undone in a moment. If all those Archvillains are freed from the Universal Prisonplex, they will bring such chaos to the galaxy."

"Not to mention death and destruction," Evarinia added.

Delveran nodded. "It is the responsibility of the Enforcers to see to it none of this happens. The Fellowship of Darkness must be stopped from recruiting Archvillains to their organization if the jailbreak succeeds. The bigger it grows, the more of a problem it becomes."

They eventually finished dinner. Evarinia led Delveran to her bedroom. They made love.

****

Thirty-one Enforcers joined the Tellusian troopers south of the Universal Prisonplex two days later. Trenches had been dug. Laser cannons had been set up. Fighters would join the coming battle in the morning. The defense of Acropollon was in place.

"Soon, we will be facing the enemy," Delveran began. "We will stand our ground against them. They must not be allowed to pass. The Federation and the rest of the galaxy are counting on us to succeed against them. We are on the side of right."

Universal Marshals and troopers cheered. Everyone was in high spirits.

"The Enforcers here outnumber the Archvillains who will lead the assault on the capital," Wardelorean pointed out. "That is in our favor."

"Yes," Kennedrill agreed, standing left of the Dreadnought. "But the biocreated minions commanded by the Archvillains may outnumber our troopers."

"It is irrelevant whether or not they are outnumbered," Zithell said, standing right of the Dreadnought. "What matters is how well they fight against the enemy."

"We must take the fight to the enemy," Darthan stated. "Not let them gain an advantage over us."

The day passed into night. All day the weather was good, not much cloud cover. Evening saw little activity as the defenders experienced warm temperatures. Wind blew little. Nembat was at half moon.

"This is going to be a long night," Galamagne remarked. "This waiting for the enemy is a bit nerve-wracking." The Space Chevalier patted his light sword on his belt.

"What did you do before you became a Universal Marshal?" Sharminival asked. The Energy Being sat across from him.

Galamagne took off his helmet. "I performed heroic deeds in the galaxy. Rescued damsels in distress. Went on a few quests. All in all, it was an exciting life." He put his helmet back on.

"I spent most of my time exploring the galaxy," Kennedrill said. "Met many different races in my travels. Made plenty of friends along the way."

Thayla and Medeordese lay down next to each other.

"This is not exactly a romantic setting," Medeordese joked. The Speedster touched her hand.

Thayla smiled. "Just being together is romantic enough." The Valkyrie-Enforcer returned the gesture.

Universal Marshals and troopers took turns keeping watch. The night passed uneventfully.

****

Just after dawn, the enemy came. Fighters and laser tanks advanced on their position. Archvillains led biocreated minions on the march.

"Steady," Delveran said.

Tellus fighters flew from the north. As soon as they reached the battlefield, they began shooting. Enemy fighters returned fire. The battle of Acropollon began.

"Laser cannons, fire!" Delveran commanded.

The artillery of the Tellusians did. Blast rifles followed in the hands of troopers. Some used photon bazookas on their foes.

Laser tanks fired. Some hit their targets.

Glyndalyn summoned lightning from the sky to strike the enemy. Mother Nature commanded nature against them.

The enemy kept advancing. They appeared confident about smashing through the defense of Tellus in order to get to the Universal Prisonplex.

Kennedrill pressed buttons on his powerbands and fired a variety of rays at the enemy. First he shot a heat ray and felled biocreated minions repeatedly. Then he used a blasting ray to slay more of them.

Rorbash shot fire from his mouth at the enemy. The Dragonling burned a bunch of male clones to death. He set fire to other biocreated minions.

Molton threw hot lava balls at the enemy. The Lava Being tossed some at laser tanks, but they did not have much effect on the armored vehicles.

Zorroquin shot lightning from his body at foes. The Thunderer raised his hammer and pounded the ground with Bronthorjal. It sent shock waves through the earth and tumbled biocreated minions.

Chryssina shot photon blasts from her hands at the enemy. The Light Being slayed foes with them and also hit laser tanks.

Delveran shot green fire from his hands. The High Enforcer destroyed biocreated minions and tried to burn laser tanks.

Ramairgan shot blasts from his Rod of Power at the enemy. Hermit Power hit laser tanks as well.

The Archvillains leading the assault struck. Ragnar threw his battle-axe of power into troopers and plowed them down. The magical weapon returned to his hand, and the Berserker yelled a battle cry.

Orlin appeared among the troopers. The Grim Reaper swung his scythe and felled them.

Troopers fired their blast rifles at the Incarnation, but to no effect. Death could not be killed so easily.

"The Grim Reaper is wreaking havoc among our troopers," Wardelorean said. "He must be stopped."

Ramairgan spied the Incarnation among the troopers. "I will take care of him."

Hermit Power challenged Death to single combat. Orlin accepted. The two Incarnations fought. Orlin swung his scythe at the Enforcer, who blocked the strike with his rod. Ramairgan countered with his rod, which was parried by the Archvillain. They exchanged blows, neither gaining the upper hand.

Bolan fired a photon bazooka at a laser tank. The Noble Soldier blew it up. He reloaded and took out another one.

Ragnar came face to face with Zorrorquin in the battle. They looked at each other.

"You are handy with that hammer," Ragnar said.

Zorroquin grinned. "You wield a mean battle-axe."

Ragnar smiled. "Let's see how well you do against it."

The Archvillain charged the Enforcer. Yelling a battle cry, the Berserker swung his battle-axe at the Thunderer. The Enforcer blocked the strike of the Archvillain and whipped his hammer around to hit the Archvillain. The foul being intercepted the blow and countered with a downward chop of his magical weapon. The Universal Marshal evaded the hack and swung Bronthorjal upward against the Berserker, who dodged it. Both circled each other to find a weakness in the other's defense.

A Tellus fighter got hit by a laser tank and crashed to the ground. The pilot was all right, not injured. Before the enemy could kill him, in a flash of speed Medeordese saved him and carried him back to the Tellusian lines.

Transport ships from the enemy landed more biocreated minions for the battle. More were coming. Kennedrill took off in the air with Chryssina and they went after the transport ships.

The Light Being shot photon blasts at them as Kennedrill fired a blasting ray at them. The two Universal Marshals managed to destroy a pair of them together.

Cenjuno opened her Curdatch and let out blights to attack the troopers. The Archvillain killed a number of them. Then Slennass found her and engaged the Keve in combat.

The enemy began pushing the Tellusians back. Soon they were in sight of the Universal Prisonplex. Fighters from the enemy fired on the guard towers of it and knocked two of them out.

A unit of biocreated minions accompanied Vilegast to the force wall of the Universal Prisonplex. The Gremlin planted photon bombs at the base of it. The Archvillain and the unit got clear of the spot before the explosives did their job and took out the force wall.

Biocreated minions followed the Gremlin inside the Universal Prisonplex. Troopers and a few of the Enforcers saw this and ran after them.

"Keep them busy," Vilegast said to the biocreated minions.

Battle ensued just outside the Universal Prisonplex. The Gremlin, accompanied by some robots, went through the place and found the control room that activated antipower cells that kept Archvillains. In a moment, the Archvillain planted a photon bomb and blew up the control room.

Archvillains, having been locked away over the

centuries, were freed. Prison guards tried to stop them, but the foul beings were too much. Their special powers had been restored after being neutralized in the antipower cells. They overran the prison guards and headed outside.

Chapter 32

The Enforcer Squad prepared for the showdown with the Archvillains. As soon as they were ready, the *Centaurus* took off and headed for Hawaii.

"So the Complex was hidden from the fabric of reality by a realming device," Lorliane said. "Clever."

Averroil nodded. "We will confront them on their own turf."

"No wonder we had a hard time finding their hidden stronghold," Jagathan remarked. "We finally got a break locating it."

Eneysa chimed in. "They may be expecting us."

"Then they are ready for us," Raquella stated.

"True," Vartagal agreed. "But we are ready for them."

The ship flew across the United States west. It traveled at sublight speed, not using teleport drive to get to their destination.

"Trying to arrest them will be very difficult," Severrin said. "They will put up a fight."

Isisis spoke. "That is obvious."

"They will certainly have biocreated minions of Magnemus to contend with us," Minanket said.

"Undoubtedly," Averroil agreed. "Plus there may be more cloned creatures from Quasicoatl."

"How do we breach the gateway of the realming device to get to them?" Orissa asked her fellow

Enforcers.

Rathol joined the conversation. "With the Staff of Godpower. The almighty hand of the Lord will part the way for us."

The vessel soon flew across the Pacific Ocean for Hawaii. They encountered no planes of Earth along the way.

"They may set a trap for us," Raquella remarked.

Vartagal nodded. "That is a possibility."

"We will spring any trap and disable it," Severrin stated.

Averroil turned to the Occultic Being. "Do you sense anything from Tellus?"

"Yes," Isisis answered after a moment. "Great danger. I feel the Archvillains imprisoned in the Universal Prisonplex have been freed."

"Has Tellus been conquered?" Eneysa asked.

"No," Isisis replied. "There is a battle going on at Acropollon. I also sense Federation forces getting closer to eliminating the energy barrier that has contained Tellus."

"How did the invaders manage to bust out all those Archvillains imprisoned in the Universal Prisonplex?" Vartagal asked no one in particular.

No one answered the Great Archer. The mood on the ship turned somber. They neared their destination.

"Woe to the galaxy," Raquella murmured. The other Universal Marshals agreed with the Gothic Being on that.

They arrived at Hawaii. The ship landed south of Hilo in the countryside.

"May God see us succeed in our task," Rathol prayed.

Some of the Enforcer Squad armed themselves with blast rifles from the armory. The Shepherd led them out of the ship. The ramp closed behind them.

The countryside looked beautiful. Overhead the sun shone in an almost cloudless sky. A few birds flew overhead. They viewed stands of trees. Plenty of wildlife as well.

"This is paradise," Eneysa remarked.

"Aye," Jagathan agreed.

The wind was calm. It was late morning. The Enforcer Squad walked a little way.

"It's a shame they won't come out and face us here," Severrin said. "They have the advantage in their hidden realm."

"They are probably waiting for us," Minanket surmised.

"Likely," Averroil agreed.

Rathol halted the Enforcer Squad near some hills. The other Universal Marshals got behind the Shepherd as he raised the Staff of Godpower.

"By the almighty hand of the Lord," Rathol intoned, "the way shall be opened for us. We will enter their secret land."

A white beam shot from the Staff of Godpower and parted the fabric of reality before them. On the other side of the rift, they could see machines parked and the Complex. Rathol led them into the demesne established by the realming device. The opening behind them closed.

"They must know we're here," Lorliane said.

Severrin agreed. "You think they would have a welcoming committee for us."

"I expect we will see action soon," Raquella remarked.

Just then, three robots appeared and shot at them with lasers. Minanket turned into a molecular wheel and bowled them over, disabling them.

The Enforcer Squad reached the front entrance to the Complex. Jagathan raised the huge door by sheer strength, and they entered the place.

A voice over the intercom spoke to the Universal Marshals. It belonged to Magnemus.

"Welcome to our humble abode. We were expecting you. Sorry, we were not able to greet you on your arrival in person."

"Show yourselves," Vartagal said.

Magnemus continued. "We will not do that. You have trespassed into our realm. We cannot allow you to leave."

With that, biocreated minions charged down the main corridor of the Complex at them. The Enforcer Squad defended themselves.

"They do not want a direct confrontation with us," Averroil stated.

"Cowards," Vartagal spat.

Biocreated minions fired blasters and blast rifles at them. Members of the Enforcer Squad returned fire with their own weapons.

Jagathan tangled with a big robot. The Titan-Enforcer hammered the droid with his fists and knocked it around. It opened a chest compartment, and a circular saw extended out to try and cut the Universal Marshal to pieces. He grabbed the robot, lifted it into the air, then slammed it down to the floor and smashed it. It stopped operating.

Minanket turned into a molecular spear and went through a bunch of androids. That disabled them. The

Molecular Being repeated this maneuver with some cyborgs.

Severrin shot bronze beams from his eyes and destroyed mutants. The Colossus flew at biocreated minions and knocked them over.

Rathol wielded the Staff of Godpower and fried clones in white fire. The Shepherd led them forward.

More and more biocreated minions kept coming. The Enforcer Squad fought on.

"They must be hiding someplace in here," Eneysa said.

Isisis sensed the Archvillains. "They are in the Complex. I feel their presence."

"We have to fight our way to reach them," Procules stated. The Robot-Enforcer shot lasers from his eyes at biocreated minions.

From a pair of automatic doors to the side near Rathol a mutant jumped out, grabbed the Shepherd, and pulled him into a chamber. The Enforcer swung the Staff of Godpower and freed himself from its grasp. Then the mutant grabbed the Staff of Godpower and fought him over it.

Rathol responded by sending fire into the body of his adversary and burning his foe to ashes. The Universal Marshal left the room and rejoined his comrades.

"Are you all right?" Orissa asked the Shepherd. The Sylph-Enforcer used wind power against their enemy.

"I am fine," Rathol answered. "They tried to take me out. They failed."

Jagathan hammered the floor with a fist, and biocreated minions fell. The Enforcer Squad reached the halfway point down the long passageway.

"There are so many of them," Raquella remarked.

The Gothic Being fired a blast rifle and shot biocreated minions down.

Minanket spoke. "Magnemus has mass-produced them. They appear countless in number."

"Didn't the previous High Enforcer send you to arrest the professor on your first assignment as a Universal Marshal?" Lorliane asked the Molecular Being. The Ice Being shot ice beams from her hands and froze biocreated minions.

Minanket frowned. "Yes. But I was unable to apprehend him. He disappeared from public, and I was not able to find him. He resurfaced after ten long years."

Severrin addressed the Occultic Being. "Can you sense where the Archvillains are hiding exactly?"

"I will try." Isisis felt for their presence again. "The control room of the Complex."

"Where is the control room located?" Minanket asked.

Isisis paused. "In the back of the Complex."

The Enforcer Squad wiped out the biocreated minions. The corridor, at the moment, was clear. Then they heard howling ahead.

"That cannot be good," Raquella remarked.

Now a pack of large, two-headed wolves ran at them. Cloned creatures of Quasicoatl.

"I have seen such beasts before," Vartagal said.

Raquella turned to the Great Archer. "Where?"

"On my native world of Mazza," Vartagal replied. "And on a few other planets."

A two-headed wolf leaped at Jagathan. The Titan-Enforcer caught it and hurled it against the wall hard to his left. Then he grabbed the beast from behind around the waist and snapped its spine, killing it.

Severrin shoulder-charged a jumping two-headed wolf and knocked it to the floor. The Colossus then broke the necks of the cloned creature, slaying it.

Vartagal loosed two arrows in rapid succession at a two-headed wolf and buried the shafts between both sets of its eyes, snuffing its life. The Great Archer prepared to do the same thing again.

Lorliane shot ice beams from her hands and froze a two-headed wolf to death. The Ice Being did the same with another one.

Rathol shoved the top end of the Staff of Godpower in the left mouth of a two-headed wolf. The Shepherd blasted the cloned creature from the inside, and its body exploded into chunks.

Raquella and Averroil shot and killed two-headed wolves with blast rifles. Minanket changed into a molecular saw and felled a pair of them. Eneysa shapeshifted into a huge three-headed dog, fought and killed one, and then changed back into her natural state.

The Enforcer Squad ended the threat from the pack of two-headed wolves. None of the cloned creatures remained alive. They continued down the passageway.

Ahead in the corridor, black beetles swarmed up the walls. They made a chittering sound.

"Oh, dear," Averroil muttered.

Orissa turned to the Chakra Being. "What are they?"

"Scarabs," Averroil answered. "Flesh-eating insects."

Isisis spoke. "I sense the handiwork of Gordred behind this attack."

The Enforcer Squad halted as the swarm advanced on them.

"What do we do about them?" Raquella asked the

other Universal Marshals.

Rathol stepped forward. "I will deal with them." The Shepherd raised the Staff of Godpower and shot waves of fire at the swarm. The flames burned it to a crisp.

"The Archvillains are pulling out all the stops against us," Severrin remarked.

Averroil nodded. "One labor after another."

"Aye," Jagathan agreed. "We are being sorely tested at each turn."

Isisis frowned. "They are not finished with us yet."

Just then, monsters came lumbering up the passageway. More of the handiwork of Master Horror.

The Enforcer Squad met them head-on. Soon the Universal Marshals clashed with them. A monster that looked like a two-legged alligator snapped its jaws at Jagathan. The Titan-Enforcer evaded its bite attempts and belted it. The creature swung around and whipped its tail at the Universal Marshal and struck him in the chest. It had no effect on him. Then he grabbed its jaws and bent them outward until its jaws broke, thus killing it.

The battle with the monsters lasted for a time. Those minions of Gordred proved tough to kill. After the fight was over, the Enforcer Squad eventually reached the back of the Complex.

They stood before the automatic doors to the control room. A force field was erected to prevent their entry.

"I will disable the force field," Procules said. The Robot-Enforcer wheeled forward and touched it. Then he short-circuited it. "Safe to enter now."

The Enforcer Squad stepped inside the control room. It was a huge chamber with control consoles and machines. Across the control room from them stood the twelve Archvillains.

Magnemus looked directly at the Molecular Being. "My old friend."

"You should not have turned to evil," Minanket stated.

"I had little choice," Magnemus countered. "My biocreation work was being hampered by so many laws and regulations on Aruvenor. A scientist must have freedom in their chosen field, not be so restricted."

No more words were said. A fight began.

Namprey shot silken threads from his fingertips and antennas at Severrin. The Nodrone cocooned the Colossus. But the Universal Marshal responded by shooting bronze beams from his eyes, melting the stringy fibers, and freeing himself.

Jagathan tackled Quasicoatl. The Cloning Creature tried to bite the Titan-Enforcer to get some of his cells for cloning material. But the Universal Marshal stopped him each time and struck his orifice repeatedly with fists.

The battle went back and forth. Neither side got the upper hand. Then Magnemus used his special powers and lifted the Enforcer Squad by antigravity in the air. Rathol countered by using the Staff of Godpower to return the Universal Marshals to the floor.

Sorrent struck. Using her special powers, the Gwillion cast a glamour and made many images— multiple copies of the twelve Archvillains there—and surrounded the Enforcer Squad. This bewildered the Universal Marshals.

"They're not real," Avverroil said. "This is a grand illusion."

Isisis used her special powers and undid the glamour with the law of magic reversal. The images disappeared.

But the Archvillains were not there.

"Where did they go?" Eneysa asked no one in particular.

Isisis felt the presence of the foul beings. "They are escaping."

The Enforcer Squad ran out of the control room back up the main corridor of the Complex. When they finally got outside of the structure, they spotted a ship taking off. It was the *Technokado*, the vessel that belonged to Magnemus. A rift opened in the air, and it flew through the hole. Afterward, the rift closed.

The ship left Earth. After flying a distance, it engaged its teleport drive and vanished from the solar system.

Chapter 33

Delveran sensed what happened in the Universal Prisonplex. Archvillains freed from long captivity. "Oh no."

The battle of Acropollon continued. Tellusians kept fighting the enemy to not be overrun. Their fighters engaged the enemy in aerial combat.

Bolan blew up a laser tank with a photon bazooka. The Noble Soldier dropped his weapon as a male cyborg charged him. Trevarre pulled out an army knife from Earth and met the attack. The biocreated minion swung his blast rifle at the Universal Marshal and missed. Seeing an opening, Bolan slashed the exposed neck of his adversary, and blood spilled. His foe fell to the ground and died.

Ramairgan still tangled with Orlin. Hermit Power swung his Rod of Power at the Grim Reaper, who blocked it with his scythe. They circled each other.

"You are doomed," Orlin said. The Archvillain knew the jailbreak of the Universal Prisonplex succeeded. "Death will come to the Enforcers."

Ramairgan shook his head. "The Universal Marshals will live and ultimately stop you."

The foul being brought his scythe down to split the skull of the Universal Marshal. Hermit Power raised his Rod of Power sideways and caught the blow. They shoved against each other.

"You cannot win," Orlin said.

Ramairgan smiled. "We shall see about that."

The two separated and circled each other again, looking for a weakness in the other's defense. Zorroquin and Ragnar remained locked in combat. The Berserker kept swinging his battle-axe of power at the Thunderer and did not land a blow. The Universal Marshal had the same result with his hammer.

"Do you hear those cries of freedom from your Universal Prisonplex?" Ragnar asked. "You failed."

Zorroquin pounded the ground with Bronthorjal, and the force of the blow sent the foul being reeling. The Thunderer leaped at the Archvillain and brought his hammer down to crush the skull of the foul being. But the Berserker recovered in time and intercepted the blow.

"You are no match for me," Ragnar stated.

The Berserker swung his battle-axe of power upward at an angle to slice the Universal Marshal. Zorroquin parried the strike. The Thunderer countered by thrusting his hammer straight at the heart of the Archvillain and connected. It caused the foul being to move back a few steps.

"You are a worthy adversary," Ragnar complimented. "But I will win this fight between us."

Glyndalyn kept raining lightning from the sky down on the enemy. Next, Mother Nature changed tactics and cracked the ground open under their foes and swallowed biocreated minions and a few laser tanks into the earth. Then she summoned tornadoes and wreaked havoc among the enemy.

Hellob struck. The Gorgon turned some Tellusian troopers to stone. The Archvillain caught the attention of Glyndalyn, and the two fought.

The foul being tried to turn the Universal Marshal to stone. But the Enforcer seemed immune to it. Hellob backhanded Mother Nature in the face. The blow stunned Glyndalyn briefly, and she retaliated with one of her own. The two locked arms and shoved against each other.

Kennedrill used his freeze ray on biocreated minions and iced them. The Interstellar Pilgrim flew at a laser tank, lifted it in the air, and crashed it on the ground. Now the Universal Marshal found himself surrounded by robots. The Enforcer blasted them with plasma rays from his powerbands and destroyed them.

Lethesis attacked some land troopers and sent them flying all over the place. The Wildcat leaped and stomped them to death. Turning, the Archvillain saw Zithell not far from her. The Amazon just finished taking out a few androids with her light sword.

The foul being charged the Universal Marshal. The Enforcer swung her light sword to cut Lethesis in half, but the Wildcat jumped over the strike and somersaulted in the air to avoid it.

"Bitch," Lethesis said after landing on her feet.

Zithell came at the Archvillain and tried to slice her again, but with the same result. The Universal Marshal put away her photon weapon on her belt and delivered a front kick to the foul being, catching the Wildcat by surprise. Lethesis responded by jumping at the Amazon to stomp her. But Zithell stepped forward and caught the Archvillain. The Enforcer proceeded to squeeze the foul being in a bear hug.

Lethesis clapped the ears of the Universal Marshal, who released her grip. The Wildcat did a sweep kick to Zithell, and she went to the ground. The Archvillain tried a flying stomp on the Enforcer. But the Amazon rolled out of the way and got back to her feet.

The two ran at each other. The Amazon, the bigger woman, knocked the Wildcat to the ground. Then Universal Marshal grabbed her by her feet and spun her around, making her dizzy. The Enforcer let go and hurled the foul being to the earth.

Lethesis stood up again. The Wildcat screamed in frustration. She stalked the Amazon this time, leery of her. Zithell moved cautiously as well.

Ulleric fired rays from his hands at biocreated minions. He scored on them. The Dynaman flew at a bunch of mutants and bowled them over. A laser tank bore down on him. The Enforcer jumped on top of it, opened the hatch, and pulled out two clones, one driving the armored vehicle, the other operating its laser weapon. He got out of the way as a laser cannon shot it and destroyed it.

Meanwhile, back at the Universal Prisonplex, Archvillains tasted freedom as they stampeded out of the place. Vilegast directed them to board the transport ships landing in the yard. Archvillains piled in the spacecrafts.

"There are too many of them," Medeordese remarked. "We cannot stop all those Archvillains escaping."

Thayla agreed. "Could we slow them down?"

"Probably not," Medeordese replied. "They outnumber us way too much."

Thayla got an idea. "What about disabling those transport ships?"

"That might work," Medoerdese said. "How do we do that?"

Just then, robots attacked. They did not get the

chance to try and stop the transport ships. Once full, they took off.

More biocreated minions arrived on the scene. The Speedster and the Valkyrie-Enforcer, with troopers, held their ground. Another transport ship, loaded with Archvillains, took off.

Galamagne came to the aid of his fellow Universal Marshals. The Space Chevalier shot blasts from his gauntlets and pulverized foes. He pulled out his light sword and slashed into the enemy, destroying them.

Thayla stabbed a clone in the chest with her sword, killing him. The Valkyrie-Enforcer ducked under a punch thrown by a robot who almost caught her off guard. She whirled and cut its head off.

Medeordese flashed around the enemy. He knocked a bunch of clones down. The speedster avoided strikes against him by foes very easily, too fast for them to catch him. He managed to rip a blast rifle from an android. With a weapon in his hand, he started shooting biocreated minions.

"Those Archvillains escaping are thinking not but fleeing this planet," Galamagne remarked.

"They're not interested in taking part in the battle," Medeordese added.

Thayla dispatched a male mutant. "Maybe fortunate for us."

Medeordese frowned. "It's a shame we cannot arrest them again under the circumstances."

More transport ships, full of Archvillains, took off. All those spacecraft headed for space, like the previous ones.

Delveran saw the transport ships flying away. The High Enforcer felt dismay at the event. He could do nothing about it. Resigned, he returned to the battle.

A laser cannon exploded after being hit by a laser tank. This injured some troopers. Another laser cannon shot the laser tank that had done damage and blew it up.

Darthan fired his blast rifle at biocreated minions indiscriminately. The Marveltrooper threw a photon grenade at a bunch of clones and it exploded and sent them flying. The Enforcer ran up to a laser tank, climbed on top of it, ripped open its hatch, and threw a photon grenade into it. It exploded after the Universal Marshal jumped to safety. He ran back to the Tellusian lines and resumed firing his weapon.

Slennass knocked the Curdatch from the hands of Cenjuno, stopping the Archvillain from unleashing any more blights on the troopers. The Keve pushed the Huntress aside and reached for the box on the earth. Before she could get it, the Universal Marshal kicked her and doubled her over. The Enforcer grabbed for the Curdatch herself. But the foul being tackled her, and they wrestled on the ground for it.

Wardelorean fired a pair of missiles from his shoulder armor. One struck a laser tank and destroyed it. The other exploded in a bunch of androids and disabled them. The Dreadnought wielded a blast rifle and shot more biocreated minions with it. He stood near the High Enforcer.

"We need reinforcements," Wardelorean remarked.

Delveran shot green fire from his hands and charred some mutants. "There are none at hand. We must not let them take Acropollon."

Sharminival fought the enemy not far from the Grand Universal Marshal. Energy beams shot from her body and slayed foes. A male cyborg fired a blast rifle at the Energy Being, and the Universal Marshal absorbed the blast. The Enforcer retaliated and shot an energy beam from her hand and destroyed him.

An enemy fighter took a hit from a Tellusian one and crashed to the earth. More fighters on both sides got hit and suffered the same fate.

Neisie charged a robot and stabbed it with her horn. This short-circuited the droid. Being a magical creature, the Unicornling used her bony, pointed projection to kill them, occultic energy power running through it to aid in slaying them.

Lucane held a blast rifle and shot at biocreated minions. The Peryton felled his fair share of foes. He silently prayed to the powers of light and dark that Tellus would win the battle of Acropollon.

Brinivere also wielded a blast rifle. The Cellular Being shot biocreated minions left and right.

Voltar shot electricity from his hands and shocked biocreated minions. The Electrobeing electrocuted them to death. He spotted a laser tank getting close and sent electricity into it and disabled the armored vehicle.

Delveran paused in firing green fire from his hands. He sensed something. Federation forces finally eliminated the energy barrier! Help was on the way.

****

Federation ships destroyed the enemy vessels holding in place the energy barrier, thus eliminating it. Battle in space raged again.

Battlecruisers fought space destroyers. Federation fighters joined the battle, particularly taking on enemy fighters. Laser fire and antimatter torpedoes hit targets.

Transport ships carrying Archvillains docked inside space destroyers. When enough of the spacecraft landed inside them, the space destroyers engaged teleport drives and disappeared from the Sagittarian Sector.

Other space destroyers kept fighting the Federation ships. One enemy vessel took repeated hits and finally exploded. Battlecruisers took some pounding. Fighters on both sides got destroyed.

Another space destroyer exploded. A battlecruiser took too much damage and retreated.

Slowly the Federation forces decimated the space fleet of the Archvillain organization.

The Federation sent armed beings to the surface of the planet to aid the Tellusians. A few fighters joined them.

****

"Finally," Wardelorean said. "Reinforcements."

Delveran breathed a sigh of relief. The High Enforcer felt taxed.

Federation forces landed and attacked the enemy from behind. The tide of battle began to turn in favor of the Tellusians.

Arboron extended one branch and stabbed through a line of clones, killing them. The Treeling-Enforcer retracted his limb and stepped on a mutant.

Findall used a sling and hurled exploding rocks of magic at the enemy. The Habble-Enforcer hit his targets and felled a bunch of cyborgs.

Estephone slashed a male clone to death. The Horae-Enforcer continued her offensive and took out more biocreated minions.

Federation forces, comprised of humans, humanoids, and aliens, fired blasters, blast rifles, and photon bazookas and threw photon grenades at the enemy. Biocreated minions and laser tanks turned around to face them. The enemy was caught in a cross-fire between Tellusian defenders and Federation forces.

Brutalos grabbed troopers and crushed them in his four arms. Arboron saw this and charged at the Kraken. The Universal Marshal was bigger than the Archvillain, even though the foul being was a giant himself. They clashed. Brutalos tried to wrap his four arms around the trunk of the Treeling-Enforcer to crush him. Arboron whipped his branches and blocked the attempts.

"You are living wood," Brutalos remarked. "Brittle and easily broken."

Arboron snorted. "You are out of your element."

The Kraken clubbed the Universal Marshal in the head with a fist. This did not have any effect on the Treeling-Enforcer.

"I will snap your branches like twigs," Brutalos said.

Arboron whacked the Archvillain in the body with a branch. The Universal Marshal then followed that with one to the head. The foul being did not feel a thing.

Before the two could lock together in close, Brutalos got teleported to a space destroyer. In fact, all the Archvillains in the battle did. Once all the foul beings were aboard, the ship engaged its teleport drive and vanished from the Sagittarian Sector.

Eventually the Tellusians and Federation forces triumphed. On Tellus, the enemy was annihilated. In space, the remaining vessels of the space fleet of the Archvillain organization were destroyed. So were the enemy fighters.

"We have victory!" Galamagne shouted.

Wardelorean grinned. "At last."

A cheer arose from the victors. There would be a celebration.

Chapter 34

The Enforcer Squad explored the Complex. They found a zoological chamber full of caged creatures first.

"These poor animals will have to be set free," Eneysa said.

"Yes," Procules agreed. "The Federation will have to transport them to different worlds for their natural habitats."

"They must have suffered abuse by the Archvillains," Lorliane remarked. "Particularly at the hands of the Cloning Creature and the Scientific Being."

The Universal Marshals moved on and entered Biolaboratory Two. They heard bird cries and monkey chattering. The biome of a rain forest in the huge chamber impressed them.

"The animals in here will also have to be set free and returned to their natural habitats on Earth," Raquella said.

"What do we do about the realming device?" Averroil asked his fellow Enforcers.

Minanket answered. "It will have to be dismantled. This demesne will have to be eliminated."

Next, they entered a laboratory full of scientific equipment, including vertical tubes with small creatures in them full of water.

"This is where Magnemus bioengineered living forms," Minanket said.

Rathol fumed. "He played God."

"What is to be done with the Complex?" Raquella asked her fellow Enforcers.

Severrin answered. "It is to be demolished."

The other Universal Marshals agreed with the Colossus. They moved on to another room with some inoperative robots in it.

"These droids must never be activated," Procules stated. "They would obey only the Archvillains if operational."

They came upon a chamber with bionic parts. Here, cyborgs were put together.

"These biocreation facilities in the Complex are topnotch," Minanket remarked. "It's a shame they were used for evil instead of good."

The Enforcer Squad explored all the rooms in the Complex. They saw the armory, recreation room, mess hall, private quarters, and more. There were no clues to where the Archvillains disappeared to after the fight with them.

After the Enforcer Squad was done looking through the Complex, they went outside again. Overhead, the glowglobe in the sky shone brighter. The atmosphere processor continued to work.

"Now what?" Orissa asked her fellow Enforcers.

"We shall return to the ship," Rathol replied. "We have seen enough."

The Shepherd raised the Staff of Godpower, and a white beam shot from it. A rift appeared as the fabric of reality parted. They went through the hole. Afterward Rathol closed it.

The Enforcer Squad walked back to the *Centaurus*. It was now afternoon.

Back onboard the vessel, the Enforcer Squad ate in the mess hall. The mood was good.

Averroil addressed the Occultic Being. "Can you sense what has happened on Tellus?"

Isisis closed her eyes. After a moment, she opened them. "The invasion of the planet is over. Tellus is victorious."

"Good news," Lorliane remarked.

"However," Isisis said, "the jailbreak of the Universal Prisonplex succeeded."

"We will learn everything about what happened on Tellus when we get back home," Minanket said. "We will also file our report to the High Enforcer and the Federation Department of Justice."

Rathol joined the conversation. "My wife will be happy to see me upon our return."

"My family will, too," Vartagal said. The Great Archer ate a beef sandwich on wheat bread. He drank a dark beer.

Jagathan spoke. "My family is back on my home planet."

"We could all use a vacation," Lorliane said.

They all agreed on that. Their mission had been a long one.

"It will be nice to see our fellow Enforcers again," Raquella stated. The Gothic Being had no family to return to.

"Tellus will probably celebrate the victory over the invaders," Orissa said.

"As will the Federation," Eneysa added.

Severrin nodded. "We may arrive in time to join the celebration."

"If not, we can do it here," Raquella said.

Lorliane consumed flavored ice treats. "We did save the Earth from the Archvillains."

"Aye," Jagathan agreed. "We stop them from destroying the Terran world."

Vartagal voiced a thought. "Do you think the Earthlings will want to become members of the Federation?"

"Maybe," Minanket responded. "That is up to the Federation to consider the possibility."

"Bolan would love that," Lorliane stated. "Being from Earth, The Noble Soldier could visit his home planet."

"The Terrans would likely welcome him as a hero," Lorliane said.

After they had a meal in the mess hall, the Enforcer Squad went each to their private quarters. Later they ran a check on all systems of the ship. All functioned normally.

Raquella worked the communications console. She received instructions from the High Enforcer on Tellus. The Gothic Being informed her fellow Universal Marshals of his orders.

The Enforcer Squad returned to New York City and held a press conference again. They told the Terrans that the Archvillain threat to the planet was no more. Though the Universal Marshals did not arrest the foul beings, the danger to Earth by them was diminished. It was unlikely that the Fellowship of Darkness would return to the Terran world after suffering such a defeat.

Earth celebrated. The Enforcer Squad was honored. Parades were held. The Terran world thanked the Universal Marshals for what they had done for them.

The Enforcer Squad experienced a little bit more of

the culture of Earth. They got introduced to video games, particularly superhero ones. Some of the Universal Marshals tried their hand at it. Severrin proved to be the best player among them, winning every time.

The President of the United States, on behalf of the Earth, submitted a formal request to the Enforcer Squad. It involved a petition for the Terran world to become a member of the Federation. The Universal Marshals would give it to the proper authorities after they returned to Tellus.

The Enforcer Squad said farewell to Earth. They would not forget their visit to the Terran world. The Earthlings would never forget about them.

Ready, the *Centaurus* took off and left Earth. After putting some distance between it and the planet, it engaged its teleport drive. The ship returned to Tellus.

Chapter 35

Around Tellus, they celebrated the victory over the invaders. They partied like there was no tomorrow. Even the Enforcers got into the act.

There would also be funerals held for those who died in the war for Tellus. Both military and civilians. None of the Universal Marshals suffered any casualties in the battles that had taken place.

****

At his home in Acropollon, Wardelorean celebrated with his family and friends. The Dreadnought feasted with them in his backyard. His son Rajah, nine years old, ran up to him.

"Father, why are we doing this?" Rajah asked.

Wardelorean smiled. "To remember the day when our world triumphed over an enemy bent on conquering us. Good won over evil."

His daughter Saria, eight years old, addressed him. "You are a hero."

"You could say that," Wardelorean agreed.

His wife, Helana, went over to him. "Are you all right?"

"I'm okay," Wardelorean replied.

Helana was concerned. "You seem a little bothered."

Wardelorean sighed. "At times during the battle of Acropollon I thought all would be lost."

Helana hugged him. "Everything turned out well in the end."

Wardelorean was not so sure of that. He made no comment on her last statement.

****

Some of the Universal Marshals celebrated in the mess hall of the Justiceplex.

"One for our side," Galamagne said. The Space Chevalier downed a glass of ale.

"It was close," Zorroquin remarked. "We were pushed to the brink of defeat."

"True," Voltar agreed. "We somehow managed to pull out the victory."

Findall raised a glass of wine. "Hail to Tellus! Hail to the Enforcers!"

"Here, here," Lucane said. The Peryton drank mead.

The Universal Marshals sang the national anthem of Tellus. It roused patriotism in them.

Medeordese downed a root beer. "This is more like it."

"Let's go for a walk," Thayla said to the Speedster.

"All right," Medeordese responded. He put down his glass on the table.

The Valkyrie-Enforcer and the Speedster walk hand in hand out of the mess hall. They went outside and walked along the shore before the Angranadan Ocean. It was early evening.

****

One who was not celebrating with everyone was Delveran. The High Enforcer sat in his office in a sullen mood. Just then someone buzzed him outside his office.

"Come in," Delveran said.

Evarinia entered. "Why are you not celebrating?"

Delveran frowned. "We might have won the battle, but the war is far from over."

Evarinia came to stand by him. "You think you have failed."

"We did," Delveran responded, getting up from his chair. "The jailbreak still succeeded. Despite the fact that we defeated the space fleet and invading forces of the Archvillain organization. Now the galaxy will be terrorized by all those Archvillains freed from the Universal Prisonplex."

Evarinia touched his arm. "I'm sorry."

"Centuries of Archvillains arrested gone," Delveran said, very upset. "I am worried that the Fellowship of Darkness will recruit all those foul beings freed to its organization. They outnumber the Enforcers by a hefty margin."

"And you fear that they will try to seek revenge on the Universal Marshals," Evarinia finished for him.

Delveran grimaced. "Yes."

Evarinia rubbed his shoulder. "You need some fresh air."

Delveran nodded. They left his office and walked out of the Justiceplex hand in hand.

****

Next morning, the Enforcer Squad waited for Delveran in the briefing room of the Justiceplex. The High Enforcer entered and sat down.

"Here is our report," Minanket said. The Molecular Being handed the Grand Universal Marshal a disc. The High Enforcer would look at it later, and it would be filed away.

"What happened to the Archvillains on Earth?" Delveran asked.

Lorliane answered for the Enforcer Squad. "We had them until they pulled a trick on us. Then they fled the Terran world."

"We did prevent the Archvillains from destroying Earth," Raquella added.

Delveran smiled. "Bolan will be happy to hear that."

"The Earthlings have given us a petition for membership in the Federation," Isisis said. The Occultic Being handed the document to the High Enforcer.

Delveran nodded. "I will see to it that it is given to the Federation president for debate in the Federation Assembly."

"Maybe Bolan can speak on behalf of his native world before the Federation Assembly," Averroil stated. "Naturally, he does have a vested interest in the matter."

"I will ask him if he wishes to," Delveran promised.

"Do you have new assignments for us?" Eneysa asked.

Delveran breathed deeply. "No. You can take some time off. You deserve it."

In unison, the Enforcer Squad responded. "As you say, High Enforcer."

****

Rathol was teleported to the spot where his wife and the other shepherds camped, east of Paradar, near forestland. He entered their tent, and she rushed into his arms.

"I am glad you are home, my husband," Shebeth said.

Rathol smiled. "It is good to be home again."

****

Delveran was teleported to the office of the Warden in the Universal Prisonplex.

"The control room of the antipower cells is being repaired," Thurjen said. He sat in a chair behind his desk. A telescreen hung on the wall right of him.

Delveran nodded. "The Defenseplex is being rebuilt, and a new warding device will be installed in it."

"I was wrong about an ultimate threat to the Federation," Thurjen admitted. "Now all those Archvillains will have to be arrested all over again."

"That will be very difficult, in light of the Fellowship of Darkness," Delveran stated.

"At least the Criminals and Villains in here didn't escape," Thurjen said.

"Yes," Delveran agreed.

They talked for a while. Then Delveran left the Warden and returned to the Justiceplex.

Stopping the Archvillain organization remained the number one priority for the Enforcers. The High Enforcer started sending Universal Marshals on new assignments. He hoped that the thousands of Archvillains out there, roaming the galaxy, would not band together and become the next supreme evil. But he was afraid it would happen and could spell doom for the Federation and the Enforcers.

A word about the author...

Stephen M. T. Greene was born in Lowell, Massachusetts in 1959. He received his B.A. Degree in Liberal Arts/Writing from Vermont College of Norwich University and his M.S. Degree in Creative Writing from Columbus University. His publications include poems in three poetry anthologies and four stories in a fiction anthology, which he also edited, *Tales of the Unknown*. In addition he writes plays, teleplays, and screenplays. He enjoys movies, music, sports, martial arts, video games, and reading. Currently he lives in Pennsylvania.